THE
SAME SWEET
GIRLS

Also by Cassandra King

Making Waves

The Sunday Wife

Cassandra King

THE
SAME SWEET
GIRLS

Doubleday Large Print Home Library Edition

HYPERION

New York

ISBN 0-7394-5085-9

**This Large Print Book carries the
Seal of Approval of N.A.V.H.**

*To the Same Sweet Girls, for all the years together.
I had better get the crown for this.
And always, to Patrick.*

Acknowledgments

First, a disclaimer. There is a real group, the Same Sweet Girls, but none of us would ever carry on like the shameless hussies in this book. We are really, truly sweet. All of us were exemplary students at Alabama College, where we were shining models of southern womanhood, never getting into trouble with the dean of women. The real SSGs have never partied or drunk too much, never gossiped, and certainly never flirted. We do not listen to nor tell dirty jokes, complain about our husbands, give unwanted advice, or quarrel with each other. No one comes from, or has, dysfunctional families.

And we are all truly happy for our reigning queen, even though we know she does not deserve the crown as much as we do.

Thanks and gratitude to three honorary SSGs: Marly Rusoff, my agent; Leslie Wells, my editor; and Ellen Archer, my publisher. Mihai Radulescu, for the computer help: You are a Same Sweet Guy.

Special thanks for the assistance of Deborah Arnold, a gifted gourd artist from Sedgwick, Maine; and for the medical expertise of another Maine friend, Dr. Lanier Summerall.

Deep love and gratitude to the family: my boys, the girls, the grands, the King family, and the Conroy clan. And to the wonderful friends who share the journey, know that I love you, each and every one.

Camerado, I give you my hand!
I give you my love more precious than money,
I give you myself before preaching or law;
Will you give me yourself? Will you come
    travel with me?
Shall we stick by each other as long as we
    live?

WALT WHITMAN, from "Song of the Open Road"

THE
SAME SWEET
GIRLS

1

Corrine

BLUE MOUNTAIN, GEORGIA

ALTHOUGH WE CALL OURSELVES the Same Sweet Girls, none of us are girls anymore. And I'm not sure that any of us are now, or ever have been, sweet. Nice, maybe, and polite, certainly. All southern girls are raised to be nice and polite, can't be anything but, regardless of how mean-spirited we might be deep down. The illusion of sweetness, that's all that counts. We don't have to be sincerely sweet, but by God we have to be good at faking it. Southern girls will stab you in the back, same as anyone else, but we'll give you a sugary smile while doing it.

The question is, are the Same Sweet Girls

sweet? Hardly. But one thing's for sure: We're the same. We are the same complicated, screwy, mixed-up, love-each-other-one-minute and hate-each-other-the-next group of women we were when we met thirty years ago. I guess we were sweeter then, at age eighteen; we were certainly more naive and less sophisticated. I'd like to say virginal, but that wouldn't quite be true. Not of everyone. Okay, I was. Unlike the others, I was fresh off the farm, as wide-eyed and gullible as a newborn calf. But a couple of us were already damaged, innocence long gone. Those of us with a trace of naïveté left at age eighteen were soon to lose it; we just didn't know it then. I can promise you this: Not a single one of the Same Sweet Girls has a smidgen of it left today.

We're the same, but we're also different, if that makes sense. The group—the SSGs, we call ourselves—formed when we were in college together, roommates, suite-mates, tennis or lab partners. We got our name from a silly little incident that we still relate to each other, telling the story over and over as though we haven't heard it a million times already. Finding ourselves away from home for the first time, in the intimate environment of an all-girls' school, we became friends for life. We forged our clique then, our group of six girls, and we became closer than sisters. We scheduled classes together, stayed up half the night gossiping and giggling, went home with each other during weekends and holidays. As close as we were then, however, we were only truly bound together when one of us was lost, three years after graduation. When you're in your early twenties and invincible, death is a life-changing experience, a sobering wake-up call unlike any other.

I clung to the Same Sweet Girls then, loving them as I'd not done before. Before, life was one big party, the whole basis for our friendship; afterward, we were tightly bound, as though knitted together with unseen but indestructible threads. In tears, we stood apart from the crowd of mourners at the grave of one of our own, linked hands, and promised to remain friends, to always be the Same Sweet Girls we were then. Five felt like such an odd, lopsided number that we moved quickly to fill the gap, becoming the magic six again. Too quickly, some of us thought later. But . . . that's another story, for another time.

Today the six of us do not live in the same

place; some of us are geographically separated by hundreds of miles. But somehow, we manage to stay as close as we were when living in the same dorm, all those years ago. Some years I've seen the others only at our biannual get-togethers, in early summer and late fall. There have been times when job or family obligations kept us apart. After graduation we started our careers, then we married, had babies, raised families. Things like sick children, school plays or Little League games, proms, funerals, weddings, graduations would keep us from attending our gatherings. Inevitably, when that happened, we grieved our absence from the group as though we'd never see each other again. Now that we're older, for the most part our kids grown and gone, we see each other more often, and we're all more aware of the passing of time, the shocking awareness that one day we'll attend a gathering of the Same Sweet Girls, and it will be our last one.

When I'm describing the Same Sweet Girls to other people, I usually tell them it's helpful to group us in twos. Lanier and I were former roommates, as were Julia and Astor; then there's the odd couple, Byrd and Rosanelle.

(Poor Byrd, getting stuck with Rosanelle, but there again, that's another story.) Paired like that, we seem like polar opposites, but we aren't, really. I'm considered the weird one of the group, and I'll admit I've earned that honor. Most people think artists are weird, anyway, but me—I'm a gourd artist. As the other SSGs say, with much eye rolling, how many of *those* do you know? My former roommate, Lanier Sanders, doesn't do weird, being not only a former jock but also a nurse, which is such a prosaic profession for someone like Lanier. Lanier would have been a doctor—a good one—had she not flunked out of medical school her first year. Not because she's dumb; although she struggled in the humanities, Lanier's plenty smart in math and science. Here's the thing about Lanier—lovable as she is, she will always find a way to screw up her life. Almost fifty years old, and she is still doing it. But I don't have any room to talk, since I've been pretty good at that myself.

Like Lanier and me, Julia and Astor were college roommates. The school we attended, the Methodist College for Women in Brierfield, Alabama (nicknamed The W), paired you up; you didn't get to choose like you do in most schools, the Methodists preferring to mix their poor scholarship students in with the more privileged ones. If it hadn't been for the incident our freshman year that made us the Same Sweet Girls, I'd never have gotten to know Julia Dupont or Astor Deveaux, either one. Unlike me, a shy little art major, both Julia and Astor were hot stuff on campus. Classically beautiful in a Grace Kelly sort of way, Julia Dupont was from a wealthy old family in Mobile. Her mother had gone to some fancy boarding school with the dean of women, which was how Julia ended up at The W. It was a year after we became friends before we discovered the real reason Julia was there. Thirty years later, it still surprises me.

What to say about Astor Deveaux? How about, she and I have a rather complicated relationship. I'm not sure what kind of weird chemistry there is between us, but it's been going on since the first day we met, in an Interpretative Dance class. Lanier accuses me of not even liking Astor, but that's not quite true. I don't trust her, I'll admit, and we've had numerous clashes. But like everyone else, I'm fascinated by her. From Lake Charles, Louisiana, Astor Deveaux came to

The W on a dance scholarship and intrigued everyone on campus. None of us Alabama hicks had ever seen anyone like her; we'd certainly never seen anyone so talented. Astor went on to dance on Broadway, until she got too old to get good parts. Then she moved back to Alabama, unfortunately. See?—that's what I mean. I'm always making cracks like that about Astor, and I'm not even sure why. But one thing I do know—I've got better sense than to turn my back on her.

I group Byrd and Rosanelle together because they're the most normal ones of the Same Sweet Girls (which isn't saying a whole lot, believe me). Byrd McCain is plain and simple and unpretentious. We've nicknamed her Mama Byrd, a role she fits to a tee. She certainly plays it well, and if on occasion Byrd plays it too well, giving out advice, being uptight or disapproving . . . we always forgive her. She's that lovable. Rosanelle Tilley is another story, but she's not really one of us. She's who we inherited after Byrd's roommate, one of the original six, was killed in a car wreck, and we felt the need to fill the gap. Rosanelle's also the one who unintentionally gave us our name, the Same Sweet Girls. This will tell you every-

thing you need to know about Rosanelle—
she's flattered that we named our group
after something she once said, not realizing
that, as usual, we were being ironic and
facetious. Thirty years have gone by, and
she still doesn't get it.

It all sounds so serious, telling it like this,
but it's anything but. Over the years, we've
developed a lot of silly rituals that I'm embarrassed to tell other people about, especially
now that we're almost fifty years old. We
crown a queen and have royal edicts and all
sorts of stuff like that. Each year the crown
goes to the one who can prove that she's the
most deserving. And what does she have to
do to land the coveted crown? Why, be the
sweetest one of all, of course. She cam-
paigns all year for the crown, then has to convince the rest of us that she's done enough
sugary deeds to earn the coveted title. The
highlight of our summer weekend is when
each of us summarizes our campaign for the
crown during a ten-minute presentation. Like
the pope, the queen is elected by secret bal-
lot. Naturally, the first year everyone voted for
herself, so we had to change the rules. It's not
considered a sweet thing to do, to vote for
yourself, and if you do so, you're disqualified.

Even more embarrassing, we have our own coded language that we call Girl Talk. It's been going on for so many years that it's hard to remember where most of it originated. The punch lines of popular jokes make the rounds, but we tire of them and they fall by the wayside, due to our overuse. Our most enduring Girl Talk comes from stories we repeat ad nauseam, year after year. Lanier provided one of the lines we use most often by telling us the story of the elderly woman who was a patient of hers. When Lanier took her vital signs and asked her how she was feeling, the lady said, "Terrible, just terrible. My rheumatism's worse than ever; I can't lift my arms; my back's killing me; and I can't walk without hurting. But it's being so cheerful that keeps me going." The other two most popular Girl Talk lines were provided by Astor, years ago. When she lived in New York, her best friend was a gay dancer named Ron. Astor would take Ron shopping with her because if she picked out the wrong thing, Ron would shake his head sadly and say, "Oh, honey, *no.*" On the occasions Ron didn't go with her and she showed up wearing one of her mistakes, Ron would sigh, roll his eyes, and say, "Girl, what were you *thinking*?"

With the Girl Talk, the crowning of the queen, the royal salute, the procession, and the edicts, our get-togethers have become ritualized to the point that they're pure theater, and anyone peeking in a window at us would swear we're all crazy as loons. Which we are. One of these days, we'll stop being the Same Sweet Girls and start calling ourselves the Same Crazy Fools, I suppose. Some would say that day is fast approaching. But in the meantime, we'll be the Same Sweet Girls, who aren't girls anymore, and who aren't sweet and never have been. We'll keep crowning our queen and going through our rituals and loving each other and sometimes hating each other, because we've done it so long it's become a part of us. It's a big part of who we are and how we got to be that way. It's where we are today and how we got from there to here. It's our story.

2

Lanier

DAUPHIN ISLAND, ALABAMA

MAMA ALWAYS CALLED ME sassy, and bless her heart, my smart mouth nearly drove her to drinking. If you looked up "sweet old southern lady" in the dictionary, there would be a picture of my mama, wearing pearls with her apron. For some reason I have Mama on my mind today. Guess because it's been several weeks since I've gone to Selma to visit her in the nursing home. I feel bad when I visit her and worse when I don't. Last time I was there, she didn't know me from a houseplant. Poor Mama. Sometimes I think it was having me for a daughter that made her lose her mind. It's all my fault.

Maybe it's the dolphins jumping in the bay this afternoon that make me think of Mama and Daddy and the so-called good old days of my childhood. Actually, they were. Good old days, that is. Sometimes I think I ought to make up some dysfunctional stuff so I'll fit in with everyone else. The Same Sweet Girls say I had the best childhood of all of us, and I reckon they're right. Truth is, I didn't think about it one way or the other when I was a kid. I just lived it. I was raised in a pretty little town, Selma, Alabama, which later got famous for the civil rights stuff. But in the fifties when I came along, it was just home, where my grandparents and most of my relatives lived, and where my daddy was a judge. Mama was a homemaker and did the country club and the Episcopal church ladies and all that stuff. Actually, I spent about as much time at the country club as Mama did because I played tennis and golf all the time. So guess I had one of those—what do you call it?—idyllic childhoods.

We spent most of our summers here, on Dauphin Island, in this old fishing cabin where I've been staying the last three months. As I stand on the back deck and watch the dolphins playing around in the bay, I remember naming this place when I was eight. Lord, that's forty years ago now! Five acres of prime waterfront real estate on Mobile Bay, this property and cabin had been in Daddy's family for years without being named anything, just called the Brewer place by the locals. When we piled in the car and drove three hours south to get here, we just said we were going to Dauphin Island to our fishing cabin. (I thought it was "Dolphin" Island until I was ten.) I pitched one of my fits, insisted the property needed a name, and we should call it Dolphin Cove. Damn if Daddy didn't go for it, even making a sign in his workshop and hanging it up on the gatepost. The thing's still out front but I've got to fix it, because it's loose and flops around whenever the wind blows hard. When I first moved in here, it banged around in a rainstorm and liked to have scared the devil out of me.

I watch the dolphins jumping around, bobbing up and down like they're showing off for me, and I raise my wineglass to them in a salute. Not a coincidence that I named this place Dolphin Cove—I've always loved dolphins. They're like pure magic to me, and I used to swim with them when I was a kid.

The Same Sweet Girls don't believe that, even Corrine. First time the SSGs met here, everyone got so excited when they saw the dolphins that they almost fell off the pier. "I swam in the bay with them when I was a little girl," I told them, not dreaming they'd think I was bullshitting them. When everyone pooh-poohed me, I jumped right into the bay with all my clothes on—of course I'd had a few drinks—and swam out to where the dolphins were. I spooked them splashing around, and they took off like I was the guy who chased that big whale we studied about in American Lit. What was his name, Captain Arab? The book was *Moby-Dick,* I know, because I called it Mo' Big Dick, just to aggravate Byrd, who was in class with me that semester. Anyway, with the SSGs yelling at me to get my butt back to the pier, *right then,* I tried to grab a dolphin and almost drowned myself. Corrine screamed bloody murder and poor Julia cried until I managed to crawl back on the pier, soaking wet and sober. It was one of those things that was funny afterward but not at the time—Corrine actually grabbed me by the shoulders and shook me, like she was my mama or something. In an attempt to lighten things up, Astor said, "Girl, what were you *thinking*?" but nobody laughed, even me.

I tried to explain to Corrine that I have a thing for dolphins, like they're my soul mates or something. I figured Corrine of all people would go for that, since she's into all sorts of New Age stuff. But she was too scared and mad to listen to me. I said maybe I was a dolphin in a previous life. And Corrine said, "Yeah, Lanier, guess that's where all the crazy karma comes from." Maybe she's right. If so, I must have been one bad-ass dolphin.

I wait until the dolphins disappear from view, moving further and further out to sea, before turning away and going back into the cabin. I've put this off long enough, by God. I *have* to get the house cleaned up. It's a disgrace. For three months I've lived here like I was on a camping trip or something, and the place is a wreck. The big weekend is coming up, the annual gathering of the Same Sweet Girls, and the girls will have a hissy fit when they see what a mess the cabin's in.

The SSGs love this place almost as much as I do. The first summer after graduation, when we decided to have our first SSG get-together, we had it here. I had to beg; everyone wanted to go to Gulf Shores instead.

I promised them we could go to the beach whenever we wanted to, since Gulf Shores is not that far. Once everyone got here, I was scared they wouldn't like it, since it's so isolated. Although it's *real* pretty here, there's not a blame thing to do except sit on the deck or the pier, watch the dolphins and seabirds, gossip, and get drunk. Dixie Lee was alive then, bless her heart, and she said, "And the bad part is . . . ?" which kind of broke the ice.

We didn't go to the beach the whole weekend, we just lazed around the cabin laughing and talking and drinking rum punch. Well, we did a little crabbing, too, the girls surprising me by enjoying that so much, something I'd done all my life. They loved catching the crabs, thought they were *so* cute, but did not like cooking them. Corrine grabbed my arm and stopped me when I started to drop one of the squirming crabs into a pot of boiling water. She's always been too tenderhearted, which is part of the reason she's had such a sad life. I ended up throwing the crabs back into the bay and going into town to buy crabmeat for my she-crab soup. Corrine wouldn't even taste it and still won't, to this day.

I get the mop and the bucket and the

Clorox and Mr. Clean and start cleaning up. Before I tackle the house, I make myself go down to the pier. Daddy added a little gazebo-like thing with benches—another project from his workshop—and all the fannies that have sat on the benches over the years have worn them smooth as driftwood. But the benches are grimy and nasty now, so I spray them with Fantastik and wipe them off with paper towels. The walkway of the pier is white-speckled with seagull doo-doo, making it look like a crazy artist flung a paintbrush over it, so I unwind the hose and wash it off good. The queen's promenade down the pier is a Same Sweet Girl tradition, one of my favorites. We can't have the queen slipping on seagull doo and busting her royal ass, can we?

It takes me a couple of hours and several trash bags to clean up the cabin, it's such a mess. Don't know how I've let it get so bad in such a short time. The cabin's real simple, what a decorator would call rustic. Julia once called it shabby chic, but Astor muttered, "Guess I missed the chic part." There's one big central room, with plank walls and pine posts from the floor to the ceiling. The kitchen area's sectioned off from the sitting area by a counter that doubles as an eating bar. The back of the room is the best because of the floor-to-ceiling glass doors and windows looking out over Mobile Bay, with all the sofas and chairs turned to face the great view. On either side are the bedrooms, two on each side. That's it, except for the deck in back, where the steps lead down to the bay.

Plopping down on the old wicker sofa, I try not to break my arm patting myself on the back. It looks good, clean as an angel's underwear, as Mama used to say, but living here now, rather than just vacationing, I see that it leaves a lot to be desired. Truth is, it's pretty tacky. Both Mama and my grandmother furnished it with their throwaways, a few "beachy"-looking pieces thrown in, like the wicker sofa and rocker. I don't know how much longer I'm going to be camping out here, but I ought to fix it up, make it not only more comfortable but prettier. My house in Reform, now that's what you call well decorated. Ought to be; Paul and I paid a fortune to that hotshot decorator from Columbus, Mississippi, to fix it up, after we restored it. *Paul and I . . .* better not go there now, or I'll end up squalling again, and I won't get a thing done. I stand up, hands on hips, and look around. I'm not sure of the best approach for a makeover. Repainting the walls? Putting rugs on the bare floors? Nuking the whole place and starting over?

I go outside and down the wooden stairs to the storage area under the house. Since it's on stilts, there's not only a parking area under there but also lots of room to store stuff, which Mama did after Daddy died, before she got sick and ended up in the nursing home. But rummaging through it, I don't find anything I like, except a big pink ceramic lamp that looks like a tallywacker. Being the mean person I am, I put it in the room where Rosanelle always stays, she and Byrd. Poor Byrd, getting stuck with Rosanelle every time, as though it was Byrd's fault that Dixie Lee was her roommate and Rosanelle the replacement. Once I had too much rum punch and horrified everyone by saying that the worst thing about Dixie Lee dying was how we ended up with Rosanelle taking her place. (Obviously, this was one of those times when Rosanelle didn't come.) My comment even shocked Astor, who's pretty unshockable, and everyone agreed I'd never be crowned queen again, saying such terrible, unsweet things. I felt real bad about it, I swear I did, because I didn't really mean it. I like Rosanelle fine, bad as she gets on my nerves. Truth is, I'm not a sweet person, but most of the time, I'm able to fake it pretty good.

I get this wild hair up my butt and decide to decorate, not just clean up. Except for a few nice pieces of Corrine's artwork, her gourds that look like fancy vases and bowls, everything here is so tacky I can't stand it anymore. I load up three big boxes—old-timey chenille bedspreads, plaid and floral throw pillows, faded rugs that look like they survived the Civil War, they're so old—and haul them to Mobile, to the Goodwill thrift store. Then I shop, going to Pier 1 Imports and blowing a whole month's paycheck. I buy bedspreads in Indian batiks and a red-patterned throw from the Himalayas to spruce up the sofa. I get kilim floor pillows and a green-edged sisal rug. The sales clerk, a skinny college girl with little-bitty ears pierced about fifty times, talks me into getting these *precious* hanging lamps that she calls "jewel-globed," telling me the colors are amethyst and ruby and emerald. I've always been a sucker for talk like that. Taking her advice, I buy enough scented candles to burn Mobile to the ground and smell good doing it. In a fancy kitchen store at the Outlet Mall, I splurge on bamboo placemats and at least a million baskets, every size and shape imaginable. On a roll, I can't seem to stop myself buying stuff. I've always hated to shop, which caused Paul to swear I was lacking in some essential female gene, but today, I see why it's considered such fun. By leaving the hatch open in my car, I'm able to take home two five-feet-tall ficus plants in sea-grass baskets as well as half a dozen hanging spider plants. If I can't decorate it, I'll hide it.

By nine o'clock that night, I'm worn out. I've only stopped once, to eat dry granola from the box, standing up by the sink. I emptied the fridge when I cleaned it, and my cupboards are bare; how they'll be till payday. I've never had to worry about money before, never in my life, and I feel guilty how I've always taken things for granted. You know, things like groceries and the light bill. I've found out in the last few months that nothing makes you feel poorer than being hungry. Because I haven't had to think about it in the past, I do dumb things like spending all my money buying jewel-globed lamps instead of groceries. Tomorrow I'll have to hit the crab pots again, just to have something for supper. Once the SSGs get here this weekend, though, there will be plenty to eat because our dishes have become part of the ritual.

For a bunch of weight-conscious women, we eat like field hands when we get together. Julia will have her chef fix that great chicken salad with red grapes and toasted pecans in it, which I could eat by the gallon, and she'll also bring her pimento cheese. The other girls make sandwiches out of it, but I've been known to sit cross-legged on the floor with the bowl of pimento cheese in one hand and a spoon in the other. Mama Byrd brings comfort food: garlic-grits casseroles and her tomato-and-Vidalia-onion pie. I ate a whole one the first year, all by myself, so since then, she's been bringing half a dozen, one for each of us. First time she brought that many, Astor made me mad by saying that Byrd brought one pie for the SSGs and five for me. That wasn't what pissed me off, actually; it was the way Astor rolled her eyes and carried on about me eating a whole pie. I stuck out my tongue at her and she said no wonder your ass is so big and I said you can kiss mine, and she said she'd better get started, then, because it'd take her a while. We ended up having a pure-tee fight about it.

The next year, after we'd all graduated, we had the gathering here again—the beginning of the tradition—and Astor flew in from New York with a cheesecake from some famous Yankee place up there. Since then she always brings the desserts. Not that Astor cooks them; she's about as domestic as a bird dog. Recently, she's been bringing healthy, sugar-free stuff that we all hate, things like tofu and fruit with Sweet'N Low on it. Take last year. Astor brought a *prune* cake from a new bakery in Birmingham and told us it was sweetened with fructose or something. After supper we got about half-crocked and took the cake down to the pier, where we broke off chunks of it and fed the fish.

After a thirty-minute shower (Oh, God, how will I pay the water bill?), I go to bed on new sheets from the Ralph Lauren outlet. They feel as soft as a baby's behind, which they'd damn sure better, at fifty dollars a sheet. A breeze, tasting of salt and smelling of the ocean, blows in the opened windows (that way I don't have to run the air-conditioner), and I doze off. When the phone rings, I can't think what the sound is, what has jerked me out of sleep. I think it's the alarm and I've got to be at the hospital. When I grope for the phone, a catch in my back surprises me, what I get for getting down on my all-fours and scrubbing the floors, like a pure fool. A good deed never goes unpunished. I answer without turning on the lamp. "Yeah?"

"Lanier? You there?"

It's Astor. I fall back on the pillow, wishing I hadn't answered. Conversations with Astor can be exhausting; she's nothing if not high maintenance. "I'm asleep," I tell her, throwing in a yawn for good measure.

Her laugh is skeptical. "Oh, bull," Astor says. "Don't give me that. You've got someone with you, right?"

"Listen, can I call you back in the morning? I cleaned up the house and . . ."

"Someone's there," she repeats, ignoring me. "Who is it, Roland Pierce?"

That wakes me up. "*Not* funny, Astor. Even for you, that's a low one."

"Calm down, Sidney Lanier," she sighs. "Don't get your panties in a wad." Astor tells everyone that she always does yoga while on the phone, so I picture her twisted like a pretzel, the phone hooked up to headgear. "I'm calling to see if you knew that Byrd has gone to Blue Mountain to pick up Corrine," she says.

I sit up against the wicker headboard, pulling a pillow behind me. "Byrd's gone to Corrine's? Why would she do that?" Our travel is habitual. For our get-togethers here, Corrine drives from Blue Mountain to Birmingham to Byrd's house, and they travel together to Mobile. Since moving back to Alabama, Astor's been going to Montgomery and picking Julia up. Rosanelle drives down by herself, since she usually visits with other alumni groups. That way, she can write the weekend off as part of her job. In October, when we meet in Blue Mountain, we reverse the process, me going to Birmingham to travel with Byrd, Julia picking up Astor. Only a few times have there been any variations in our patterns. Byrd driving to Blue Mountain to pick up Corrine is definitely weird. For some reason—maybe because I'm only half awake—it makes me uneasy.

"I have no idea why Byrd would do that," Astor says, with that breathlessness she gets when she's either excited or nosing around in somebody else's business. Why Byrd picking Corrine up would interest Astor is beyond me, except she's so nosy. Since moving back she's been in hog heaven, all wrapped up in the boring little dramas of our lives. She goes on to say, "When I called Byrd tonight, Buster told me she'd gone to Blue Mountain to get Corrine. I was afraid that something might be wrong."

"Nothing that I know of. Corrine's car is a piece of crap, as you know, so maybe Byrd got it in her head that Corrine wouldn't make it to Birmingham. Probably nothing more than that." I'd almost fallen for Astor's dramatics again, gotten myself all worked up. "Guess we'll find out this weekend," I add, yawning.

"If Corrine decides to be her usual murky, mysterious self, we won't. And quit yawning, Lanier, you're making me sleepy. Oh, did I tell you, I'm leaving for Julia's right after my afternoon dance class so her chef can fix those crab cakes of his, just for me?" The way Astor emphasizes "just for me" in a playful, little-girl voice irritates me for some reason. Makes it sound like I'm supposed to be jealous or something. Determined not to let her get to me again, I say, "I love going to Julia's now, with all those servants and chefs and bodyguards hanging around."

She giggles. "Especially the bodyguards, huh? If I were Julia, I'd go after—oops . . . somebody's beeping in. Hang on a minute." Astor's back in less than that time, breathless. "Nobody I need to talk to now. Thought it might be the nursing home."

"Anything new with Mose?" I hold my breath guiltily. I'm too tired to hear it tonight.

"Guess you could say that. Earlier today he watered the potted plants on the front veranda, in full view of a group of visitors."

"Yeah? That's a good sign, if he's taking an interest in gardening—"

Astor snorts. "He peed in them, Lanier. Can you imagine? The esteemed Mose Morehouse, rising up from his wheelchair and pissing in a flowerpot on the veranda of St. Mary's. Oh, crap—another call coming in. I'd better catch this one."

"Talk to you tomorrow," I say, relieved she's going, though the image of Mose and the flowerpot breaks my heart.

"Okay. And, Lanier? Give Roland Pierce a kiss for me." Cackling like a wicked witch, Astor hangs up.

I put down the phone and swing my legs over the side of the bed, sitting in the dark. Sometimes Astor can be more irritating than Rosanelle, which is saying a mouthful. I've been fascinated by Astor since we first met, but she can be one royal pain in the ass. Here's what is weird, though. Something about Astor makes you overlook that— which we've all done, again and again. Well, all of us except Corrine, that is. I don't get it, whatever it is between the two of them. Sometimes I think Corrine actually dislikes Astor, but then we'll all be together, laughing and talking and carrying on, and I'll wonder where I got such a notion. One of the Same Sweet Girls couldn't dislike another one, could she? We'd kick her out of the group, since it wouldn't be *sweet,* and you can't be an SSG if you're not sweet. It's an oxymoron, or whatever you call that thing. I wasn't particularly good in English class.

Corrine and I met Astor Deveaux the first day of Interpretative Dance class, our freshman year at The W. We'd heard of Astor since she arrived on campus, of course; everyone had. Anyone out of the ordinary stood out at The W, and Astor was anything but ordinary. She'd come to The W on a dance scholarship provided by some rich alum who'd made a name for herself on Broadway. We'd heard there was competition all over the southeast for the coveted scholarship and that the girl from Louisiana who got it was really something. After college, Astor went on to dance on Broadway, too, and the SSGs always planned on taking a trip up to see her in a play, but we couldn't get everyone together for that. Too much trouble. Some of us went on our own, though.

Even before our dance instructor introduced Astor as the scholarship winner who'd be assisting her in teaching the class and Astor made a theatrical bow, I knew who she was. Had to be. Since I'd never seen a real live Cajun before, I stared at her wide-eyed. "That's her!" Corrine whispered, nudging me with her bony elbow. Then she leaned over and whispered again. "If that girl's a Cajun, Lanier, I'll kiss your behind." I tried to shush her, but she added, "Bet you *anything* she's a phony." From that moment on, before they ever spoke to each other, the die was cast for Corrine and Astor's up-and-down relationship.

I pick up the phone to call Corrine, find out why Byrd is picking her up, but don't. It's an hour later in the north Georgia mountains; Corrine will be asleep. Even in college she kept odd hours. First night, I figured I'd have to go to the housing council the very next morning and request a new roommate, much as I liked Corrine. Night and day we were, literally and figuratively. But I decided to give it a little longer, giving me time to get used to Corrine's weirdness. Which wasn't just her bedtime hours, believe me. For one thing, Corrine was the first person I'd ever met who had problems with clinical depression, something I knew nothing about. I wasn't sure if that meant she'd spend a lot of time sitting and staring like a zombie, or if she'd talk to herself or something. God, I was so ignorant then! I knew The W would put me with a scholarship recipient, but I wasn't expecting an art major, which was as strange to me as clinical depression.

Then, to top it off, I found out that Corrine's "medium" was gourds. Gourds! I laughed my hiney off when she told me, but it shut me up when she hauled in a bunch of gourds that she'd won all sorts of prizes with and decorated our room with them. I'd never seen anything so cool! Matter of fact, I wouldn't have even known they were gourds if she hadn't told me. She'd carved or painted them in all sorts of really neat-looking designs. She'd even made musical instruments from some of them, little flutes and sitars and stuff. It used to make me feel really bad for Corrine when she had to sell one for spending money, because you could tell that she was attached to everything she made. She was snooty about it, too, refusing to give in to requests to make those crafty-looking gourds you see, the ones decorated like Santas or birdhouses, though she could've made a lot of money doing so. Corrine's stuff was real art, and sure enough, after graduation, she went on to become sort of famous as a gourd artist. Which still sounds funny, to tell you the truth. To this day, I can't even say the word "gourd" without getting tickled.

Both Astor and Rosanelle have told me—in strictest confidence, of course—that they think Corrine's crazy as a loony bird. Talk about the pot calling the kettle black! One thing about Astor, though. She and Corrine have their little clashes, but deep down, I can tell that Astor really admires Corrine. I know for sure that she likes Corrine a whole lot better than Corrine likes her.

The reason I know how Astor feels about Corrine is this: At our get-togethers, the SSGs are always playing these silly little games, stuff like "If you wrote your autobiography, what would the title be?" Well, one year Astor said, "Let's describe each other by using literary characters instead of adjectives." Most of the time, I like the games a lot, but for some reason, that one struck me as the stupidest idea yet, and believe me, Astor's come up with some lulus. When I pooh-poohed it, Astor told the others that I didn't want to play because I wasn't smart enough. She said that I didn't know any literary characters or adjectives, and I said, "Oh, yeah—is that right, Lady Macbeth, you frigging bitch?" I thought Julia was going to fall off her chair laughing. I ended up playing the stupid game anyway, and Astor said that Corrine was Annabel Lee, which I thought was perfect. The reason is, Corrine is really pretty but in an unearthly sort of way, if you know what I mean. What makes her look kind of ghostly is her being so pale, with big round eyes, silver and clear as water. Then she's got this long, curly, reddish-blonde hair, exactly like the picture of Annabel Lee in the American Lit book we used as sophomores.

I realize I can't call Corrine this late because she's been feeling puny lately, had some kind of bug. Which might be—it hits me—the reason Byrd has gone to get her. Corrine left me a couple of messages when I was working nights last week, saying she might not come to the SSG gathering this year since she couldn't seem to shake whatever was ailing her. Because of her being a New Ager, she's been to psychic healers and herbalists and stuff, but they haven't helped. I'd pooh-poohed the idea of her not coming, calling her back and telling her she'd never get the crown again if she didn't. And we haven't talked since. I'd just assumed she was coming. Assumptions, Paul used to say; you can't assume things in our profession. Got to have proof. He sure took that a whole lot more literally than I ever dreamed he would.

Paul. Almost every night, before going off to sleep, I have to stop myself from calling Paul, just to hear his voice. Sometimes I literally grab one hand with the other to keep myself from picking up the phone. But tonight I have it, right here. I punch in the numbers and wait for the ring. Since I'm no longer in the house to screen the calls, his service usually answers. But ever so often, I get him instead. Like tonight. My breath catches when he answers, and I say, "Paul?"

Must've had an all-nighter at the hospital last night, otherwise he wouldn't be in bed already. "Paul?" I repeat.

"Who's this?" He's answered without thinking, sleep-dazed. I know him so well. Or so I thought. So I thought.

"Paul, it's Lanier."

"Who?"

I clear my throat, and speak louder. "It's me, Lanier."

The sound I hear is the rustling of the sheets as he moves across the bed to hang up the phone. "Paul—wait! Please, don't hang up!" It's too late. Hearing the click of the receiver, I throw the phone down. Before I know it, I'm crying again, though I haven't cried over him for days. Weeks, maybe. I've been doing so much better. Serves me right. I had to hear his voice again, didn't I? No matter that he hates my guts, that he can't stand the sight of me or the sound of my voice, I had to twist the knife. Fumbling around on the bedside table, I find a tissue, wipe my eyes, and blow my nose.

Jesus, I'm such a slow learner! Either that, or a masochist. Haven't I found out, over and over, that I can't talk to Paul, Lindy, or Christopher without boo-hooing? Christopher calls occasionally, and I always cry, even after his most recent call, a happy one to tell me about his tennis scholarship to Vandy. He's such a jock that I used to worry he couldn't deal with emotional upsets, yet he's handled this better than any of us. Lindy, on the other hand, won't return my calls or answer my letters. Everyone tells me she just needs time, that she'll come around if I let her grow up a bit. She just turned seventeen, and it's been harder on her than any of us.

I can't go back to sleep now; I've gotten myself all worked up, calling Paul and thinking about the kids. Pushing the pillows behind me, I sit up in the bed, yelping at the pain in my lower back, and open the drawer to the bedside table. Fumbling, I pull out my lesson book and fountain pen and wipe my eyes. Since I'm awake anyway, might as well write in my book. I've neglected it lately, being so caught up with settling into my new life. Plenty I need to add to it, that's for sure.

Corrine gave me the lesson book as a joke, sort of, with neither of us having any idea how I'd take to it. It was a few years ago, at a Same Sweet Girls gathering at Corrine's place in the mountains, when she brought out the book and presented it to me. "Lanier, I found this at an antiques store on Tate Mountain," she'd said, "and knew it was perfect for you."

Being Corrine, she'd wrapped it in artsy-looking parchment paper that she'd tie-dyed, or something, herself. I was disappointed when I unwrapped it, failing to see what made it so perfect for me, while the other Same Sweet Girls oohed and aahed politely. It was a child's old lesson tablet, made of heavy cardboard, with the blue-lined pages stiff and browned around the edges; the kind of writing tablet I guess our grandparents practiced cursive writing in. The neat thing about it was the way Corrine had added to it—matter of fact, it took me a minute to figure out she'd done it, that she hadn't found it that way. The ivory-colored cover was real old and antique-looking, and "LESSON BOOK" was printed in dark calligraphied letters. Above that, Corrine had added "LANIER'S." Dead center, she'd written, "When the pupil is ready, a teacher appears."

"Okay, Lanier, here's the thing," Corrine had said, sitting beside me on the floor and opening the lesson book. "You tell us how you're always screwing up, right?" *"Right!"* the Same Sweet Girls yelled together, before I could open my mouth. Ignoring me giving everyone the finger, Corrine continued. "You've got to help the rest of us out. It's your duty to our friendship. I got this for you to put your life lessons in. Think of all the important lessons you've learned over the years from your screw-ups and record them for posterity." She handed me a fountain pen. "I got this to go with it and put purple ink in it. Real sweet of me, wasn't it?"

"Kiss my fanny," I'd said indignantly, and everyone booed me. "I'm not going to do it! It's not only that I'm a lousy writer, but I never learn from my mistakes, no matter how many times I mess up." I tossed the book in Corrine's lap, pouting.

But Corrine made me take the stupid little book back and kept telling me to just give it a try, that I'd come to love writing in it. I knew what she was trying to do, of course, so I resisted, like I've always resisted anything good for me, from spinach to studying. But the little book was so cute—and I'd never written with a fountain pen, much less one with purple ink—that I told myself I'd at least write my name in it. Then a couple of days later, I picked it up and wrote down something that my mama used to say, something the Same Sweet Girls loved and quoted over and over when I read it to them: *Honey, it will either work out or it won't.* Having it in writing kind of inspired me, so that whenever I got myself in a mess, I'd take out the little lesson book and read over that line again—it will either work out or it won't. Yep. That was sure the gospel truth. One day, in a snit, I wrote: *I keep doing the same crap over and over and expecting it to turn out different each time.*

The entries began to expand, and once I was so startled on rereading an entry that I called Corrine, excited. "Listen to this, girl-friend," I'd said. "I think I've discovered the source of all my problems! Here's what I wrote in that stupid-ass book you gave me. All my problems can be summed up in this one line." "Let's hear it, then," Corrine had said, and I'd read, *"I thought I was doing the right thing at the time."* I knew I'd hit home when Corrine, after a pause, burst into laughter. Once she told everyone, I was assigned the role of the official scribe of the Same Sweet Girls. Every time we get together, I have to read them what I've written.

Tonight I look back over the last entries as I think about what needs to be said before the gathering, what I can write to share with everyone. Lanier's Life Lessons. A few months ago, when Paul kicked me out of the house and I ended up here at the cabin, I'd written, *The Moving Finger writes "You're Screwed," then moves on.* Tonight I nibble on the tip of the fountain pen, frowning, before finally writing: *Any landing you walk away from is a good landing.*

I put the notebook back in the drawer, then yawn and stretch, trying to get the kink out of my back. Getting to my feet, I stumble to the kitchen for a drink of water, feeling my way. Then on to the bathroom to pee. When I come out of the bathroom, something catches my eye, and I move to the window that's across from my bed. Leaning over, I stick my head out, squinting without my contacts to see through the thick foliage. What I see scares me, and I grip the windowsill. I'll be damned—a light is on in the house next door. But—it can't be!—the house has been empty for years. Just yesterday, a Realtor who was one of Mama's old friends called me, asking if I'd ever thought about putting Dolphin Cove on the market. Somehow, with me and her yakking about various things, the subject came up, and the Realtor told me that the Picketts had not sold their property next door. Mrs. Pickett died a few months ago in a nursing home in Mobile—hadn't I read it in the papers? she asked. She said the house was unoccupied, what with the Pickett kids all over the world and poor Mrs. Pickett dying in a nursing home. Said she'd tried to get the Picketts to put the house up for sale, but no. She'd repeated herself, so I'm sure that I heard her right: A shame it was, a real shame that such a nice house, such an *important* house, should be empty.

I sink back in my bed, a little shaken, and pull the sheet over me against the strong salt wind. For the first time, I have second thoughts about my impulsive decision to move here. Pretty as it is, and as much as I love it, it *is* isolated. Everyone—the SSGs especially—told me I was crazy, a single woman living here alone. It was Lanier and her foolhardy behavior again, they'd said. Fools rush in where angels fear to tread, blah blah blah . . . as though anyone would ever mistake me for an angel. Well, I've been a fool going on fifty years now, all my life, and it's not very likely that things are going to change at this late date. If I weren't so sleepy, I'd pull my lesson book out again, and that's what I'd write.

3

Julia
MONTGOMERY, ALABAMA

WHAT I LIKE ABOUT marble floors is the sound my heels make, the *click! click!* as I walk from one wing to the other. Since moving into this mausoleum, I've come to appreciate the oddest things.

Unbelievable what it takes for me to get off for a weekend; unbelievable how much I look forward to going. The things from an ordinary life you take for granted: sleeping until you want to get up, then going into a kitchen, a regular *kitchen,* and fixing yourself what you want for breakfast. It's been two years since I've opened a box of Special K myself, or spooned yogurt out of the container, or poured half-and-half from its carton instead of a silver pitcher. Oh, I can do that now, any-time. It's the hassle of explaining why I'd want to that defeats me. And then, the incredulous look from Joe Ed, wondering why I'd do something for myself when some-one else is eager to do it for me. I can do it if I pay the fiddler. Take what you want, the old saying goes, one of my mother's favorites. *Take what you want from life, then pay the price.* If it weren't such a cliché, I'd tell Lanier to put it in her lesson book. I could fill up that lesson book with my mother's say-ings, easily. The old girl is never at a loss for words.

The breakfast with the reporter from Huntsville is over, and I have an hour before meeting with my assistant and the gardener, planning next week's floral arrangements. Then another hour before the luncheon with the Democratic Women for a New Alabama. I won't need preparation time for that; after two years the standard speech is branded on my brain. That gives me a couple of hours. Barely. If His Highness hadn't issued a royal command, it'd be more like two and a half. Maybe I'll still have it—usually it takes Joe Ed less than fifteen minutes to hem-haw around until I figure out what he wants. He has it down to an art. It's amazing what years of practice can do for you.

I glance down at my watch, which is so heavy and diamond-studded that it actually hurts my wrist. Poor Joe Ed; he has tried for so long to buy class, not realizing it's not for sale. Mother rolled her eyes when I opened the watch on Christmas morning, and I knew, with a petty satisfaction, that Joe Ed had not asked her advice before buying it. Astor helped him pick it out, meeting him and his entourage at Goldberg's in Mountain Brook Village, and hearing that was all it took to get Mother's eyes rolling again, and sure enough, as soon as we were alone, she let me have it. I *must* not let Joe Ed shop for me; he has the most appalling taste; and if he insists, I *must* send her with him in-stead of one of my (here she sniffs, turning her nose up) *friends*. Mother never says anything against Astor in front of Joe Ed, certainly not since Astor married Mose Morehouse. Watching the old girl struggle for political correctness threatens to be my undoing, and I have to hide my smirks. Joe Ed knows what his dear mother-in-law is doing but can't afford to offend her, so I keep a straight face every time the two of them blather on and on about Mose, what a treasure to the state of Alabama he is. Mother inevitably says how much she admires Astor and how touching her devotion to Mose is, and just as inevitably, she looks at me meaningfully. Hand it to old Estelle d'Iberville Dupont, she is nothing if not predictable.

Thank God Cal is on duty today. He clicks off his walkie-talkie and replaces it on his belt when I enter the outer office. He's the only one of the troopers who will make eye contact with me. The widespread stories—though I doubt their veracity—that one of George Wallace's wives slept with half the state troopers assigned to guard her husband naturally make them nervous in my presence. The SSGs love to flirt with the troopers, trying to get their attention like tourists do with the guards at Buckingham Palace, but I've never been anything but professional with any of them. Except for Cal, I can't understand the SSGs' flirtations, since most of the troopers look like drill sergeants with their shaved heads, bulging muscles, and bull necks. Many of them are former football players at Alabama or Auburn, including Cal, who'd been Joe Ed's favorite receiver when he was quarterback at Alabama. Cal the Creek, Bama fans called him, not only because he "cut like a creek" through his defenders, but also because he was half Creek Indian, having been raised on a reservation in Florida. Both Cal and Joe Ed left the gridiron gimped up, however; Cal walks with a slight limp and Joe Ed has had back surgery twice.

"How's my favorite first lady?" Cal smiles politely as he steps to Joe Ed's door and opens it for me. "Behaving yourself?"

"Not if I can help it," I reply. "How about you, Lieutenant Hawkins?"

Cal shrugs. "Same old same old. Maybe we'll have another terrorist attack, liven things up around here."

I laugh, shaking my head. Last Saturday night some drunken fool had crashed his pickup into the brick wall surrounding the grounds, setting off alarms and bringing the full force of the state troopers running, guns drawn. Cal had radioed Joe Ed, waking us up, to stay in our quarters until further notice. Police scanners all over the city picked it up, and word got out that the Governor's Mansion was under a terrorist attack. Afterward, when Cal came by to assure us that it was nothing, Joe Ed had insisted he join us for a nightcap. Things changed that night between Cal, my husband's longtime friend and bodyguard, and myself. Even though I'd been acquainted with Cal for years, we didn't hang around in the same circles, so I didn't really know him very well. But that night we became friends. After Joe Ed excused himself to go to bed because of an early-morning breakfast meeting, Cal and I stayed up an extra hour, drinking Chivas Regal and talking late into the night.

"Your girlfriends' weekend starts tomorrow, right?" Cal asks as I pass him entering Joe Ed's office. When I nod, he says, "What is it you call yourselves—the Sweet Old Girls?"

I roll my eyes. "The Same Sweet Girls. The *SSGs,* who will die when I tell them what you called us. The closer we get to fifty, the more sensitive we are about a certain three-letter word."

He winks conspiratorially. "Sure you ladies don't need a bodyguard?"

"They couldn't stand the thrill of having you around, Cal."

"Aw, have a heart, Julia. I haven't been in

the presence of that many beauty queens since Bama." He nods to Joe Ed, seated behind his desk. "Here's Mrs. Stovall, Governor, punctual as always."

I turn before Cal closes the door, saying, "Still half a bottle of scotch left, Cal. Stop by and help me finish it off sometime."

"Joe Ed asked me to come by tonight." With a mock salute, he closes the door behind me.

Two aides are with Joe Ed, but they scurry out when I arrive, bowing and scraping. They're baby-faced, clean-cut, dressed for the role in their dark suits and stylish paisley ties. Since Joe Ed's been in politics, his assistants get younger looking every year. Joe Ed stands until I sit down in the leather chair next to his desk. Chairs are placed strategically around him; I rate the more intimately placed one by virtue of being first lady.

"Coffee?" Joe Ed presses a button before I have the chance to decline, and his secretary, Ruth, appears with a huge tray, bearing a silver coffee service. None of us talks, except for the exchange of pleasantries, then *thank you,* and *you're welcome.* After Ruth is gone, I raise the delicate cup, embossed with the seal of Alabama, and sip the coffee reluctantly. I had too many cups at the breakfast, which is why my hands are shaking.

I feel Joe Ed's eyes on me and raise my eyes. "What?" I say, trying not to sound defensive. I have no idea why he's summoned me.

"You look so pretty, Julia," he says softly. "I like the new outfit. That color's good on you."

I look down at it, forgetting what I put on. It seems like I've been up for days instead of hours. I've dressed in a silk pantsuit in a pinkish-ivory color, which I'd bought because it showed off the really spectacular necklace Mother had handed down to me on my forty-seventh birthday last month. It's an antique diamond-and-pearl choker, the pearls so old they've turned a pallid shade of pink. In the drawing room of the family home in Mobile is a portrait of my namesake and great-great-grandmother wearing the necklace, and I've always liked it. Funny Mother giving it to me this year instead of saving it for my fiftieth, the milestone one. Maybe she thought one of us wouldn't be around then. "Glad you approve," I say, relaxing, smiling at him for the first time. I'd assumed he was upset about something and needed my shoulder to cry on, thus the early summons.

"Julia, when you leave tomorrow for Dauphin Island, I'm going to visit Bethany," Joe Ed says, putting down his coffee cup and looking at me defiantly. Joe Ed had his fiftieth birthday this year, but you'd never know it. Except for a receding hairline, he looks exactly as he did when we met almost thirty years ago: sandy-haired, broad-shouldered, all-American. With an easy grin and shining blue eyes, he was incredibly good-looking then, but that wasn't what attracted me to him. In those days, before the political world affected him, Joe Ed was such a sweet-natured young man, so polite and earnest. The golden boy of southern politics, he is now at the apex of his looks and power, his destiny. Except for Bethany, he has led a charmed life. Bethany . . . the dark spot on his cloudless horizon.

I place my cup and saucer on his desk so I won't drop them with my shaky hands. "Joe Ed, you *cannot* do that."

His blue eyes flash. "I'll be damned if they'll tell me I can't see my own daughter." His jaw, square and tight, juts out, and his face flushes. When Joe Ed gets angry, he looks like a little boy.

"It's the only way Bethany can adjust," I remind him. "If you go there, she'll put in to come home with you. And she can't stay with us forever. She's eighteen now, Joe Ed. I beg you, please don't do this." Then I realize this is exactly what he wants me to say. He knows he can't go. It's too important that Bethany settle into the Helen Keller Institute. Not for us, but for her. *For her.* Joe Ed needed me to remind him, thus the early-morning summons. He said he was going so I would tell him that he couldn't.

He puts his hand over his eyes and I soften toward him. Rising from the chair, I go and kneel beside him, placing my cheek next to his, which smells of his expensive aftershave. I put an arm around his shoulder. "We've done the right thing. You know that. We've done the right thing."

He nods wearily, then sighs. "Yeah, I know. I just didn't know it'd be so hard." After a long, painful moment, he sits up, resuming his gubernatorial dignity. I stand, watching him. It's Joe Ed's deep love of our daughter, our fragile, handicapped daughter, that makes me love him. On and off, through the years, there have been times when I've felt nothing on the good days, something close to hatred on the bad ones, and despair on the others. But his devotion to Bethany will bind me to him, always, in spite of everything else. I'm reminded of that whenever his love of Bethany hurts him in all his soft places.

I put my hand on his shoulder. "Parents' weekend in a few weeks, remember? Dr. Uptain assures me that Bethany will have made so much progress by then we won't know her." When he doesn't speak, I continue. "Sweetheart, I've got to run. Don't forget, Astor's spending the night here so we can get off early in the morning, and you said you'd have a drink with us before your meeting."

Joe Ed's face brightens. "Something to look forward to." He gets to his feet, gives me a peck on the lips, then lowers his eyes to study the pearl choker. "Your mama's gifts always make mine look pitiful by comparison," he says. *Which is exactly what she intends,* I think. But I keep that hurtful observation to myself.

Astor's in rare form tonight, charming both Joe Ed and Cal Hawkins, who showed up together in our sunroom at six o'clock, the cocktail hour at the Mansion. Took me a minute to recognize Cal dressed in khakis and a short-sleeved denim shirt rather than his gray state trooper's uniform, with his crow-black hair neatly combed. At first I was touched to see that he'd obviously spruced up for the occasion, but that changed quickly to dismay. When he and I stayed up and talked last Saturday night, Cal told me for the first time about his separation and impending divorce from his wife. I'd already heard from Joe Ed that Cal was devastated, that he and his wife, Rita, a much-sought-after decorator in town, had been married since college days and seemed to be devoted to each other. However, Rita had fallen in love with a much younger man who came to install a computer system in her store and had left Cal for him. When telling me the story, Cal was composed and unemotional, but the pain in his dark eyes told me how hurt he was. I'd tried to console him, saying that surely Rita would come to her senses before the divorce went through. Since Rita, like me, was approaching fifty, she probably needed to be assured that she was still attractive; hence she'd taken up with a younger man. Men do it all the time, I'd told Cal, who looked startled before laughing, as though I'd told the funniest joke on the planet. I'd urged him to send Rita flowers, along with a sweet letter telling her how much he missed her. Now I'm a tad uneasy, seeing how Cal keeps glancing over at Astor. I hope Joe Ed's bringing him along didn't send the wrong message, make it appear we were trying to set him up with Astor. *Oh, dear.*

"Astor, tell Cal how you women got your name," Joe Ed is saying, after we've laughed about Cal calling us the Sweet Old Girls this morning. "You'll love this story, man."

Astor has center stage, perched on a wicker stool, a flute of champagne in hand. The glassed-in sunroom is my favorite in the Mansion because it's small and cozy, unlike the rest of the wing containing the family's quarters. The rattan furniture is cushioned in bright tropical prints, and an overhead fan turns, stirring the air perfumed with dozens of gardenias in hanging baskets. Astor begins her story with a coy smile, saying, "Okay. At The W, Cal, we had to attend convocation every Thursday morning. Freshmen were assigned seats so the much-feared dean of women, Dr. Pate, could keep an eye on us from her perch in the balcony."

Cal is the perfect audience, and he whistles and shakes his head. "Everyone at Bama called The W a nunnery, didn't they, Governor? Being a girls' school run by Methodists, it had a reputation for strictness."

"Oh, it was," Astor assures him. "In the fifties, sixties, and seventies, Dean Pate ruled with a white-gloved hand."

Joe Ed turns to Cal. "She was an old friend of Julia's mama, Cal. Think Mrs. Dupont let loose in a school of two thousand young ladies and you'll get the picture."

"Scary thought," Cal smiles, rising to pour himself another scotch. Joe Ed had dismissed the trusty, preferring to serve the drinks himself when we have just a few friends in, but Cal felt comfortable enough to help himself.

Astor tilts her head to look at me, pushing her dark hair behind her ear. "Actually, the friendship with Dr. Pate got you into The W, didn't it, Julia?" I freeze, and she realizes what she has said. Quickly, her face flushing prettily, she mouths "Oops," then turns back to Cal. "As I was saying, we had assigned seats at convocation. We all hated going since it was usually some boring politician—sorry, Joe Ed—who spoke. We groaned and moaned and bitched, but quietly, sending each other notes, so we wouldn't get in trouble with Dean Pate."

Astor pauses for effect. She's in her element, with two attractive men hanging on her every word. Astor is not what you'd call beautiful, but she attracts more attention than any beautiful woman I've ever known. I've seen people on the street stop dead in their tracks when she walked by. Since she was a professional dancer, her every movement seems to be set to music. It's impossible not to notice her, partly because she's overly dramatic, always striking poses and talking with her hands, gesturing grandly. When we were in school together, Astor, my roommate and the most exotic creature any of us sheltered southern belles had ever seen, set the style on campus. We all wanted to look like her, with her dark olive skin, stick-straight black hair, and long, slanted eyes. To me she looks even better now than she did then. Today she's particularly striking in cropped, pencil-slim black slacks and a skimpy black sweater, with high-heeled sandals on her shapely feet.

"This convocation," she continues, cutting her dark eyes to Cal, tossing her silky hair, which brushes her shoulders, "we had a special speaker—a senior, Rosanelle Tilley of Eufaula, Alabama. She'd returned to The W after spending a year traveling, reigning as the National Maid of Cotton. She paraded on stage decked out in her crown and a white evening dress and long, trailing train—one-hundred percent cotton, of course—and in her arms she carried a bouquet of white roses and cotton bolls."

Cal laughs, but Astor holds up her hand to continue. "Rosanelle parades up and down the stage, giving us her queenly wave, while the pianist plays 'Stars Fell on Alabama.' Then, she tells us all about her reign as Maid of Cotton, going on and on for about an hour till we start to get bored and drift off. But—here's the way she closes her speech." Astor stands and puts her champagne flute on a glass-topped table next to her, grabs a daisy from an arrangement there, and poses, flinging her head back and holding the daisy clutched to her as though it were the rose and cotton boll bouquet Rosanelle carried that day. "Even though I've been all around the world during my reign as National Maid of Cotton," she says, in an exaggerated southern-belle drawl, fluttering her eyelashes, "and even though I've met with kings and queens and heads of state, I want all of you to know that I'm still the *same sweet girl* I've always been."

At the punch line, Joe Ed and Cal laugh appreciatively. Astor replaces the daisy and sits back down. "That woke us up! I thought Julia would explode trying to keep from laughing out loud. And the two girls sitting next to us, Lanier Brewer and Corrine Cooper, got tickled, too."

"But the worst was Byrd. Byrd and Dixie Lee, don't forget," I remind her.

"I'm getting to that. Byrd was the one who got us in trouble," she says, and Cal leans forward, his glass in hand forgotten, the ice melted.

"Byrd?"

Joe Ed answers him. "Real name Elizabeth Byrd, but the girls always called her by her last name. Her husband Buster is a big supporter, Cal—owns McCain International in Birmingham. You know him."

Cal whistles. "Sigma Nu president, a year ahead of us at Bama?" He turns to wink at me. "Your friend sure married well."

Astor and I exchange glances, but at this point, she doesn't tell him how Byrd came to marry Buster. Instead, she turns to Cal and continues her story. "We were all fighting to keep from giggling and catching the eagle eye of Dean Pate, but Byrd wasn't able to hold it in."

"Literally," I add, getting into the story as though I hadn't heard it a hundred times.

"Byrd laughs so hard that she pees in her pants," Astor says. "And who catches her but the feared Dean Pate, who has left her perch in the balcony to come storming down and find out what the hell we're doing, carrying on like that in convocation. So Dean Pate marches over and grabs all six of us by the arm—one at a time, of course—and pulls us out of the auditorium. We go to her office, where she chews us out for an hour before calling our mamas."

"We were on dorm restriction for six weeks, but it bound us together," I say.

Astor nods. "Sure did. School had only been in session a couple of months then, so we really didn't know each other well. But after six weeks restricted to the dorm while everyone else was out partying, we were inseparable. We called ourselves the Same Sweet Girls, and we had our first SSG reunion a year after graduation. That was over twenty-five years ago, and now we get together twice a year, the beach in the summer and the mountains in the fall."

"They've got these ridiculous rules and rituals they go through," Joe Ed says, and Astor and I both gasp, pretending to be offended.

"Ridiculous?—how can you say that, Joe Ed?" Astor cries. "One of these days we'll get the legislature to declare our queen the ruling monarch of Alabama, then you'll be sorry."

"You have a queen?" Cal asks, and Joe Ed puts his hand over his eyes. "Please don't ask any more, Cal," he says with a groan.

Astor leans toward Cal. "You are in the presence of royalty. If you think Julia's only claim to fame is being a successful author and the first lady of Alabama, you're wrong. She is the reigning queen of the SSGs."

"Okay, I'll bite," Cal grins. "How do you get to be queen?"

"Oh, we have very precise rules," she

says, wide-eyed, tossing her head. "We campaign all year, and we're in hot competition against each other for the coveted crown. The queen of the SSGs has to prove she's been the sweetest one for a whole year."

"We have a royal salute and a throne, the presentations, and the victory promenade down the pier," I add. "The reigning queen counts the ballots, then crowns the new queen. We got the crown at Mardi Gras, several years ago—"

"And it's the tackiest thing you've ever seen," Joe Ed interrupts. "If the press ever sees Julia in it, my career will be down the toilet."

"I'm going to ignore that remark," I say, "and assure you, Cal, that the crown is fabulous. It's almost ten pounds of rhinestones and looks stunning with the scepter, which used to be Rosanelle's drum majorette baton. Now it's decorated with streamers and topped with cotton bolls and sugar cubes."

Cal holds up his hand, laughing. "I get the picture. I had no idea our first lady belonged to such a group of wild women."

Shaking his head, Joe Ed rises to take

Cal's glass from his hand. "Enough. You ladies are going to run off my old buddy with these crazy tales. I've got time for a short one, then gotta run. Astor, Julia, more champagne?"

We hold up empty flutes and Joe Ed refills everyone's glasses, then stands by my chair to finish off his. Sipping his drink, Cal turns to Astor. "Are y'all still the original group? The same six of you?"

Astor and I lock eyes, then she raises her champagne glass and studies it thoughtfully. "No. We've lost one of us. Then we gained one. Not to replace her, but—"

"Not as a replacement," I interrupt. "But she came along after Dixie Lee was . . . killed in a car wreck, three years after graduation." I clear my throat. "You've met her, Cal, the replacement. The original Same Sweet Girl, Rosanelle Tilley. Dixon, now."

Cal's eyes widen in surprise. "That woman who does your alumni stuff? I've seen her here on lots of fund-raisers, of course. *She* was the Maid of Cotton?"

I nod. "She stayed on at The W, got the job of alumni director, and in that capacity, came to Dixie Lee's funeral. We all got drunk afterwards and told her why we called ourselves the Same Sweet Girls. Instead of it offending her, she was actually flattered. She never got the irony and was so taken with the idea that she not only wrote us up in the alumni magazine, she also started coming to our get-togethers. She's not one of us, really, but none of us has the heart to tell her." I shrug, sipping my champagne. "Wouldn't be very sweet of us, would it?"

Joe Ed puts the glass down with a thud. "Cal? You gonna stay around and visit with the ladies, or you want to walk out with me?"

My breath catches when Cal, under pretext of finishing off his drink, cuts his eyes over to where Astor is perched on the stool. I stand up quickly and take Joe Ed's arm. "Run along, sweetheart. Astor and I will walk Cal out."

When Joe Ed has gone, I take Cal's arm and lead him into the sitting room, with Astor trailing behind us. I stop in front of the mantel and point to the painting over it. It's huge, three feet by five, sweeping all the way to the ceiling. Folk art, oil on canvas, it shows an old-timey cotton field at harvest time, with brightly dressed black field hands at work, a mule-drawn wagon in the background piled high with white cotton. "I don't know if you've ever noticed this, Cal," I say.

He looks up at it. "It's a helluva painting. You've got others like it here, right?"

"And in the museum, too. But did you know that Astor's husband painted it? Mose Morehouse?"

Cal whistles. "Mose Morehouse? I've heard of him."

"He and Astor met in New York, right, Astor? The night he was honored by the American Academy of the Arts." I smile at Astor, but her face remains expressionless, as though she's trying to figure out where I'm going with this story. "It was *so* romantic," I continue. Astor may not know where I'm heading, but I do. "Mose was in a wheelchair, still is, I'm afraid, and Astor was so attentive to him that he fell in love with her and they were married a few weeks later. The SSGs were thrilled, not just because Astor had found such a wonderful man, but also because she moved to Mose's house in Birmingham and we got her back with us, finally." I give Astor another big smile before turning back to Cal. "I thought you'd find that story interesting."

Cal stands with his hands on his hips, looking up at the painting, until Astor comes to stand beside him. Side by side, Astor and

Cal look alike, I notice, with their exotic looks, the chiseled cheekbones and smut-black hair, their tight, muscular bodies. Cal is a more attractive man than Mose, no question about it. But somewhere in the back of my head, I can hear my mother: *You make your bed, you lie in it.*

Cal cuts his eyes over to Astor, then back to the painting. "So you're married to Mose Morehouse, Astor? I had no idea," he says, then whistles softly, shaking his head. "I'll be damned."

4

Corrine

BLUE MOUNTAIN, GEORGIA

I FALL IN LOVE with every gourd I do. I spend days—weeks!—working on a gourd, and it becomes a part of me. Every time I sell one, I feel like I'm selling a little piece of myself, which I am, in a way. The hardest to part with are the ones I've raised myself, from seedlings. Not that I grow all the gourds I work with, by any means. Most of the gourd artists I've met over the years don't grow their gourds themselves, leaving that up to the professionals. Which makes a lot more sense than my way, I guess, but growing them is part of the process for me, the beginning of my art.

All of my pieces are special to me, but the one I'm working on now . . . I can't even begin to describe the way I feel about it. What most people don't know about gourds (when I say things like that, Lanier always says, *everything,* is what!) is this: They have magical powers. No, really; they have. Truly, truly magic, in the old mystical, mythical sense of the word. There's a lot of lore concerning gourds, which goes way back to ancient days. They figure prominently in some biblical stories. In a famous fresco, John the Baptist is baptizing Jesus, using a gourd to pour water over his head. The first gourd that I sold in a gallery other than my own was a handle dipper I engraved, duplicating that scene.

In a graduate course in Native American Studies that I took in the fall after I left The W and came to the mountains, I got intrigued with the Native American use of gourds in sacred rituals, especially healing rites. That's why some of my better-known pieces feature Native American icons, even though I'm not Native American myself. The piece I've been working on, on and off for several weeks, is another Native American design and may be the most special one I've ever done. That's not bragging; that's just the way I feel about this gourd.

When I first saw it on the vine last year, I knew it was going to be special. Not only was it flawless and an unusually bright green color, it was large for a kettle gourd, almost two feet tall, so I had to fashion a sling for it as it ripened. I kept returning to the trellis day after day to check on it, already drawn to it beyond all the others, which I could never explain to a layperson. It's just a feeling you get when you work with gourds. This kettle gourd was so special I was tempted to pick it early and force the maturing process, but I restrained myself because there's always the chance of it rotting or shriveling. After bringing it in from the trellis, I let it dry until this spring. After I cleaned and prepared it last month, I spent two or three days holding it in my lap and meditating on the design. Several years ago, the first time Lanier caught me cradling one of my gourds and meditating, she wigged out, convinced I was every bit as loony as she had suspected. She and I laugh about it today, especially about how she begged me not to *ever* tell the other SSGs how I come up with my designs.

Today, in my studio, I put on my leather work gloves, then take up my wood-burning tool to make permanent the design that I've drawn freehand on the kettle gourd. Then I'll do some carving to bring it into sharper focus. The final step is my favorite, the painting in of the colors. At this stage, I'm never sure exactly which colors the design will call for. Of course, smart-mouth Lanier says all I have to do is hold the gourd in my lap and ask it. If only it were that easy! This kettle gourd, though, will speak to me as all my gourds do (I'd never tell Lanier that), and I'll know the palette by the time I begin painting it.

By midday I'm exhausted, having been working since daylight. I decide to call it a day and go into the gallery, see how Culley's doing. Since he got home from college in late May, he's been opening up for me at ten every morning, allowing me more time to work in my studio. At first I didn't want him to, afraid he'd get bored with the work and quit. Our relationship is still so fragile that I don't want to do anything to push him away. But so far, he's surprised me by taking to the running of the gallery in a way I never expected. As long as I allow him to bring his guitar and practice between browsers, he appears to be as happy working in the gallery as a pig in slop.

Standing in the front of the gallery looking out the windows, I watch the onslaught of tourists with the mix of emotions all of us in this touristy little mountain town experience. If it weren't for them, we wouldn't be here. I can barely handle the overhead as it is. Except for the Christmas festival, I do no business in the winter—none—so I close every January and February. But here it is the first week in June, and they're out in full force. I watch two busloads from a senior citizens' center in Marietta as they unload, the women in their pastel pantsuits and sun hats, the men in plaid bermudas and sturdy walking shoes. Cute, they're all so cute, I tell Culley. I swear to God, I will kill myself before I ever become *cute* in my old age. "Not a chance, Mom," Culley says, which I'm not sure how to take.

By two o'clock, when Culley and I finally have time to grab some lunch, a few items have sold, unusual for so early in the season. In addition to a couple of pieces of pottery I sell on commission for other artists, some of my gourds sold, too. A large, loud woman bought the tiny sennari gourd engraved with dogwood blossoms and inlaid with mother-of-pearl. I put a pretty price on it, too, for such a small piece—one hundred forty dollars—but she didn't even blink. When two of my painted bluebird houses sold at fifty-two dollars each, Culley looked at me for my reaction, after the customers left. I told him how I'd added the birdhouses reluctantly, strictly to cater to the tourist trade and to bring in added income. My gallery is here to sell pieces of art, I said snootily, not local crafts. Plenty of places for that, but not that many for local artists to sell their works. When I bought the gallery from a former teacher of mine, it was called the Fielding Gallery. I'd renamed it The Golden Gourd, planning to specialize in gourd art, but had ended up showing a lot of local painters and potters as well. Another thing I'd done to survive. After years of refusing to make anything just to attract tourists, I gave in after a bad season when I thought the bank was going to foreclose. During that season I found out something about myself: Over a lifetime of doing so, I've grown rather fond of eating. I've learned that principles are not nearly as tasty as bacon and eggs.

"You had lunch?" I ask Culley. No one's in the shop now, so he's got his guitar out, his reddish-gold, shoulder-length hair falling over his face as he hunches over, long fingers moving on the strings. At least he got my hair, otherwise I'd think his daddy cloned him. He's playing "The Seven Bridges Road," but I don't comment. Instead of that god-awful punk stuff he usually plays, I'd suggested the other day that he explore mountain music. Not exactly there, but a step in the right direction.

"Not hungry," he responds without looking at me as he rocks slowly back and forth, his eyes closed. His eyelashes cast shadows on his cheek, lashes a girl would kill for. He cut them off with manicure scissors when he was ten. Now he has three earrings in one ear and a cross dangling from the other and has been known to paint his nails silver. Today he's wearing his usual tattered jeans and a black T-shirt that says "Normal People Scare Me."

I'm not going to insist. I don't want to see him bristle, turn away from me. "Me, either," I say instead. "But I'm getting weak, so guess I'll walk up to Molly's and get me a smoothie." When he doesn't respond, his eyes still closed, I start out the door. Before pulling it to, though, I turn, unable to resist after all. "Sure I can't bring you anything?"

"From Molly's?" He opens dreamy aqua-green eyes, just like his father's. "Yeah. How about a tofu sandwich on soy bread with a side of wheat sprouts and alfalfa?"

"Smart-ass," I mutter to myself, pulling the door to. Just before it's closed, Culley calls out, "Hey, Mom, forgot to tell you. One of your fruitcake friends called, said she was coming to get you."

I stick my head back in the door. "Byrd called again?"

He plays another verse, singing in a low voice about a seven bridges road. "Yeah," he says finally. I wait, decide he's not going to say anything else, eyes closed again and his head moving up and down as he sings, like one of those bobble-head dolls. I close the door and step out on the sidewalk, warm already with the day's heat.

Paper cups of red wine in hand, Byrd and I walk the wooded trail along the ridge, the one that follows the flow of Shoal Creek. It's so peaceful here, and so beautiful. God, how I love these mountains, the foothills of the

Smokies! I fell in love with this place the first time I saw it, when I was in college and I came here one weekend to visit Miss Fielding, my old art teacher from high school, who'd retired and moved here. I knew then that if I ever had the opportunity to live in the mountains, I'd do it. On days like this, when the late afternoon sun turns the whole valley gold, I wish I were a poet instead of an artist. Maybe then I'd have more of a chance of expressing my awe and gratitude at being able to live in the midst of such beauty. I try to say it through my art, but always feel like I fall short. I stop and hold my arms high in a salute. Thank you, thank you, O God of the heavens, I feel like shouting. Byrd, practical little Byrd, walking ahead of me, stops and waits. As soon as I said let's take a walk, she changed into pink-and-white Nike shorts, shirt, and running shoes. I swear, I love Byrd, but she's so *perky*. When I told her I meant a stroll, not a power walk, I had to listen to a fifteen-minute lecture on the health benefits of walking, not believing Byrd actually used those dreaded words: At Our Age.

I'm winded and weak, just from the climb up the trail, but I don't tell Byrd, don't want to bring on another lecture. Based on her concern, I know, but still. I'll get Molly to mix me another of her herbal spring tonics. Usually they cleanse me, make me feel so much better, but I've tried everything this time, with no luck. "Let's sit here a minute, Byrd." I nod toward a fallen hickory limb, big as my body, beside the trail. We're overlooking Shoal Creek here, and it's cooler.

Perched high on the log where it branches off, Byrd can't possibly know how much she looks like a plump little bird. A snowheaded, pink-crested warbler. Since I've known her, I've envied her hair. Beginning with startling white streaks that appeared in her teens, Byrd's hair had turned pure white by the time she was forty. She keeps it too closely shorn for my taste (a punk cut, Culley calls it), but it suits her. "Just for a minute," Byrd says, sipping her wine. "Then we've got to get you packed."

I roll my eyes. "I told you, I don't feel up to going this time." I've been a coward. I'd not planned on going to the SSG weekend, but I wasn't going to tell anyone. Except Byrd—I had to tell her since I always drive to Birmingham and ride down with her. It was when I asked her not to tell the others until she got there that Byrd got stubborn, refused to let me off the hook, and insisted she'd come get me, if that was what it took.

She sighs, giving me a start when I realize how much it sounds like those martyred sighs my mama used to come out with. "Corrine, I didn't drive all the way up here to argue with you." God, she's even talking like my mama now! We don't call her Mama Byrd for nothing. "You're not feeling well because you're working too hard, so I'm driving you to the coast, and that's all there is to it. You won't have to do a thing but rest."

"Not true. I'll have to put up with Astor." I feel bad as soon as the stricken look crosses Byrd's face. She hates any kind of conflict, does everything she can to make things run smoothly, make everybody happy. "Just teasing," I amend.

"Poor Astor." She sighs again. "Bless her heart, she has such a cross to bear. My circle added her to our prayer list, just last week. I don't see how she's going to hold up."

My turn to sigh. That's what I get for lying, pretending I was only teasing about Astor—now I have to hear what a saint she is. Serves me right. "How are Buster and the kids?" I ask brightly. Anything to change the subject.

Byrd's the only SSG who's a grandmother, has been for a couple of years. Technically, they're her step-grandchildren, but no one thinks of them that way, never has. When Byrd married Buster McCain a year after Dixie Lee was killed in the car crash, Dixie Lee and Buster's two kids were toddlers, nine months apart. Byrd had been teaching kindergarten in Mountain Brook since graduation, living in a garage apartment near Dixie Lee and Buster, she and Dixie Lee closer than ever. It was Byrd who'd coached Dixie Lee through childbirth classes instead of the squeamish Buster; it'd always seemed like the kids were half Byrd's anyway. Ironically, on the day that a drunk driver ran a red light and plowed into Dixie Lee's station wagon, she was leaving her doctor's office with the news that she was pregnant again. Instead of heading home to tell Buster, Dixie Lee had called Byrd to say she was stopping by with some news. She never arrived; Byrd and Buster learned what Dixie Lee's news was from the doctor's report found in the wrecked car. It seemed right that Byrd and Buster would come to love each other, united by their grief and the kids, and it's worked out well for them. Eventually they all merged, Dixie Lee and Buster's two kids and Byrd and Buster's three, close together in age, all looking a lot alike. Five kids, and now two grandchildren! Good thing Buster has more money than God.

Byrd won't let me off the hook. "Everybody's great, but don't try to change the subject. It's none of my business, granted; but . . ."

"That's never stopped you before," I interrupt.

"But I keep hoping you'll work on having a little more compassion for Astor."

"I know. I'll never get the crown this way."

Byrd frowns and studies me. "This is serious, Corrine. Astor needs us now. Not just our prayers, but our support. Our *love*. Our special SSG love for each other."

"Oh, please," I moan.

"No, I mean it. Poor Mose—"

"That I can agree with. Poor Mose."

Her jaw set (Mama Byrd again!), she plunges on, both of us looking at the creek instead of each other. "It's so pitiful. Poor

Mose doesn't know he's in this world," she says.

"Then he's lucky, because he doesn't have to know he married Astor. Who, by the way, in case you've forgotten, deliberately set out to ensnare him."

"How can you be so heartless? That man has pure-tee lost his mind!"

"I'd lose my mind too if I had to live with Astor."

"Corrine!"

"Byrd, Mose didn't have much of a mind left when he and Astor met. He was seventy-five years old and she was forty-two. Don't give me that bless-her-poor-heart shit. She married him because he is famous, because he's black, because he's rich, and because she figured out how to turn him on. Wheelchair sex, remember? She told us all about it, that fall we were here—right here in my cabin—after she first met him in New York. Astor is paying the piper, is all."

Byrd holds her hand up to stop me. "Now, Corrine, be fair. Astor's told us a million times that she didn't marry Mose for his money. His estate will go to his children, and Astor'll get very little."

"Here's where I have complete faith in Astor: I'm sure Mose's family set that up to protect him from women like Astor, but I'm equally as sure that she'll find a way around it."

"Why do you think Astor has to teach those dance and yoga classes?" Byrd practically screeches. "She wouldn't if she didn't need the money."

"Crap. She doesn't need the money. She's too old to dance on stage now, but she still wants an audience. She has an adoring one with her students, is all."

"I want you and Astor to be friends." Byrd picks at something on the tree trunk, her head lowered. "She gets on everybody's nerves at times, but . . . well, we all love her in spite of that. That's all I'm asking."

Oh, that's all? But, since I hate to upset Byrd, I promise that I'll try being nicer to Astor if that's what she wants.

"What I really want is for you to come to the SSG weekend, Corrine. You need to get away from here. You're run down from working too hard."

I don't say anything, and Byrd's face is troubled, her eyebrows drawn together. She wants everyone to be sweet and happy, always has. But she's so dear, and such an innocent, I can't stay aggravated with her. I rub my face wearily, then relent. "Okay, tell you what. I'll come with you," I say. "I've been worried about Lanier and need to see for myself how she's doing since moving to Dauphin Island. Let's go back to the house, and you can help me pack."

During the long drive from Blue Mountain to Dauphin Island, Byrd tells me all about her family, catches me up on the three girls and two boys, the sons-in-law, the daughters-in-law, the new grandchildren. They all sound so happy, so prosperous and successful, so—what?—so damn wholesome. They have family portraits made for Christmas cards; they go on vacations together at Gulf Shores or Seaside; they're real active in the Episcopal church. I realize that Byrd could never imagine some of the things that have happened in my life, never. Not that she wouldn't be sympathetic. She'd say, "Bless your heart, Corrine honey," and she'd put me on her prayer chain, but she couldn't comprehend any of it. None of the SSGs could.

I've been carsick twice, unusual for me, and Byrd's pulled her BMW wagon over for me to toss my cookies on the side of the road, once right after we crossed the state line and the other between Auburn and Tuskegee. "How appropriate," I say weakly, sipping the ginger ale Byrd bought to settle my stomach. "The deeper I get into my beloved home state, the sicker I become."

Byrd keeps her eyes straight ahead on Interstate 85 as she says, "You haven't been back home since your mama's funeral, have you, hon?"

"Now that Mama's dead, I will never go back."

I feel her eyes cut over to me, then back to the highway. "But, your daddy . . ."

"Byrd," I say. "Drop it, okay?"

"Okay, okay. Sorry. Oh! Did I tell you that Jennifer passed the bar exam? Buster took everyone out to Highlands Bar and Grill to celebrate, including all the in-laws. I can't believe we have a restaurant like Highlands in Birmingham, can you?"

"Never been." Fighting the urge to baptize the side of the road again, I suck harder on the straw, swallow the fizzy ginger ale hopefully.

"No kidding! Then you've got to come for a visit soon. Buster asks about you all the time. He adores all the SSGs, of course, but you're his favorite."

It's a lie, one of Byrd's little white lies intended to make me feel better. Julia and Rosanelle, the beauty queens, are much more the kind of women Buster admires. He is too much of a good old boy to do weird, or to admire women who lose custody of their children. Bet he liked Lanier as long as she was behaving herself, safely married to a respectable doctor, but probably doesn't think much of her now. And Astor—Buster is a limousine liberal like a lot of businessmen nowadays, but I can't help but wonder if, deep down, where the genes of his Confederate ancestors lurk, he doesn't have a problem with Astor's marriage to a black man.

Once we pass Montgomery, Byrd insists that I sleep the rest of the way. We've caught up, having talked about everything and nothing. She puts on a CD, Roberta Flack singing "Killing Me Softly with His Song," an oldie reminiscent of our days at The W. I close my eyes and put the seat all the way back, hoping to sleep, to get to feeling better. Before I doze, though, Byrd has one more comment. "I was thrilled to see Culley and you together," she says.

"Ummm," I murmur. "Things have been a little better this summer." I don't say much about Culley to any of the SSGs, not wanting to tell them that I'm superstitious, afraid of losing him again if I push my luck. It's only been in the last three years that Culley and I have had any sort of relationship at all.

"What about Miles?" Byrd asks. "How are things between the two of you?"

I answer her with my eyes closed, my head propped on my denim purse, leaning on the door. "Just peachy. We get together and bake cookies, all the time. Things couldn't be better."

Byrd laughs lightly. "Oh, girl, you're so crazy! You don't have a prayer of getting the crown, I'm afraid."

"Not a hope. Now shut up so I can sleep."

But I don't sleep. I doze on and off and think about Miles, wishing Byrd hadn't brought up his name. Byrd, with her expensive, made-to-match clothes and her orderly life, her days of playing golf at the country club and attending the Mountain Brook Episcopal Church on the weekends—what would she say if I told her the truth about Miles? She'd probably wreck the car, she'd be so horrified.

5

Julia
MONTGOMERY

I DON'T KNOW WHY I wake up at one A.M. When Bethany was younger, I got up to check on her so often that waking all through the night became a habit. However, since she has outgrown her childhood ailments, I've gotten so I sleep the sleep of the dead, as though to make up the lost hours. Since we've been in the Governor's Mansion, Joe Ed has developed the habit of getting up a lot during the night, going to his office to work when he can't sleep. I may wake up when he leaves, but I always go right back to sleep. Tonight he hasn't even come in from his meeting yet; sometimes the party meetings go on until the wee hours. I'm wide awake, even though I've only been asleep a couple of hours. After Astor and I finished our supper—she'd ordered a double serving of our chef's famous crab cakes, even though she normally eats like a bird—we took our dessert wine and coffee and went to the sitting room, where we stayed up until eleven talking. I asked for decaf, but maybe they brought us regular coffee instead. Whatever, I don't think I'll be able to go back to sleep, so I get out of bed, put my robe and slippers on, and start for my office, which is two doors down. I rarely get up in the night to work, but since I'm wide awake, might as well work on the chapter I'd hoped to finish up before the weekend but haven't gotten to yet.

When Bethany was little, I wrote stories for her in which the main character was—surprise—a girl named Bethany, partially deaf and blind. On a visit to interview Joe Ed for a book on southern politics, a reporter from New York saw one of the stories and insisted on sending it to his publisher. That was the beginning of the Bethany Stories—*Bethany Learns to Tie Her Shoe; Bethany Practices Table Manners; Bethany's First*

Day of School—and the beginning of my career as a writer of children's books. I've published half a dozen children's books and one book for adolescents, and I'm now halfway finished with a new one. Since Joe Ed was elected governor, I don't have time to work on them like I used to.

It's when I open the door leading out of our quarters that I hear the noise, the click of shoes on the marble floors. At first I think it's Joe Ed, coming in from his meeting, but then I know. Even though the guest rooms are way down the hall, I realize that it's Astor, leaving her room. I wait, wondering if she's on her way to the little kitchen area next to our bedroom, where we keep a fridge well stocked. But then it's unmistakable, the sound of her footsteps going down the back stairway. Hesitating only a moment, I go to the spacious corridor outside our quarters, the one that leads to the stairway. Sure enough, even though it's dark except for the recessed night-lights lining the baseboards of the corridors, I can see Astor as she disappears around the bend in the stairs. Where could she be going? The door at the foot of the stairs leads outside, and she's been here enough to know it's not safe to roam the grounds at night; you could get shot as an intruder. Once outside, how would she get back in?

Instead of calling out to her, I follow Astor down the stairs, quietly, staying far enough behind that she doesn't hear me, even though I feel like a fool. My curiosity over- rides my good sense, and I realize, with a shock, that if I stopped Astor and asked where she was going, she wouldn't be truth- ful with me. Even though we've been friends for thirty years, there is so much about Astor that she keeps hidden away, and I feel, sud- denly, as if I don't know her at all.

Before going out the door at the bottom of the stairwell, Astor stops and tinkers with the lock, and I pause on the stairs, crouching so she can't see me. I wonder if she's fixing the alarm so it won't go off when she re-enters, and if so, where she learned how. She goes out the door, closing it quietly behind her, and I wait a few seconds before following her, giving her time to get far enough away not to see me. When I peer outside the door, I see her, even though she's in the shadows and still in her all-black outfit. She's moving steadily next to the dark-leafed camellia bushes that surround the Mansion, heading toward the back wing. I don't have to close the door behind me to watch her. There are spotlights all over the grounds in the back, placed at the bottom of the towering magnolia trees and shining upward on the trunks, but Astor stays in the shadows. Suddenly she veers to the right, knocks on a hidden back door with her knuckles, and almost immediately, the door opens enough to let her in. There's no mistaking the man who opens the door; it's Cal Hawkins.

I turn and go back inside, up the stairway and to my bedroom. It makes no sense, none at all. First of all, when did Cal and Astor plan their little assignation? I was there the whole time they were together. Okay, even supposing that she—what?—slipped him a note with her cell phone number on it, it still doesn't make sense. The secrecy I can halfway understand; Astor enjoys her role as devoted wife to a sick old man, and if Cal is trying to get Rita back, maybe he doesn't want anyone to tell her he's seeing a married woman. But why go to the back wing? Cal doesn't live there, but there are quarters for the bodyguards if they need a place to stay on the grounds, so I guess they could use it for a tryst. But why go to the trouble of disengaging the alarm, if that's indeed what Astor was doing? Should I tell Joe Ed what I've seen? I slip back into bed, my mind in a turmoil. One thing's for sure: I won't ask Astor about it on our ride to Dauphin Island tomorrow. If she's gone to such lengths to be so secretive about a one-night stand, then it's pretty obvious she has no intention of confiding in me.

6

Corrine
BLUE MOUNTAIN/DAUPHIN ISLAND

I DOZE ON AND off on the trip to Dauphin Island, even though Byrd forgets I'm trying to sleep and talks to me every now and then. I murmur something in response until her voice blends in with the hum of the tires on the highway and the rhythmic beat of the oldies station on the radio. I wish Byrd hadn't asked me about Miles, hadn't stirred those old memories. I want to put it behind me, my whole sordid life with him. If it weren't for Culley, I'd wish I'd never met Miles, never fallen in love with him. *When the pupil is ready, a teacher appears.* I wrote that in Lanier's lesson book because I believe it. As

I told Lanier when I gave her the book, I believe that all life experiences are sent our way to aid us in finding the right path. My life with Miles put that philosophy to the test. For life to have sent Miles as my teacher, I must have been so far off the path that I was wandering in the wilderness, hands outstretched like a blind person, trying to find my way back.

I met Miles Spaulding in a way that no woman should ever meet a man—in the psych ward of the hospital, a few months after I went to live on Blue Mountain. It wasn't the first time I'd tried to kill myself, but it turned out to be the last. Partly because of Miles, I'll give him that. As Mama used to say, give the devil his due. I was sitting on the side of the bed, waiting for the therapist who'd been assigned to me to come in and introduce himself and set up a time for a follow-up in his office. They wouldn't release me until it was worked out. I'd gotten impatient waiting for him, so I was brushing my hair, which was long enough then to hold out at arm's length to get the tangles out. With the careless vanity of youth, I was taken with the way the sun from the window next to my bed was turning my hair to a crackling, gold-and-red fire in my hands. I even played with it as I brushed, like a child instead of a twenty-two-year-old who'd just graduated from college. Over and over, I held my hair up and let it fall in silken sheets, rippling through the brush. I heard the sharp intake of his breath at the door before I saw him.

"Jesus Christ, would you look at that," Miles Spaulding said, and I turned to see him and the doctor who'd treated me in the emergency room. My doctor, a frizzy-headed woman with black-rimmed glasses, laughed.

"Told you she was a sweet little thing," she said. "Miss Cooper, this is Miles Spaulding, who's been assigned to you. I'm leaving you in his capable hands now, okay?"

Miles sat in the chair across from me, crossing his long legs casually, and I looked at him wide-eyed. He was the most fastidious, elegant-looking man I'd ever seen. With his silver-gold hair and dreamy blue-green eyes, he reminded me of Peter O'Toole in *Lawrence of Arabia,* a movie I saw over and over in college. If it weren't for his rather overpowering sexiness, he'd be too beautiful for a man. Back then everyone smoked, and

I watched as Miles Spaulding smoked a cigarette as though making love to it, his long fingers caressing it, his full lips pulling on it sensuously. He tossed his head back, exhaled the cigarette smoke, then stared at me with those amazing eyes before asking, "Miss Cooper, tell me: Do you want to die, or do you just no longer want to live? They are two different things, you know."

I'd never heard a voice like his before, cultured and sophisticated, almost British. I'd never known anyone like Miles Spaulding, either; he was an alien being to me. He'd come to Blue Mountain to open up his own therapy practice after having interned at the county hospital, where he'd fallen in love with the mountains. He'd been raised in Atlanta, his father a philosophy professor and his mother a music teacher, both at Oglethorpe College. His family was poor but proud of their advanced degrees, the kind of intellectual snobs I hadn't encountered in my limited experience at The W, where the faculty was mostly women with degrees from Peabody and Milsaps. Miles had gone to Oglethorpe, then to Emory for his graduate work.

"I don't really want to die," I told him, surprising myself. I'd thought for years that I wanted nothing more. This was the first time I'd tried pills and was shocked to find out that they hadn't worked when I regained consciousness in the emergency room, after my stomach was pumped. I'd awakened sick and miserable, horribly so, with tubes in my nose and hostile nurses holding me down to poke an IV needle in, hard. "Too bad she didn't succeed," one of them said to the other. When I started to cry, to call for my mama, another nurse told me to shut up. "Most folks here want nothing more than a chance to live, and you pull a stunt like this," she hissed.

"So you don't want to die after all?" Miles Spaulding asked, and I hung my head. He read my chart, his exquisitely arched eyebrows raised. "You're an artist, I see. You've just moved here to work for a former teacher who has a gallery in town. And you're from Alabama?"

When I nodded, he studied me. "Ah. That explains why you did it, then. An Alabama girl." When I stared in surprise that he could tease me at a time like this, he smiled, his eyes glittering playfully. With that smile, I was a goner. Falling in love with Miles Spaulding,

I forgot why my life had seemed so hopeless that I wanted out of it.

The first time Miles and I made love, he pushed me facedown over his desk and entered me from behind, his hand tight over my mouth so the patients in the waiting room wouldn't hear us. Had it not been so intensely passionate, so forbidden, the unfamiliar pain would have been a turnoff. Naively, I'd been totally unprepared for this sort of thing to happen between us. It hadn't occurred to me that Miles Spaulding would be interested in me, and I was content to worship him from afar. After I began going on a weekly basis to his office in the town of Chickasaw, fifteen miles from where I lived in Elijah, it was as though I existed just for those appointments.

Miss Harriet Fielding, my former teacher who'd retired to open her little gallery in Elijah and hired me fresh out of college to help run it, had been puzzled by the change in me. Since I'd moved to town and rented a room from her, I'd been quiet, depressed, and miserably unhappy, so unhappy I'd tried to overdose. Not only had I moved away from everything familiar to me, I'd dropped the boyfriend I'd had all through college, a young man who ran the bookstore in Brierfield. Once I met Miles Spaulding, I thought the poor guy was a pathetic loser, and I'd cruelly hang up on him when he called me, begging to know why I no longer wanted to see him. I told Lanier that I'd fallen in love with my therapist, and she had hooted. "Surely you can come up with something more original, Corrine," she had laughed, then damn if she didn't go and fall in love with her supervisor, a doctor at the medical school where she'd gone after The W. Lanier's crush was a tad more complicated than mine, as I pointed out to her, since she'd made the Lanier-like mistake of marrying an old boyfriend—I swear I can't even recall his name now!—right before starting medical school, but that didn't last any time at all. Lanier had planned on becoming a doctor, but she gave it all up to marry Dr. Paul Sanders and settle down in Podunk, Alabama. For years she shocked everyone by her contentment with running a clinic with Paul, raising their family, going to church and scout meetings. When she got bored and restless and threw it all away, the SSGs said, yep, the old Lanier is back.

Although I'd built my whole identity on

being a free spirit, an artist, it didn't bother me one whit that I'd become a cliché, a patient who saw her therapist as savior. I was a cliché in another way as well; having never been in love before, I was a starry-eyed fool. Looking back on that time now, I see it as addicts probably see their obsession with the fix. Oh, it was intoxicating, I have to admit, better than booze or pills. Every time Miles opened the door to his office and stuck his golden head out, indicating the time had come for my session with him, my heart hammered in my chest. My face grew hot and my throat closed up as I stumbled past him. I couldn't look at him when I first seated myself across from him and he took out the file with his notes on my craziness. It always took him a while to warm me up, to make small talk until I relaxed enough to confide in him.

It humiliates me now to remember the gifts I brought him. I'd already started the garden that would later become a passion, and I brought him baby lettuces and spinach, tiny stalks of asparagus, slender spears of carrots. I baked, too, chocolate brownies and oatmeal cookies and tea cakes like my grandma used to make. I'd painted Miles little containers from some of my ornamental gourds, which he put on his desk and used for pencil holders. Oh, God, how transparent I must have been to him, this country girl only four years away from the farm! If I could go back now and shoot the naive fool I was then, I'd do it.

For several months I didn't see Miles outside his office, though I dreamed of nothing else. Literally. I'd wake up in the night burning hot and trembling after those dreams of him, dreams where he held me in his arms and told me I was beautiful, that he couldn't get me off his mind. I didn't make the connection at the time; had no idea that those nights of imagined passion were brought out by our sessions, where he questioned me about things I'd never talked about with anyone.

"Corrine," he'd said the second or third time I was in his office, "we need to explore some things that might make you uncomfortable. I'm not sure you're ready for this yet, but it's necessary for your treatment. Do you think you can trust me enough to confide in me?"

I was more than eager to show that I trusted him. "Oh, yes, sir, Mr. Spaulding," I'd replied, trembling. I only referred to him as

Mr. Spaulding, even though he'd said to call him Miles. He had gotten up from his chair and come to sit beside me on the couch, where he leaned toward me and spoke in a soft voice.

"I suspect that you were sexually abused as a child, and that's why you have such a poor self-image. Am I right?" His eyes had held mine and I couldn't look away, even though my face burned.

"N-no, sir!" I'd gasped. "I swear I wasn't." In the household of my childhood, there were only two males, besides my little brothers. I was twelve when my grandfather, who'd lived with us, died, and he was an invalid. My father was a cold, hard-bitten man who had never even hugged me that I recalled.

"I expected you to answer that way because I suspect that you've suppressed the experience. So, here's what we should do, Miss Cooper." As though calming a frightened animal, he put his hand on my arm. His voice—how I loved his beautiful voice!—was low and soothing. "Over the next few weeks, we're going to explore some feelings you may have suppressed and see if we can uncover the traumas."

If only those therapy sessions could be

suppressed now! I cringe thinking back over them and realizing what an innocent little fool I was. I'd been raised in the sticks of Coffee County, Alabama, on the most dismal little farm imaginable, although there was a lot of competition for that honor all around me. It was twenty miles to the nearest town, ten to a school. My family was white trash, pure and simple. That ignorant, poverty-stricken South had been my only history until an art teacher, Miss Harriet Fielding, came to our school and took an interest in me. My life had been pretty harsh until an art scholarship got me two hundred miles north, to Brierfield and The W. Inexperienced beyond belief, I was putty in the hands of a man like Miles Spaulding.

I could tell when I disappointed him, like when Miles put his hand on my arm and asked if I could describe the first time I had sexual fantasies. If I didn't answer in a way that satisfied him, he would keep prodding me until I stammered around and came up with something that made his eyes shine. "Ah, yes!" he would say, nodding at me. "Let's explore that a bit more." He was always scribbling away on the pad he kept in his lap, nodding, and saying things like,

"Good, Corrine. Very good! Now, let's take it a little further." The first time he touched me, other than to place a hand on my arm or on my back to lead me out of the office, was a week before the lovemaking over the desk. At his prodding, I was trying to describe the feelings I had had the first time I let a boy put his hand on my breasts. As I stammered around, I lowered my head and my hair fell forward, partially covering my face. I was glad because I was so embarrassed, but Miles reached out and pushed my hair back behind my ears. He leaned real close to me to do so, and his breath came out in little gasps, which surprised me. "The first time I saw you," he said, voice soft, "I wanted to get my hands in your hair. Even though you are not a great beauty, Corrine, you have the most beautiful hair I've ever seen. I've never seen that color before." I'd stammered something—probably thank you, although now I'd like to *hope* not—and looked down at my hands as he kept stroking my hair, pushing it back from my face. "What were you saying about that boy after the homecoming dance?" he asked, still breathing in those ragged gasps that I was too inexperienced to recognize. I thought he was asthmatic.

"J-just that he was the first to . . . ah, actually put his hand inside my blouse." I thought that Miles's hand touched my breast as he pushed my hair back. Then he reached across me to push back the other side, and this time there was no doubt. I shivered at his touch, but, dumb me, I was sure he didn't mean to.

"You have rather small breasts," he said. In the style of the seventies, I was wearing a long gauzy skirt and a thin tank top, with no bra, so it was pretty evident. I blushed and nodded glumly, since I was flat as a hoe cake. I glanced up to see Miles's eyes on my cleavage—or lack thereof—with disgust, I was sure. Instead he smiled. "Don't look so downcast. I find small breasts extremely erotic."

"I thought all men liked . . . ah . . . big boobs."

"You'll find out, Corrine, I'm not like other men," he said. I was also to find out that Miles Spaulding was a master of understatement.

The following week, our session was over and I stood up to leave. I was shaken; Miles had made me describe the fumbling experiences I'd had with my boyfriend in Brierfield, such as they were. It seemed odd that Miles appeared more shaken than I did. He was behind me as I moved toward the door, and that's when his arms suddenly came around me, pulling me to him. For a moment I almost swooned, sure that this was to be the romantic moment I'd dreamed of, when he'd hold my face in his hands and tell me he was wrong, that I really was a beauty and that he had fallen in love with me. Instead, his hand went into my hair roughly, and he pushed me over his desk, never facing me at all. Rather than my usual long skirt, that day I'd worn a miniskirt, making it easy for him. "Oh, God, Corrine," he murmured breathlessly as he pushed my panties to the side, "you've gotten me more aroused than I've ever been!" He was quick, his breath hot in my ear, his thrusts pushing me painfully against the edge of the desk. When it was over, he kept his face buried in my hair while I sobbed, my face in my hands. He turned me around and kissed me, long and deep, his tongue halfway down my throat, before handing me his handkerchief. Then, pushing me away, he whispered for me to go straight to the bathroom down the hall and clean up. "No one will notice," he said, smiling down at me. "It's not unusual to leave here crying." When

I stumbled out the door, he put his head out and said, for the benefit of the receptionist, "Same time next week, Miss Cooper."

I spent the most miserable week of my life trying to decide if I loved Miles Spaulding or hated him. I couldn't decide if I was elated or degraded. I was a mess by the time I went for the next session, but Miles was totally professional, never once alluding to what had occurred between us. More than that, he was detached, removed from me in a way that he'd not been since the first time I met him. That was all it took to make me long for him, make me want to do anything to please him. Two weeks later, when I thought we'd exhausted the subject of my limited erotic experience, he asked if I'd ever performed oral sex on a man. He was breathing in those asthmatic little gasps again. "God, no," I'd cried, raising my hands to cover my face. "I wouldn't even know how to." Wrong answer. By the end of the session, my sexual education would be complete, but my sordid saga with Miles Spaulding was just beginning.

When we pull into the driveway of Lanier's beach house, Byrd blows the horn, grinning from ear to ear. I've dozed on and off the whole trip, and now my head hurts and I'm nauseous again. "Oh, goodie," Byrd squeals like a little girl, "everybody's here!" She opens her door, waving happily when they begin to appear at the top of the steep front steps, Julia and Astor and Lanier, drinks in hand. As always, Julia looks elegant, tall, thin, and ash-blonde, dressed in white linen pants and a gray sleeveless sweater. Beside her, Astor is her usual stunning self, her black hair slicked back in a chignon and a smug smile on her face. When her eyes meet mine, she raises her glass of wine, and, honoring my promise to Byrd, I resist the urge to return her salute with my middle finger.

Lanier starts down the steps, looking like shit warmed over, like she hasn't slept in weeks. When I first saw Lanier Brewer from Selma, Alabama, descendant of the famed poet Sidney Lanier, daughter of a well-to-do judge, and my newly assigned roommate at The W, my heart had sunk. She looked so girl-next-door wholesome that I despaired. Even worse, she was a jock, on both the tennis and swim teams. Why would The W pair an artist with an athlete? I'd wondered. Lanier's thick brown hair was tousled and bobbed like a flapper's from the twenties, the way she wears it still, perfect with her freckles and gap-toothed grin. She wore no makeup and was dressed in gym shorts and a polo shirt. In the seventies the campus of The W was full of artsy-looking girls with long straight hair and granny glasses, and I had to get Scout Finch for a roommate. The moment Lanier opened her mouth, however, I saw I was wrong. Lanier Brewer turned out to be what my mama called a "pure-tee sight."

"Corrine Cooper?" Lanier said, looking me over from head to toe as I stood in the door with the suitcases Miss Fielding had given me for graduation. "Where are you from?" Coffee County, I'd told her, blushing. Twenty miles from Opp. "Opp?" she'd screeched. "Not where they have the Rattlesnake Rodeo?" I'd nodded and she'd laughed. "Godalmighty damn," she'd said, "it's worse than I thought." She pulled me into the room and closed the door behind us. "Bet you could use a drink," she said, and I blurted out, "Don't tell me they serve drinks here!" Lanier's bubbly laugh was great, and I loved the way she threw her head back, her hands on her hips. "Not unless the grape juice in the communion cups ferments," she said. "But I keep vodka in my Clearasil bottle. Won't do a thing for your pimples, but it will sure as hell cure the Coffee County blues."

Today Lanier opens the car door for me, sticking her head in and giving me a long hug. "You look like you've been dipped in shit and rolled in cracker crumbs," she says, patting me on the back.

"Thanks a lot," I say, pulling myself out of the passenger seat. "You look even worse."

"If that's true, y'all better call Dr. Kevorkian," Lanier says. "You're not going to believe what's been going on with me, Corrine. I can't wait to tell you about it. I've got it all written down for you, in the lesson book."

"Can't wait. I forgot to bring a fun read for the weekend." My suitcase feels heavy, although I brought almost nothing.

Lanier suddenly throws her arms around me, holding me tight. "Oh, Jesus, I'm so glad you came. I need you now, roomie. I've fucked up my whole life this time, Corrine. For real, this time."

I start toward the house with my suitcase, Lanier behind me carrying the herbs Byrd and I hastily gathered from my badly neglected garden. It was the first time I hadn't had my fresh vegetables to contribute. "What else is new, Lanier?" I say, shaking my head sadly.

7

Lanier

DAUPHIN ISLAND

IT TOOK ME A while to get up the nerve to investigate the light at the Pickett house next door, and I didn't go over there until the day before the SSG weekend. Because I've always been so reckless, folks think of me as brave, which is not the same. But my freshman year at The W, during what has come to be called "the incident of the Girl with the Flaming Hair," I found out what a chickenshit I really am.

The senior dorm at The W was haunted. When The W was built there was only one dorm, Wesley Hall, named after the founder of the Methodist church, good old John

Wesley. Wesley—the dorm, not the preacher—has these big spooky halls and wings and hidden staircases. Story goes, on a stormy night long, long ago, one of the coeds, candle in hand, goes down a hidden stairway, sneaking out to meet her lover. She's a babe and has this long flowing hair—golden blonde, naturally. Just hearing that, you can figure out what happens next: The long hair catches fire and she's trapped in the stairway, where she burns to death. Serves her right for sneaking out like that, and I'm sure the ghost of old John Wesley nods in approval when she dies screaming in agony. Anyway, the Girl with the Flaming Hair became a famous ghost story in Alabama, and legend at The W was, if you took a candle and went up that stairway at midnight during a storm, you'd meet the ghost coming toward you, her hair on fire.

What kind of nitwit would want to see that sight? It scared the crap out of me to even think about it, but of course, the SSGs dared me. Since I was a bigger fool than coward in those days—not that things have changed much—I took the dare.

Part of the deal involved sneaking into Wesley Hall, which was hallowed ground because the seniors didn't allow us lowly freshmen there. One November evening when it started thundering and lightning like crazy right after supper, we knew this was it, the night the daring Lanier Brewer of the newly formed SSGs, camera in hand, would make freshman history by taking pictures of the Girl with the Flaming Hair.

Sneaking out of the freshman dorm, Tutwiler, was much easier than getting into Wesley Hall because of a weird feature of The W: spiral fire escapes. Each dorm had them, enclosed fire escapes that you slid down like slides, making fire drills a hoot. They were off-limits otherwise, but that never stopped any of us from taking a joyride every now and then. Problem was, there was no way to stop your fall, and you came barreling out right on your ass. The first week of school, Dixie Lee, braying like a donkey, came flying down the fire escape and landed right at the feet of the college president, Dr. Lumby. Dr. Lumby, acting quickly, put Dixie Lee on room restriction for a whole week. Byrd was far enough behind her that she could wedge her feet against the sides of the fire escape tube and crawl back up, which is exactly how we figured we'd get into Wesley.

At midnight the SSGs dressed in black and slid down the fire escapes of Tutwiler without a problem. The storm was keeping everyone in, including, we hoped, the seniors and the campus security force, all two of them. We ran across campus to Wesley, where we proceeded to crawl *up* the fire escapes. The rain had us wet enough that the slide was slippery as snot, but we made it, me and Byrd and Dixie Lee and Astor and Julia. I should've suspected something when Corrine wouldn't come with us, claiming she was claustrophobic, but I was more trusting in those days.

What I didn't know was, as we sneaked in Wesley on one side, Corrine was crawling up the fire escape on the other, her long, white nightgown under her raincoat, and with a flashlight covered in red crepe paper, designed to hold under her chin and look ghostly when she met me on the hidden stairwell, long hair flowing. Although she was already pale as a haunt, she'd put white makeup on her face and ringed her eyes in black. The SSGs had planned their little dupe of me carefully except for one thing: At the time, they didn't know what a chickenshit I was. We sneaked into the hidden stairwell; I slung my camera around my neck and lit my candle. Then, with the SSGs on the landing waiting for me, I began to creep my fanny up the stairwell, scary-looking as the halls of hell with only the candle to light my way. Soon as I turned the bend where I could no longer see the SSGs, I looked up into the darkness. Sure enough, a ghostly figure in white appeared above me, with a zombie-like stare and long hair in flames. I let out a screech, then proceeded to faint dead away, falling over and rolling down the staircase. I could've become a whole new legend if the candle hadn't gone out.

The SSGs managed to drag me to the fire escape, still out cold, and we made our get-away before the seniors caught us. Problem was, we got our asses out of there so fast that we forgot Corrine. When the seniors, in their gowns and curlers, came running to investigate the bloodcurdling scream and the strange noises, Corrine had no choice but to stand her ground, looking ghostly and holding the flashlight under her chin. The seniors who ran up the dark stairwell went into hissy fits, screaming their fool heads off as they scattered like baby chicks, which gave Corrine the chance to make a run for the fire escape, back to Tutwiler. The next day the whole campus talked of nothing but the appearance of the Girl with the Flaming Hair. My candle was found on the stairwell, proving once and for all that the ghost really did exist. When the story was picked up by the *Birmingham News* and reporters swarmed the campus, we met in my room and swore to never tell *anyone* what really happened that night.

Since then I've had better sense than to do anything that stupid, till the other day. The very next night after I see the ghostly light in the Pickett house, I can't help myself—I get up and look to see if it's still there. Sure enough it is, dim but definitely *there*. Only way I can get back to sleep is with two double vodkas, straight, and the next morning I go to work with a hangover. When I drive back on the island at sunset—no dolphins greeting me today—I pull into the driveway of the Pickett house next door. I don't get far. Sure enough, the gate to the property, which I remember as always flung wide open, is padlocked.

At home I get out of my uniform and into my cutoffs and a T-shirt. Without noticing till I had it over my head, I'd picked up one Lindy gave me for Mother's Day last year that says "If Mama Ain't Happy, Ain't Nobody Happy." Pain hits me like a punch in the stomach, tears sting my eyes, and I jerk the T-shirt off and poke it in the back of the drawer.

After pouring a glass of Kendall Jackson Chardonnay (from a bottle I'd hidden from myself in an attempt to save it for the weekend), I head down to the pier. With the seagull shit gone, it's sure nicer sitting out here and watching the sunset. Still no dolphins. Hope it's not my bad karma acting up. When the sunset's gone, I start back to the house before the lights come on on the pier. One of the last things Daddy did before his heart attack was to rig the string of lights along the pier to come on at the same time every night. I'd like to stay down here at night and watch the lit-up boats on the bay, but I need to get a couple of loads of laundry done before the SSGs get here tomorrow.

There's only one place on the pathway down to the pier where you can see the Pickett house, through the branches of the water oaks. I'm not even looking on purpose; I just happen to see it. It's still daylight, yet there it is again—the weird light in the house. Looks like it's not an electric light but a candle. Suddenly, I'm transported back twenty years, and it's the Girl with the Flaming Hair all over again.

I don't know what makes me do it, any more than I know what made me go along with the idiotic idea of seeing the ghost in Wesley Hall that night. I cut through about a million snakey-looking ferns under the water oaks until I reach the fence separating our property from the Picketts. Grabbing a supporting post, I clear the fence easily, though my days as a jock are long gone. I only want to peek in a window and see if I can tell what's going on. What if a devil-worshiping cult is using the deserted house, burning black candles and chanting while they sacrifice virgins or something? Well, if that's the case, I'm perfectly safe.

Unlike Dolphin Cove, the Pickett house is their family home, a really cool-looking place. Much bigger than ours, it sits in the middle of palms and water oaks, with big old porches in the back, facing the bay. From the looks of things, no one has been here for a long time. It's definitely deserted, the lawn overgrown and creepy looking. Like most of the houses in this area, part of it is elevated on stilts to protect against flood waters, and under the house on this side, I spot just what I need, hanging with the crab traps and fishing poles: a stepladder!

Scanning the yard to make sure no one's here, I place the ladder against the side of the house, under the window where a light glows. It's been many years since I've been in the Pickett house, but I'm pretty sure this is the kitchen. Maybe the devil worshipers use the stove to boil their cauldron of toads and spiders and stuff, or whatever it is that makes up a witches' brew these days. No standing and stirring over a campfire for modern witches, I'll bet. They may even use a microwave, for all I know. When I climb the ladder, which is much ricketier than it looks, I see why the light has looked so dim—the window's filthy. Finding a Kleenex in my pocket, I spit on it and clear a little peephole in the dirt, then strain my neck, trying to see in. I don't exactly hear anyone come to stand underneath me on the ladder, but I sense it, and the hairs on my neck stand up. My heart pounding, I turn and look down.

At first he doesn't say anything, looking up at me with his hands on his hips, his legs apart. Then he squints and says, "Still spying on your neighbors, Lanier?"

I'm so surprised that my legs give out and I sit down on the top of the ladder, staring at him with my mouth wide open. It's been at least ten years since I saw him last. "Jesse!" I gasp. "Jesse Pickett—my God—is it really you?"

"Don't get so excited at the sight of me that you fall off the ladder and bust your ass," he says dryly. "Which looks pretty good for a fifty-year-old. I got a real good view from here."

"My ass is not fifty for two more years, when yours will be sixty, if I remember right." I start down the ladder backward, still staring at him. "Jesus, Jesse, this is unreal. What are you doing here?"

When he rolls his eyes and hoots, I say sheepishly, "Guess you're the one who should be asking me that question, right?"

"Lanier, honey," he drawls, shaking his head, "nothing you do can surprise me. I admit, seeing you on a ladder looking in my window ranks, but hell, I've caught you doing it before."

I jump to the ground and go into his open arms for a hug. My face buried in his neck makes it easier to hide my shock at his appearance. "I was only twelve last time I peeked in a window at you," I say, hugging him tight and patting his back. "But I will admit that I was trying to see you naked."

I expect him to laugh, to keep up our bantering. But with his arms so tight around me that I can hardly breathe, Jesse Pickett, known to his many fans as Jesse Phoenix, world-famous balladeer and songwriter, says, "Thank God you're here." Then he breaks down and cries like a baby.

By holding him up like an old man—which is what he looks like now—I manage to get Jesse into his house, him still boo-hooing, those harsh, racking sobs that men do. What I see once we're inside shocks me speechless, not the usual state for me. We climb the back steps and past the porch, going into a large, open living area that's instantly familiar to me, though I've not been in it for years. I half drag, half pull Jesse until I manage to get him to a couch. For such a slender, wiry man, he feels heavy as a walrus. All the time, I'm speaking to him in a calm voice, saying things like, "Hey, it's okay, Jess, honey. Let's just get you inside. I'm going to help you; lean on me and I'll help you." I've seen plenty of patients lose it, even seen some have what my mama called a nervous breakdown, but even so, I'm scared, not so much by Jesse as by the condition of the house. Something weird is going on here.

When I get him on the couch, Jesse lets go of me and buries his face in his hands. Because it's almost dark, I ease over to turn a lamp on but nothing happens; I'm not sure if the electricity has been cut off or if the bulb's just out. Half-burned candles are on the wicker coffee table in front of us, the candlelight that I've been seeing at night. A box of matches is there, too, but I don't want to move far enough from Jesse to light a candle. Not yet.

I lean over Jesse and put my arms around his shoulders, laying my head against his. His once-dark hair is thin and gray-streaked now, the back part long and pulled into a little ponytail. He looks real bad, almost like a street person. *Homeless.* Maybe that's what he feels like, with his mama dead, all his family gone. "Jesse?" I whisper. He's quit his boo-hooing but still has his face buried in his hands. I've always liked his hands, so strong looking, with long slender fingers. I notice he has on a hammered silver ring with a turquoise stone, but no wedding band. Last I read about him, seems like he'd remarried after his divorce to another singer, but I'm not sure. "Jesse?" I ask again.

His voice is muffled. "Guess it'd be better if you go home, Lanier. Looks like I'm not in any condition to see anybody after all."

"I'm not leaving you like this! I'm a nurse, Jess. I can help you."

His laugh is bitter, but he raises his head and fumbles in his jeans pocket till he pulls out a handkerchief and wipes his eyes. Then he blows his nose and puts the handkerchief back into his pocket. "Can't nobody help me. I'm too fucked up."

"Amen to that," I agree. "What in hell is going on?"

Instead of answering me, he rubs his face and looks around. "Is it dark already or have I gone blind?"

I smile, lighting a couple of candles on the coffee table before easing back beside him on the couch. "My guess is, with no one living here, the electricity's been cut off."

He nods. "Hadn't even thought about that."

"Jess, how long have you been here?"

He shrugs wearily. "Hell if I know. A week, maybe?"

With the candles giving some light to the dark room, I dare to look around. Beer cans and whiskey bottles are everywhere. Empty whiskey bottles. Stinky old cigarette butts are all over, squashed out in big old ashtrays. "You been alone?" I ask.

He chuckles. "Oh, yeah. Just me and old Jack Daniel's."

I keep prodding, even though he won't face me, looking down at the floor instead. "You eaten anything today?"

When he doesn't answer, I put my hand on his arm and shake him. "Jess? If I go to my house and get something, will you eat it?" Still no response, and I shake him again. "Come on. Do it for me, for old times' sake." Kneeling in front of him, I make him look at me. His eyes are bleary, and it's obvious he hasn't shaved in days. His face looks like he's been living the sad ballads that have made him famous. "Jess? You know what? You're the first boy I ever loved." I knew from the first time I saw him that Jesse Pickett was something special, sitting out on the pier playing his guitar and singing his mournful songs.

To my surprise, this brings a halfhearted grin. Smiling, he looks like the sweet young man I had such a huge crush on as a kid, before he left home for good, setting out for Nashville to seek his fortune. I've kept up with his career, attending his concerts when I could, going backstage a couple of times and meeting his band, reminiscing about the good old days on Dauphin Island. I took Paul and the kids to meet Jesse following a concert in Biloxi. That was the last time I'd seen him, over ten years ago now. He found both fame and fortune when he left Mobile Bay for good, but from the looks of things, he'd sure not found much happiness.

"I remember you tried to get me into your britches one time when you was nothing but a girl," he says finally, and there's a gleam of the old Jesse in his eyes. "Scared the shit out of me. I ran like a devil-woman was after me. Judge Brewer being your daddy, I figured I'd be a dead duck for sure."

As a child, I was always getting into mischief, but in spite of that was as innocent as a kitten. If Jesse had been a different person, he could've easily taken advantage of my crush on him. I smile, remembering. "You broke my heart, Jesse Pickett. Mr. Jesse Phoenix. My first love."

His eyes, reddened from crying and too much booze, hold mine. "The ones who got away are the lucky ones, honey. Believe me."

"Oh, yeah? Funny, the men I've been married to say the same about me."

On the way back to the Pickett house, a Pyrex dish of hot chicken-noodle soup in hand, fresh out of the can, I plot ways to help Jesse. If I can get him to trust me, surely he'll let me take him to an internist I've become friends with at the hospital, and she can see that he gets help. He's about as bad off as anyone I've ever seen, though I'll admit my experience is pretty limited. Paul's clinic in Pickens County treated mostly physically sick folks, not too many fucked-up ones. If only I could call Paul, ask him what to do. . . . Be a little hard, though, since he hangs up the phone every time he hears my voice.

Good thing I've brought a flashlight. The candles have burned down and the house is dark and scary as a tomb. It's a pure miracle that Jesse hasn't fallen asleep with the candles burning and set the house on fire. *World-renowned balladeer and songwriter, Jesse Phoenix, burns to death in his family home on Dauphin Island after passing out dead drunk. His biggest hit was, appropriately, "Lost in a Land Called Lonesome."* I find Jess sprawled across a bed in the back bedroom, conked out.

"Jess! Get your behiney up and eat this soup. You're going to croak if you don't eat something." After lighting a candle on the bedside table, I shake him, pulling him halfway over so that he's facing me. He's clutching a Jack Daniel's bottle like a teddy bear, but I pry his fingers loose and toss it in the trash can, along with about a million others. I take the candle, go to the bathroom and wet a washcloth, then, kneeling next to Jesse on the bed, wipe his face with the cold cloth until he opens his eyes.

"Lanier? I'm bad sick, honey. Bad."

"I know. But I told you, I'm going to help you. Now get up and eat this soup."

He throws an arm over his face. "Gotta sleep this off first. I 'preciate you bringing the soup, though. That was real sweet. You're such a sweet little girl, Lanier."

"The same sweet girl I've always been.

Listen to me, Jess. I can help you if you'll let me."

He raises up on an elbow and looks at me. "You want to help me, honey? You mean it?" Somehow he's gotten himself out of his jeans and dirty T-shirt and is lying there in his boxer shorts. I'm surprised that his body still looks good, that his shoulders are as muscular as when he and I used to swim together off the pier. I'd expect him to be flabby and wasted, the shape he's in. "Best way to help me would be for you to go back home and let me drink my fool self to death."

I shake my head. "Can't do it. Not that I give a damn about you, but I like your music too much."

"Ha. How long has it been since I've written anything?"

"Too long."

He falls back on the wadded-up pillows behind him, then surprises me by giving in. "Goddammit, Lanier, you always were a pain in the ass. What kind of soup?"

Jesse eats the lukewarm Campbell's like it's the finest soup du jour. I'd brought along some saltines, too, so I crumble in a handful. By the time he gobbles it up, he starts to look like a human being again. Thanking me, he hands over the empty bowl and I give him a glass of water, which he sniffs. "Plain old water?"

I hit him on the shoulder. "Drink it and shut up. You're bound to be dehydrated." I've already spotted his pills on the bedside table, and I pick up a sleeping pill I recognize as being safe. The others are uppers and downers, all prescription. "Do you take these every night?"

He lays his head back on the pillow, closing his eyes. "Naw. Believe it or not, I've never been much of a pill popper. All that crap's easy to come by, but my drug of choice is Jack Daniel's. With a little Dr. Heineken as a chaser."

"Take two of these sleeping pills and sleep as much as you can for a couple of days, you hear? I've got a bunch of company this weekend, but I'll stop by and check on you. When the weekend's over, maybe we can talk. Okay?"

I expect him to protest, to tell me to leave him alone, to get lost, like he used to when I was a little girl and he couldn't shake me. Instead, he takes my hand and laces his fingers through mine. "My sweet little girl, if you're so damn determined to help me, stay with me awhile, till I go off to sleep. Do you mind? One reason I drink so much is I'm scared to go to sleep. Can't decide if I'm afraid to sleep or afraid to wake up."

I prop up next to him, my head cushioned on a pillow. After kicking my sandals off, I glance over at him. "Jesse? I'll lay down with you till you go to sleep, but nothing else, you hear?"

He chuckles, squeezing my hand. "Hell, honey, I can't remember last time I was able to get it up. You got nothing to worry about."

Leaning over me, he pinches the candle out with his fingers, and when I gasp, he explains. "Get your fingers calloused enough from years of guitar playing and you can do it, too. Thought you'd like the moonlight better. Pretty, isn't it, coming through the window like that?"

"Hmm," I murmur, looking at him in the moonlit darkness. He's closed his eyes, even though he's still hanging on to my hand for dear life. "Jess?" Now seems as good a time as any to approach him about the internist, but, without opening his eyes, he reaches up and puts a finger on my lips.

"Shhh. Thank you for staying with me, Lanier. I owe you."

"I want you to get better so you can write me a song. Nobody's ever written me a song before."

He doesn't say anything for a minute, and I wonder if he's gone to sleep. Then his voice comes out of the darkness, breaking my heart. "My songwriting days are over, honey," he says. "I'm washed up. I've destroyed that, like I've destroyed everything else in my life that's worth a shit."

I squeeze his hand and sigh. "If that's the truth, then you and me are cut out of the same cloth, Mr. Jesse Phoenix."

The Same Sweet Girls carry on about the way I've fixed up the house, swearing I'm just trying to get the crown by making it so nice. Julia rearranges the two rockers so they're on either side of the sofa, then pulls a table over to set a lamp on. "Nobody will believe I had the first lady of Alabama for a decorator," I tell her, and Julia smiles at me, crinkling up her gray eyes. She's loosened up since she's been here, not as uptight as she was when she and Astor first arrived. Julia's always been quiet and aloof, but today, her panties were in a real wad, for some reason. I wondered if she and Astor had some kind of fuss on the drive down, since each seems to be avoiding the other.

Once Corrine asked me if I thought Astor was jealous of Julia, which had never occurred to me. If it's true, that doesn't make Astor the Lone Ranger, though. A lot of people are envious of Julia, and not just because she's a successful author and the first lady. There are a lot of other reasons to envy her. Julia's not only the skinniest woman I've ever seen, she's nice as pie, and really, really beautiful, in a classy, diamonds-and-pearls sort of way. Plus, she's married to Mr. Southern Politics, Joe Ed Stovall, who's still as hot as he was in college, when he was the hottest thing at Bama. I think he's a perfect match for Julia, even if everyone says Julia married beneath her. My daddy used to say that all southern women think they married down. In spite of her being so beautiful and having such a hot husband, I don't envy Julia myself. I can't imagine her fishbowl existence and the pressures on her, and that's not even counting the problems with Bethany.

Byrd's puttering in the kitchen, putting away all the food they've toted in. I'm trying not to put any significance on the fact that

Corrine has brought nothing from her garden this year but basil, rosemary, and tarragon. Not only does she raise a lot of the gourds she paints, she also has a great garden and always brings all sorts of stuff to make fancy salads with. (Naturally, Corrine's a vegetarian but not one of those pious, self-righteous ones.) When I ask if her vegetable garden kicked the bucket this year, Corrine nods her head but doesn't elaborate.

"Hey, y'all," Byrd calls out. "Everybody brought bananas, it looks like." She points to one of my new baskets that she's filled and placed in the center of the counter. "Now what on earth will we do with so many bananas?"

"Well, we could always eat some of them," I say, grinning, and Julia hits me on the arm with a throw pillow while the others hoot and holler.

"Oh, Lanier, you're so *bad*," Julia laughs. "You'll never get the crown!"

"If Lanier gets the crown this year," Byrd says, "anybody can."

"Does anyone know if Rosanelle is coming?" Corrine asks from a rocking chair, facing the back windows and looking out over the bay. Since her arrival, she's collapsed into a rocker and sipped ginger ale. Byrd whispered to me that she drove over to pick Corrine up because Corrine had been sicker than she'd let on. I knew she'd had a bug or something but hadn't been too worried till now, when I saw her. She looks awful.

"Not if we're lucky," I say, bringing about another chorus of hoots. I hold up my hand to stop them. "She called earlier, and she's on her way."

As if on cue, Rosanelle Tilley Dixon flings open the door and sweeps into the room. "Ta da! I'm here," she grins.

As usual, Rosanelle has a new do, her platinum hair real short and stylish, with bangs sweeping to the side, just below her cheek. Looks like she's had her already-white teeth whitened again, or maybe it's just the contrast with her bright lip gloss. She's dressed fit to kill in an expensive-looking plum-colored suit and suede heels. I've never seen anyone wear so many bracelets, and they jangle like mad when she gestures, which she does all the time, getting on my nerves bad. Tie her hands and she'd be mute.

"Oh, Byrd," Rosanelle cries, hugging her so hard that Byrd almost loses her footing,

"You look just precious—precious! I admire you so much for letting your hair go natural like that. Takes a lot of courage. If I did it, I'd look a hundred years old."

Rosanelle spots Julia standing by the table and rushes to her, arms out. Fortunately, Julia has the table to hold on to when she's grabbed. Rosanelle's gardenia perfume floods the room, and I cough, wishing I had a gas mask. "Julia, *darling*! How's my favorite first lady?"

"Just fine, Rosanelle. How are you?" Julia tries to back away, probably stifling from the perfume, but Rosanelle holds tight, grasping her arms.

"I just heard that you and Joe Ed had to put poor little Beth Ann in the Helen Keller School. You did the right thing, honey. My heart goes out to you." Rosanelle is patting Julia's shoulder hard enough to bruise it, while she stands with an appropriately concerned look on her face, her head tilted in sympathy.

"Thank you, Rosanelle," Julia says serenely. "And it's Bethany."

"What?" Rosanelle blinks her big blue eyes, her long lashes heavily mascaraed.

"Bethany, not Beth Ann."

"Oh! That's what I meant. Bethany. And listen, I'm calling you next week about hosting the Montgomery chapter for us in August. The W is counting on you."

Corrine doesn't get up to greet Rosanelle, though they wave and smile as they greet each other. Rosanelle's glance passes over her and lights on Astor, who's just coming out of the bedroom, where she's been closed off, talking on the phone to the nursing home where Mose is. "Rosanelle, you're here!" Astor smiles, and she and Rosanelle hug like they haven't seen each other for years. Rosanelle gets on Astor's nerves as much as she does the rest of us, but Astor's such a big hypocrite she always acts like Rosanelle is her long-lost twin or something.

"How is poor old Mose?" Rosanelle asks, her brow wrinkled in concern. Poor old Mose, my foot. I hate the way Mose, one of the most gifted artists in Alabama, has become an object of pity since he's turned old and senile. I hope I don't live long enough for anyone to say of me, And how is poor old Lanier?

Now Rosanelle is pouring it on, telling Astor how much she admires her loyalty to her poor dear husband. One thing Corrine's always pointing out to me: Kiss-ass though she might be, Astor has a way of turning on you, cutting you down, which you don't realize till you're bleeding all over the floor. I figure Astor will let Rosanelle prattle on and on, then she'll come through with one of the little zingers she's known for. Sure enough, draping herself over the arm of the sofa and looking concerned, Astor asks, "Are things still pretty rough at The W, Rosanelle?"

"Rough? I don't know what you mean, rough?" Rosanelle blinks her eyelashes rapidly, her hand at her throat.

With her hair slicked back in a chignon and gold hoop earrings hanging from her ears, Astor looks like a flamenco dancer. She tilts her head as she regards Rosanelle. "I've been concerned about your job security, is all," she says, her voice sugary-sweet. "Everyone's saying that the new vice-president is cleaning house, firing people left and right. I worry about both you and Bob." Rosanelle's husband Bob is also an administrator at The W, recently appointed to provost. Bob is perfect for her, one of those toothy, back-slapping southern men slick as a politician. A Bill Clinton type, in more ways than one, or so I've heard.

"Oh, no—no. There's absolutely nothing for anyone to worry about, I can assure you. I've had my job for almost thirty years," Rosanelle says, her jaw tightening.

Astor reaches over and pats her arm. "Well, if we can do anything, let us know. We can write letters of support or whatever."

"We'll be glad to, if it will help," Julia chimes in. She's taken out the ingredients for the rum punch and is standing at the cabinet mixing everything in a big pitcher, fresh pineapple juice and lime and mint and lots and lots of spiced rum. As queen, Julia shouldn't be fixing our drinks, but she's always mixed the punch. She says that she's a royal who's also a populist, whatever that means.

"Thank you, but that will not be necessary," Rosanelle repeats. I get it over with by crossing the room and giving her a hug, knowing what she'll say to me, and she doesn't let me down. "Oh, *Lanier*! Bless your heart, I've been so worried about you since you and Paul split up. How are your poor, poor children?"

Corrine sort of gasps, but I don't flinch. "Actually, they're doing real good," I tell her. "Christopher called me just the other day to say he's gotten a tennis scholarship to Vandy next year."

This brings cheers and congratulations all around the room, but Rosanelle stays on course. I know exactly where she's headed. "How nice. But what about Lindy?"

"What about her? She's only seventeen, so she won't be going off to college for another year." I'm deliberately misunderstanding her, and she knows it.

"I mean . . . how is she managing without a mother?"

"She has a mother, Rosanelle, and you're looking at her."

Rosanelle wags a finger at me. "You know what I mean, Lanier."

Before I can respond to that, Julia stops her stirring and says, in a loud voice for Julia, "Really, Rosanelle! Surely you know that's a painful subject for Lanier, so let me answer: Lindy will be fine. I talked to her recently, and she tells me that she's beginning to cook for Paul and Christopher, which is good for her. Helps her become more independent. This has been rough on everyone, and it's a very sad situation, granted, but there's a lot of potential for growth and self-discovery for all concerned."

After that, everybody gets real quiet till Astor, from her perch on the arm of the sofa, snickers. We all turn to look at her, and she waves a hand in the air as though to erase the sound of her giggles. "Oh, God, I'm so sorry, Julia! But you sound like *Chicken Soup for the Soul* or something. Next thing you know, you'll be hosting one of those radio shows where folks call in for therapy." Rising, she comes to stand by me, putting her arm around my shoulder and leaning her head against mine. She's a full head taller than me, so she has to bend to do it, but as usual, she looks as graceful as a heron. "Lanier has had such an awful time, Rosanelle, honey. If only you realized how she's suffered over the past three months, you wouldn't be drilling her."

"How could I?" Rosanelle looks genuinely hurt. "Lanier has not told me a blooming thing. All I've heard is gossip, gossip, gossip! I have a very active alumni group in Pickens County, and you won't believe what they're saying."

"Oh, yeah, I will," I say with a hoot of laughter. Rosanelle would faint dead away if she knew that most likely everything they say is true. I went from being the darling of Reform, Alabama, to becoming the bride of Satan.

Standing in the center of the room, Byrd moves quickly to get things back under control, actually clapping her hands like a camp counselor herding a bunch of misbehaving campers to their next activity. "Listen up, everybody! Raise your hand if you're ready for a glass of punch, and I'll bring you one."

I don't know exactly how, but Byrd has managed to dissipate the tension in the room. After we raise our hands and Byrd takes the count, I point out the window. "Okay, everybody—the sun's about to set," I say, excited about my favorite time of the day. "Ready for us to take our punch and go sit on the pier, Your Majesty?"

"Wait!" Rosanelle squeals. "Let me run and change first."

"Please don't change, Rosanelle," I say dryly. "We like you just the way you are."

"Ha ha, Lanier. Always joking around," Rosanelle responds. "Won't take me but a minute, girls." Byrd hurries over to help with the suitcases—Rosanelle always brings two or three—and they head to the back bedroom, where Byrd already has her stuff.

"Take your time," I call out, managing to keep a straight face when Corrine rolls her eyes to the ceiling.

8

Julia
DAUPHIN ISLAND

SITTING ON THE PIER with our plastic glasses of rum punch in hand, the Same Sweet Girls begin the first of our rituals: the pronouncement, the reading from the royal scribe, and the queen's salute. As reigning queen of the SSGs, I get the seat of honor, the royal throne, which Lanier and Byrd bring out for me. As Lanier unlocks the padlock on the storage shed that Judge Brewer added to the covered part of the pier, Corrine says, "I've never been able to figure out why you keep it locked up, Lanier. It's not like anyone would steal it."

I gasp in mock horror, my hand at my

throat. "My ears must be deceiving me—a lady-in-waiting dares to insult the royal throne?"

Rosanelle wags a finger at Corrine. "Not very sweet of you, Lady Corrine. You'd better plea for a royal edict of forgiveness, or you'll never get the crown again." Rosanelle has loosened up considerably since having a couple of rum punches. She's out of her expensive business suit and into linen pants and a loose shell in a becoming shade of rosy-coral, with matching sandals on her dainty feet. She still has her pearls on (come to think of it, so do I), but her face is flushed with the rum, and her bangs are flapping on her cheek, thrown around by the warm salty breeze blowing over the bay. She looks quite pretty, like a former beauty queen should, and I remember her as she was that day in convocation thirty years ago, her hair stiff as papier-mâché and her makeup flawless. Four years older than us, she's already in her fifties. Astor told me once in strictest confidence that Rosanelle had her face lifted on her fiftieth birthday.

Lanier gets on one side and Byrd on the other; then, struggling, they bring out the royal throne. A triumphant flourish is provided by Astor, who stands and bows before me, singing out, "Ta dee da!" Bent over like old women with the weight, Byrd and Lanier lug the throne to its traditional place of honor, centered in front of the benches that Lanier's told us a million times she scrubbed and scrubbed for us to sit our royal fannies on. Of course I quickly reminded her that I'm the only one with a royal one. The throne is an old commode that Lanier's father had brought down a few years ago, intending to add it to the enclosed area where he'd put a shower, Lanier told us, teary-eyed. After he died, the SSGs claimed it. Byrd made a sequined cover for the lid and a padded velvet one for the seat, in the royal colors of purple and gold, and Corrine painted the names and reigns of the queens each year on the tank, in purple calligraphy. When Byrd remembered her grandkids had left a Burger King crown in her car, Corrine painted "Royal Throne of Her Majesty, Queen of the SSGs" on it, and we glued it on top. Take my word for it, it gives new meaning to the word tacky.

As reigning queen, I have to wear the crown at all the royal functions this weekend, so I sit on the throne and take the crown from its hatbox, the original one that's looking shabbier and shabbier each year. When I put on the heavy crown, it knocks down the better part of my French twist, as well as hurting like everything, and I make a face. I've been hitting the rum punch pretty hard, too. Normally I drink very little, a couple of scotch and sodas, maybe, but on these SSG gatherings we all let our hair down, both literally and figuratively.

The scepter is kept in a cardboard cylinder, and I remove it, holding it high for everyone to pay homage to. The ladies-in-waiting applaud and bow as they take their seats on the benches around the royal throne. The scepter is my favorite. It was Rosanelle's baton when she was drum majorette at Eufaula High School, and we've decorated the knob on top with cotton bolls, sugar cubes, and purple-and-gold streamers that flap in the strong breeze. The complete costume—crown, scepter, and train—looks fabulously campy, but I don't get to wear the train until tomorrow night, when we have the queen's promenade and the crowning of the new queen. "Okay, you *sweet* ladies," I say, raising the scepter high. "Now for the pronouncement."

The queen's pronouncement always accompanies the bringing forth of the throne, crown, and scepter. Standing, I hold the scepter up and we all shout the queen's pronouncement in unison: "Balls, said the queen. If I had 'em, I'd be king!" Then, I return to my position on the throne and say, "Let the royal scribe come forward for the reading of the lesson."

With a bow, Lanier steps up beside the throne, her little lesson book in hand. The ritual of having Lanier read from the lesson book is a fairly new tradition, begun only a couple of years ago, when Corrine gave Lanier the book as sort of a journal and Lanier astonished all of us by writing some really thought-provoking things in it. I've noticed that some of her observations don't sound like much on first hearing them, but afterward, they've stayed with me. Her first lesson, *It will either work out or it won't,* I wrote on a card and taped to the mirror of my vanity. When I read it to Bethany, she loved it so much that she printed it for me in large letters on a piece of canvas, and now it's framed and hanging over the mirror.

"Okay, Your Majesty and all you floozies-in-waiting, listen up," Lanier says. "Here it is."

She clears her throat and reads in a loud, clear voice: "Any landing you walk away from is a good landing."

There's a silence while we wait for the rest of it, but Lanier closes the book with a flourish, bows to me, then resumes her place with the other ladies-in-waiting. Corrine's the first one to get it; her face lights up and she begins the applause. Lanier looks pleased with herself, in spite of Rosanelle's puzzled frown and halfhearted clapping. I can tell that Rosanelle doesn't get it, but I think Lanier has done it again. I can't wait to tell Bethany what the lesson was this time, because it's certainly true in her case.

"That was splendid, O royal scribe," I tell Lanier. "A hard-earned lesson that life has taught you, and one we will all benefit from. Now for the next ritual." I hold the scepter above my head. "Let us begin the royal salute."

Like everything else, the salute follows a pattern that has developed over the years, and Byrd always begins it. Curtsying, holding out the edge of her shorts as though it were the hem of a long skirt, Byrd stands before me. "Your Majesty," she says, "you've been the sweetest queen the SSGs have ever had. You are so much sweeter than that disgraceful queen we had last year." Since I was queen last year also, Byrd has done well, and we applaud her.

Now, according to the royal edicts, I have to respond in kind. "Thank you, Lady Byrd. I'm so glad to see that you have on shorts. Next time you pee in your pants, you can just hold out the legs and let loose." Grinning, the girls applaud appreciatively.

It's Corrine's turn. "Your Majesty," she says, standing and bowing before me, "I read the profile that *Time* magazine did on you last week, and they got it wrong, saying you pushed Joe Ed into running for governor. Everyone knows it was your mama instead." Corrine smiles and gives the victory sign at the applause she earns, but she has no idea how close she's come to the truth.

"Such a *sweet* salute, Lady Corrine," I say. "Although you claimed to be sick this afternoon, Her Majesty suspects you got an early start on the rum punch." Again, smiles and applause, and I notice that Astor applauds longer than anyone. That odd thing between Astor and Corrine is always lurking in the background, and you never know when it will flare up. But you know that eventually, it will.

When Rosanelle takes her place, I see Corrine and Lanier exchange glances. Once, I said to Corrine—sort of joking—that Astor and Rosanelle do the ironic salute better than the rest of us, and Corrine said it comes naturally to them, is why. "I've been meaning to thank Your Majesty," Rosanelle says, her voice somewhat slurred, "for that *lovely* reception you hosted last month at the Governor's Mansion in honor of the Montgomery alumni chapter. I didn't realize you could get such good boxed wine at Wal-Mart's."

"Why, thank you, Lady Rosanelle," I respond, bowing my head. "I knew you'd be right at home with anything from Wal-Mart's. And I loved the dress you wore to the reception. Isn't it nice that pretty clothes come in larger sizes now?" The SSGs applaud enthusiastically, maybe overdoing it a tad, since Rosanelle has put on a little bit of weight lately, her curvy figure becoming even more Rubenesque.

Red-faced (taking us seriously again), Rosanelle returns to her place, and it's Lanier's turn. Before her curtsy to me, Lanier says in an aside to the others, "I'm fucked," and Astor mutters, "You can say that again." Clearing her throat and straightening her shoulders, Lanier plunges in. "Your Majesty, your royal bearing is an inspiration to all of us ladies-in-waiting. But I wonder if the unbelievable number of rum punches that you've had has anything to do with how crooked your crown is."

I straighten the crown, but when I look at Lanier and raise the scepter for my response, I can't help it; I get tickled. "I'm sorry, Lady Lanier," I laugh, "but this is too easy."

Corrine comes to Lanier's rescue by applauding loudly. "I think that says it all," she declares, but Astor holds up a hand. "No fair!" she protests, her voice loud. "Lanier can't get off the hook that easy. Ask her about Dr. Roland Pierce."

A stunned silence follows, broken only by Byrd's gasp, which comes out as more of a hiccup. Cutting her eyes to me, Astor puts a hand over her mouth before turning back to Lanier. "Oh, Lanier, honey!" she says. "I can't believe I said that. I must've had more punch than I realized."

"Bull," Corrine murmurs under her breath, her eyes narrowing as she stares at Astor. It's well known that Astor, being so into dance and yoga, drinks a lot less than the rest of us. Lanier is staring at Astor, and I can tell by the look on Lanier's face that Astor has betrayed a confidence. I know that she did, actually; Astor told me about Lanier's affair with Dr. Pierce before Lanier told me. Lanier said she was only telling me, Astor, and Corrine, but she didn't want Byrd or Rosanelle to know.

I quickly raise the scepter and point it toward Astor. "Since you called attention to yourself, Lady Astor, come forward for your salute now."

Her head held high, Astor steps forward and curtsies much more elaborately than any of us. She's changed clothes, dressing in an off-the-shoulder peasant blouse and long silk skirt. Like everything Astor wears, it's fabulous looking, right out of a smart New York boutique, but she's way overdressed for the occasion, making the rest of us look like bumpkins in our comfortable linen pants and shorts outfits. All of us are wearing our fabulously tacky pins that spell out SSG in rhinestones pinned right over our hearts—except for Astor, who's pinned hers to her hip, on the tie of her wraparound skirt. Predictably, Corrine whispered to me that evidently Astor got confused as to where her heart was located.

"Your Majesty," Astor says, her arms thrown wide, "I admire your courage in being out here in the open, in full view of terrorists. We've all been so worried since the terrorist attack on the Governor's Mansion a couple of weeks ago."

"What?" Corrine gasps, and we wait until Lanier tells her what happened. The only one who lives out of state, she hasn't heard about the incident that had everyone in Alabama laughing for days. On hearing the story, Corrine joins in the laughter, and I'm relieved to see her cheeks flush with color. She has the most incredible milk-white skin, translucent and creamy as a camellia, but earlier I was really concerned about her, she was so pallid. Even her lips were colorless.

Astor tilts her head sideways and smiles a wicked smile at me. "I thought surely Your Majesty would insist on bringing Lieutenant Hawkins, your favorite bodyguard, to protect you."

"Whoa." Byrd grins, jerking her head up. "Intrigue in the Governor's Mansion! Did y'all see that sexy movie where Kevin Costner was Whitney Houston's bodyguard?"

Rosanelle says, her eyes glazed, "Honey, that Lieutenant Hawkins can guard *my* body any day of the week."

"Oooh, Rosanelle, listen to you, girlfriend,"

Byrd squeals. Rosanelle's hair is even more windblown now, and her speech is slurred. She's definitely drunk. Not that I needed more proof. She's the last one of us to make a remark like that.

I don't know what makes me say what I do to Astor, since I've vowed not to let her know that I saw her the other night, but I hear myself saying, "I wouldn't dream of trespassing on *your* territory, Lady Astor. Besides, I'd have to get you to show me how to fix the alarm on the side door. Couldn't have it going off when I sneaked out to meet Lieutenant Hawkins, like you did last night."

It's rare that Astor is at a loss for words, but it's obvious that I have dropped a bombshell right in her lap. Her dark eyes widen and she takes a step backward. "D-don't be silly, Your Majesty," she stammers. "I didn't sneak out of the Mansion last night." Her laugh sounds weak. "Where'd you get such a ridiculous idea?"

"I followed you," I tell her. I hear the startled gasps of the SSGs, then a rustle of whispering. Astor's so dark you wouldn't think the color could drain from her face, but it does. The stunned silence is broken by Corrine's burst of laughter. It's contagious, and the rest of them join in, with Rosanelle clapping her hands in glee.

"Oh, Julia—that's a good one! You had me going for a minute," Rosanelle cries, wiping her eyes.

I turn my head from Astor and raise the scepter high above my head. "I declare the royal salute is now officially over for another year. Thank you, my dear ladies. You all were very, very sweet this year."

9

Corrine
DAUPHIN ISLAND

LANIER LOOKS LIKE SHE'S going to jump out of her skin when she sees me, sitting on the back steps in the moonlight, waiting for her to return. I watch her turn off the flashlight when she clears the fence beyond the clump of palms and make her way through the moss-hung oaks to the back of the house. "Jesus Christ, Corrine!" she whispers, dropping down to sit beside me. "You scared the crap out of me. You look like the Girl with the Flaming Hair sitting here in that white nightgown."

"I was faking sleep when you sneaked out of bed." I don't tell her I'm sick again, can't sleep. No point in worrying her. I got up to meditate, see if I could reconnect with the healing powers of the universe. Evidently, I've lost that lately, for some reason. I lean back on the steps, and even though the strong wind blowing in from the bay is wonderfully cool, the steps hold enough of the day's sun to warm me through my thin gown and robe. I'm not suffering from the heat this summer as I usually do. I've been almost cold lately, like an old person. "Don't tell me you have that bodyguard of Joe Ed's hidden in the house next door, the one Rosanelle is hot for," I say.

Lanier giggles, then takes the glass of port from me, the one I've poured to see if it will settle my stomach. It doesn't. "I see you found Julia's expensive port," she says, then turns it up and drinks it like water, wiping her mouth on the back of her hand. "Sorry. I didn't mean to finish it off." She sticks her tongue in the tiny glass and licks the sides. "Hmm . . . best port I've ever had."

"Help yourself," I say dryly. "Want to take the bodyguard a glass?" Pulling her gray hooded sweatshirt close, Lanier turns her head and looks at me. It's dark, lit only by a half-moon, but I can see her fairly well.

"Oh, hell, Corrine, it's Jesse I went over there to see, but don't tell the others. I found him there yesterday, in bad shape." She sighs deeply and throws her head back to catch the breeze.

"Jesse? Jesse *Phoenix*?" I couldn't be more surprised if she'd told me that it was, indeed, Joe Ed's bodyguard that she sneaked out to meet in the dark. I knew that Dolphin Cove was next door to Jesse Phoenix's boyhood home, of course; we'd joked about it for years. At various gatherings we'd gotten out the binoculars and spied on the house, trying to get a glimpse of him, even though Lanier told us he was never there. I finally got to meet him, several years ago when Lanier and I went to one of his concerts in Atlanta. Lanier told me she'd had a tremendous crush on Jesse as long as she could remember, and that night, I found out why. Although not a good-looking man, Jesse Phoenix was a charmer, with lots of charisma and a whimsical sweetness. By the time we left the backstage, I was halfway in love with him, too, and I bought all his albums. If he had nothing else going for him, those beautiful songs of his would've been enough. I look at Lanier once what she said sinks in, and ask, "What on earth is he doing there?"

Lanier shrugs. She's propped on her elbows; her eyes are closed and her head falls back languidly. "Damn if I know. I can't get anything out of him except how fucked up he is, which is obvious. The electricity's off in the house and it's a wreck. Whiskey bottles and beer cans everywhere."

"You think he's an alcoholic?"

"If not, he's missed his calling."

"His mother died, right?" Lanier nods, her eyes still closed. "I read that a few months ago and thought about you," I say in a low voice. "The time you told me how upset you were when Jesse left home and nobody knew where he was, till his first album came out." We're quiet a minute, then I look over at her suspiciously. "You're not fooling around with him, are you, Lanier?"

"Not yet." Lanier grins, that impish, gap-toothed grin of hers that has always gotten her into trouble. Anything ever out of line in class or in the dorm, all it took was Lanier to grin and she'd get the blame for it. I can't help myself; I smile and shake my head.

"God, you're hopeless. You'd better stay away from Jesse Phoenix, girl. That's all you need now."

"Oh, Lord, please don't throw me in that briar patch!" Lanier laughs, and I poke her with my elbow to shut her up, looking over my shoulder at the dark, sleeping house.

"Listen to me, Lanier," I say. "I hope now you'll see that you cannot confide in Astor, after her remark about Dr. Pierce."

"I thought you were going to have a stroke," she says, running her hand through her short brown hair. "It pissed me off, too, but . . . that's Astor for you. It just slipped out. She didn't mean to say anything."

I rub my face wearily. It's beyond me, how everyone not only forgives Astor for everything but also makes excuses for her. Maybe it's just me; maybe I'm a mean-spirited person. "I'm not going there with you yet again," I tell Lanier, "but I will say this: It was obvious that everyone knew about you and him. And where do you think they heard it if not from Astor? Byrd's reaction told me she knew."

Lanier's eyes are on me, and I can tell she's considering the possibility that Astor has violated her trust. She turns her head away and looks out over the moonlit bay, then shrugs. "I figured word would get out eventually. That doesn't necessarily mean Astor told. Folks know that Saint Paul must have kicked me out for a reason, right? I mean, think about it. Like Rosanelle said this afternoon, gossip, gossip, gossip."

I stop her by holding up my hand. A wave of nausea causes me to feel hot and faint, but I'm determined to have my say before returning to bed. "Well, I'm not going to plow that ground again, however . . ."

"I love your earthy way of putting things, farm girl," she grins, putting her arm around me. "And I love you. I know you're just trying to protect me, honey. But it's too late."

"Don't say that! It's not true. I know that Paul will take you back. He's too good a man not to." I don't tell her about the letters I've written Paul, begging him to reconsider. Lanier always teased him, calling him Saint Paul because of his good nature, but for the past few months, his hurt has killed that part of him, or so it seems. Saint though he might be, he hasn't been able to forgive Lanier's indiscretion with a colleague. I turn back to her and say, "Lanier, you made a mistake, a big one, granted, but . . ."

"A *mistake*?" Her laugh is low, but bitter.

"That doesn't even come close to describing what I did. As we used to say in church, I have sinned and fallen short of the glory of God."

I close my eyes and quote from memory: *"'We do earnestly repent and are heartily sorry for these our misdoings, the remembrance of them is grievous unto us, the burden of them is intolerable.'"*

Lanier nods soberly. "Damn right."

I smile at that response, so typically Lanier. "But it's being so cheerful that keeps you going, right?" We both smile, then I say, "Did I tell you that I'm going to church again?"

"Are you? That's good! In college you went every Sunday and seemed like you got a lot out of it. A lot more than the rest of us." Lanier puts an arm around my shoulder. "But then, you were into all kinds of spiritual stuff in those days. Still are, I guess."

I shake my head. "I've been trying to find my way back. I think that has a lot to do with whatever it is that's ailing me."

Lanier was right; I'd always been drawn to the spiritual world, like the proverbial moth to the flame. When Miss Fielding took me under her wing in high school, she'd often gotten me to spend the weekends at her house by telling Mama she and I were working on an art project. Miss Fielding would take me to her church in the little town of Geneva on Sunday mornings before returning me to the farm that afternoon. I'd been raised Pentecostal, where the preacher shouted and scared me to death, and the congregation fell out in the aisles, speaking in tongues. In Miss Fielding's little Episcopal church, they read beautiful words from their prayer books, led by an elderly, white-collared priest who was as dignified as my preacher was common. After the Holy Eucharist, drinking the blood and eating the body of Jesus Christ, I filled up with the love of God. I felt like I was incandescent with His light as I made my way back to the pew.

When I ended up at a Methodist college, I went to chapel every Sunday. No prayer books, but they had holy communion, very similar to the Eucharist, and I found the same peace there I'd found in the little church in Geneva. However, when I married Miles, I quit going to the Episcopal church in Elijah, the one I'd been attending with Miss Fielding since my move there. Miles scorned all organized religion and convinced me that my piety was yet another example of my provincial mind-set. Over the past few years, I've mostly explored alternative approaches to spirituality. However, a few weeks ago I found myself longing for that incandescence I lost so many years ago, and I returned to take the Eucharist again.

I slide my arm around Lanier's waist, and she puts her head on my shoulder. "Lanier?"

"Hmmm?"

"I love you, too, even if you are seriously screwed up." She laughs, and I get to my feet. "Come on, let's go in now and see if we can get some sleep. Big day tomorrow. Bet you anything Astor gets the crown."

"One thing for sure," Lanier says as she pulls herself up and dusts off the back of her pants, "ain't a chance in hell that I will."

10

Julia

DAUPHIN ISLAND

WHEN I PUT THE crown on Astor's dark head the next night, I catch Corrine's eye and wink. She and I had sat on the deck after breakfast and talked for a few minutes this morning, and Corrine had said she was sure Astor would get the crown this year. She'd said something else that really touched me. Corrine had told me that she couldn't believe she'd almost missed out on this weekend. Outlandish and moronic as it is, year after year it always turned out to be more fun than anything else in her pathetic life—she'd sworn—which made me feel sad for her. Both of us agreed that it's become more than a silly ritual that has taken on a life of its own. Corrine and I agreed that we always laughed more, teased more, and enjoyed ourselves more at the SSG weekends than on any other occasion. If we ever decide it is too ridiculous, that we've outgrown it or become too weary to continue, we'll miss out on something that has become an important part of us.

The SSGs spent the better part of the afternoon decorating the pier, draping purple and gold streamers from it, positioning gold candles along both sides, putting the royal throne in its place at the pier's end. Another tradition: The queen has to contribute a new decoration each year, and I've had to do it two years in a row. Last year I'd brought hundreds of purple irises from the greenhouse of the Governor's Mansion. We'd strewn them along the pier for the promenade, afterward throwing them out into Mobile Bay, where they floated on the dark waters like some kind of exotic water lilies. But this year I surprise everyone with sparklers, something I've not seen since childhood. Astor helps me with them— evidently she's decided to overlook what I did to her yesterday with the salute—and she not only sticks sparklers in the tops of the pier posts, but also gives everyone one to hold in her hand. That night after supper, with the pier all lit up with the candles and the string of lights along the posts, we position ourselves with our cameras and sparklers. Soon as I leave the deck and start down the steps toward the pier, Astor scurries around lighting the sparklers on the posts, as well as the ones in our hands. Byrd turns on the tape player to a nauseating version of Wayne Newton singing "Ain't She Sweet," and the SSGs wave their sparklers wildly, leaving bright streamers of fire in the dark night.

I absolutely adore dressing up in the queen's getup—the crown, scepter, and cape with the long train. The crown by itself is bad enough, huge and gaudy with rhinestones and fake jewels dangling from its little points, but the cape is beyond tacky. Byrd made it several years ago when she was queen, of iridescent purple satin with a gold lining, its train trailing several feet behind, making it hazardous to walk in. Byrd bordered the edges with a boa of bright-purple ostrich feathers, making her royal majesty look like a tart from a grade-B movie.

Flashbulbs flash and everyone cheers and waves their sparklers as I promenade down the pier. I admit that I'm proud of the way I perform the queenly wave, which I think is one reason I've been chosen queen more than anyone. No one can do the little stiff-wristed movement of the hand better, except for Queen Elizabeth herself, whom I copied it from.

It's obvious to everyone that Astor's going to get the crown this year. Once I'm seated on the royal throne, each of the SSGs gives her presentation, trying to convince the others that she's been the sweetest of all, the one most deserving of the crown. Each of us is only allowed ten minutes, and she has to allow time for two things: one, to make her case for what she'd do if she were queen, and two, to answer a "serious" question from the reigning queen.

Byrd begins. She describes all her babysitting details, telling us how sweet she was even when the grandchildren refused to go to sleep or eat their suppers or take baths. She says she'll promote world peace if she's fortunate enough to be queen. Then, she answers my question of which historical figure she'd most like to have dinner with by answering, Jesus Christ. The SSGs applaud her halfheartedly, and I'm sure each one believes that her presentation is surely much better.

I think Lanier might have a chance when she forgoes her presentation, throwing herself prostrate at my feet and begging for mercy. I notice that even Rosanelle laughs and laughs. Everyone is more relaxed tonight; for some reason, there's always some tension when we first arrive, which gradually dissipates over the weekend. It's the same the last weekend in October, when we meet at Corrine's house on Blue Mountain.

Rosanelle's presentation is typical of her—serious rather than tongue-in-cheek—and I have to keep myself from yawning as she lists her achievements during the past year: being asked to be on the vestry of her church, getting an award from her garden club, taking stuffed animals to the children's hospital, teddy bears at Christmas and bunnies on Easter. I marvel every year that Rosanelle has never gotten our irony, that she actually writes up our get-togethers in her little newsletters as though we were a real alumni group. Matter of fact, it's become part of the ritual—when we get her newsletters through the mail, we call each other to hoot over her efforts to make us sound legitimate. Lanier summed it up after ten years, when it finally dawned on us that Rosanelle just didn't *get it.* "She has us by the balls, so to speak," Lanier had said, one of the times when Rosanelle didn't attend and we sat around trying to decide what to do about her. "We're sweet, right? Booting Rosanelle out wouldn't be a sweet thing to do. None of us would ever get the crown again if we did."

We all sat looking at each other in bewilderment until Lanier added, "Maybe God sent us Rosanelle as a true test of our sweetness."

Corrine asks me if she can follow Rosanelle, which she does. I give her permission to change the order when she tells me that her presentation is lame because she hasn't worked on it any since being sick so much lately. Corrine outlines all her good deeds this past year: not murdering Culley when he had yet another orifice pierced, not murdering him when he got a crown of thorns tattooed on his butt ("At least it's a crown," Lanier contributes); not murdering Miles when he threatened to cut off payment of her health insurance, although ordered to

by the divorce court; and especially not murdering Miles when he told Corrine the argument he's taking to the judge: that he
shouldn't have to pay her health insurance
because of her pre-existing condition,
severe depression. The sympathetic gasps
of the SSGs seem to energize Corrine, and
she says that when she's queen, she'll campaign to make Prozac free to everyone, and
the SSGs—myself included—applaud enthusiastically. Drawing a question from the box
kept under the commode seat, in the toilet
bowl, I ask her if she could do one thing to
make the world a better place, what would it
be? "Why, make everybody as sweet as I
am," Corrine responds, and Lanier whistles
and applauds loudly. But I suspect Corrine
has lost at least one vote when Rosanelle
frowns as she scribbles notes to herself in
the little organizer that she's never without.

Astor's presentation comes complete with
costume changes, various hats and acces-
sories that she's brought down in a tote,
pulling out different ones to illustrate the
many "sweet" roles in which she's been
cast in the past year. As a fairy godmother to
her step-grandchildren, she dons sequin-
studded wings and a wand; as a shining star

to her dance pupils, she sticks her face through a cut-out cardboard star; as an inspiration to her yoga classes, she contorts into a Salute to the Sun; but she clinches it by presenting herself as an angel of mercy tending to Mose, putting on a halo and wings. I see both Byrd and Rosanelle wiping their eyes and know Astor's won, even before answering my question. If she could have one wish granted by a genie, she'd wish that poor Mose could give his beloved state of Alabama just one more of his paintings. You can hear Rosanelle sniffling all the way to Mobile, and she jumps up and hugs Astor when the votes are counted and I remove the crown and put it on my successor.

Afterward, freed of the crown and cloak that are both so heavy they were beginning to give me a headache, I seek out Corrine. Leaning against a post, she is by herself in a dark spot on the pier where she can't be seen by the others as they gather around Astor, taking dozens of pictures for our scrapbook. I put my arm around her and lean my head against hers.

"You turned out to be prophetic, Lady Corrine," I say, smiling.

"I just hung my head over the pier and

puked," Corrine says. "Which I did on the trip over here, also." She turns her head and looks over at the SSGs, where Astor is posing for pictures, her arms raised high in triumph as flashbulbs flash. "Difference is," she adds, "this time, it wasn't caused by car sickness."

11

Corrine

DAUPHIN ISLAND

IT COULD BE THAT we're all hungover the next morning; I'm not sure. Saturday night, after the promenade, the presentations, and the crowning of the new queen, we bring out champagne, this on top of the rum punch we'd already had during our cocktail hour. Whatever it is, the tensions of the first day are with us again, zinging here and there like electric currents. Always just minor things, nothing you can really put your finger on.

I didn't drink Saturday night since I wasn't feeling well and had lost my supper right after the crowning. But even so, I feel sluggish and hungover the next morning. It doesn't help that I have an unsettling encounter with Astor before breakfast. I've gotten up early, as is my habit, and everyone else is asleep. Lanier, sleeping beside me, is actually snoring. I get into my clothes, sweat-pants and a T-shirt, a denim shirt tied over my shoulders against the early-morning chill, and leave the house without a sound, pulling the glass doors behind me.

Early morning on the bay is so beautiful that it takes my breath away. A white mist floats cloudlike over the water and obscures the point where the sea meets the sky. Even though I know it will be sticky-hot by noon, it's cool now, and I put my arms through my denim shirt, pulling it close. When I sit at the end of the pier, leaning against a post with my legs dangling over the water, I offer a prayer to the God that I've abandoned the last few years. I want to come home, to find again that awesome love that I've never found anywhere else. I want it so bad that it's an ache, a real ache, and I put both hands over my heart. Tears slide down my cheeks as I raise my head to the heavens. The mist obscures the sky, but I don't doubt for a moment that it's there, just as I know that God is, too. Not necessarily in the heavens, because I believe that God is everywhere, but I like the image. I've always loved the image of a hand reaching through the clouds, Michelangelo's painting on the ceiling of the Sistine Chapel. Man is barely moving to lift a hand, but God is actually straining in an effort to meet him. Today, I feel like the hand of God is reaching out to me, and I feel relieved. It's still there. The love that I turned my back on after being shamed into thinking myself crazy for even considering it, is still there. All I've got to do is claim it.

I realize I'm no longer alone on the pier—literally rather than metaphorically this time—and look over my shoulder. It's Astor, moving toward me through the mist like the angel of death. It's not having lived in New York all those years that inspires Astor to wear so much black; I think she wears it to match her heart. She has on her yoga suit, black tank and sleek tights that hug her long legs like a second skin, and an oversized silk kimono in ivory and black, with Oriental letters block-printed on it. The kimono is not tied at the waist, and it flaps behind her like the graceful wings of some sort of giant bird. The breeze coming off the bay lifts her hair, which is loose on her shoulders, and she looks like she's moving on the wind, floating like a leaf caught in a gust.

Neither of us says anything when Astor reaches the place where I'm seated, then stops, right beside me. She has a black nylon tote in her hand, a smaller version of the one she carried her stage props in last night. Still without saying a word to me, she unzips the tote, reaches in, and pulls out a slim red mat, which she unfurls and sits on cross-legged, next to me but facing away, toward the east. She places her hands on her knees, palms up, then arches her neck, her face turned upward and her eyes closed. I look at her flawless profile, the chiseled cheekbones and high, arched eyebrows, the wide, full-lipped mouth, then smile in spite of myself. Evidently she's going to launch into her meditative stances as though I'm not here, though she could have sat anywhere on the hundred-foot-long pier.

"Good morning, Corrine," I say. "Am I disturbing you? Do you mind if I sit here and contort? Why, no, Astor. You go right ahead. Don't mind me at all."

Her eyes still closed and her long neck arched in what has to be a painful position, Astor doesn't say anything for a full five minutes, then her low, throaty voice sounds amused. "It didn't occur to me that I needed your permission to sit on the pier, Corrine," she drawls.

Her meditations evidently concluded, Astor opens her eyes and rises. She stands tall and inhales until her chest expands, then raises her arms straight up, her elbows close to her head, her stomach concave. Her bones like liquid, she bends until her nose is between her knees, her palms flat on the mat. She arches her back like a cat, her stomach so flat it's against her backbone, her body in a perfect U shape. Easing her legs behind her, she sinks slowly down, flat on the red mat, then raises her head like a snake peering out of a hole. I watch in amazement as she sticks her tongue out, flat against her chin, goes back into the U shape, then rises majestically, her arms high above her head. She bends her head back against her spine so that her long hair brushes against her butt. Having saluted the mist-shrouded sun, she sits back on the mat, cross-legged.

"Bet you can't bend over far enough to kiss your own behind, can you?" Astor surprises me by asking, with complete seriousness.

"If I could, I'd never fool with a man again," I reply, with a grin.

"Just think what you'd be missing." Coyly, she smiles at me and tucks a glossy strand of hair behind her ear.

"Besides a lot of heartache?" I glance over at her. "Are you through with your contortions, Astor?"

"For the time being," she murmurs, then turns her head to look at me. I can't help it; I avert my gaze to the horizon, where the mist is lifting, burned off by a hazy white sun. Since I first met Astor, I've been uncomfortable under her direct gaze. She has a way of studying you that's unnerving, as though she's able to pick up on your hidden, shameful thoughts, thoughts that she carefully files away to be used against you at a later date. She reminds me of Miles in that way. Both have the ability to hone in on what you'd prefer no one knew about, let alone them. As a therapist, Miles is trained to ferret out that part of you; with Astor, it seems to come naturally.

Astor stares at me so long that I finally turn my head and meet her gaze. "What?" I say, more sharply than I intended. I've learned in the past that it's a mistake to let

Astor know she gets under my skin, so I usually ignore her as much as possible.

Astor shrugs. "I'm just trying to figure out why you've turned against me, Corrine. It hurts me that we're not close anymore. But even so, I love you as much as ever."

I look at her in astonishment. "I haven't turned against you, Astor. I've never liked you."

She laughs lightly, as though I'm teasing her. Which I am, of course, and she knows it. I'm not going to let her off that easily, however, and I say, "You know good and well why I steer clear of you, Astor. If I were you, I'd let sleeping dogs lie."

Astor widens her eyes innocently. "Surely you don't blame *me* because of that time with Miles!"

"Silly me, thinking close friends don't go after each other's husbands. Though in hindsight, I should have left you and Miles alone. I've never known two people who deserve each other more."

"Oh, thanks a lot! Guess that tells me what you think of me, since you make no secret of your dislike of him. That really hurts my feelings, Corrine." Astor lowers her head, then blinks her eyes rapidly. To make sure I get it, she dabs at the corner of her eyes with her index finger. Her fingernails are lovely, long and unpainted, naturally white-tipped. Bet she spends more on manicures than I do on food.

I sigh, rolling my eyes. Next thing you know, she'll be performing her poor wounded Astor number, and Lanier, Byrd and the rest of them will jump me for being mean to her. "Seriously, Astor," I say, "next time you're between husbands, I think you should consider Miles. He has a new wife, but infidelity's not a big deal with him. Something else the two of you have in common."

Astor abandons her halfhearted attempt at crocodile tears and studies me again. "So that's the real reason you've turned against Miles. I've always wondered if he cheated on you." Dry-eyed now, she doesn't even try to hide a sly smile. "It has little to do with him being a shit to you, does it? You're just plain jealous, aren't you?"

"And I thought I was hiding it so well. Yep, I really envy his new wife. She doesn't know what she's in for, but I'm beside myself with jealousy thinking about him having her committed, then taking her child away from her, should she be unlucky enough to have one with him."

Of course Astor's instantly on that remark, like a fly on cow plop. "Unlucky?" she gasps, placing her hand to her throat, as though mortally wounded. "I had no idea that you consider yourself unlucky to have had Culley."

"Culley's the unlucky one, with the parents he has." Weary, I rub my face, then raise my head to watch a blue heron rise from the marshes at the edge of the water and float over the bay, the same smoky-blue color as the heron. I don't want to think about all of that now and wish I hadn't let Astor put a damper on my morning. I'm tired of her, tired of her games and postures and devious-ness. I wish to God that I hadn't reacted to her taunting. She can always get to me, no matter how firm my resolve to ignore her.

"If you don't forgive Miles," Astor astonish-es me by saying, her tone pious, "then you'll become more bitter than you already are. Not a very attractive quality as you age, you know."

I can't help myself; my face flushes. Before I can respond, my mouth open, Astor continues in that fake, sugar-sweet drawl of hers that irks me about her as much as any-thing else. "You should be nicer to me,

Corrine. I have lots of contacts, and I know at least half a dozen eligible men I could fix you up with. Smart, artsy men, who have to fight women off. Wouldn't take but a word from me, and they'd be knocking your door down."

Astor's dark eyes blaze when I throw back my head and laugh in astonishment. "You can laugh if you want to," she spits out indignantly, "but one day, you'll be begging me to help you out. I just hope when it happens, your looks aren't gone for good."

"Astor, I'll say one thing for you," I say, shaking my head. "You never fail me. Just when I think you can't surprise me . . ."

She leans toward me, laying a hand on my arm, and her long hair falls forward, over her shoulders. "If you'll listen to me, Corrine, I can help you. You know that it's been five years since Mose has been a real husband to me, but I've learned to channel my energies in other ways. I—"

I hold up a hand to stop her. "Please, Astor, it took me all day yesterday to get over my car sickness. I don't want to start puking again this morning."

She ignores me as though I haven't spoken. "There's nothing wrong with innocent lit-

tle flirtations, not a thing. I'd never be unfaithful to Mose, but . . ."

"*Flirtations?* Yeah, right. Guess you
sneaked out of the Governor's Mansion to
play Parcheesi with the bodyguard, huh?
Who won, by the way? Did you give him a
good game?"

Astor's voice becomes so indignant that
I stare at her in surprise. "Julia was just
teasing, Corrine. God! You're worse than
Rosanelle taking everything seriously. It was
part of the silly salute. No one else thought
a thing about it."

It's my turn to smile slyly at her. "Oh, I
don't think Julia was teasing, *Mrs.* Morehouse. She was a bit too convincing for that.
Only thing I can't understand is why you
acted so weird about it. When you were married to that sleazy actor, you used to tell us
about all your little affairs in salacious
detail—"

Astor interrupts me, her face flushing.
"You're so cruel, Corrine! Surely you recall
that the only reason I cheated on Steve was
that he screwed anything that moved, male
or female. Mose is the love of my life. I might
flirt with other men now, but just for fun. I'd
never be unfaithful to Mose."

"Oh, bull," I say, with a snort. "Think I've forgotten the inauguration, when all of us were flirting with Lieutenant Hawkins? You said he was the sexiest man you'd ever seen, and you'd love to get him in the sack. I know you, Astor—if you want something, you go after it."

Her look is scornful. "Sure I flirted with Cal Hawkins, but I was just playing around, having fun. Do you honestly think I'd go to bed with an uncouth man like him? *Please*. I've been with several of the most high-powered men in New York, and I've married both a well-known Broadway actor and a famous artist. Cal Hawkins? A nobody." Astor tosses her head, dark hair flying about her shoulders.

I eye her skeptically, wondering if the disdainful look is for real or another of her poses. "So you're not attracted to him, then?"

She shrugs, then smiles a slow smile. "Oh, he's plenty hot. But he's a nobody. Power has always been a bigger turn-on for me. Power, money, fame . . ."

I can't believe she's saying it out loud, what I've always accused Astor of, what the others have jumped me for saying about her.

Naturally, she says it when nobody's around. And just as naturally, she'll deny having said it. Or say she was having me on. Another thing about Astor that drives me crazy: She always leaves a door open so she can weasel her way out.

"So, let me see if I have this right." I squint as the sun rises higher and hold my hand to shade my eyes as I study Astor. I'm not just being mean to her, I'm sincerely curious. I've always wondered what makes her tick. "In spite of Cal Hawkins being hotter than a jalapeño," I continue, "you find someone like . . . say . . . Joe Ed more your type." As soon as I say it, quite innocently, I'm suspicious. I wouldn't put anything past Astor. Not only did I catch her practically making out with Miles when we were still married, I've seen her flirt with all of the SSG husbands. I tilt my head and squint at her. "You wouldn't go after Joe Ed, would you, Astor?"

Astor jumps to her feet, her eyes blazing and her cheeks pink. "How dare you accuse me of such a thing! The very idea—Julia's been my best friend for thirty years."

I stare up at her as she towers over me, her black-and-ivory silk robe flapping in the strong breeze, her hands on her hips. "Julia said . . ." I begin, swallowing hard, "Julia said she followed you, watched you sneak out to meet Lieutenant Hawkins. But—maybe it wasn't him you met; maybe it was Joe Ed instead. I'll bet Julia saw Cal Hawkins letting you in so you could meet Joe Ed, is what happened . . ."

"That's utterly ridiculous," Astor hisses, but she keeps her voice low, so no one in the sleeping household can overhear us. Hands on hips, she leans over me. "You are really sick, you know that? Sick! Miles was right about you—sometimes you act like you're crazy. No wonder he had you locked up so many times. I'm surprised they ever let you out of the loony bin, but if you don't watch out, you'll be back. And this time, it will be for good."

Twirling around dramatically, Astor takes two steps as though to leave, then turns back and leans over me again. Her face, twisted in anger, is not pretty now. "You listen to me, Corrine. I love Julia more than anyone, and she has her cross to bear with poor little Bethany. So help me God, if you say one thing to her about this idiotic notion of yours—"

"I'd never say anything to Julia! And I

didn't accuse you, Astor. I just wondered, since I've seen you in action so many times before." Despite her claims of love and devotion to Mose, I don't believe for a second that Astor's been faithful to him the past five years of their marriage. Joe Ed, though . . . I'm not so sure about him. I don't trust any politician, since they all seem to fool around a lot. I don't really know Joe Ed that well. He seems like a good man, but political power can have a negative effect on anyone, I've observed. On the other hand, Joe Ed and Julia have been married for years, and he obviously worships her. He may not be the sharpest knife in the drawer, but he'd know that Julia would never forgive him for an affair with her best friend. Especially carried on right under her nose, in the Governor's Mansion. Joe Ed has spent his whole life building his political career, finally getting where he wants to be; he'd never jeopardize that for a fling with Astor, would he? And Astor—flirt though she is, she knows where her bread's buttered, and she's bound to know Julia would cut her off forever if she slept with Joe Ed. With her usual cunning, Astor seems to sense the exact moment doubt creeps in, and she pounces on it.

"You owe me an apology," she says, her voice shaky. Then, to my surprise, she kneels in front of me, getting right in my face. Her voice changes to the breathless, sugary tone that's her trademark. "You know, Corrine, I'm really worried about you. You seem to be on the verge of another nervous breakdown, and I think you need to go back into therapy as soon as you get home."

"You're the one who needs therapy, Astor, not me."

She throws back her head and laughs. "Honey, you'll never catch me in therapy. I'm afraid I might turn out like *you*."

"What are you two laughing at?" Byrd's voice interrupts us, and both Astor and I turn our heads to see the SSGs heading toward us. Byrd leads the way, perky as always in her pink Nike outfit, this time topped off with a matching windbreaker. Her white hair gleams in the morning sun, and a smile lights up her face, no doubt in her joy of finding me and Astor having such a good time together.

Rosanelle is the only other one who's all dressed up and groomed, dolled up in another short-skirted suit, this one white, with a black-and-white scarf draped around her neck, the ends flapping in the breeze. She'd told us last night she had to leave first thing this morning, driving to an alumni luncheon in Pensacola. "Hello, Queen Astor and Lady Corrine!" she calls, waving, picking her way down the pier in her black-and-white heels. Lanier looks hungover, her short hair tousled like a little boy's and her eyes bleary. Barefoot, she's pulled on a pair of cutoffs and a gray T-shirt, which is inside out.

Surprisingly, the ever-elegant Julia looks almost as bad. Her hair is loose on her shoulders, her face obscured by a big pair of sunglasses, and she's dressed sloppily for Julia, in sweatpants and an oversized T-shirt left over from the election, which says in big black letters: "Give Joe Ed the Job, Alabama!" Julia had sent both me and Culley one, and Culley had taken a Magic Marker to his, adding "Hand" before "Job" and wearing it constantly until, thank God, it fell apart.

"We came down to get y'all for breakfast," Byrd announces when she reaches the spot where Astor and I are huddled. "Bloody Marys are waiting in the kitchen, m'ladies."

"That's Queen Astor to you, peon," Astor says, standing erect, back to her old self.

Byrd drops into a deep curtsy and Lanier, standing next to her, groans.

"Bloody Marys? How about Alka-Seltzers?" she says, shielding her eyes.

"Hair of the dog, Lady Lanier," Byrd says, then reaches out her hand to pull me up. "Come on, Lady Corrine, we can't have the going-away breakfast without your tradition-al herb omelets."

I brush off the seat of my pants and start following them back to the house. Every-one's moving slowly, stopping to admire the view, pointing to the herons in the marshes, talking quietly so as not to disturb their nests. Byrd leads the way, talking animated-ly to Rosanelle and Astor. Julia slows down to wait for me, then drapes an arm over my shoulder. "You feeling better today, honey?" she asks me.

I nod, keeping my eyes averted. In Julia's presence, I feel guilty and disloyal for my suspicions about Joe Ed and Astor. In spite of any questions I might have about Joe Ed's character, Julia has remained loyal to him. The night of his first senatorial victory, Julia had too much champagne and told the SSGs something I found really interesting. She said she'd told her husband that if he ever let politics change him, she'd leave him. She was completely unemotional, telling us about her ultimatum to him as though saying she'd demanded he quit smoking, or maybe lose a few pounds.

Joe Ed and Julia were the golden couple long before they became the first family, going back to our college days. Joe Ed was a big football star, playing in the pros in Dallas before being injured and returning to Alabama to marry Julia, go to law school, and enter politics. Her father had been a big-time banker, and Joe Ed's daddy, newly rich with a mobile-home factory, was one of his top clients. Joe Ed was really something back then, his broad-shouldered, golden-haired picture in the papers and the sports magazines all the time. So it was easy for everyone to understand why the beautiful, classy Julia Dupont would fall for him. Easy for everyone but me, that is. I was probably the only SSG—and we were all bridesmaids in one of the biggest weddings the state had ever seen—who couldn't believe it when Julia married Joe Ed. I have never thought that she loved him and once shocked Lanier by saying so. "You know good and well why

she married him, Lanier," I'd said, then surprised both of us by bursting into tears.

With her head close to mine, Julia
squeezes my shoulder. "You're not lying to
us, are you, Corrine?" she says, her voice
soft. "You're not sicker than you're telling
everyone, are you?"

"I wouldn't lie about something like that."

"Yes you would, if you thought we'd worry."
To my surprise, Julia stops me, pulling me
close in a hug. "I couldn't stand it if anything
happened to you, Corrine. I swear I couldn't!
You've *got* to promise that you'll see a doctor next week if you're not better. Promise?"

"I will, Julia. I promise." Even though the
big, brown-tinted sunglasses obscure her
eyes, up close I see that her face is pale and
puffy. I wonder if she's been crying, and say,
"Julia? Are *you* okay?"

"Me?" She laughs lightly, but it doesn't
ring true. "Of course I'm okay. Why wouldn't
I be?"

"Maybe . . . the thing with Bethany?"

She shakes her head. "No. I'm very much
at peace with that. I would've put Bethany in
the school a long time ago if Joe Ed had
agreed. But, now . . ." She lets her voice fall,

then glances over at me. "It's going to be so good for her to become independent. It's a good thing we've done, I know." With her hair down, Julia looks much more vulnerable. Almost fragile, which she definitely isn't. Of all of us, Julia's the most imperturbable, the one the rest of us rely on when we fall apart.

"Hey, you two lesbos," Lanier calls out from the wooden walkway to the house. "What are y'all whispering about?"

Astor stops and stares at Lanier. "Have you ever considered the concept of political correctness, Lanier? You're such a blunt instrument."

"Oh, ex*cuse* me, Your Royal Majesty," Lanier snaps. "Maybe I could take some lessons from you."

Julia chuckles, her arm around my waist as we continue our walk down the pier. "Uh-oh," she says. "We've been together long enough, haven't we? The weekend always ends just in time."

12

Julia
MONTGOMERY

ON THE RIDE HOME from Dauphin Island to Montgomery, I catch myself studying Astor's profile as she drives. She feels me looking at her and glances my way, a sphinx-like smile playing about her lips. Had I not known Astor for thirty years, I would have assumed silicone injections were responsible for her full-lipped pout. Joe Ed once remarked that Astor had the sexiest lips he'd ever seen. "What?" she says. Her eyes are obscured by narrow, silver-rimmed sunglasses, pink tinted, very *Vogue*-ish.

I turn my head and look out the window. The most boring stretch of I-65 in Alabama, with nothing but pine trees, pine trees, pine trees. God, I hate pine trees. From the CD, the song playing is "What I Did for Love." *"Chorus Line,"* I say to Astor, suddenly remembering. "The last time I saw you dance." Joe Ed was a state senator then, and we left Bethany with his parents for the trip to New York. Afterward we went to a trendy restaurant with Astor and Steve Gold, her husband at the time. Steve, the beautiful but egomaniacal actor who couldn't stop himself from smirking at our southern accents. I was afraid Joe Ed was going to punch him out before we'd finished dinner, proving that we were the uncouth Alabama rednecks Steve assumed us to be.

Astor snorts. "Big fucking deal. I was one of hundreds." She's wearing black, as usual, a skimpy black T-shirt with a short denim skirt, and flip-flops, the kind you get for ninety-nine cents at the drugstore. If I had legs like hers, I'd wear heels every day, even with shorts. Her hair is slicked back in a low ponytail, held with a rubber band. Very classy, very Astor. Unadorned, she makes the rest of us look like we try too hard, fixing our hair and coordinating jewelry with our outfits.

When Astor sings with the CD, I look her way but turn to the window before she can catch me studying her again. Two hours into the trip now, and neither of us has mentioned the tension between us. I won't bring it up—I still can't believe I said that about her sneaking out to meet Cal Hawkins. An unspoken SSG rule: no reality checks. Everything has to be *sweet*. Sweet, always. In the past, that's suited me fine. I survive life by slow-paddling down the river denial.

I haven't been able to put my finger on why Astor's sneaking out to meet Cal bothers me so much, but I've thought of little else. Astor's had plenty of affairs, extramarital and otherwise, which she's told the SSGs about, in great detail. Every year, after the crowning on Saturday night when we are all about half-soused, we get into our pjs or gowns, night cream heavy on our faces, and stay up till early morning talking, talking. This year, we did the same—except for Corrine, who'd gone to bed early—but we talked of inconsequential things, as though nothing was going on in our lives except the cute new outfits we'd bought, the great movies we'd seen, the anti-aging makeup everyone has to try. Even Lanier, who needs us now more than ever, blathered on and on about the fun time she had had fixing up the cabin. Not a word about Paul or the man who caused her to lose him. I didn't talk about this past week, the momentous move of Bethany to Talladega, and Rosanelle said nothing about worries over her job. Byrd did reveal that she and Buster were going to nutrition classes together at the Mountain Brook medical center because Buster's cholesterol was so high. She had blown it off, laughing, telling us a story that had us all laughing as well, about Buster stopping by Baskin-Robbins after the class and eating a hot fudge sundae, with the pamphlets about stir-frying tofu bulging from his back pocket.

Suddenly it occurs to me why I confronted Astor, why her secret assignation bothers me. It's not that she cheated on Mose, a sick old man who deserves better. Frankly, I never expected Astor to be true to him, or to anyone. No—it's that she didn't tell me. Even though she's told me more than I ever wanted to know about her past flings, for some reason, Astor did not want me to know about this one.

When I look again at Astor, who's still

singing, moving her head back and forth, something else occurs to me. I don't know her. Astor Deveaux, whom I roomed with for four years, maid of honor in my wedding and one of Bethany's godmothers, is a stranger to me. I don't know what makes her tick, what she feels. I don't know if she really loves Mose or if she married him for other reasons, as Corrine insists. As though she senses my thoughts, Astor turns to me and says, with a melodramatic sigh, "What I've done for love, no one will ever know." I laugh lightly, but she continues, surprising me. "But you, Julia? What have you ever done for love? I mean, really?"

Astor's tone irritates me, the mocking emphasis on *you,* the skeptical raising of an eyebrow. She's implying that since I come from a privileged background, my life has been a cakewalk. When Astor first moved back to Birmingham, she'd shocked me by saying the only thing that mattered was money and power. She went on to say that she'd always envied me because my family had both. I'd surprised myself with my vehe-ment reaction, which caused a strain in our relationship for several months. I'd raised my voice, something I rarely did, telling Astor that all the money in the world wouldn't make Bethany whole.

I stare at Astor before replying, "I assume you mean besides anything I might have done for Joe Ed?" It came out sharp and defensive. The SSGs have always been curious about my role as a politician's wife, the public life I live. That it's a path I've gone down willingly has convinced them I must love Joe Ed more than anything.

"Besides Joe Ed," she qualifies, the same self-satisfied smile playing about her lips. It's hard to picture Astor without that odd little smile of hers, a look that drives Corrine crazy. Last year, at the autumn SSG weekend, we were all sitting around the fireplace at Corrine's mountain house with our cups of hot rum punch. Suddenly Corrine startled everyone by jumping to her feet and turning on Astor. "Dammit, Astor—stop smirking at me," she'd said, and we'd all laughed nervously. But Corrine wasn't joking. She'd flounced out of the room, going to bed and leaving us to make jokes about menopause and mood swings while Astor kept smiling and looking pleased with herself, though no one dared asked why.

"There was never anyone else," I say, and again, it comes out sharper than I intended. I know what's coming next.

"Not even that Mexican boy, when you were seventeen?" Astor says, and the smile doesn't change.

"Certainly not him. God, Astor, you know that. I've told you a hundred times."

"I know, but I've never believed you," she replies, with a light laugh, glancing my way. "And it's Queen Astor, not God."

"Keep your eyes on the road," I snap, peevish. "So many big trucks on this stretch it scares me to death."

"You're the one in a hurry to get back. What kind of dinner are y'all going to tonight?"

"Just a get-together after church with some couples from the legislature." I reach over to turn down the CD. Evidently a collection of Broadway hits, since it's playing "Tomorrow" now. One of Bethany's favorite songs. It was the greatest blessing, when we discovered she wasn't totally deaf. "Bethany loves that song," I hear myself telling Astor. "She loves all music. Did I ever tell you what happened when I took her to the John Denver concert, when she was six?"

Astor shakes her head. "Seems like you

told the SSGs that Denver singled her out somehow?"

I smile, remembering. "Bethany had just gotten the hearing aids, and she and I, we'd worked on that song, 'Sunshine,' over and over. John Denver ended his concert with it, and up until that point, I wasn't sure how much Bethany had heard or seen, even though we were in the front row. But when he sang 'Sunshine,' Bethany stood in her seat and started signing the words. I was astonished but was even more surprised when John Denver spotted her and stopped the concert. He brought the audience to its feet when he had her come onstage and sign as he sang. She was so adorable, with her blonde pigtails and big smile. So proud of herself. Everybody was boo-hooing, including John Denver. He took us backstage afterwards, and Bethany was on cloud nine. A few years later, when he died, she went to pieces. I still can't listen to 'Sunshine.'"

Astor reaches over and squeezes my hand, and I brush tears from my eyes. "Didn't mean to do that," I say, embarrassed.

"Hey, no prob," Astor smiles, then adds, "Sunshine always makes me cry, too."

* * *

In bed that night, with Joe Ed snoring beside me, I think about my lie to Astor. Of course I'd loved the Mexican boy, Jesus Perez, as only a seventeen-year-old can. He absorbed my every waking moment and tormented my dreams at night. Funny, I still think about him, still wonder what happened to him. I've even thought of looking him up, finding out if he's alive or dead. Selfishly, I'd assumed my life was the only one ruined; of course it must have been much worse for him. Finding out about him would be no problem; my assistant could do it without blinking. Tomorrow I could ask her, and she'd bring me the report, clipped neatly in a manila folder. No one, not even Joe Ed, would have any idea why I'd ask for information on a Mexican boy I knew thirty years ago.

Funny, my mother had been the one to hire Jesus Perez, based on an enthusiastic recommendation from Father Laurence, the Jesuit priest who depended on Mother and rich women like her to support his various missions. Bringing needy young men from foreign countries and enrolling them in the Jesuit-taught Spring Hill College was one of Father Laurence's pet projects. Not just another freshman from a foreign land, Jesus had special skills, according to Father Laurence. The young man had a way with flowers. Landing in Mobile, Alabama, with its lush gardens of azaleas and camellias, was a godsend for a poor boy like Jesus, until he came to work the lavish grounds of the Dupont house on Spring Hill Road.

Mother, bless her snooty, old-Mobile heart, had her nose high in the air when she introduced me to Jesus after I got home from school my junior year of high school, a hot September afternoon. The car pool—I can't recall who now—dropped me off at the end of our driveway with its avenue of moss-draped oaks, and I went over to see what Mother was doing at the lily pond, find out who was with her. I can still see her, how she looked that day in her floppy garden hat. For yard work, Mother had on flat shoes and slacks instead of her usual dress and heels.

"Julia, this is Jesus Perez, whom Father Laurence sent to work in the gardens," Mother said. She pronounced it "Jesus" instead of the Mexican way, "Hey-sues," and I giggled. Then I blushed, looking at Jesus Perez, who stared at me like I was un-dressed, rather than properly clad in my school uniform from St. Mary's. He was unlike anyone I'd ever seen, with his blue-black hair and skin almost as dark as R. J.'s, the old black man who'd worked in Mother's gardens for years. I could see R. J. out of the corner of my eye, pushing a wheelbarrow our way. I stuck out my hand to Jesus, much to Mother's disgust, and called him Hey-sues. *"Como está, Jesus. Salud,"* I'd said, showing off my second-year Spanish skills. In the months to follow, I was to become very proficient in Spanish.

I was the one to seek Jesus out the next time we met. From my room on the second floor of the house, I watched him every time he came to work in the gardens. By going to the rarely used rooms on the third floor, I could see all over the grounds behind the house, beyond the tennis court, to the edge of our yard, the high, iron-lace fence covered in jasmine and rambling roses. There were two pre–Civil War outbuildings out there, a potting shed and a storage house. My broth-er and I played in them as kids, until R. J. scared us off, telling us there might be snakes and black widows there.

Jesus took his breaks by the potting shed, I soon discovered. I'd watch him, sitting and eating from a brown sack and drinking a Coke, then smoking leisurely, often stretching out on the sweet-smelling grass to nap. One Saturday, after I made sure that Mother had gone to her ladies' luncheon and Daddy to the golf course, I approached Jesus as he sat cross-legged on the grass behind the shed. Having practiced my best Spanish accent over and over, I asked him for a cigarette, saying I'd just run out.

He shook one out of a package of Marlboros, then grinned at me as I sank beside him. The reason I remember wearing pink bermuda shorts and a white cotton shirt was, I couldn't get the grass stains out and had to take them to school to throw them out, afraid our maid Elsie would find them. "I speak English," Jesus said to me, lighting my cigarette. "The nuns taught me when I was little boy." When he cupped his dark hands over mine to block off the breeze, a bolt of desire shot through me, clear to my toes.

"Yes, but you speak like a Yankee," I teased him, trying not to choke. I'd never smoked a cigarette in my life.

Jesus smiled, and I thrilled at the whiteness of his perfect teeth against the dark creaminess of his even-more-perfect skin.

"You are Yankee, no?" His voice wasn't like any of the local boys I knew, even the ones who went off to prep school in New England.

Giving him my most indignant look, I said, "Of course I'm not! I'm a southern belle."

"A bell? You mean, ding-a-ling bell?" We laughed together, then Jesus said one word that melted me. "You are called Julia?" No one had ever said my name like that; no one has since. *Jule-lee-ah*. Mesmerized, I nodded, and Jesus looked at me intently, his black eyes liquid and serious. "Jule-lee-ah," he said, his voice rich as cream, "I will teach you to smoke the cigarette, no?"

In the glorious autumn weeks that followed, Jesus taught me to smoke a cigarette, holding the smoke in my lungs as I inhaled, rounding my lips and letting it drift out on the exhale. I took to holding the cigarette lightly between my lips so I could use both hands to cup his hands as he lit my cigarettes. Any excuse to touch him. It was weeks before he touched me, and I was beginning to think maybe he didn't like me after all, despite the way he looked at me with those black-fringed eyes. I had no idea, of course, that he was terrified of me, of what could happen between us. Seventeen years old, I already had a well-deserved rep-utation as a snow queen, aloof and un-approachable, freezing out the fumbling adolescents whom I'd dated. I'd only been allowed to date for the last year, and that was to go to well-supervised parties, dances, or church events. The only boy I'd kissed was Bucky Rodgers, who got so excited he passed gas, effectively spoiling the moment.

Once the winter months came, Jesus didn't need to come to work as often. We had R. J. and others to keep the grounds up; Jesus was a horticulturist, not a yard boy, or so I liked to think. He came after school occasionally and every other Saturday morning to work with the camellias and Mother's orchids on the sunporch. I could tell Mother liked him, often coming on them with their heads bent together over a plant, dis-cussing bonemeal and mealy bugs and peat moss. When Mother or Daddy was around, Jesus never spoke to me, only nodding politely before returning to his work. No one knew that when the coast was clear, I'd head to the bench behind the potting shed, where Jesus and I would sit smoking our ciga-rettes, talking and laughing like any seventeen- and eighteen-year-olds, any-where in the world.

It was cold weather that eventually did us in. Like most coastal areas, it doesn't get cold very often in Mobile, but when it does, it's a damp, biting cold that chills you to the bone. On a miserable gray day in January, Jesus and I got so cold on the bench that we carried it inside the shed. Jesus lit a small fire in the bottom of a huge old pot, the first chiminea to hit Mobile. He then pulled a woven cotton blanket from his backpack and wrapped it around my shoulders. "I'm a Mexican girl now," I told him, laughing. Taking me by surprise, he reached out and stroked my flaxen hair, held back from my face with a velvet band.

"No. You are the southern belle, Jule-lee-ah," he said. Had I not laughed nervously, he would have kissed me then, I'm sure, rather than making me wait for three more weeks.

Had Jesus and I taken lighter fluid and thrown it on the chiminea fire, it would have had a similar effect. We couldn't stop with kisses, couldn't stop putting our hands all over each other, couldn't get enough of being together. Once I smuggled blankets to the shed, as well as a lidded basket to hide them in, the outcome was as inevitable as the tide.

Somehow I got through the dreary school days, living my life as though in a dream. I was young and in love with the most beautiful, exotic boy in the whole world, and I could think of nothing else. My snow-queen reputation grew as I distanced myself more and more from the crowd I'd grown up with. It was only when I caught Mother eyeing me sharply that I made myself go out with friends, to movies and school plays and parties. I even let another boy, not the windy Bucky this time, kiss me when we parked in front of my house after a movie, but I felt nothing. I felt nothing with friends, at school, even going to mass, though I'd once thought of becoming a nun. It was only with Jesus that I felt anything, and what I felt was so powerful it swept me away, down a swirling, dark river. So swept away was I that I'd missed three menstrual cycles before realizing something was wrong.

You'd think with me being so thin, so tall and willowy, my expanded waist would have been immediately noticeable, but unbelievably, I'd missed five periods and school was out before I could no longer wear my uniform. It was the early seventies, when even in uptight Mobile, fashions relaxed from the belted shorts and tucked-in shirts my closet was filled with. As soon as school was out, my girlfriends and I went to downtown Mobile to buy loose sundresses, even though Mother disapproved. I faked a twisted ankle to get out of tennis, which I'd played religiously since I was little. Hobbling on an ankle wrapped with an elastic bandage, I managed to relax the erect posture Mother insisted on, further helping to disguise my swelling middle.

I told Jesus nothing about the missed periods, and we continued to meet every week in the potting shed. I had no idea that Jesus was as naive as me, a good little boy from a strict Catholic home. Although he kidded me about gaining weight, he had no idea what I was hiding from everyone, including him. Once the semester was over at Spring Hill, Father Laurence got Jesus a summer job at Bellingrath Gardens, and he only came to our house on Saturday mornings. The weather hot, Mother and Daddy were often home then, so Jesus's and my time together became harder to pull off. We were in despair, and in whispered phone calls, we plotted ways to meet. At the time, it didn't occur to me to suggest we actually date, meet somewhere like normal teenagers, go to the movies or the beach. Without ever putting it into words, we both knew it wouldn't be tolerated. I'd grown up with racial prejudice and knew that to many Mobilians—even my own parents—Jesus was even less acceptable than a black person. I'd snapped at my brother Andrew, home for Christmas holidays from Notre Dame, for asking Mother who the wetback was in the gardens, only to have Mother reprimand me for raising my voice to Andrew, rather than him for his racial slur.

In June Mother and Daddy went to Europe for two weeks, and Jesus and I got careless. He had the bus from Bellingrath Gardens drop him off at our house after work, and we'd hide out in the airless potting shed until dark, when he'd walk to his dorm room at Spring Hill College, several blocks away. Andrew was home from Notre Dame for the summer, and although he spent most of his time at the country club, we had to be careful.

We weren't careful enough, as it turned out. It was so hot that day, still in the nineties at dusk, when Jesus and I lay together on the blankets in the shed. We'd made love in spite of the heat, in spite of the sticky, suffocating air in the windowless shed, which made it almost impossible to breathe. I had been wearing my favorite sundress, a loose cotton floral that buttoned up the front, making it easy not only to slip out of, but to disguise my condition. I was lying down, my dress crumpled under me, and Jesus was beside me, his hands on my breasts. On one elbow, he raised himself over me and smiled down. "Too many of the chocolate malts for you, Jule-lee-ah," he said, shaking his head sadly. Poor innocent Jesus; it'd been easy to convince him the reason I'd gotten so thick around the middle was my addiction to ice cream.

I laughed. "Will you still love me if I get fat, Jesus? *Muy gorda?*" Jesus laughed, too, but I never heard his answer. A shadow filled the door, and I gasped. Before I knew what was happening, Andrew was inside the shed and had lunged forward, grabbing Jesus and throwing him off of me.

"Goddamn wetback," Andrew yelled, his fist smashing into Jesus's face, the beautiful face I loved. "What are you doing with my sister?"

"No, Andrew!" I screamed, struggling to my feet, pulling my dress around me. Jesus had his shirt off but his shorts half on. When Andrew pulled him up to hit him again, his shorts fell to his ankles, making it more diffi-cult to escape the blows. Built like Daddy, Andrew was heavy and broad-shouldered, while Jesus, like me, was thin and willowy, with bones small as a child's. He crumpled like a rag doll under my brother's assault, his arms over his head in a futile attempt to pro-tect himself.

Crying hysterically, I grabbed Andrew from behind, wrapping my arms around his to stop the blows. "Run, Jesus," I yelled. *"Run!"*

In the few seconds I held Andrew at bay, Jesus somehow managed to get to his feet and button his shorts. Bleeding and trem-bling, throwing me a look of such concern it broke my heart, Jesus hesitated until I screamed again. "For God's sake—get out of here!" And he did, running, stumbling and falling, crying. Andrew shook me off easily, but I could feel his hesitation, deciding whether to pursue Jesus or confront me. He turned to me, grabbing my arms and shak-ing me, his blond hair falling over his forehead. His face was beet-red and his eyes wild.

"Did he rape you, Julia? Tell me the truth," he said, shaking me.

I collapsed, burying my face in my hands, shaking, crying. "No, no—I love him, Andrew—I love him!"

I'll never forget his face, that look of disgust and repulsion. My jovial big brother, who'd always adored me. Before I knew what was happening, he'd drawn his arm back and slapped me, knocking me to my feet. "You stupid idiot," he spat out. "Get your clothes on and get in the house. Then I'm calling Mother and Daddy to get their asses home. They can take care of you, and as soon as I find out where that wetback went, I'll take care of him."

My room at the monastery was all white, austere, like a cell, reminding me of something you'd see in an old World War II movie. It consisted of a cot with a white blanket, a single small dresser with a lamp, and a straight-back chair. A crucifix hung on the wall, directly across from the bed. A door led to the balcony, and I would go out there, sitting on a wooden bench and looking out over the grounds, breathing deeply of the hot, sweet-smelling air. Huge live oaks draped with Spanish moss were adorned with the stations of the cross, making a path of devotion for the faithful. I was there two days and two nights before I walked to the end of the balcony and down the stairs to the ground floor, then into the courtyard, enclosed from the outside world by a stone wall. I went to the gazebo and sat, my hands folded in my lap, and watched as a black-robed Sister entered the gardens, moving as silently as a dark ship gliding over a still sea. I watched as she knelt by the Sacred Heart statue in the center of the courtyard, praying the noon Angelus as the song of the chapel bells floated in the air. There were about a dozen Sisters at the monastery, and I'd observed them the times I'd gone to the dining room, eating at a table by myself as they gathered at their one long table, passing the food around family-style. One of them, Sister Theresa, I recognized, since she'd opened the gates for me the night I'd arrived, desperately ringing their bell. In the dining room, Sister Theresa had filled a plate and brought it to me. She'd motioned for me to join them, but I'd shaken my head and lowered my eyes. I couldn't sit with them yet, not until the purpled swelling on the side of my face went back to normal.

The Sisters of the Visitation Order were cloistered, so they didn't speak to me, thankfully. When I'd arrived two nights ago, after having slipped out from my house, I'd begged Sister Theresa, protected from me by a nook with a glass partition, to send for Mother Margaret Mary, whom I'd known all my life. Without a word, she'd motioned to her left, to the room set aside for communications with the Mother Superior. I sat on the edge of the bench facing the cubicle with its iron-lace grill until Mother Margaret Mary appeared, looking so old and frail that I burst into tears. Through the grill, she reached her shaking, age-spotted hand out to me and I grabbed it with both of mine, then fell on my knees. "Please, please . . . can I stay here?" Even though she'd refused at first, she relented when I reminded her that my parents were in Europe. My face hadn't swollen up then, and I prayed she'd think I was just going through some kind of teenage crisis. In the end, she'd probably agreed just so I'd let go of my death-grip on her poor old hand.

I wanted more than anything to stay hidden away, cloistered like the Sisters who lived in the monastery, their whole life devoted to prayer and contemplation. I was on the third floor of the old dormitory, locked in, completely alone but not a bit scared of the spooky, shadowy halls. For the first few days, I was in shock, suspended in time. The Visitation Monastery was another world, even though it was less than a mile from my house. On the other side of the tall stone walls the traffic of Mobile sped by, yet my world was completely silent, except for the ringing of the chapel bells. I kept expecting Mother Margaret Mary to send for me, until I decided she was leaving me alone to work out whatever spiritual crisis I was going through. Finally, I had no choice but to request an audience with her, to ask about getting a message to Father Laurence. I had to find out what had happened to Jesus Perez, and I had to let my parents know I was safe, or Jesus would be in worse trouble if they thought I'd run away with him or something. Mother Margaret Mary allowed me to write to Father Laurence and promised she would personally see that he received my message.

After I'd been in the monastery a couple of weeks, I was lying on the cot with a cool cloth over my eyes, the balcony door open to a late afternoon breeze. Not only was I feeling sick, I'd been bleeding enough to scare me. For the first time since I'd been in the monastery, I heard footsteps coming down the hallway. I didn't think anything about it since the monastery was open for spiritual retreats, but I removed the cloth and sat up when the footsteps stopped at my opened door. Her mouth set in an angry line, blue eyes cold, my mother stood there, with Father Laurence behind her.

I have never believed that my baby died. I saw her briefly, heard her cry before she was whisked away from me, and that one sight was enough to break my heart, a wound that never healed. She was tiny but perfect, with her miniature head, her plump little arms flailing. With her stick-straight black hair, she was so much what Jesus must have been as an infant that, in my drugged state, I laughed hysterically as they took her away. I kept laughing and crying until they gave me a stronger shot, one that kept me out for two days. When I came to, I begged Mother to tell me where Jesus was, but she never mentioned his name again. Instead, she sent Father Laurence in. I turned my back on him until he relented and told me what had happened to Jesus. All he'd say was that Jesus had returned home. When I begged for his address, Father Laurence reminded me, gently but reproachfully, that Jesus knew how to get in touch with me if he really wanted to. "It's best that both of you put this behind you, Julia," he said, "and get on with your lives."

Back in my pink-and-white room at home, Mother walked in and, tight-lipped, gave me her plan for my future.

"I have been in contact with Evelyn Pate, an old friend of mine who's the dean of women at the Methodist College in Brierfield, and we have arranged for early admission for you, allowing you to skip your senior year of high school. You will enter in two weeks."

Dizzy with shock and grief, still bleeding and sick, I could only gasp, *"Methodist?"* Mother was the most devout Catholic I knew.

"Because of Evelyn, it's a place we could get early admission for you, no questions asked," Mother said, her voice cold. "There's a Catholic church in town, and I've been in contact with Father O'Hara there. An Irish priest—" she said this as though she had a bad taste in her mouth—"but that can't be helped."

"You always planned on me going to Loyola or some other Catholic college," I said, trembling.

"I had a lot of plans for you, Julia."

She turned to go out the door, and I called after her. "Mother . . . please . . ."

Before closing the door, Mother stopped and stared at me, her ice-blue eyes bitter. "I have nothing to say to you, Julia. I leave it to God to deal with you."

Two years afterward, it was Daddy, not Mother, who called me at The W one bright autumn day, his booming voice taking me by complete surprise. "Julia, I'm picking you up Saturday on the way to Tuscaloosa, me and J. D. Stovall from Fort Payne. You don't know him, but he's one of my bank's new clients," he'd said, without asking me if I had any plans. "The three of us are going to Denny Stadium to see Bama play Ole Miss. J. D.'s boy is the quarterback there. Bring a long dress, because the boy's taking you to a dance after the game. You'll like him— good-looking boy, real friendly. J. D. thinks he's got a future in politics." Had it not been for Jesus Perez, my parents would have never pushed someone like Joe Ed Stovall on me, no matter how bright his future appeared. I'd heard my mother say "nouveau riche" the same way she might say "dog turd," if such a word ever crossed her lips.

Ten years after that, Mother looked down at her only granddaughter, Bethany, who—after a long, difficult labor—was born with multiple handicaps. Neither of us had ever referred to that other baby, born black-haired and perfect, but when Mother raised her head and looked at me, her pale eyes said it all. The God she worshiped had come through.

13

Corrine
BLUE MOUNTAIN

I'VE NEVER SAID THIS out loud. I don't want to sound like a fool—or worse, Scarlett O'Hara, standing in the garden of Tara with a handful of dirt and a mouthful of radishes—but I'm convinced of its truth anyway. You can't really understand or appreciate life until you get dirt beneath your fingernails. My garden and my gourds have saved my life the last few years. I honestly believe that without them, I would not be here today. Believe me, that's something I'll never tell the Same Sweet Girls, since they all think I'm crazy anyway, but it's the truest thought I've ever had. Every time I work in my garden, plant and water seeds, then watch the cycles of growth and harvest, I'm blown away. Here's something else I won't tell anyone: I say a prayer for each seed I plant, and then I kiss it. Oh, God, Culley would *die* if he ever caught me doing it, and if he told his daddy, I'd be back in the loony bin so fast I wouldn't know what hit me.

When I got back from the SSG weekend, I was really depressed because I didn't have a vegetable garden this year. First thing I did when Byrd left was to sit on the back steps, put my head in my hands, and cry. Normally, by June the tomato plants would be staked, the squash vines spreading on the ground, and the tops of the carrots and radishes unfurling like baby ferns. And all my lettuces, in every shade of green imaginable! But this year, I've been so run-down and tired that I've had to choose between planting the vegetables or the gourds. No choice, really. The vegetables are a joy, but the gourds are my life.

Today I'm standing in my garden and crying again, like a damned fool, but this time it's not like the other day. Culley has saved my gourd vines. Knowing how puny I've been, he's come over every day after closing the gallery, not saying a word to me about it, and he's watered the young plants, pulled weeds, and trained the vines to go up the trellises. Cucumber beetles can be a problem in late June, but Culley's spread a layer of ashes and lime around the base of the plants, like he's seen me do. The vines are flourishing, big and healthy-looking, and the white and yellow flowers are glorious. He's saved my gourds, yet I'm afraid to thank him. Yesterday Culley was in the garden and I walked down the dirt path with a glass of lemonade for him. Shirtless and barefoot, he had on a pair of droopy cutoffs, which hung slightly below the top of his underwear, and I was surprised to see that he was getting a tan, since he's so fair. His thick, reddish-gold hair was pulled back in a ponytail and tied with a piece of leather. Willowy like me, Culley is lean and rangy rather than muscular and broad-shouldered, like his father. "Thanks," he said casually, after gulping the lemonade and burping, twice. "Pretty hot out here."

"You don't have to do this, you know," I said, shielding my face from the sun with my hand.

Culley shrugged, turning from me to pick

up the hoe he'd put aside when I handed him the lemonade. "It's cool. I like gardening 'cause I can get a tan doing it. No big deal."

"Culley," I said, tentatively, "I can't tell you how much I appreciate . . ." But I stopped myself when Culley pointedly turned his back to me and started loosening the soil with the hoe.

"No big deal," he said again, this time more emphatically. The way he communicates with me, most of the time, is to use as few words as possible and avoid eye contact.

"It's a big deal to me," I said. "My gourds . . ." But I couldn't say it. When Culley hit his teens, he started making fun of my gourds, rolling his eyes, saying it was embarrassing to have a mom who wigged out over gourds, of all things. A lot of his friends had parents who were artists, but they weren't as weird as me. Why couldn't I paint or sculpt or throw pots instead? I knew it was part of his rejection of me, and I understood why he did it, but it still hurt.

With his back to me, Culley began hoeing the neat rows so hard that dirt was flying, although there were no weeds to be seen. "Culley?" I tried again, reaching out to touch his shoulder. He flinched, and I withdrew my hand.

"Forget it, Mom, okay?" He stood still as a statue for a minute, then he propped the hoe against a trellis. "Think I'll go in the house and get another glass of lemonade."

"I'll get it for you," I said quickly, but he brushed past me and was gone, without another word.

This evening, I leave the trellises and arbors and head back toward the cabin, fanning myself with a floppy gourd leaf. It's still warm, even though it usually starts getting cooler here after the sun has set. Stopping on the porch, I pick up the jar of green tea leaves, crushed mint, and spring water that I put out this morning. My herbalist, Molly, seems to think drinking several jars daily will purify my system, but I haven't seen anything purifying yet. I've felt a little better today, but the fatigue's worse. Even a walk to the garden and back wears me out. I haven't gone into town, to the gallery, since I got back from Alabama, though I've gotten a lot of work done in my studio. A week ago Julia called and insisted I go to a doctor she knows of in

Chickasaw, someone whose parents live in Montgomery. She said the SSGs would show up on my doorstep and drag me there if I didn't. I know Julia's strong will, so by God, I went. I'll admit, I was weak-kneed with relief when the doctor couldn't find anything. Until that point I hadn't realized how scared I was. Finally, finally, my life's making some sense and bringing me some happiness for a change and I sure don't want to croak. Not now. Not yet.

I reported to the SSGs that Dr. Brown ran a bunch of tests and couldn't find anything. Of course, everyone had their pet theories as to what my ailment was: Byrd said stress, Julia a virus, Rosanelle said menopause, and Astor, naturally, told me it was all in my mind. Lanier said it'd been too long since I'd gotten any, was all that was ailing me. That the doctor hadn't found anything wasn't much comfort when I kept feeling so run-down, though, and I went back to Molly. Like the SSGs, she too has theories, but hers have to do with my yin and yang being out of whack.

In my favorite perch on the front porch, a wide, cane-bottomed chair that was Miss Fielding's, I sit and rock and sip iced tea. For some weird reason, I'm fine during the day—except for the puzzling fatigue—but I start feeling pukey again at night. The sickness and the nausea begin to sneak up on me as daylight fades and darkness claims the valley. I'm finding it harder not to give that a metaphorical meaning. It's almost like if I keep watch, the darkness won't come. So, like a fool, I sit on the porch until it gets really late, putting off going inside the cabin until I can't hold my eyes open. The high porch overlooks the valley of Blue Mountain, which cradles the swift-flowing Shoal Creek, which I can hear babbling away, even over the night noises of cicadas and frogs and whippoorwills. Tonight the summer air is soft and sweet-scented. Wild thyme borders the path that leads down to the stream, and its spicy fragrance is so strong I close my eyes and breathe it in, leaning my head back.

The sickness has been occurring every night—appropriately enough—at the same time as the arrival of another unwanted visitor. I hear a car approaching, down the long driveway to my house. I'm tempted not to open my eyes. It's not enough that I'm suffering, that I've been weak and wiped-out for weeks. That's not enough, is it? Guess I've pissed off the gods somehow. For some unknown reason, Miles has taken to stopping by every evening after closing up his clinic. He drives several miles out of his way in order to go through the motions of an amiable visit. I don't know what's going on with him, but one thing's for sure: He's up to no good.

I'd love to say that Miles is aging poorly, but fact is, he's still beautiful. He hasn't lost any of his silvery-blond hair, although it's thinner. The slackness under his aqua-green eyes isn't unflattering, even though it gives him a world-weary look, as does the slight stoop of his broad shoulders. His body is still as good as ever, with no paunch or excess pounds. He looks so good for his age that, watching him as he climbs the stairs, his fine-boned hand on the rail, I'm struck yet again by one of life's many injustices. Compare a woman in her sixties to a man in his, and you'll know that Mother Nature is one cruel bitch.

"Good evening, Corrine," Miles says. Appropriately enough, his voice sounds like a cross between Vincent Price and Hannibal Lecter.

Even though I'm thinking, *And a jolly good*

evening to you, too, asshole, I'm determined to keep my cool. At least, until I figure out what he's up to. I respond, "Hello, Miles." Then, in my best SSG sugary-sweet voice, "Could I get you a glass of tea?"

He declines. Two nights ago, when he first dropped by, he asked if I had anything else. I offered fresh aloe juice or goat's milk, which he also declined. The next night he brought a bottle of Merlot and we had a glass together until, as unexpectedly as he'd showed up, he got up and announced he'd be on his way. Tonight, he glances toward the opened door leading into the house. "Did you finish the Merlot?"

I shake my head. "It's in the kitchen cabinet. Help yourself."

Even though he's never spent much time here, Miles knows his way around. Several years ago, after Miss Fielding died and left me the cabin, Miles urged me to sell it. Although he thought it was just an old shack, he said it'd probably bring a nice price because it was on the side of the mountain, overlooking the creek. Although I stupidly gave in to everything Miles wanted back then, I couldn't bring myself to give up the cabin, so I kept putting off selling it. After my divorce the cabin became a refuge that helped get me through those dark days. It took me in and enveloped me, like an old quilt made by familiar hands.

Miles returns to the porch, wineglass in hand, and sits in the rocker next to me. His first comment takes me by surprise. "I hear you paid a visit to Dr. Brown a few days ago."

I raise my eyebrows. "You know him?"

Miles nods, sipping the Merlot before answering. "I've worked with him a couple of times. Good doctor, to be so young."

"Surely he didn't tell you that I—" I begin, but Miles cuts me off.

"Of course not. Karen, who files his Medicare claims? She worked for me a while. I ran into her and she mentioned that she'd seen my ex-wife."

I can't resist saying, "And you knew who she was referring to?"

Miles's face flushes. Culley told me, right after I got back from the SSG weekend, that Miles's new wife had packed up and left him, going home to Atlanta. On hearing that, I gloated like a possum let loose in a tater patch.

"Alison has filed for divorce, but it isn't

final yet. So, yes, I knew who Karen was referring to."

I refrain from asking Miles to give young Alison my phone number, in case she needs me to testify for her. Bet I can pinpoint the exact moment she left, a few months into the marriage. It was the time I should've run for my life, if I'd had any sense, which of course I didn't. I stare out into the darkness as the first wave of nausea hits. It begins at the bottom of my feet and travels upward, flushing my face, then exiting out of the top of my head. Afterward, hot flashes, cold chills, and sweating.

"Shouldn't I turn on the porch light?" Miles asks, his eyes fastened on me in the darkness.

"No. I like it this way." With the lights on, he can observe me closely like he's always done, making me squirm under his scrutiny.

"You've always preferred being in the dark, haven't you, Corrine?"

"Yeah. Lucky for you," I reply.

Instead of coming right out and saying shitty things, Miles has mastered the art of innuendo. I wonder why every time I'm with my ex-husband now, Astor's image looms before me. I swear, the two of them were separated at birth. After college I tried getting away from Astor and ended up marrying her.

"Culley graduates next year," Miles remarks casually, "yet he seems to have no idea what he'll do afterward. I've offered to send him to graduate school, but no. Typical Generation X'er, wouldn't you say?"

"Not at all. Culley will do something with his music, I'm sure. It's his passion."

Miles snorts. "I would hardly call that noise he makes music."

"He will graduate with a degree in music from Brevard, Miles." Being the spiteful person I am, I can't resist rubbing it in. Miles had wanted Culley to go to Emory, but Culley had ended up at Brevard, a fine-arts college where he could concentrate on his music. "A very prestigious school," I remind him. "He'll be fine."

"If only he were getting his degree in music education," Miles says, still peevish. "I've warned him he can't make a living with a performance degree, but he won't listen."

I keep my mouth shut, determined not to have this argument again. Instead, I lean my head back and wait for the next wave of nausea to pass. In the silence between us, I can sense Miles's mind at work, know that I'm getting closer to discovering what these nightly visits mean. It never works with Miles to come out and ask him; you have to wait until he reveals himself. Another thing he shares with Astor. "You've been pleased with Culley's running of your gallery so far, haven't you, Corrine?" he asks.

I nod. "He's pretty much taken over, which has been great for me. You wouldn't think that Culley had such a good head for business. I haven't even gone in lately."

After a silence, Miles says, nonchalantly, "I've wondered—have you considered letting him take over the gallery after his graduation?"

Aha! So that's it. Dumb me, I should've figured it out. During our marriage, Miles—a control freak—had me under his thumb; once I left he had Culley, who is sweet and pliable and easy for someone as masterful as Miles. Now things are different. I've been out of Miles's control for the past three years now, but he's had Culley. When he's home from school, Culley lives with Miles, since his place is so much bigger—not to mention nicer—than mine. But after graduation next year, Culley will be gone—unless Miles can find a way to keep him here, on Blue Mountain.

I shake my head. "No. It's been great having him work for me these past summers, but I can't afford anyone full-time. And even if I could, I wouldn't hire my son. He's going away from Blue Mountain, Miles. Surely you know that." I'll admit, I can't wait for Culley to be away from his daddy's influence.

"Not necessarily," Miles says mysteriously. Another thing he's good at, keeping you guessing what he's talking about. Not necessarily he doesn't know, or not necessarily Culley won't leave Blue Mountain?

I don't have the energy or desire to figure it out. Reluctantly, I stand to go inside, though I want to stay longer in the sweet coolness of the night. Other than flat-out asking him to leave, however, I don't know how to get rid of Miles if I stay on the porch. After years of hostilities and not speaking to each other, we've finally re-established diplomatic relations. So I say, again nauseatingly sweet-toned, "I'm not good company tonight, Miles, so I'm going to bed early. Please excuse me."

His manners impeccable as always, Miles stands. In the darkness his eyes glow and burn, iridescent. Years ago, when I loved him, the glow of his eyes seemed like the fire of opals to me. Now I find them predatory, like those of a mountain cat. "Are you sick, Corrine?" he says, regarding me seriously. "Tell me the truth."

"No. I've had some problems"–no point in lying, since he knows about my visit to Dr. Brown—"but all the tests came back negative."

"What kind of tests?"

I shrug. "The usual battery. My white count was a little elevated, but nothing else showed up." I don't tell him about the questionable results of a couple of them, which the doctor wants to repeat in a few weeks.

"At least you went to a conventional doctor instead of your usual hokey herbalists and shamans," Miles says with a sardonic smile. "But, I have to tell you, I don't have much faith in those diagnostic tests. I've known too many people who . . . ah . . . well, you know." He lets his voice trail off, but the implication is clear.

"The tests don't show anything, but they kick the bucket a few months later, anyway," I say dryly, finishing the cheerful thought for him.

Miles clears his throat, his eyes on me like lasers as he says, "One reason I was worried when I heard about your visit to the doctor, Corrine, is something I warn all my patients about."

"And what is that?" I dare to ask.

"I tell them to take great care, because eventually, your biography becomes your biology."

I let out a hoot. "If that's the case, I'm a dead duck."

Taking a sip of his wine, Miles continues to regard me intently. "I wouldn't say that, but as a therapist, I'd suggest you explore the connections."

I stare at him in surprise, wondering if he's as oblivious to his role in my biography as it sounds. Surely not. Before I can figure it out, though, he extends a hand. A handshake, as though we're business partners? Instead of shaking my hand, he holds it tightly in his strong grip. "Well," he says smoothly, "off to bed for you, then. I'll be on my way, soon as I finish my wine." And releasing my hand, he sits back down.

I don't want to leave him on the porch while I go inside, but the only other choice is to stay with him, which I don't want to do, either.

Unsure, I shrug, then go to the kitchen and take the ginger pills that Molly gave me for the nightly nausea. I turn out the light in the kitchen but not the lamp in the sitting area, since that would leave the Prince of Darkness sitting on the porch unilluminated, and I couldn't see when he leaves. My bedroom's in the loft, where I change to my white cotton gown, soft as flannel with age. After washing my face and brushing my teeth, I braid my hair, then go downstairs to the living room to peek and see whether or not Miles is gone.

He's gone, and I stand chewing my lip, trying to decide if I want to sit on the porch again or try to sleep. On my bedside table, in addition to relaxation tapes, is a concoction of dried lavender and goldenseal that Molly mixed up as a sleep aid, but it hasn't helped much lately. I need my sleep tonight; tomorrow I'm working on a couple of giant Indonesian bottle gourds that have finally cured enough for me to carve. I'd love to be rested up, able to give them my full attention, always preferable when I'm carving or using the saw. Shrugging, I turn off the lamp and start back toward my room. I've only taken a few steps when a figure steps out of the darkness. "Corrine?"

My hand goes to my throat, and for one scary moment, I think a mad axe murderer has broken in. Then I see it's only Miles. "Jesus, Miles, you scared the crap out of me!" He moves in so close that I take a step backward. "I thought you'd gone," I laugh nervously.

"Corrine?" Miles—who's never at a loss for words—sounds tentative and uncertain. "I was wondering . . . could we talk?"

"T-talk?" I stammer. "Well, ah—not tonight. I'm really tired."

Suddenly he's even closer, bringing the clove-sweet smell of his aftershave, which brings on another wave of nausea, and I reach backward, steadying myself on the arm of the couch.

"Corrine," he says, his voice husky, "I made a terrible mistake in my marriage to Alison."

I refrain from saying that I sympathize, having made a terrible mistake in my marriage to him. I attempt to back away even more, but the couch stops me. I halfway sit on it, but Miles reaches out and takes both my arms, pulling me to him. "Miles . . . wait, now. I don't think . . ." I begin, but he bends his head as though to kiss me. Startled, I jerk away, hitting my hip painfully on the wooden arm of the couch. "Miles, don't!"

His hands grasp the back of my head so that I can't move this time as his mouth comes down over mine, and his kiss is rough, bruising my lips. Trying to pull away from him, I fall backward on the couch, down on the cushions. Miles is halfway on top of me, and I'm struggling against him, pushing away his hot, wet mouth. "Stop it right now— what do you think you're doing?" I gasp.

"Corrine," he whispers, his breathing heavy, "I've never stopped loving you. God, I've wanted you so bad lately!"

Unbelievably, he grabs the top of my cotton gown, pulls it down, and fastens his mouth on my breast. When I start flailing at him with my arms, he raises his head long enough to look up as he grabs my wrists and holds my arms above my head, pushed painfully against the wooden arm of the couch. When I cry out, "Stop—stop!—you're hurting me," he tightens his grip on my wrists even more.

"You like it rough, don't you?" he says with a soft laugh. "It was always best when you fought me." He lowers his head again and covers my mouth with his. His kiss is so rough, so bruising, that tears spill out of the corners of my eyes. Holding my wrists above my head with one hand, Miles uses his other hand to push my gown up around my waist. When he reaches to unbutton his pants, I twist sideways, throwing him off balance.

"Miles—please, please—don't do this!" I start crying, remembering too late that my begging and crying always had the opposite effect, turning him on even more.

But to my surprise, he goes slack and his grip on my wrists relaxes. With a sudden movement, he's gotten up and is standing over me, tucking his white oxford-cloth shirt into his gray linen trousers, rebuckling his black braided belt. For one scary moment, I think he's going to use the belt on me, as he's done before, and I freeze. Although it's dark, I can see his face in the moonlight, his eyes glittering as he looks down at me. Finally he speaks, his voice trembling. "I want you back, Corrine," he says. He states it like a simple fact, like you might say you want a glass of water or a bowl of ice cream.

Straightening up, I lean against the arm of the couch, clutching my gown like a panting heroine in a Harlequin romance. "Have you lost your mind? I'd never go back to you—never!"

His laugh mocks me. "You belong to me, Corrine. It's that simple. There will never be anyone else for either of us." He turns to go, almost to the porch when I stop him.

"Wait a minute! Listen to me—don't come back here. I don't want to see you again!"

Miles pauses by the door. "Culley will be disappointed to hear that. He's been really pleased that you and I have been getting along so well, having a drink together every night. He'll be sorry to hear that you've asked me not to return."

"Then I'll tell him the truth."

Again, the mocking laugh. "Now *that* would be a first for you." His silhouette is framed in the door, with the star-filled blackness of the valley behind him. "Same time tomorrow night, then?" He pauses before going down the steps, and I can see his teeth gleaming white as he smiles. "I'll bring another bottle of Merlot."

Lanier is the only one I tell about Miles's move on me. I need her perspective, the way Lanier, with her caustic wit, can cut to the heart of the matter. The scariest part about last night was not the fear I felt, or the pain, or the certainty that Miles was about to force me into a sexual encounter that I didn't want. Instead, it was the moment of weakness when I did want it. It made me literally sick to realize that I almost gave in to him.

"Oh, godalmighty, Corrine," Lanier sighs the next morning when I call her. "Don't tell me you're using that as an excuse to beat up on yourself. Gimme a break."

I'm lying on my bed with a cold cloth over my forehead, feeling weak and shaky. "If I'd let Miles make love to me last night, I would've killed myself this morning. I swear it!"

Lanier laughs her wonderfully naughty laugh. "Surely I told you that after me and Ethan divorced, we screwed more than we did when we were married."

"Ethan? I thought that was Mike. I can't keep your husbands straight, Lanier."

"That one's easy. I didn't marry Mike, we were just engaged." Even though it was an old SSG joke about Lanier and all her husbands, actually she'd only had two. "Ethan and I were divorced the year I was in medical school, remember?"

Of course I remember; Lanier was married to Ethan when she fell in love with Paul. In spite of Jesse Phoenix, Mike What's-his-face, Ethan Edwards, and at least a dozen others, I'm certain that Lanier has never loved anyone but Paul Sanders. Can't blame her; Saint Paul is every woman's ideal man in so many ways: sweet, sensitive, funny, and nice-looking, too. You could hardly expect him to be all that and overlook Lanier's fatal flaw as well, I guess.

Lanier continues, telling me that she would run back to Ethan whenever she thought it was hopeless with Paul, and she and Ethan would end up in the sack. "So don't be so hard on yourself about Miles, honey. It's been too long since you've had any."

"That's because I lost my taste for it—so to speak—after Miles."

"I understand that, but it's been three or four years. Maybe you should have . . ."

"But, Lanier—with *Miles*?" I cry, flinging the washcloth off and sitting up. "After what that asshole did to me?"

There's a pause, and Lanier's voice loses its playful tone. "Oh, honey, you're right. I shouldn't even tease you about Miles. I'll never forgive him for what he did to you. One of these days, I hope you will tell Culley what he made you do."

I put the wet cloth back over my eyes. "No. I'll never tell him."

"I understood when Culley was a child." Lanier sighs, then takes a deep breath. "But he's old enough to understand now. All those years, when he turned against you . . . I wanted to tell him so bad."

Tears leak out of the corners of my eyes, and I wipe them away with the washcloth. "I don't want Culley to know anything about that time, Lanier. I have every intention of taking that nasty little secret to my grave with me."

14

Julia
MONTGOMERY/TALLADEGA

JOE ED HAS BEEN strangely quiet tonight, uncommunicative. He's trying to sleep but is so restless that I put the book I'm reading on the bedside table and turn off my lamp, in case the light's bothering him. It's the first time he and I have been alone together for any length of time since I watched Astor sneak out to meet Cal. After much deliberation, I've made up my mind not to say anything about it, not with Joe Ed's worries about Bethany added to his ever-present job stresses. Besides, I've had a few days to rethink the incident, get a different perspective. Even though Cal used poor judgment in allowing Astor to sneak out to the back wing, I'm convinced of his loyalty to Joe Ed; he's proven it. Cal got a congressional citation when Joe Ed was campaigning and a former mental patient came after him with a gun. Though no shots were fired, Cal threw himself in front of Joe Ed and wrestled the gun from the crazed man.

Not only that, I know about Astor's past affairs, which always have an element of intrigue and danger in them, evidently part of the turn-on for her. Once in New York, she'd had sex with a man in the bathroom while a party was going and the man's wife knocked on the bathroom door. And at The W, with one of her professors: Astor told us about performing oral sex on him in his office—not after hours, but while classes were in session, right down the hall. Although Cal used poor judgment, I'll bet anything that Astor was the one to insist on the intrigue of sneaking out like that, having their affair in the Governor's Mansion. It's just like something she'd do.

"Joe Ed? Is anything wrong?" I ask finally, after he turns over yet again, repositioning his pillow for the umpteenth time.

"Just tired, is all," he mutters. "Glad you had a good time with the girls this weekend."

I close my eyes, trying to sleep, too. Maybe I'm overreacting. Joe Ed and I have been together over twenty-five years, and I know him like the back of my hand. He's not a complicated man. He's easy to read, as predictable as the cycles of the moon.

My thoughts flit like butterflies in a flower garden, landing here and there. In replaying scenes from the weekend, I can't get Corrine's listlessness and unhealthy pallor out of my mind. I'm more worried about her than I was in the past, with her suicide attempts and stays in the psych ward. I'm going to call her tomorrow to insist she see a doctor. She's into all that New Age business, using herbalists, acupuncture, things like that rather than conventional medicine, so I'll have to be insistent that she goes to a regular doctor rather than a spiritual healer or something. Joe Ed and I know a couple here in Montgomery whose son just took a job as an internist in Chickasaw. If I can get her an appointment . . . "Joe Ed?"

I can tell he's not asleep, although his eyes are closed and his breathing regular. I know him too well. *What is going on with him? Is it Bethany, or what?* "Joe Ed?"

"Goddammit, Julia," he grumbles, turning his back on me. "I'm tired. Can't it wait till tomorrow?" His voice is peevish, irritated.

That convinces me. One of the main reasons I married Joe Ed was his easygoing nature, such a contrast to the demanding, tense household I was raised in. His big rowdy family, as down-home and country as corn bread, was a welcome refuge from the Mobile society that had almost stifled the life out of me. The only thing Joe Ed asked of me was that I play the role of the perfect politician's wife, which I was born and bred to do. A few years ago, Corrine upset the SSGs by an offhand remark about how Joe Ed and I seemed more like business partners than husband and wife. Unlike the others, I knew exactly what Corrine was saying. Our relationship has evolved to a comfortable partnership over the years, one that works for both of us. A lot of people warned us that campaigning together would be a real strain on our marriage, but it made us closer instead. We were working for a common goal, and the campaign trail ended up being our best time together. When Joe Ed snaps at me, something's definitely wrong.

I turn on my side, away from him. There is something about Governor and Mrs. Joe Ed Stovall that none of the SSGs know. It's something that Corrine couldn't have possibly known when she made that offhand remark about us. If the SSGs knew, they would be shocked and full of disbelief. While it's true that Joe Ed and I have an amiable relationship that works well for us, what no one but the two of us knows is this: We are not lovers, and we haven't been for years.

I didn't realize how damaged I was when I met Joe Ed. I had not let a boy touch me since Jesus Perez had gone out of my life. Unknowingly, my mother had done the perfect thing by sending me to an all-girls' school, placing me in that intimate environment of companionship and acceptance. I'd never had sisters, and my friends in Mobile were carefully chosen for me, based on their parents' position in society. The W was exactly what I'd needed at the time. I think I'd have had a nervous breakdown if I'd gone anywhere else. When I first got to The W, I was a zombie, going through the motions of living but not feeling anything. Mother had pulled strings with Dean Pate to assure me a "suitable" roommate, and it had backfired on her. I didn't care who was assigned to me, could have cared less, but found it amusing that Dean Pate put me with Astor. Evidently, she thought it would please Mother immensely since Astor was on a dance scholarship, and Mother was a well-known patron of the arts. As it turned out, Mother was appalled, but Astor was the perfect roommate for me. She was so self-absorbed that she didn't notice I was one of the living dead. And she was so flamboyant and fascinating, with all her lovers and little dramas, that I forgot my own misery just watching the melodrama of her life. By the time the SSGs formed, I was surprised to find that I was happy again, surrounded by the camaraderie of girlfriends in a way I'd never been. Becoming one of the Same Sweet Girls saved me.

My high-school reputation as a snow queen was nothing compared to my first year at The W. An all-female school attracts males like bees to pollen, and the campus of The W was always swarming with boys from the other colleges in the Birmingham area, as well as Bama and Auburn. I dated; it was impossible not to. I went to dances and concerts and plays and movies and parties, but I wouldn't even let the poor guy with me hold my hand. Instead of my behavior discouraging the young studs of Alabama, I became a challenge, I suppose; Astor heard that bets were taken in fraternity houses all over the state as to who could get into my pants first. I was asked out more than any girl on campus, then accused of being either frigid or a lesbian. Neither was true; there was just a vast emptiness where my capacity to feel passion had once been. When my daddy took me to the University of Alabama to meet Joe Ed Stovall, I dutifully packed a long dress for the dance after the football game, but without a smidgen of curiosity about my date, even though he was the hottest thing at Bama since Kenny Stabler and Joe Namath.

Joe Ed turned out to be totally different from the fumbling, drunken boys I'd dated before; totally different from what I expected. Not a sports fan, I didn't expect to enjoy the football game that afternoon, but I did because I hit it off so well with Mr. Stovall. Joe Ed's daddy was such a character, loudmouthed and fun-loving, constantly jumping to his feet and cheering drunkenly, hugging everyone around him. He kept looking at me and saying, "Hot damn—wish I was twenty years old again. My boy's gonna up and die when he sees you!" Such a contrast to my elegant father, who could barely hide his dismay. "That's my boy!" Mr. Stovall would yell whenever Joe Ed scored, and slap my father on the back, once so heartily that my father's cigar went flying out of his mouth. Several times I had to cover my mouth to keep from giggling.

After the game, when a swaggering Mr. Stovall took us to the field house to meet his son, I figured that Joe Ed Stovall would be a loutish country boy, a younger version of his father. Instead, I met a strikingly handsome young man with old-fashioned, courtly manners and an undeniable magnetism, and I watched in amazement as he charmed the socks off of a roomful of reporters as well as my haughty father. When I was introduced to Joe Ed, it was like a scene from a romantic movie. Joe Ed stopped dead in his tracks and stared at me, his blue eyes wide. Later, he told me that ever since he was a little boy, he'd had a vision of the woman he'd one day meet and love. When I appeared in that noisy, crowded field house, he knew immediately that that woman was me, and he said he was struck dumb that I'd appeared so unexpectedly.

That night Joe Ed and I went to the victory dance, but his admirers swarmed all over him, fraternity boys wanting to talk about the game and sorority girls—most of them quite beautiful—just wanting him. When he whispered to me, "Let's get out of here," I didn't realize he'd taken my hand until we were walking across the moonlit campus, under falling autumn leaves. Ordinarily, I would've pulled away, but instead I laced my fingers through his, and I smiled up at him when he squeezed my hand, both of us grinning in relief to have escaped the mob scene.

We hid from everyone under the low sweeping limbs of a flaming-leafed dogwood tree, where we sat on a bench and talked until midnight, time for Joe Ed to take me back to the University Club where our daddies were staying. Joe Ed was fascinated by my upbringing in Mobile society, a lifestyle he couldn't even imagine. I was equally as interested in hearing about his childhood, how he'd been raised in Fort Payne by uneducated parents, good country people who just happened to be multimillionaires because of the success of their mobile-home factory. He wanted to go into politics because he was idealistic and believed he could make the world a better place. There was something about his boyish enthusiasm and innate sweetness that reminded me of Jesus Perez, so I agreed to see him again. On the shadowy porch of the University Club, Joe Ed held both my hands in his, his eyes glowing as he looked down at me, but he didn't try to kiss me goodnight. It was only after he'd left and I'd gone inside that I realized I wouldn't have pulled away if he had.

It took a year after becoming an SSG before I trusted them enough to tell them about Jesus and the baby; it was even longer before I told Joe Ed. Perhaps because of the differences in our backgrounds, Joe Ed treated me like I was made of fragile porcelain or something. He kissed me on our second date and I didn't pull back, but it had to be obvious to him that I wasn't exactly responsive, either. Instead of turning him off, it made him see me as some kind of unattainable virgin. I honestly believe that's why Joe Ed fell in love with me: He developed this Lancelot/Guinevere fixation, fostered by his idealistic nature. Of course, this worked perfectly for the snow queen, until I grew so fond of him after a couple of years of dating that my conscience got the better of me. I wrote him a Dear John letter, saying I could no longer see him because I wasn't what he thought I was.

The Sunday after I'd mailed the letter, I returned to the dorm after going to mass in Brierfield, and I found Joe Ed waiting in the lobby. I knew he'd gotten the letter because he'd called afterward, but I wouldn't go to the phone. I'd sent Astor to the phone booth to tell him that I couldn't talk, that I was in bed with a migraine. I was supposed to have gone to Bama on Friday night; when I didn't show up, Joe Ed called again, but I still refused to come to the phone. Since he hadn't called back since then, I'd assumed he'd accepted our breakup. He stood when I entered the lobby and said, "Julia, we need to talk." His eyes were red and his shoulders slumped, and my heart went out to him. He looked terrible, like he hadn't slept since getting my letter.

As on our first date, we sat on a secluded bench, this time under a low-sweeping ginkgo tree. It was spring, and The W was known for its beautiful campus with old brick streets, designed by the same architect who built Williamsburg. But Joe Ed and I didn't notice the flowering dogwood or the sweet-smelling roses bordering the walkways. I cried and told him everything. I told him the reason I'd written him the Dear John letter was because of Jesus Perez and the baby. I said he deserved better than me, that he deserved someone he could idealize and cherish. Joe Ed brushed my words aside like annoying gnats. He held me so tightly I thought surely I'd be crushed and said none of that mattered, that he wanted to marry me.

"I can't marry you, Joe Ed," I'd said as I wiped my eyes with his handkerchief. "I can't marry *anyone*. There's something wrong with me, don't you see that? If I could love anyone, it would be you. You deserve someone who can love you and respond to you. I wish it could be me, I really do. But I'm beginning to think I should become a nun instead."

"If you'll marry me, Julia," Joe Ed had said, "I swear to you, you won't regret it. I'll love you enough for both of us, and I won't push you into anything you don't want. One day I plan to be a state senator or governor, and I want you by my side when I do. We'll have a good life together."

Trying to be fair to him, I resisted. I tried dating other guys for a while, but I was even more miserable. The SSGs told me I was out of my mind to turn Joe Ed down. I found I missed him, much more than I ever dreamed I would. I missed his sweetness, his gentleness, his quiet good nature. Between him and the SSGs, my resistance was worn down, and a few weeks later, I told Joe Ed that I'd marry him. "But not on your terms," I said to him, the summer after my junior year. "You deserve more than that. If I marry you, I'm going to love you, and I'm going to be a good wife. You wait and see."

Joe Ed is still waiting. He was unable to shake his idealistic, virginal image of me, evidently; either that, or he was afraid of scaring me off. Whichever, he was the one to insist we wait until our honeymoon to sleep together, and until then, he seemed content. In a moonlit hotel room on the island of St. Thomas, we finally—after three years of dating and chaste kisses—made love. Afterward, while Joe Ed slept, I slipped out to the balcony, where I huddled in the white moonlight and cried. I promised myself that next time, I wouldn't freeze up. I'd love Joe Ed the way he deserved to be loved, so help me God.

I wasn't able to keep that promise, going cold every time Joe Ed touched me. I didn't understand it, since I knew now that I loved him, but I couldn't talk about it to anyone, especially Joe Ed. Eventually, both of us began to accept the lack of passion in our lovemaking, which occurred more and more infrequently. Once I discovered I was pregnant with Bethany, Joe Ed didn't touch me at all, and after she was born, our sex life became nonexistent. As the years went by, I never discussed it with Joe Ed; neither did I ask him if he slept with other women. He was so full of life, so beautiful, so *sexy,* that I assumed he did, but I didn't want to know.

Tonight I wonder if that is what's wrong with him, if he's seeing someone else. I know politicians have ample opportunities; I've seen women coming on to Joe Ed, even with me standing right beside him. A lot of his political buddies, senators and representatives and other governors, have picture-perfect families, with loving wives; but they have their mistresses on the side. I really can't blame Joe Ed if he turns to someone else, can't blame him at all. But as perverse as it sounds, I don't want him to. I hate myself for being like I am, but I know that in spite of my coldness, my lack of passion, it would kill me if Joe Ed loved someone else.

His back turned to me, he's asleep now, no longer pretending. Carefully, so that I won't wake him, I move over until I'm pressed lightly against him and put an arm around his waist, still as trim as it was thirty years ago. I've always loved his shoulders, so broad and strong, and I lay my cheek against his back, inhaling the sweet smell of his skin. Close to him, I match my breathing with his until I fall asleep.

For years, Joe Ed and I have not touched each other, but we have been lovers in my dream life. It shocks me that I cannot respond to him face to face, alone in our bed with his arms around me, but in my dreams, it's different. Tonight, in my dream I'm moving through the darkness of the Mansion grounds at night, the magnolia trees illuminated with hidden lights turned to shine on their trunks. Carefully, so no one will see me, I approach the back wing. When I'm sure I haven't been followed, I move quickly to a door that's hidden in the tangled darkness of wisteria. Looking over my shoulder, I knock quietly on the door. A man opens it, and I step inside, closing the door behind me. He takes me in his arms, and his mouth is over mine, hungrily. With a hand inside my blouse, he pushes me against the wall, where he makes love to me until I cry out again and again, my legs locked around his waist. I bend his head to mine, and my hands go into his hair, crow black and shining, straight as a stick. Tonight in my dream, it's not my husband I make love to. It's Cal Hawkins, his oldest friend and bodyguard.

In the middle of July, I'm surprised to answer a knock on the door of the sitting room and find Cal Hawkins there, even more surprised when he tells me he's come to escort me to the prearranged weekend with Bethany at the Helen Keller Institute in Talladega. "But— I thought you were with Joe Ed," I say. Joe Ed had flown to Atlanta yesterday; he was meeting me at the school today. I'd never known Cal not to accompany Joe Ed on a flight.

Cal shrugs. "Boss man changed his mind. Decided instead of Lieutenant Robinson taking you to Talladega, he wanted me to." I motion him in, but he declines, standing in the door instead.

I shrug, too, then return to the dressing room to get my purse, overnight bag, and the care package for Bethany. I don't want to ride in a car with Cal, making small talk, all the time purposefully not meeting his eyes. I awoke from my dream about making love to him that night full of shame and guilt, and I've avoided Cal ever since. I have no idea what the dream meant, why I put myself in Astor's place, sneaking out to meet him, unless it was the SSGs joking about him a couple of weekends ago. I've never thought of Cal that way before, and now I can't face him. Although I've not planned on working on the drive to Talladega—it only takes an hour and a half—I get my briefcase and laptop. I can sit in the back and work on a speech I'm giving next month in Birmingham, at a national convention of health-care professionals, a talk to promote my pet project, aid to the handicapped. I've given variations of it so often that it doesn't really need additional work, but this way, I can avoid Cal.

The campus of the Helen Keller Institute for the Deaf and Blind is such a lovely environment it reinforces my determination that

Bethany be here. I would've had her here at a very young age if Joe Ed had not been so adamant about keeping her at home with tutors. Only because she begged him for playmates did he eventually allow her to attend one of Montgomery's elite private schools, which caused him to lose some support in the elections. A politician has to support his state's public schools. Joe Ed is pliable, easily led and molded, but he absolutely refused to budge on Bethany, in spite of opposition from me, my parents, his father, and his advisors. I realized how strongly Mother felt about it when she suggested I threaten to take Bethany and leave if Joe Ed wouldn't give in and send Bethany to the Helen Keller Institute; threaten, not actually do it, of course, since that would rather defeat the purpose. But I could never use Joe Ed's devotion to his daughter—overprotective and misguided though it might be—as a weapon against him, and Mother knew it.

It's easy to find Joe Ed and Bethany; Cal leads me to the front of the administrative building where the largest group is gathered. As we approach, I gasp, then look at Cal. His jaw is clenched and his dark eyes narrowed.

"Oh, no," I say in a low voice. "The press is here." "Son of a bitch," Cal mutters, and I realize that today's been turned into a media event. Dr. Uptain, the president of the Institute, had assured me over and over that Bethany would be protected; he'll be as upset by this as I am. No, I know who's responsible—Joe Ed's closest advisors. Joe Ed will be furious but unable to do anything except smile and pose for pictures with Bethany and Dr. Uptain, say a few words for the press. He'll chew out everyone afterward, but—what good will that do? What's done is done.

Perversely, I'm almost glad the media's there when I take Bethany in my arms as though she's been gone a year rather than a few weeks. The presence of the press keeps me from breaking down at the sight of Bethany, and I'm able to smile instead, even get in a few words about my work on behalf of the handicapped and about the new book I'm working on. I can say to them sincerely that Bethany looks prettier than I've ever seen her. She's so tiny, barely five feet tall, and so small-boned that she looks more fragile than she is. Today she finally looks grown up, wearing makeup for the first time and showing off a new haircut. Her baby-fine blonde hair, which has been easier for her to manage in a long braid, is now blunt-cut and shoulder length, very becoming. Bethany's always been self-conscious about her thick glasses and hearing aids, but they're a lot less noticeable with her new look, her hair soft around her pretty face. Flashbulbs go off as Bethany keeps saying, "Mama, Mama, I missed you," over and over, her arms tight around my neck. She communicates mostly by signing, but she's always talked at home with me and Joe Ed. When Bethany finally releases her hold on me, she flings her arms around Cal. Since she was a little girl, she's loved Cal, who's always teased her, playing with her and treating her like a normal kid instead of the way so many do with the handicapped. Cal kisses her and says, "Have you told the boys here that your Uncle Cal will beat them up if they so much as look at you?"

"Oh, don't worry—they can't see," Bethany giggles, shocking the news media, who exchange startled glances once they figure out what she said.

"Good thing," Cal tells her. "I'd hate to whip

up on a bunch of gimps with all these reporters here."

"I have a boyfriend now, Cal," Bethany
says, grinning up at him. I notice, though,
that she doesn't look at her daddy when she
says this. Joe Ed's head jerks up sharply,
turning away from his conversation with Dr.
Uptain and staring at his daughter in dismay.
The reporters obviously didn't understand
what Bethany said—Cal and I are used to
her voice but most people aren't—that
caused her daddy to stare at his daughter
like that. When one of the reporters asks
Bethany to repeat herself, she signs instead
of talking, giggling mischievously as the
reporter frowns and shakes his head in frus-
tration, putting his notepad aside.

"I can't wait to meet your new friend," I
say quickly, taking Bethany's hand. "Come
on. Let's go on that tour you've been prom-
ising me."

The weekend turns out to be a success in
spite of getting off to such a bad start with
the unexpected presence of the media.
Sunday, because he's going from here to
Washington, Joe Ed has to leave after lunch

in the Institute's cafeteria, a special occasion for us. Although we don't have a chance to talk, it's obvious to me that Joe Ed leaves happy, since he's now free to visit Bethany any time, once she's survived the critical first month away from her home. I observe that he's uncomfortable around the new boy-friend, although he pretends otherwise. Scott Simms turns out to be a shy, sweet boy not much bigger than Bethany, who laughs good-naturedly when Cal tells him he'll break his neck if he isn't good to Bethany. Bethany has to sign the message to Scott, who's not blind but totally deaf. When we say our good-byes and Scott Simms takes Bethany's hand to lead her away, I can't stop the tears. I turn my head away to wipe my eyes, and Cal pats my shoulder awkwardly.

"Scott can be her eyes now," I say, swallowing hard, and Cal grins.

"Yeah, but he'd better remove his skinny little arm from her waist or I'll have to break it."

I laugh and turn toward the car. "Let's get out of here."

The weekend has relaxed me toward Cal, and we're friends again. Not only have I put the embarrassing dream out of my mind, I've forgiven Cal for Astor, even excused him.

I've seen Astor in operation before, and less vulnerable men than Cal have given in to her. At one time when she was between husbands, I even thought she was coming on to Joe Ed. When I teased her about it, she surprised me with her indignation that I'd even suggest such a thing. Since the SSG weekend, I've seen no evidence that Astor's affair with Cal is ongoing, so I assume it must've been a one-night stand. Astor and I met in Birmingham for lunch just last week. A couple of times, I almost asked her about Cal, but held back, still convinced she'd lie to me. After lunch the two of us went to St. Mary's to see Mose, and Astor couldn't have been more attentive and loving with him.

Taking my elbow, Cal leads me back to the car, but when he holds the door open for me, I pause. "Cal? Will you take me to the lake house?" We've kept the lake house that Joe Ed's daddy gave us as a wedding present as our retreat, away from the madness of our public lives. Located on Lake Martin, a couple of hours from Montgomery, it's secluded and hidden away, and suddenly I long to be there, more than anything.

His eyes widen. "The lake house? You

mean, just for the afternoon?" Before I can answer, Cal adds, "It'll be almost dark before we can get there."

"Not for the afternoon. I want to stay tonight."

"Tonight?" Cal's eyes move over me in my suit and heels. "But—you don't have anything but dressy clothes with you, do you? Surely you're not going to wear those heels to the lake."

"We keep plenty of stuff there."

Cal looks skeptical. "Didn't you tell me on the way down that you have a breakfast meeting in the morning?"

I shrug. "I don't care. I want to go to the lake house."

He puts a hand on my arm. "Whoa, now. Number one, Joe Ed would kill me if I took you there and left you alone, and number two . . ."

"I won't be alone. You'll be with me."

Cal laughs nervously. "Yeah, right. Number two . . . goddamn, Julia! You made me forget what number two was."

I laugh, too. "Okay, then, how about this? You take me to the lake house and leave me, then someone comes and picks me up in the morning. If they get there by six . . ."

But Cal cuts me off, shaking his head adamantly. "No way. I told you, Joe Ed would have my head if I left you there by yourself."

I shrug again. "Looks like you'll have to stay with me, then."

"I can't tell if you're serious or not, Julia. But if you are, then you know I can't do that, either."

"I'm completely serious. And you know the guest house where you guys stayed last time we went? You'll be there, in the guest house, and I'll be in the lake house."

Cal rolls his eyes, then unhooks his phone from his holster. "Let me call Joe Ed, see what he—" but I put my hand out to stop him, grabbing his wrist before he punches in the code.

"No! Please, Cal . . . you know what Joe Ed will say."

"Yeah, I know he'll fire my ass if I let you do this. Let's think this out, Julia. What about next weekend? You could—"

"Next weekend Joe Ed will be home. I want to go now, by myself."

He grins triumphantly, thinking he's got me. "But you won't be by yourself if I'm there."

"Okay. Then take me back to the Mansion.

Soon as we get there, I'll get in my goddamn car and drive to the lake house. *By myself.*"

Cal raises his eyebrows in surprise. My determination shocks him; it shocks me. Suddenly, I want to escape to the lake house more than I've ever wanted anything. "Jesus, Julia," Cal says. "You're serious, aren't you?"

"I'm going, Cal, one way or the other."

"I don't have any other clothes, either. I've slept in my uniform before, but it's not my first choice, believe me."

"The least of our worries. Joe Ed's got plenty of stuff there, and y'all are the same size."

He sighs and shakes his head, his hands on his hips. "Hell, I'm fifty now. I can take early retirement, maybe. Be hard to get a job after being fired from the governor's staff, but Wal-Mart can always use another security guard, I guess."

"I'll take full blame. I'll tell Joe Ed I was so upset over seeing Bethany with a boyfriend that I couldn't face anyone at the Mansion."

Cal shakes his head in exasperation. "You're taking advantage of my good nature, not to mention our friendship. But you know that, don't you?"

I nod. "I certainly do. I'd never ask Lieutenant Robinson to do this."

Muttering, "Shit. Fuck. Son of a bitch," Cal, his face dark, motions toward the backseat of the car. "Okay, goddammit. But you'd better write me a good recommendation to Wal-Mart."

15

Corrine
BLUE MOUNTAIN

I HAVE A WEIRD affliction that has been both a blessing and a curse in my life. When I was a teenager, Miss Fielding gave it a name: the beauty disease. Having the beauty disease, I was initially attracted to Miles Spaulding because of his looks. I find that pretty shallow, even though Miss Fielding made me understand that a hunger for beauty was not something to be ashamed of. "Art is beauty, Corrine," she'd said to me, "even when it represents something less than lovely. Art and beauty are the same. When you're crafting art, you're celebrating the beauty of life."

At first I didn't understand that her notion

of art and beauty was a paradox. "But so much of the world isn't beautiful, with all the suffering and poverty and stuff!" I'd responded. "You mean artists should only produce pretty things?"

My ignorance made Miss Fielding stern. "Certainly not. But it's the role of the artist to search for loveliness and illuminate it. You can't ignore all the pain and suffering and evil in the world, Corrine, and you'll never be untouched by it. But you can choose beauty. Always, you have that choice."

When I'd told my major professor at The W that I was going to be a folk artist because of Miss Fielding, he'd hooted. He'd said that she was obviously a deluded Romantic, spitting the words out like bitterweed. Whether it was a silly notion or not, I was too afflicted by the beauty disease to care. My hunger for beauty made me miserable growing up, but it led me where I needed to go, and it keeps leading me today.

The thing is, I wasn't raised like the other girls at The W, Julia and Lanier, Byrd and Rosanelle, even Astor, who tried to keep her family situation mysterious. None of us ever went home with Astor, who told us she'd been raised by her grandparents in a decaying mansion in the Louisiana swamps after her mother, a great beauty, died of a broken heart without ever revealing her father's identity. What a crock! Astor's story was right out of Tennessee Williams, and I never believed a word of it. Except about the grandparents, who never came to any of the plays or dances Astor was in but did show up for her graduation. Not only were they about a hundred years old and half senile, which I'd be too if I had had to raise Astor, they were ignorant country people like my folks. Astor pretended to be horrified that they'd made the long trip, fooling everyone but me. I could tell that she was just plain ashamed of them.

The SSGs knew about my family situation and why I never invited anyone to Tobacco Road for the weekend. I figured a visit to a sharecroppers' shack would hardly be a fun trip for them, and my family wasn't the friendliest in the world, either. I also knew that the other SSGs were not used to having squirrel or possum and black-eyed peas and hoecakes for dinner, and that was on a good day. Growing up, I went hungry more often than I care to remember.

I'm not sure at what age I knew that I was

hungry in another way, a way having nothing to do with food. The land my daddy farmed was poor and dismal. Instead of rich black soil, Coffee County had white sand and red clay, baked hard by the sun of south Alabama, right across from the Florida line. In that cheerless setting, I sought out sources of beauty wherever I could find them, which is how my love of gourds came about. The only flowers my poor, beaten-down mama planted were stinky marigolds to protect her vegetables from bugs; those and gourds, which grew on a fence erected to keep the hogs out of the garden. It'd be romantic if I could claim that Mama raised the gourds as a creative outlet, decorating and using them to brighten our pathetic lives, but I'd be lying. Mama made water dippers and martin houses from the gourds, but she never saw their beauty, letting most of them rot on the vines. As a little girl, the gourd vines, spilling riotously over the fence, became my playhouse, a place I escaped to and dreamed in, living in a make-believe world. Mama showed me how to dry and clean the gourds, and they became my toys first and my art projects later. Once Miss Fielding began giving me art supplies, I experimented with the gourds and made lovely containers and musical instruments from them. If the ugly, hard-shell gourds, brown and moldy after they dried, could be made into something beautiful, I decided, then art really was miraculous. Miss Fielding, taken with my fascination with gourds, gave me a book about the folklore associated with them, which I read till the pages fell apart. When I read that in some cultures gourds are considered magical, my imagination took off. If that were the case, I decided, my magical gourds would provide me a way to a better life. Turns out, I wasn't far off the mark.

It wasn't an easy journey. I'd grown up being ridiculed by my family as useless and dreamy-eyed. Although I loved my poor mama, I pitied her more, and my daddy was a bitter and mean-spirited man, whom I had little affection for. When I got the scholarship to The W, instead of being proud, my family scorned me, telling me not to come home if I got uppity or a "big head." Every time I returned to face their ridicule, it brought on depression and self-loathing, which sank me down so low that I tried to escape by slitting my wrists. Shortly after graduation and my move to Blue Mountain to work in the gallery with Miss Fielding, I went home for another dismal visit. I returned to Blue Mountain depressed enough for one of my suicide attempts, and that's when I became the patient of Miles Spaulding.

An old saying in Coffee County goes, marry in haste, repent in leisure. The SSGs couldn't believe it when I told them that Miles and I had gotten married since we had not even dated before then, not in the regular way. Lanier shocked me by bursting into tears when I called to tell her that Miles and I had gone to the probate judge after one of my therapy sessions, gotten married, and were deliriously happy. Her first reaction, which we later joked about, was, "But, Corrine, you've never even seen his *house!*" "I'm seeing it now," I replied. "I've moved in, and it's just fabulous. He designed it himself, and it's made of cedar and glass, real modern. I can't wait for you to see it. It's on the mountaintop, and you can almost see Miss Fielding's cabin from here." "Maybe when I meet Miles, I'll feel better about this," she'd sniffed, and I'd laughed. "You're going to love him, Lanier. He's so wonderful and so good-looking, and he absolutely adores me."

I didn't tell Lanier that I'd had my first

twinge of doubt right after we married. When Miles drove me to his mountaintop house and I'd stood gaping at it, he'd come around the car and taken me in his arms. "I never imagined that you had such a house," I'd said.

"You'll find out this about me," Miles said, laughing, "I'm a hedonist. I like nice things." He kissed me roughly, bruising my mouth as all his kisses did, then looked down at me, eyes glowing. "And I like having such a wide-eyed, innocent wife. You're like Alice in goddamn Wonderland, Corrine. Turns me on, thinking about what I'm going to teach you. I'm going to spend the rest of my life teaching you things."

"Do you really love me, Miles?"

"I love you so much that I'm going to devour you," he'd answered. "I'm going to consume you. You belong to me."

Sexy as it sounded, I wasn't sure I wanted to be devoured, but I didn't tell Miles that, since I figured he was speaking metaphorically. At the time I was too awed by his house—now mine, too—overlooking the waterfall that fell into Shoal Creek in the valley, the creek that ran by Miss Fielding's cabin several miles away. My beauty disease came full circle when I realized how far I'd come from my hideaway in the gourd vines that grew on the fence next to the sharecropper's shack, the fence put up to keep the hogs out of the vegetable garden.

The first time I rebelled against being consumed by Miles's love for me should have served as a warning flag, but I was young and in love then—not to mention ignorant and naive. Oh, we were happy at first, like all newlyweds everywhere, I imagine. The SSGs came over for a reception Miles's clinic gave for us—this was long before we started gathering here every October—and everyone seemed to be as taken with Miles as I was, which validated my marriage. My new husband lavished presents on me, often surprising me with a new item of clothing or jewelry or piece of artwork, and the SSGs were impressed. Blue Mountain is an artsy place, with sophisticated folks from Atlanta having mountain houses there, and at first, Miles seemed proud that his wife was an artist. We entertained and were entertained by collectors and other artists, and my work began to flourish. Since there was no place to plant a garden in the rocky soil on the mountaintop, I kept my gourd vines in Miss Fielding's garden; she insisted I share her studio, so I worked there daily. Miss Fielding's specialty was ceramics, but soon her gallery was selling my gourd pieces as fast as I could produce them. Gourd art by Corrine Cooper—I kept my professional name—was hot, and I became rather well known, even earning a citation from the American Folk Artists Guild. After years of fighting depression, I was finally happy and productive.

Unused to being the belle of the ball, several months after Miles and I married I had too much to drink at a Christmas party and danced with every man there. Miles watched me all night, and stupid me, I kept smiling at him over the shoulder of my partners, thinking he was admiring the way other men clamored for his wife's attention. After the party we returned to the house and I hung my new wrap in the hall closet, a stunning black velvet cape that Miles had given me. I took off my heels and was walking upstairs, outside our bedroom, when Miles called out to me. He was standing beside our bed, unbuttoning his shirt. "Come here, Corrine," he said softly.

Walking a little unsteadily, I went to him, barefoot. Unsmiling, he reached out and took the long, black-sequined scarf from around my neck, the one he'd given me to match the cape. I'd worn it with a ruby-red velvet dress, not my color with my reddish-gold hair, but also a gift from Miles. "You looked lovely tonight," he said. "This scarf is good on you."

"Why, thank you," I replied, smiling at him drunkenly. "I'm sure I'll wear it to every Christmas party we go to."

Miles motioned toward the bed. "Lie down, Corrine."

"Let me get my dress off," I said, but shaking his head, Miles took my arm, rather firmly, and sat me on the bed. "Lie down," he repeated, and like a fool, I did.

"Now. Hold out your hands," he commanded. Uncomprehending, I watched as he took the scarf and wrapped it around my wrists, binding my hands together. "Now you can't get away from me," he said, his jaw clenched.

"I don't want to get away from you, silly," I said, with a light laugh. "But you've gotten the scarf too tight. It hurts."

With a quick movement, he pulled my arms over my head and tied the scarf to the bedpost. I couldn't have been more surprised if he'd started tap dancing. "Miles? What in hell are you doing?" I gasped. Moving even more quickly, he yanked the red velvet dress up around my waist, then I watched in shock and disbelief as he took his belt off and raised it high. "Have you lost your mind?" I screeched, which changed to a scream when the first blow of the belt landed on my thigh.

"You're *my* wife, Corrine," Miles yelled as he struck me on the legs and hips with the belt. "Mine—mine—mine! I don't want you ever touching another man!" His eyes were wild with fury as he yanked his pants off and straddled me. A walking kama sutra, Miles had taken me in all sorts of different positions, but he'd never forced me before. Struggling, I fought against him as best as I could with my arms tied to the bedposts, but he was too strong. When he came and collapsed beside me, he wouldn't untie me, even though I cried and begged him to, the scarf cutting into my wrists. My crying seemed to turn him on even more, and he took me again, then began hitting me with the belt until I was so stunned, bruised, and dazed that I either dropped off to sleep or passed out.

I woke up just as daylight was coming in the windows over our bed. Groaning, I moved painfully, then saw that Miles had untied my wrists, which were purple and swollen. The ruined red velvet dress was in a heap on the floor, though I had no recollection of taking it off. When I turned my head, Miles opened his beautiful blue-green eyes. Before I could move, he took me in his arms and held me to him, stroking my wild, tangled hair and kissing my forehead. "Oh, my darling," he whispered as I sobbed hysterically into his chest, "I don't know what came over me! Seeing you with all those men at the party made me go crazy, I guess. Can you ever forgive me?"

"You hurt me!" I cried, like a indignant child.

"Shh . . . shh, now. I love you, Corrine, so much that I can't share you. You've got to promise me that you'll never look at another man. Promise me!" And he kissed me, tenderly this time, careful not to hurt my bruised and bleeding mouth.

It was the first time Miles had been tender with me, and I caved in. Kindness got to me, of course, as it always does with women. His secret weapon, if only he'd been able to see that. Feeling guilty and miserable that I'd made him unhappy, I swore that I'd never do anything to make him jealous again.

A couple of years after Dixie Lee was killed, I returned from a Same Sweet Girls gathering in Alabama still high from seeing everyone, which was more important to me than ever. Astor was in New York—thank God— but the others all lived in Alabama, close enough to get together for lunch occasionally, and I realized how much I missed that. Miles and I had finished dinner and were having our coffee on the back deck as I told him about all of the silly rituals that were evolving. "I'm queen this year," I said, smiling, "so I suggested that we start meeting on Blue Mountain, maybe in October. As queen, I get to make those kinds of decisions." When Miles had met the SSGs, he'd liked everyone, especially since they'd stroked his ego by flirting with him and telling him how much they envied me, so I figured he'd like the idea of them meeting here. I yakked on and on about how important their friendships were to me, but I failed to read the chill in Miles's eyes. Finally he stopped me cold by saying, "Am I to assume that you'd rather be with your friends than your husband? You leave me alone all weekend then have the gall to return and rub it in."

"Don't be ridiculous, Miles," I replied nonchalantly, but the look in his eyes scared me. "I've got to unpack," I said, hurrying upstairs before he got any more furious. I was in the bathroom when he flung the door open, eyes glinting.

"Come to bed, my darling. I just want to be with you, is all," he told me. But in bed together, he seized me and kissed me so roughly that I pushed him away. "Stop it, Miles," I said. "I want you to make love to me, but not like this."

Flinging himself from the bed, Miles turned on the lamp and started getting dressed. "You have no idea how many women throw themselves on me every day," he said, brushing the tousled blond hair off his forehead. "Many of my patients are beautiful women, and unlike my wife, they seem to find me desirable. You don't want me, well, fine. I can go out and find plenty of women who do."

A slow learner, I should have known that Miles didn't take well to sass. "You obviously have no scruples about sleeping with your patients," I said dryly.

Miles stopped buttoning his slacks to glare at me. "You're changing, Corrine. I don't know you anymore."

"Don't tell me I'm not the same sweet girl you married." A mistake, and one I paid for. Instead of putting his belt into the belt loops, Miles doubled it and walked toward me, slapping it on his palm. I sat up in bed and tried to stop him. "If you hit me with that damn belt again, Miles, so help me God, I'll leave you!"

Miles was on me before I could get away from him, kissing me so hard that my lips bled. "I don't want it this way," I yelled, jerking my head free. "I want you to be gentle with me!"

He laughed, imprisoning me with his arms. "Guess what? I don't give a shit what you want. You belong to me, and I'll do what I please with you."

It ended as before, with me crying and pleading, turning him on even more but unable to stop myself. When he was spent, falling on me with a cry of triumph, I waited till he was asleep, then squirmed out from under him. Dressing quickly, I slipped out of the house and went to my studio in the back of Miss Fielding's cabin, letting myself in quietly so I wouldn't wake her. If Miles wanted to stay married to me, he'd have to change. I wouldn't go back to him unless he promised to stop the brutal lovemaking. He'd hurt me tonight as badly as the last time; my breasts were sore, and I was bruised and swollen, with red welts on my thighs from the blows of his belt. Not only that, I was bleeding, even though it wasn't time for my period. Much as I loved Miles, I swore I wouldn't go back to him if he didn't change.

I went back, but not because Miles promised me anything. It turned out that I was pregnant with Culley, and stupid me, I thought that would change Miles, turn him into a kind and gentle husband. I doubt I'm the first woman to make that mistake.

Culley was born in April, the first spring in many years that I hadn't planted my gourds. I had a rough pregnancy, so between Miles and the doctor, they convinced me not to garden. When the baby came, I thought, I'd be balancing diaper changes and breastfeeding with my gardening and artwork, so why not take a rest?

Or so I thought. When Culley was a few weeks old, I took him with me to the garden behind Miss Fielding's cabin, put him in a sling bundled next to my breasts, and pulled up the old vines from last year's harvest. It turned out to be an unusually warm day, and Culley got a bit too much sun. Miles freaked out, scaring me to death. He rushed Culley to the pediatrician, who—like Miles—chewed me out for taking Culley out in the sun. As a new mother, I was uptight and unsure of myself anyway; it didn't take much to shake my confidence. I decided being a mother was more important to me than being an artist, so Culley was four years old before I returned to my studio.

In those days I didn't have a whole lot of self-awareness (not that I've changed that much). My art was so much a part of me, something that had been a part of me for so long, that I had never thought consciously about doing it or not doing it. It was simply what I did. Miles was being the perfect husband, and he was a doting father to Culley. I was taken with my golden-haired, precocious son, getting into motherhood in a big way, but something was missing from my life. I was as lost as a star drifting away from its constellation. It had been four years since I'd planted my gourds and watched them take root and sprout, tending them until they spread into vines, pollinating them by hand. It'd been too many years since I'd plucked the dried gourds from the trellises and arbors I'd built for them, soaked and scrubbed them, then taken a knife and saw and engraving tool and paint to transform them. One thing I'd discovered about motherhood—when Culley was away from me, my arms literally ached for him. In the same way, my fingers began to ache for the feel of my gourds, for my knife, and for my paintbrush. I had to get back to my work.

I took Culley with me to my studio, but a lively four-year-old in a place with knives and jigsaws and paints and cleaning fluids wasn't going to work. After a few nerve-racking days, I gave up. Miles came home one evening to find me circling ads in the Chickasaw paper. "And what does my beautiful wife need?" he inquired, pouring each of us a glass of wine. "What has your devoted husband failed to provide?" He leaned over and, pulling my long, loose hair back, kissed my neck.

I smiled, content. Culley was sitting at my feet, pretending to read the new book that his daddy had just brought him. "Oh, I'm just looking for a sitter," I said, putting the paper down and rubbing my eyes. "I'd rather have someone come in and stay with Culley while I work than take him to daycare."

It was as though the temperature in the room dropped twenty degrees. Miles froze in his tracks, his eyes cold as opals, and stared at me. "You're not leaving my son with a sitter, Corrine. Period. You can forget that." His full-lipped mouth was drawn into a tight line.

Dumb me, I said, "But, Miles, I can't take him to the studio! It's too dangerous . . ."

"Damn right it's too dangerous. I forbid you to take him to your studio again. I've had nightmares thinking what could've happened these last few days."

"But . . . what am I going to do, then?"

"I think that's obvious. I'm a psychologist, and I can tell you that a child needs his mother full-time. Being left with sitters at this crucial age is why so many kids are so f-u-c-k-e-d up." He glanced down at Culley as though his son, looking up from his book to watch his parents wide-eyed, would know what he was spelling.

I gave in, telling myself I'd wait until Culley was in school, only a couple more years, rather than blame myself if my son turned out to be a psychopath. What I didn't count on was the return of my depression, creeping up on me like the monsters Culley imagined lying in wait in his dark bedroom at night. The joy I'd felt in my new life—my husband, my beautiful home, and my adorable son— dimmed bit by bit, like a light with a short in it that flickers until it goes out.

For several months I went through the motions of a normal life but gradually, I lost even that, sinking further and further into joylessness and despair. One winter night Miles came home for the third night in a row to find the house cold, no dinner prepared, and Culley parked in front of cartoons on the TV screen. Seeing me lying on the sofa crying into a damp tissue, Miles lost it.

"Corrine? Tell me what's wrong with you," he demanded, standing over me with his hands on his hips.

Culley turned his head from the TV long enough to tell him, "Mommy's been crying all afternoon, Daddy. Maybe she's sick."

"Sick, hell," Miles growled, grabbing me by the arm and pulling me to my feet. "Look at you! Your hair's a mess and you're wearing the same dirty clothes you wore yesterday."

"Leave me alone," I sobbed, but Miles pulled me up the stairs. Culley ran after him and grabbed his leg when Miles had to pry my fingers from the stair rail.

"Don't, Daddy!" Culley cried. "Mommy doesn't want to go with you."

"Go back to the living room," Miles snapped, "and turn off that goddamn TV!" Shocked, since his father never raised his voice to him, Culley scurried off, and Miles dragged me into the bathroom. After removing the grimy sweatsuit that I'd worn for two days, he shoved me into the shower.

The shower was exactly what I needed, and I let the healing waters pour over me, staying under the stream so long that the hot water ran out. I turned the water off, pushed my wet hair back from my face, and reached for the shower door. Through the glass, I could see that Miles was leaning against it, and tapping on it, I said, "Move, Miles. I need to get out."

"Water therapy," he said but didn't move.

"I'm cold, Miles. Let me out." When he refused, I banged on the glass door and yelled at him until Culley came running in to see what was wrong. Through the wavy glass, I saw Miles pick Culley up and hold him as he leaned against the glass. Upset and confused, Culley kept pleading, over and over, "Let Mommy out, Daddy. She's cold, and she's crying. Let her out!"

I shivered and cried, huddled in the corner of the shower, until Culley started crying, too; then Miles moved away. I waited until he went out of the bathroom, slamming the door shut, and then I came out, wrapping myself in a towel, shaking and scared. When I heard the front door slam, I ran downstairs in time to see Miles's silver Mercedes spinning out of the driveway, Culley in the passenger seat, heading down the mountain drive that wound up to our house. Dazed and horrified that Culley had witnessed such a scene, I sank down on the stairs and cried. Sniffling, stumbling, I went back upstairs to the bathroom to dry off and pull myself together. Even though I figured that Miles was only driving Culley to the McDonald's in town, I was terrified that he was taking him away from me.

I was combing the tangles out of my hair when the bathroom door flew open and Miles stood there, his face red and his eyes blazing.

"Where's Culley?" I cried.

"I took him to Jane's." At my gasp, he rolled his eyes. "Oh, don't worry. I told her that you'd gotten sick and it'd upset Culley. I didn't tell her what really happened." Jane was one of the nurses at the clinic, and the only person Miles trusted to babysit Culley, the few times we'd left him to go out.

"Go back and get him," I demanded. "I'm fine now. I was just depressed . . ."

"Bullshit!" Miles snarled. "I've locked up patients in the same shape you were when I got home. You were bat-shit crazy."

"No, it's my depression, Miles. You know better than anybody the problems I've had with it. Guess I should go back on my medication."

"Depression, my ass. I know depression when I see it. You were practically catatonic. If I ever see you like that again, I'll have you put away."

"Over my dead body." I started past him. "I'm going to get Culley."

I'd reached the door when Miles grabbed my hair, hanging wet down my back, and yanked me back. My cry of pain was all it took to turn him on again, after the past five years of infrequent, perfunctory sex. Determined not to give in to him, I made the mistake of resisting. I fought him harder than ever, scratching his face and flailing at him with my fists. But, as before, he overpowered me, tying me to the bedposts and using his belt on me. I didn't go for Culley that night; I was too bruised and swollen for him to see me. The next evening, I was still in bed, dazed and staring at the ceiling, when Miles brought Culley home and told him that his mommy was too sick to see him.

After that night, my depression developed into a pattern. True to his word, Miles had me locked up, several times. When I could, I'd call Lanier or Julia, who'd drive over to see if I was really as crazy as Miles told them. Much of the time, I stayed sedated, too doped-up to fully function. I became a Stepford Wife instead. I gave up my garden and my art, but otherwise, I appeared to be a normal human being. Miss Fielding died and left me the cabin, and the SSGs started meeting there the last weekend in October. Once Miles came over to say hello to everyone, and later on, I caught him and Astor huddled together, whispering and touching hands, and both of them jumped apart when I walked in. What neither of them could possibly know was how little I cared, even though it wasn't the first time I'd caught Astor flirting with a husband of an SSG; I'd seen her coming on to both Joe Ed and Buster. Again, my depression had gotten so bad that I was just going through the motions of living. Culley, my sweet-natured, gregarious son, provided me with the only source of joy in those dark times. But when Culley was thirteen, even that was taken from me.

There was another bad period, when I was practically catatonic, and Miles had me locked up for a month. This time he'd had enough, and he filed for divorce when I was released. He testified that I was unstable, suicidal, and manically depressed, unfit to raise a child. In spite of the testimony of my friends, the judge granted Miles full custody of Culley, and I was given rare, supervised visits, supervised by my psychologist-husband. If Miles decided I was too crazy to see my son, even those weren't allowed me.

After several months of living alone in Miss Fielding's cabin, I called Miles and told him I wanted to talk to him when Culley wasn't there. "He has a scout camping trip this weekend," Miles told me. "Come over Sunday afternoon."

I sat facing Miles on the beige leather sofa in what used to be my living room, with its glass walls looking out over the fog-shrouded mountains, and forced myself to stop trembling. Taking a deep breath, I began. "Miles, I want to come home."

I didn't flinch when Miles smirked at me, as I knew he would. I wasn't sure when I'd stopped loving him, but it had been a long time ago, I realized now. He took a sip of red wine, smiling that half-smile that used to drive me crazy with desire. With those dreamy eyes of his, he studied me. "What makes you think I'd have you back?"

"Because the few times you've allowed me to see Culley, you have to pry his arms off me when I leave. He tells me that he's begged you to let me come home. You have him now,

Miles, but one day, he'll resent you for this. I'm miserable, Miles, and so is Culley."

"I'm delighted to hear that you're miserable, Corrine, after all the misery you've caused me. All I wanted was to cherish you, but you've treated me horribly, throwing my love back in my face," Miles said, lighting a cigarette and regarding me through the smoke. "Now you want to come back." Surprising me, he leaned forward and caressed my cheek with the back of his hand. "Do you love me, Corrine?"

"Let me show you how much," I said boldly, hating myself for the lie. Moving quickly, Miles put out his cigarette and pulled me to him.

"Could it be like it used to be with us?" he asked. I nodded my head, and Miles laughed. I was sure he was about to mock me and throw me out, but instead, he began moving his hands over my body. "You have no idea how much I still want you, Corrine! I've had other women since our divorce, but there's no one else for me, and there never will be." He took my hand and placed it between his legs, closing his eyes and moaning. "When I think about you . . . Goddamn, I think I can put up with anything to have you like that again." He kissed me, long and hard, as rough and painful a kiss as always, then looked down at me, eyes hard. "But I'm not going to let you come back, depressed and bitter and hating me—I can't go through that again."

"Miles, *please*—I promise—"

He put a hand over my mouth. "No. Absolutely not. But I will work out a deal with you, Corrine. It will be on my terms or nothing. My way or the highway."

It ended up by me selling my soul to the devil. On weekends I returned to my old house and Miles's bed. In exchange, I had to convince Culley it was the way I wanted it. I had to convince him that it wasn't his daddy's fault that I no longer lived with them. I preferred living by myself, in the cabin, I told him, so I could do my artwork. But I'd be with him on the weekends, because his daddy knew how much he missed me.

I don't blame Miles for what happened between me and Culley; I blame myself for going along with Miles's blackmail. Shocked, hurt, and disillusioned with me, Culley pretended not to care. Oh, my art was more important than he was, huh? His mother pre-

ferred not to live with him except on weekends? Well, fine. He'd show me how little he
cared, how little he needed me. My sweet little boy turned cold and silent and shut me
out of his life, and it would be years before
he allowed me back in.

The day that Culley left to go to college in
North Carolina, I went for the last time to the
house Miles and I had shared together on
the top of Blue Mountain. We stood in the
driveway waving until Culley's car disappeared around the bend, packed up and
heading for Brevard. When we started back
toward the house, I stopped at my car, and
Miles put a hand on my arm. "Don't go yet.
Come in and have a glass of champagne.
I've opened a bottle of Moët for this occasion," he said.

I opened the car door before looking up at
him. "I've got a better suggestion for that
fancy bottle of champagne, Miles."

"Pardon me?"

"As far as I'm concerned, you can take
that bottle of Moët and stick it where the sun
don't shine."

I watched in satisfaction as the color
drained from Miles's face. "Corrine . . . listen

to me," he said finally, eying me warily. "These last few years have been difficult, but I learned something. I—I love you, Corrine, more than I've ever loved anyone, and I can't let you go. Do you think we could try again?"

I shook my head. "Not a chance in hell." And getting in the car, I drove off, not once looking back.

16

Lanier

DAUPHIN ISLAND

I DON'T LOOK SO bad when I fix myself up, but I've never been a beauty like some of the others, Julia and Astor and Rosanelle. Trouble is, I don't fix myself up like I ought to. It used to drive Mama crazy that I'd rather be playing tennis or swimming than putting on makeup or polishing my nails or trying on clothes. Half the time I don't fool with my hair, still wearing it in the same old Buster Brown cut I've had since I was two. I don't own a pair of high heels, and my wardrobe is made up of T-shirts, jeans, cutoff shorts, a few denim skirts; basic black when I have to dress up. Who'd ever expect somebody like me to be such a love junkie?

I think I've figured it out. Long as I can remember, I've been addicted to junk food, stuff like potato chips and soft drinks and candy bars. It's caused me problems all my life, cavities and stomachaches and acne, not to mention a big ass that I have to jog every day to keep under control. It's taken me a long time to see the connection, but here it is: The way I'm drawn to junk food is the same way I can't resist a man who's no good for me.

None of the Same Sweet Girls has had the man troubles I've had. You might think Astor, but no; Astor loves 'em and leaves 'em. Should be a trail of broken hearts a mile long behind her, but the kind of guys Astor likes have always been users, except for Mose. Corrine is a contender, I'll admit, with that S-and-M ex of hers, but I still win. The difference is, Corrine was such an innocent she didn't have a chance with someone like Miles Spaulding, the creep. Me, I don't think I was even *born* innocent. I walk into these things with my eyes wide open, rubbing my hands in glee and drooling happily. If the crown were given for weakness rather than sweetness, I'd win it every time.

Over the years at the SSG gatherings, we've played games and taken polls and had true confessions and all sorts of silliness like that, most of them led by me. In the back of the lesson book, I've tallied up the number of feels sneaked in at parties, the illicit kisses—with extra points for tonguing—and the number of times too drunk to walk. Shocking no one, Astor blows the rest of us out of the water. We all laughed to find out that Byrd had gotten so drunk at one of Buster's company parties that she slid out of her chair and under the table. And no surprise that Rosanelle just flat flunked out, not getting any points. (Either that, or she's lying.) But the big surprise has been me. . . . I've come in a close second to Astor every blame time, which supports my love-junkie theory. Except for Saint Paul, all the men I've just *had* to have were junk food—great-looking on the surface but bad for me. They were Goo-goo Clusters, Snickers bars, Ben and Jerry's crushed-up Oreos ice cream, and that kind of birthday-cake icing made with nothing but Crisco and powdered sugar. Paul Sanders is the only meat-and-potatoes man I've ever had. Since he was so good for me, it stands to reason that I'd go for something unhealthy first chance I got. However, after my taste for junk food caused me to lose Paul and the kids, I told myself I'd never go for it again.

With that resolution in mind, I've decided to have a strictly professional relationship with Jesse Pickett-Phoenix. No more lying down beside him, holding his hand till he goes off to sleep. No more snuggling up next to him, listening to him tell me how bad his life sucks. No sirree! As a nurse and a friend, I'm helping Jesse get himself straightened out so he can go back to writing his songs, but that's it. Every time I go over to Jesse's, I come away resolved that's the way it's got to be. And here's why—when I look at Jesse Phoenix, I see a hot-fudge sundae, piled high with whipped cream and topped with a long-stemmed cherry, and that's the sad truth.

Of course, my resolve doesn't last longer than a couple of days—or nights, I should say. Jesse is doing so much better. Not that he's on the wagon yet, but he's gotten off his drunken rump and made a few steps in the right direction. First, he got the electricity turned on. Then, at my urging, he called a cleaning service to have a go at the pigpen he was living in. I made him call his manager in Nashville and tell him he was in Mobile so the manager wouldn't have the police out looking for him. The next day, Jesse took a wad of bills out of his wallet and asked me if I'd stock his fridge, getting enough for myself. Since I've finished off the leftovers from the SSG gathering and don't have anything in the cupboards till payday, I gratefully oblige. I refuse to bring him more booze, though, but damned if he doesn't call the store and have it delivered. He's still drinking and smoking too much, and he's as messed up as when I stumbled on him a few days ago, but things are much, much better. At least he's not passed out drunk all day.

Because I like to eat so much, I'm a real good cook. That always surprises people, which in turn surprises me. Don't know what folks expect—me, I'd figure anyone with an ass like mine would have to be a good cook. Getting the groceries inspires me, so I decide to bake one of my pound cakes, Grandma Brewer's famous recipe that won blue ribbons at the county fair, and send it to

Paul and the kids. I have them on my mind today more than usual. I guess because I tried to call Paul again last night, not just to hear his voice but for a legitimate reason, to ask him if he knew what could be wrong with Corrine. I've called her every day since the SSG gathering, and she swears she's better, but doesn't sound like it to me. Julia and Byrd both called, asking if there was anything the SSGs could do. Only thing I came up with—I called Culley at Corrine's gallery and gave him my number. He promised he'd call me if he got worried about his mama. When I make the cake, I mix up a double batch so I can send one to Paul and the kids, and one to Corrine and Culley.

Over at the Pickett house last night, Jesse got to talking about crabbing and how much he loved it as a boy. Slyly, I said I'd bring him some chicken necks if he wanted to crab again. I figured he'd resist, but surprisingly, he said he was going crabbing today and that he'd fix us steamed crabs for supper. I pretended nonchalance, saying casually it'd be nice not to have to cook when I got home from the hospital, because I didn't want him to see how pleased I was, how good I thought it'd be for him to get out of the house and do something—anything! Especially crabbing, because you can't be too drunk when you do it, or you'll fall in and drown your fool self. I work till six o'clock, but soon as I get out of my uniform, I throw together another recipe of Grandma Brewer's pound cake. When I mailed the packages to Paul and Corrine, the cakes smelled so good that my resolve not to eat any went straight to hell. Standing in the post office, I promised that as soon as I got home, I was making a cake for my *favorite* person, myself. Once the cake's done, I wrap it up in a dish towel, get the peaches and whipped cream I've fixed to go with it, and head next door.

"You got some crabs!" I squeal, peering into a pot on the stove. Jesse is standing at the stove with a cigarette and a glass of Jack Daniel's, but he puts the cigarette out in an empty beer bottle and gives me a hug. We've fallen into a comfortable companionship. Helps, I guess, that we only have each other right now. On the counter is a Corona beer with a half-lime beside it, so I take the lime and suck on it, then turn up the beer bottle and drink thirstily. "God, that's good," I say, wiping my mouth, and Jesse grunts and rolls his eyes. I can't get over how much better he's doing! Not only has he cleaned up, dressed in fresh jeans and shirt; he's shaved and has on Bay Rum, which smells so good I could lick his face.

"Thought I'd lost my touch," Jesse says, motioning to the bucket full of blue crabs swimming around innocently, unsuspecting of their fate. "But once I got on the dock, it came back to me, and I found the exact spot where me and Daddy used to drop the crab traps."

"You and your daddy ever make up?" I ask, leaning against the counter and sucking on the lime, washing it down with beer. Jesse's daddy had said he'd never forgive him for going off like he did, worrying the family sick.

Jess nods. "You know that song I wrote about him?"

"'My Daddy Hung the Moon.'" I smile, nodding.

"Few years ago, I sent it to Daddy and begged Mama to make him listen to it." He stops and lights another cigarette, although I cough and frantically wave the smoke away. "Quit that, Lanier. You got a better chance of getting hit by a Mack truck than dying of secondhand smoke."

"Oh, bull. And why does it have to be a Mack truck? Doesn't anyone ever get hit by another kind?"

Ignoring me, Jesse takes a drag of his cigarette and continues. "Mama said Daddy cried when he listened to the song. She got me on the phone, and both of us bawled. I was down here the very next day, and we got along great till he died. Which was a year later, to the day."

"Great story. And such a great song, Jess. I was real close to my daddy, so I can't listen to it without crying, either. Want me to make the cocktail sauce for the crabs?"

"Nope. Mine's better than yours." He takes a pair of tongs, fishes a couple of crabs out of the boiling water, then drops in a couple more.

"Is not."

"Is too."

"Bet you anything."

"Oh, yeah? When you were a little girl, you pestered me to death, always betting me a yankee dime, trying to trick me into kissing you. Remember?"

"I remember betting you I could beat you swimming from your pier to ours. And I won."

"You were such a feisty little thing then," Jess grins. "When I lost the race and tried to give you a peck on the cheek, you grabbed me and planted one on. I hauled ass, scared to death Judge Brewer saw you."

I laugh, remembering. "I'll bet more than a yankee dime on my cocktail sauce. How you make yours?"

"Catsup, horseradish, and a slug of Worcestershire sauce. Ain't no contest," Jesse says, pouring himself another glass of Jack Daniel's, straight up.

"Tell you what. If mine's better, you've got to dump out that rotgut whiskey and have a glass of wine with me. If you've gotta drink, red wine's better for you. If your sauce is better, you and me both will have the Jack."

He raises his glass in a salute. "You're on, kid."

Going to the fridge, I pull out the ingredients and mix equal parts of catsup and horseradish, then squeeze half a lemon into it. I poke my finger in a couple of times, tasting it until it's exactly right. Plopping the bowl on the counter in front of Jesse I say, "Prepare to face defeat and humiliation."

I forget the bet because of what Jesse does next. Taking my hand, he dips my finger in the bowl of cocktail sauce. Then, his eyes holding mine, he brings my finger to his mouth and sucks the sauce off, real slow-like. "Oh, yeah," he moans, sucking and slurping. "Ummm . . . you're right, baby. You win." Releasing my hand, he dumps his glass of bourbon into the sink. Weak-kneed, I lean against the counter, my eyes wide. And that's when my resolve goes right out the window, because all I can think about is how long it's been since I've had me a good old hot-fudge sundae.

I have to give myself a good shake to get my mind off sundaes and on supper instead, so I turn away quickly, studying a healthy-looking salad Jess made with the fresh tomatoes I brought. I'm plundering through the kitchen drawers, looking for picks and pliers for the crabs, when Jesse totes the salad over to the table and spots the basket I'd put there. "Hey, Little Red Riding Hood— what's in your basket?"

"A bottle of Cabernet Sauvignon, peaches that I chopped up and sugared, a jar of whipped cream, and my Grandma Brewer's blue ribbon– winning pound cake."

Jesse's eyebrows rise in surprise. "Your Grandma Brewer's still alive? Damn, she must be a hundred and fifty years old."

I laugh, pulling a corkscrew out of a drawer and tossing it to him. "She's been dead for years, you idiot. I'm the one who made the cake, from her recipe. And I won't even bet you on it because you'd lose. It's the best cake ever."

Jesse leans close to the basket, closes his eyes, and inhales the fragrance of hot pound cake spiced with mace, Grandma's secret ingredient. "Jesus, it's still hot! You just bake it?"

"Sure did." I pull up a stool to reach the wineglasses on the top shelf, which are grimy from years of not being used. "Okay, my good man," I say, after washing and drying the fragile glasses, "got our glasses clean. Now. Crabs are ready, and the salad . . ."

I stop in midsentence when I turn around and see what Jess has done at the table. Green eyes sparkling, he crooks a finger at me. "Come here, baby. I fixed our first course," he says.

"Oh, Jesse, no," I gasp. "Oh, *no*."

"Come here," he repeats. Putting a hand to my mouth, I shake my head woefully.

"Please don't do this, Jess," I groan. "Oh, please . . ."

When I don't move, Jesse saunters over, taking my hand and leading me to the table. When he pulls out a chair with a mocking bow, I refuse to sit until he pushes me down, hands firm on my shoulders.

"You know you want it as bad as I do," he whispers, his lips touching my ear, his breath hot and moist.

"You are truly evil, Jesse Pickett," I sigh, "and I hate you for this."

Laughing, Jesse gets the glasses and pours the wine. Sitting so close his knees touch mine, he raises his glass to me. "Life is too short not to do this first," he says.

On each of our dinner plates is a humongous hunk of warm pound cake floating in juicy, sugared peaches and piled high with whipped cream. Nothing to do but pick up my spoon and dig in, which I do, cussing Jesse with every sinful, calorie-laden bite.

After supper—we eat a couple of crabs and a little bite of salad once we finish our first-course dessert—Jesse and I clean up the kitchen, then sit and talk till ten o'clock. I'm afraid to leave because he's doing so much better, and I figure he'll sink back into his black despair when I do. He's animated now, relaxing and laughing. He also nurses a big glass of whiskey, which I keep an eye on, noticing that as long as we're talking, me questioning, him telling stories, he only sips it. I try to talk him into getting his guitar out of the backseat of his car—where he said it's been for weeks—saying that the least he can do to show his gratitude for the pound cake is to sing me one little bitty song. He shakes his head and says, "I told you, honey. I can't. I've lost it."

"You told me you couldn't write songs anymore; you didn't say you couldn't sing them."

I feel Jesse watching me in the darkness of the porch, where we're sitting on the swing. I've always loved his eyes, big and round and green as a Coca-Cola bottle, when he's not drunk and bleary-eyed, that is. "Can't sing either," he says, yawning and stretching. "Come on, baby. Let's go to bed."

"I've told you, Jess—I'm not going to bed with you." I look out at the stars shining over the black bay to avoid looking into those bedroom eyes of his and thinking about hot-fudge sundaes.

"And I've told you that's another thing I can't do. But I love it when you lie down with me till I go to sleep. Wish you'd stay all night, though; I don't like you being over there by yourself."

When I don't say anything, Jess takes my hand. "You're not working tomorrow, are you?"

I shake my head and give the swing a little kick. "I'll lie down till you go to sleep, but I'm not staying here all night."

"How come? I don't like you walking to your house so late. A booger's liable to get you."

"I'm not scared of boogers." Truth is, boogers don't scare me near as bad as staying all night with him.

"Then go on home now. I don't want you going later by yourself, and I mean it."

I narrow my eyes and look at him. He'll be sawing logs and won't know if or when I go home, so I pretend to give in. "Oh, all right, I'll stay."

Jesse stands up and pulls me to my feet with a twinkle in his eye. "Aha! I knew I'd get in your britches eventually."

"*Jesse!* You liar, you said—"

Grinning, he gives me a hug. "I'm teasing you, hon. Come on, Scheherazade—it's your turn."

"Who?" I ask, following behind him as he leads me by the hand to his bedroom. Glancing back, I see that he's left the whiskey.

"You know, that chick in *The Arabian Nights* who saved her life by telling stories to the king or sheik or whatever the hell he was." We get into our usual positions on the bed, Jesse propped up on a stack of pillows, me nestled in the crook of his arm. The lights are out but the windows are open, the room lit by moonlight. Once we're settled in, Jesse mutters, "Damn, forgot my glass," but doesn't go for it, and he knows better than to ask me to. He has a pack of cigarettes on the bedside table, though, and again, I go through my routine of coughing and carrying on when he lights up.

"You've gotten off the hook long enough," he says, oblivious of me dying of second-hand smoke. "I've told you all about my shitty life, but you've told me nothing about yours."

"Nothing to tell," I say, closing my eyes. Jesse's having none of it, though, and he shakes me until I open my eyes and look up at him sheepishly.

"Why are you here, Lanier? Where is that nice husband and those babies of yours?"

After a long silence, I say, "It didn't work out, Jess."

His eyes are fastened on me in the darkness. "What you mean, didn't work out? What'd you do to screw it up?"

"I can't talk about it." I turn my head away, but he puts his hand on my chin and makes me face him.

"Lanier? What did you do?" he repeats sternly.

"Shut up, Jesse. You're not my daddy."

"Where are your babies?"

I can't help it; before I can stop myself, I'm crying my eyes out. I put my face in my hands and pull away when Jesse tries to hold me. "Come on, honey," he whispers. "You've helped me so much. Let old Jess help you now, hear?"

"You can't," I say in a choked voice, my shoulders shaking. Jesse reaches to the bedside table and hands me a wad of tissues. "Nobody can."

"I said the same thing to you, remember, just a few days ago," he reminds me. "And look how much better I am, just having you to talk to. Tell old papa Jess what happened."

I cry until I can't, then lay my head on his chest and snuffle, like I used to when I was a little girl. Finally I've worn myself out, and I wipe my eyes with the damp wad of tissues. "You'll hate me," I mutter in a hoarse voice.

"I could never hate you, honey. I ain't fit to judge anyone, believe me."

"You promise?"

"Cross my heart and hope to die, stick my butt in a pie." What I used to say to him when I was ten, so I smile as I wipe my eyes and blow my nose. Jesse smokes his cigarette and waits, with me huddled next to him, sniffling away. Finally I say, "All right. But don't say I didn't warn you. It's not a pretty story."

"Know what?" Jess's voice floats in the night like the smoke from his cigarette. "Most of our stories aren't, and that's what all my songs are about, I think."

So reluctantly, miserably, I tell Jesse the whole sordid story of how I lost Paul and my children, with Jesse interrupting every now and then to clarify parts of it he doesn't understand. I start out by telling him about how I had impulsively gotten married right out of college, to an Auburn baseball player I'd only dated a few months (a hot-fudge sundae if I've ever seen one), and how that turned out to be a big mistake. After only a few weeks of marriage, I left my poor husband to go to UAB to medical school, where I promptly fell in love with Paul Sanders, the TA in my Human Anatomy course. (Imagine the teasing I took for that one!)

"Paul wasn't a sexy stud like the husband

I'd dumped, Jesse. He was a big old teddy bear instead." I fall silent, remembering that first day of lab when Paul introduced himself to the class of mouthy med students, most of whom wouldn't make it through the first year. The student next to me smirked, "Paul Bunyan, right?" Big and bearded, Paul looked more like a lumberjack than a doctor, but all of us came to adore him, he was so patient and gentle with everyone, including the smart-asses. I wasn't the only female student in class; neither was I the only one to fall for Paul Sanders.

"But he must've had something you liked," Jesse remarks, cutting his eyes to me slyly.

"Hey—I just realized Paul reminded me of *you*," I say in surprise, and Jesse snorts.

"The unsexy part, I reckon? Don't worry about my feelings."

I try to explain that I fell in love with Paul Sanders not just because he was nice and sweet-natured, but also because he was so mature and solid and different from the wild boys I'd always been attracted to. I go on to tell Jesse how Paul came from Reform, Alabama ("You're shitting me, right?" Jess laughs, but I poke him in the ribs to shut him up), and was becoming a doctor so he could go back and open up a clinic for all the poor people in Pickens County who couldn't afford medical care.

"What is he, Mother Teresa or something?" Jess teases, and I smile through my tears.

"My girlfriends call him Saint Paul. Funny thing, Jess, I didn't even go after him. I swear it! I never imagined a man as good as Paul would fall in love with me."

"Proof that opposites attract," Jesse says dryly.

"Ha ha. But, there's some truth to that. Paul was so serious and earnest, and I made him laugh. I think that's what he liked best about me. I almost lost him when I goofed around too much and flunked out of medical school, though. He was so furious that he broke up with me. Said I'd blown an opportunity not many women have—which was true in the mid-seventies—and I should be ashamed of myself."

"Can't blame him, baby. You used to always tell me you were going to be a doctor when you grew up," Jess says, and I nod sadly. "So, how'd you get him back?"

Clearing my throat and wiping my eyes, I go on to explain how I redeemed myself by not only becoming an RN but also specializing in public health so I could help Paul run his clinic, if he'd just take me back. Being so saintly and forgiving, of course he did. We got married and opened up the clinic, and we ran it together all those years. I smile, telling Jess how everybody in Pickens County thought we were the perfect, all-American family with our two perfect kids, Christopher the wholesome jock, and Lindy the serious honor student. "And we were!" I insist, my voice breaking. "I was so happy, Jesse. Bet you can't imagine me living in a podunky little town like Reform—the locals pronounce it Ree-form—and being so content, but I *was,* I swear. I loved Paul more than I ever loved anyone, even you. And I believed in the work we were doing there, me and him. I really did."

"Old Dr. Paul seemed like a great guy when you brought him backstage that time," Jess says, lighting another cigarette. "Everybody liked him."

"My girlfriends say he's the perfect man."

"Uh-oh. I smell trouble."

"No, the trouble was with me. Paul is as perfect as any of you men can be."

Jesse snorts. "How come you dumped

him then? You women whine about wanting a man like that, and what'd you do when you find one? You lose him."

"*He* dumped me," I protest, but Jesse's having none of it.

"Let me put it another way, then . . . what did you do to cause him to dump you? Screw his best friend?"

"He wasn't his best friend!" I say indignantly, and Jess gasps.

"You didn't . . ." When I try to cover my eyes with my hands, Jess pulls them away. "Look at me, Lanier, goddammit. Don't tell me you screwed around on a nice guy like him!"

"Just that one time," I mutter.

Jesse hits his forehead with his hand, groaning. "Oh, Jesus! I ain't believing this."

"You promised you wouldn't judge me," I protest, and he groans again.

"Okay, okay, it's hard as hell, but I'm trying. Tell me how it happened. But I don't want the salacious details—"

"The *what*?" I interrupt, and he puts a hand over my mouth.

"I don't want to hear about what a good lay this guy was."

"He wasn't," I cry, moving his hand from

my mouth, but he puts it right back, shutting me up.

"I don't want to hear that either. Just tell me how come you did it."

"Then keep your hand off my mouth! How do you expect me to talk if you . . ." His look stops me, and I hang my head. "Okay, okay. I'll tell you."

And I do, turning from him so he can't see my shame glowing like a neon sign in the dark bedroom. Because of me teaching public health classes at the clinic, I begin, I have to do a certain number of continuing-ed units every year. So last spring I went to Birmingham to attend a seminar given by a big-shot doctor, a guy Paul had gone to medical school with.

"I'm only telling you this next part to help explain how it happened," I say in a choked voice. "Don't think I'm making excuses, okay? But it'd gotten so that all me and Paul did was work at the clinic, which was almost too much for the two of us to handle. We hardly ever saw each other except there, and we never had meals together anymore, since somebody was always calling Paul with emergencies. The kids were gone half the time, busy with their lives, too. Instead of that making me and Paul closer, it made us work harder, without the kids home to worry about. We didn't go out to dinner or the movies or on vacation or anything. We were just too blame worn out. Eventually we got to where we didn't even . . ."

"Get it on," Jesse supplies, nodding thoughtfully. "That's how come my wife ran off with the drummer in my band, too. If a man's too tired to do it, women tend to take it personally."

"Well, I was too tired, too. Like I say, Paul's not to blame for any of this, and I don't blame Astor, either. It was nobody's fault but mine."

"Astor? That the guy you fooled around with?"

"No, Astor's my girlfriend I stayed with when I went to the seminar in Birmingham. The man's name was Roland Pierce." I can't even say his name without cringing.

"Why would you blame your girlfriend?"

"I don't, I said! I'm trying to tell you everything that happened if you'll shut up. Because Dr. Pierce was a friend of Paul's—not to mention a big shot in Birmingham society—my friend Astor *insisted* I invite him to dinner at her place. I agreed, not really thinking anything about it. Then, at dinner,

I thought Astor was trying to get him, but she's such a flirt, it's hard to tell. What surprised me and Astor both was, for some reason, Dr. Pierce seemed to prefer me over her. Astor's a knockout, so it must've been because I was unavailable and he wanted a challenge or something. I still can't figure it out."

"You don't realize how cute you are," Jesse says solemnly. "I can see how this guy would flip out over you, myself."

I try not to, but I can't help it; I blush, pleased. "Aw, Jess, that's so sweet. But to get back to my story. When Dr. Pierce asked me if I wanted to go to dinner the next night, I told him I couldn't. But Astor wouldn't hear of me turning down a big shot like him, so she called and told him I'd go." I stop and put a hand over my eyes.

"Let me guess. You ended up having more than dinner, right?"

"Oh, God, Jess! I was such a fool. If I hadn't gotten so drunk at dinner I'd never have agreed to go to his apartment afterward. One thing led to the other, and before I knew it . . . well, me and him ended up in bed. I guess I was . . . you know . . . flattered that someone like Roland Pierce would want me when he could have Astor or any other woman, I reckon. I'd never cheated on Paul before, never wanted to, but . . ." I sigh, long and loud, shaking my head. "I still can't believe it happened! I hightailed it home the very next morning, skipping out on the rest of the seminar. But as soon as Paul saw my face, he knew."

Jesse rubs his face wearily, a cigarette between his fingers. "Couldn't forgive you, could he?"

"It's more complicated than that. Paul's a forgiving man, but . . . you know I told you about him being my TA in medical school?"

He nods, his eyes narrowed suspiciously, but I force myself to tell him everything. "Well, Paul tutored me after classes, Jess, and we spent a lot of time together before it occurred to me that he liked me. I told you that I couldn't believe it! When we started seeing each other, I was so afraid of losing him that I . . . ah . . . kind of . . . *forgot* to tell him that I was married. I almost lost him then, and he wouldn't see me again till my divorce went through. Because he's such a Goody Two-shoes, he's real—what do you call it?—mortalistic?"

"Moralistic?"

"Yeah, that, too. He said he'd never have asked me out if he'd known I was married, that marriage was real sacred to him. Said if his wife ever cheated on him, that'd be it."

"Turned out he wasn't bullshitting, huh?"

I nod, brushing away the tears that roll down my cheeks. "Paul didn't like it that I'd run around with so many guys all my life, especially after I told him how I was a love junkie and never been faithful to anyone. So he made me promise before we married that I'd change. Said if I wasn't going to be faithful to him, he wasn't about to marry me. Of course I swore on a stack of Bibles and my mother's grave—even though she wasn't dead—that I would and even told him that if I ever cheated on him, he should drop-kick me out of his life. Paul may be almost perfect, Jess, but he's still a man, and he was beyond furious when he found out I'd been unfaithful. He told me to get the hell out of his life, that he couldn't be married to somebody he couldn't trust."

"He's got a point," Jesse murmurs.

"Yeah, I know. It shames me to admit that I gave up meat and potatoes for a cream puff." I sigh, long and loud, then move my head from the crook of Jess's arm to look up at him, kind of scared. "Jesse?"

"Yeah?"

"Now you see why I didn't want to tell you, don't you?" I hold my breath, hoping he says, "Don't worry, I told you I wouldn't judge you."

"You didn't tell me what happened to your babies, but I guess I can figure that out."

"I guess you can. They're not babies anymore, though. My boy's going to college next year, and my girl, Lindy, will be a senior in high school."

"I haven't seen them over at your place this summer," Jess remarks.

"They're pretty mad at me. Christopher talks to me, but Lindy . . . well, that's another story. She's her daddy's little girl, and she can't forgive me for hurting him."

Jess doesn't say anything for a long time, then he leans over me to put out his cigarette. "You still seeing that guy?"

"Roland Pierce? God, no." I close my eyes, tired now. So tired. "He's called me—I guess Astor gave him my number—but I won't talk to him. I never want to see him again."

"At least you got sense enough to leave him alone if you want your husband back."

"Would you take me back, if you were Paul?" I dare ask him, not sure I want to hear his answer.

Jesse chuckles. "Hell, no. I'd beat your ass if I were your old man and you cheated on me."

"You would not!"

"Would, too. But you got such a cute little ass I couldn't stay mad for long. And I'm betting Doctor Paul can't, either."

"You think?"

"Yeah. But he'd better hurry up and decide, though."

I snuggle back into my cozy spot under his arm. I've worn myself out with crying and telling my story, and now all I want to do is sleep. Guess I'll stay over tonight after all. Before falling off to sleep, it hits me what Jesse just said, and I ask him, "How come?"

Jesse doesn't say anything, his eyes closed, too, almost asleep. I poke him in the ribs with my elbow. "Jess? How come?"

He mumbles sleepily, "Because I might get too used to having you around, that's why. Might not let you go back to him. Now shut up and go to sleep."

Which I promptly do. But all night, I'm tormented with dreams about eating hot-fudge sundaes.

17

Corrine

BLUE MOUNTAIN

I NEED TO CALL the new gourd something, now that the design has taken shape. I'm beginning to think I'm not going to be able to part with it. Maybe that's why I'm taking so much time working on it; ordinarily, I'd have been through a week or so ago. But the design I settled on is so intricate that the carving of it is painstaking work, and I have to stop fairly often to rub my eyes and refocus. This gourd is not like anything I've ever done.

In the beginning stages of designing it, I got down my old textbooks from the Native American art course and studied the icons until something spoke to me, the way I've done in the past. I get a lot of inspiration from beadwork, especially Cherokee, which is really neat. Sometimes it's the colors and patterns of the beadwork itself that inspire me; on other occasions, inlaid beadwork becomes part of what I put on a gourd. Pottery patterns influence me in much the same way, as do the sacred motifs once used in rituals and ceremonies: wolves, bears, deer, and eagles. Although I do a lot of birds, I don't do animals except in an abstract way. All Native American history fascinates me, but I focus my artwork on the tribes of the Southeast: the Cherokee, Creek, Seminole, and Choctaw. My most successful piece, a large basket gourd a Georgia state senator bought after a showing in Atlanta, I did to commemorate the Trail of Tears. It appears to be an abstract design until you get right up to it, then you see it's actually tiny figures of the sick and dying Cherokees. The figures march around and around the gourd, in an endless trail, decreasing in number as the circle moves on. The senator, a woman whose name I've forgotten now, later wrote me a note, saying that everyone who saw the piece was moved to tears. It blew me away that others were affected in the same way I'd been when working on it. Many days I had to put it aside because the scenes tore me up.

This kettle gourd that I'm working on now is having a similar effect on me, but I don't know why. The Trail of Tears gourd featured an actual scene, which tends to have a greater emotional impact than a symbolic or abstract one. For some reason the design I sketch on the skin of the kettle gourd turns out to be made up mostly of circles, as though radiating from a sun, or the concentric waves created by a pebble thrown into water. Most of them are perfectly round, but I also found myself making some of the circles oblong, almost the shape of an ear of corn. As I worked on it, the image began to develop dimensions, sort of like the chambers of a seashell. The whole time I was sketching, I wasn't sure where I was going with it. The pattern was suggested to me after studying the photograph of a weird image in my textbook of Native American art. Outlined with crushed shells, limestone, and feathers, it's an elaborate concentric design etched in sand.

Even though I've been drawn to the

design from the time I ran across it, twenty-something years ago, I've never done anything with it. I knew I'd use it when the time was right, and only then. When I first saw it, I'd taken the book to my professor after class and asked about it. She'd said it appeared to be some sort of healing circle like the Navajos drew in the sand, but she had no idea what tribal iconography it belonged to. Although my professor didn't find it interesting, it drew me back, again and again. This is the first time that I've felt the gourd and the design idea were right for each other. When I finished the sketch, I knew I was right, especially when I sketched the top. For some reason, a spiral of vines, branching out from the circular pattern and intertwining over the top rim of the gourd, seemed right, and my pencil moved as fast as the pointer on a Ouija board. A few days later, when I finished sketching and picked up my wood-burning tool to make the design permanent, I understood why the spiraled vines had to be a part of it. I don't know what they mean, but I know it's right.

After spending several days sketching it, I spend even more engraving it. I work day after day, hunched over my work table, squinting and frowning, but it pays off, and I finally get it ready for painting. I've worked on it so much that I have a headache when I stop, late that afternoon. Exhausted, I rub my eyes, then get to my feet. My legs are all cramped up, and I'm feeling pukey again. The nausea has gotten to be a second skin, an unwelcome one that I wish I could shed. I wake up with it, work with it lurking around all day, and take it to bed at night. Nightfall is still the worst, which makes me dread it all day. Taking off my leather gloves, I put away my wood-burning tools. The kettle gourd— still unnamed—is sitting on its bed of nails in the center of my work table, so I pick it up and take it with me to the windows. In order to have the correct light in my workroom, I saved up money until I had enough to add skylights and a bank of windows. My workroom, originally a storage room, a lean-to attached to the back of Miss Fielding's cabin, has always been rather dark.

I hold the kettle gourd up to the windows, moving it to catch the light, studying the odd design etched in its skin. It's such a special piece, worth every long—often painful— minute I spent bent over it. What can I call it?

"Okay, baby," I say, holding the big gourd

close to my cheek. "I need you to speak to me. You don't want me calling you 'kettle' all your life, because you're not just another kettle. You're too special for that." Putting my nose in the top, I inhale the fecund, earthy smell of the gourd, a fragrance I love as much as the perfume of the finest flower. "You're going to stay with me, I think. How will I be able to part with you?"

A sound startles me and I almost drop the gourd as I whirl around. Culley is standing in the door frame, wide-eyed. The late-afternoon sun behind him outlines his form, and for a moment, he looks like Miles standing there.

"My God, Mom. What are you doing?" Culley's voice is sharp, accusatory. He's obviously just come from the gallery, dressed for work in his usual jeans, a faded Brevard T-shirt, and Birkenstock sandals, with his hair tied back, sunglasses on top of his head.

My face burns, and I feel like I used to when Culley was a kid and found me in bed, staring like a zombie or convulsed with tears. It scared him to see me like that, and I knew it did, which killed me. I'd get up and comb my hair and wash my face, trying to pull myself together. With a storybook or puzzle or art supplies in hand, I'd go to his room, where I'd try to get him to sit with me, to read or draw or put a puzzle together. Sometimes it worked; more often, he turned his back to me, his little shoulders hunched over as he huddled in a corner.

"Culley—I didn't hear you come up . . ." I say, foolishly.

"What were you doing?" he repeats, his eyes narrowing suspiciously.

Please don't look at me like that, I want to say. *Please, baby . . . don't look at Mommy like that.* Instead, I say, "I—ah—wasn't, you know, doing anything . . ." *Except talking to this gourd.*

Culley puts his hands on his hips, but he doesn't move from the door frame. "Are you sick again, Mom?"

I'm sick every day, I start to tell him; instead, I shake my head. "No. I'm . . . I'm fine."

"I don't mean pukey sick," he says. "I mean, crazy sick?" He's looking at me with so much disgust that I want to grab him by the shoulders and shake him. I want to yell at him, "Crazy is sick, too, son! I cannot help being crazy any more than I can help throwing up." When I don't answer, Culley sighs, rolling his eyes to the ceiling.

"I thought you were okay now, Mom. Or at least, I thought you were better. I should have known. Dad said—"

"What? What did your daddy say?" I demand, putting the kettle gourd down and taking a step toward Culley.

"Just that you've been acting weird lately. He says—"

"Oh, really? That's what he said, huh?" I don't intend to raise my voice but can't seem to stop myself.

Culley glares at me. "I'm not allowed to interrupt you, but it's okay if you interrupt me? Do you want to hear what Dad said or not?"

"No. I've changed my mind," I snap. After I fought Miles off that night, he'd returned for his nightly visit but not stayed long. Last night he didn't come at all, and as I expected, he told Culley I was going crazy again. Culley raises his hands upward in a gesture of resignation.

"Jesus Christ, Mom! Make up your mind. That is, if you've got a mind left to make up."

That makes me so furious that I grab

Culley's arm, like I used to when he was a little boy and I needed to get his attention. "You listen here, young man," I say, giving him a shake. "I'm your mother, and you are not going to speak to me like that. Do you hear me?"

Culley backs away from me, as though I'm a slobbering idiot. I release his arm and step back, glaring at him. "You need to chill," he says, sighing mightily. "You're wigging out over nothing."

"Nothing? It's nothing when my son treats me like I'm a pathetic basket case?"

Culley's face is red and twisted. "If you don't want me to treat you like a frigging idiot, then don't act like one, for a change. All my life you've been insane, and just when I think you're getting better, I come out here and catch you talking to your gourds. Your stupid, fucking gourds! Tell me that's not crazy, Mom. Tell me that's not plain old loony-tunes crazy."

I try for humor, which usually works with Culley. "I'm out of my gourd, huh?"

His disdainful expression doesn't change. "When I was ten, I thought that was funny. Now I find it pathetic."

"Oh, for God's sake, Culley! Didn't you

have any psychology classes at that snotty, thirty-thousand-dollars-a-year college we sent you to?"

Culley's blue-green eyes blaze. "Yeah, Mom, I had plenty of psychology classes—I even took an elective in Abnormal Psychology. Know why? To try and understand my crazy mother, is why."

"*Abnormal* Psychology?" I'm so furious now that tears sting my eyes, and I blink them away. "There's nothing abnormal about depression."

"Depression, my ass," Culley snorts. "I've been depressed, Mom, plenty of times. But I've never been locked up like you have. You've spent half your life in a psych ward, and you're trying to tell me that you're just depressed? What a crock!"

"You stop that kind of talk right now, young man! I can't stand it. It kills me that you have no compassion—"

Culley's face twists into a sneer. "Oh, I have no compassion?" He crosses his arms and stares down at me, his eyes cold, and he looks so much like his dad that it scares me. "Maybe you're right about that. Maybe what little compassion I had for you dried up a long time ago, when I was a little kid and needed a mother. I couldn't even bring friends home, because I never knew what condition you'd be in. Maybe all my compassion went to Dad instead, having to put up with you."

"You have absolutely no idea what you're talking about," I begin, but stop myself. No, of course he doesn't. How could he? And who have I been protecting, by not telling him? I rub my face, suddenly too exhausted and too sick to go on. "Culley, we need to talk . . ."

Culley shakes his head, his face tight, closed against me. "You know what, Mom? You're about twenty years too late to start talking to me now." Turning around, he goes out the door and slams it shut.

I stand shaking from head to toe, unable to open the door and call out to Culley, to beg him to return and listen to me. Just listen to me! I stumble blindly to a stool near the door and sink down on it. My knees won't hold me up any longer. I put my face in my hands, but I'm too dazed to cry. This is why I've been tiptoeing around Culley, walking on eggshells, every summer that he's been home from school. I've known instinctively that he was full of resentment, an old cauldron that filled up in his childhood, just waiting to erupt and spill its poisons out. I've known it, yet I've not dealt with it, not faced it. Now, what scares me most has happened. My son has left me again.

Of course, I call Lanier. If anyone would understand the pain of losing the love and respect of a child, it would be Lanier. She talks big, pretends to be tough and sassy, but I see that for what it is: an attempt to hide the shame and heartache over what she's done to Lindy and Christopher. But Lanier doesn't answer her phone. She's probably still working at the hospital. Hanging up, I wonder if she'll go next door to see Jesse Phoenix when she gets home. Lanier, self-destructing yet again, attracted to someone who's as fucked-up as she is. Last time we talked, she'd gotten back from having dinner with Jesse, and she read to me from her lesson book. Lanier can always make me laugh, no matter what kind of mess either of us is in. In the lesson book, she'd written: "Growing up, whenever I wanted something so bad I couldn't stand it, Mama would say: 'Honey, make sure it's worth the heartache.'"

"You're applying that to you and Mr.

Phoenix, huh?" I'd snorted. "Asking yourself if he's worth the heartache?"

Lanier had giggled. "Oh, I don't think I even need to ask."

"Lanier," I'd sighed wearily, "are you still getting in trouble?"

"Does Pinocchio have a wooden dick?" she'd responded. Although I tried to keep a straight face, we ended up laughing together, like we always do.

When I can't reach Lanier, I try to call Julia. Funny, how Julia and I have gotten closer lately. I've always loved Julia but felt like our backgrounds were so different that we could never connect in the same way that Lanier and I do. However, since I've been on my own the last few years, Julia has gone out of her way to stay in touch. Julia's assistant answers, which surprises me, since I dialed the private number and didn't expect anyone to be working on a Sunday afternoon. "Julia's not in?" I ask, after identifying myself.

Julia's assistant, young and efficient and brisk, sounds harried and overworked. "Julia's out of town, Miss Cooper, but I'll leave a message that you called."

Oh, what a shock that she's not in, I

almost say. Julia stays out of town half the time, going to all sorts of meetings with Joe Ed, playing the role of the perfect politician's wife. It gives me a perverse pleasure to say to the snooty assistant, "That's okay. I have her cell phone number." I call but don't leave a message after all, suddenly ashamed that I've bothered Julia, as hectic as her life is.

Lying down on the bed in my room, I put a wet cloth over my eyes, hoping the nausea will pass before I lose what little I've eaten today. It's funny that I called Lanier and Julia but don't even consider calling the others. Maybe I should, though, to get the full range of reactions to my fight with Culley. From Lanier there's humor, which always lightens the mood, no matter how gloomy things might be. Julia provides the soft touch, the compassionate shoulder to cry on, the murmuring words of sympathy. And Byrd—sometimes Mama Byrd, with her disapproval and little lectures, is exactly who I need to talk to. Rosanelle furnishes the rose-colored glasses, which is great when paddling down the river denial. Even Astor, with her sly put-downs and innuendos, can provide the right perspective on some occasions. Being with Astor helps me see the dark side of things, if nothing else.

Yesterday, she had surprised me by calling me, supposedly to see how I was feeling, if I'd heard anything from the tests the doctor ran. As usual, our conversation was disconcerting. After we'd talked a moment, I found out the real reason she'd called. "I think you should know, Corrine, that I had the *strangest* phone call last night," she'd declared breathlessly, the drama queen in full swing.

Nothing to do but ask who called her, though I didn't really care. Astor couldn't wait to tell me. "Imagine my surprise," she'd cooed, "when I answered the phone and found it was Miles! Why, I can't even remember the last time we talked."

"And what did your evil twin want?"

"To talk about you, of course. He wants you back, Corrine. I couldn't help but be touched by how much he loves you. I think he's really suffering over you."

"Music to my ears," I'd said. "I hope he suffers even more."

"He called to ask me if I'd talk to you, see if I could convince you to give him another chance," she'd said, as eager as a hound dog baying a rabbit.

"Isn't it funny that he called you, Astor, instead of Julia or Lanier?"

"Well . . ." Her voice took on that little-girl wheedling that has always grated on my nerves so bad. "He said that Julia and Lanier don't like him very much."

"That's not true," I'd told her, and she'd gurgled happily.

"Which is exactly what I told him!"

"Truth is, Julia and Lanier hate his guts. Listen, if Miles calls you again, would you give him a message for me? Here's what he needs to do to get me back: He needs to sit and hold his breath until hell freezes over. Will you give your dear friend Miles that message for me, Astor?" And I'd hung up.

Lying on my bed with the wet washcloth over my eyes, I hear the sound of a car approaching the house, coming down the long dirt driveway. Then the slam of a car door, and footsteps on the log steps leading to the porch. I hold my breath, knowing it's Miles stopping by for his evening visit. Surely he won't come upstairs when he doesn't find me waiting for him on the porch. Too sick to get up and ward him off, I lie still and start praying, hoping he'll go away. The last place I want him to find me is sprawled out help-less on the bed, too weak to fight him off. My heart goes to my throat when I hear his footsteps on the stairs leading to my bedroom upstairs. I cringe when I hear him call out, "Corrine? Corrine, are you here?"

No, I'm not, I want to answer, *Even though my car's parked in its usual place, that doesn't mean I'm home. On hearing that you were paying me another of your special little visits, I ran away. I disappeared. I died. I vanished into thin air.*

Then I hear it, the rap of his knuckles on my bedroom door, and I release my breath in a long, agonizing sigh. "Corrine? Corrine?"

The door squeaks open and his footsteps approach my bed. I don't move the cloth from my eyes as I say, weakly, "Miles, I'm sick. I don't feel like having company tonight, okay?"

Of course he's having none of that. "What's wrong with you?" His voice is sharp, without a shred of concern. He thinks I'm faking it, I realize, to avoid him. Maybe I should puke on his shoes to convince him that, although I'd do most anything not to see him, this is for real.

"Ah . . . touch of food poisoning, I guess."

"Bullshit." I hear a couple of creaks on the old pine floorboards, then the washcloth is jerked from my face. And there he is, bloodthirsty old Count Dracula, rubbing his hands in glee and staring down at my neck, fangs bared. "Jesus Christ!" Miles says between clenched teeth, and I'm shocked at the expression on his face.

"What?" I dare ask.

"Look at you, Corrine. You look dreadful."

"You're just saying that to make me feel better, aren't you?"

Grabbing my wrist, Miles checks my pulse, scowling. His aqua eyes are dark and troubled. "Your heartbeat's running away. Get up. I'm taking you to the emergency room."

My heartbeat and blood pressure sky-rocket when you're around, I want to say, but instead I tell him, as calmly as possible, "Oh, no, you're not. I'm not going. I've been through all that, and they didn't find anything, remember?"

Hands on hips, Miles glares down at me. "And you might remember I told you that doesn't mean a thing. Let's get you in, let them check you out. If you want me to, I'll call Dr. Brown, see if he can meet us there."

I have to think fast, knowing how forceful Miles can be. Without blinking, I tell him a bald-faced lie. "I—ah—have an appointment with Dr. Brown tomorrow. It can wait till then."

"First thing in the morning?"

I nod, praying he won't ask me what time, but it's worse. Instead, he thinks a minute, then says, "Good. I'll pick you up and take you. That way, I can talk to Dr. Brown myself. You've got to find out what's wrong, Corrine. This has been going on too long."

Now I have to think even faster. "I don't need you to go with me. A—friend is taking me."

Miles's eyebrow shoots up. "A friend? Who?"

"No one you know. Just . . . a friend." Please, dear God, don't let him ask me who. My only real friend here is Molly the herbalist, and Miles knows she doesn't go for conventional medicine, that I wouldn't ask her to take me to a doctor. I can't tell him that it's one of the SSGs, either, since no one lives that close. If they were going to take me, they'd have to be here now.

Miles's eyes narrow as he stares down at me. "A friend, huh? I can always tell when you're lying, Corrine."

"Why would I lie about that?" I dare to ask.

"I know why. You can't fool your husband."

"Ex-husband, Miles."

"You're seeing someone, aren't you?"

"No. I'm not seeing anyone. It's just . . . a new friend. Someone I met recently . . ."

But Miles is having none of it. "So that's why you turned me away the other night. You're seeing someone else. I hope he knows your history."

"Of mental illness?" I say, my blood pressure shooting up another hundred points. "I'm sure you'll be glad to fill him in, like you do Culley. I really appreciate your telling Culley that I'm acting weird again, Miles. That was decent of you, making your son think his mother's sick again. You never let me down, do you?"

"Culley's more aware than anyone of your mental illness, Corrine, since he's suffered through it his whole life." Before I can fire off a retort, Miles surprises me by raising his arm and looking at his watch. "Oh, God, I forgot the time," he says. "I didn't come for a visit tonight, actually; I was stopping by to see if you wanted to come with me to hear Culley perform at the coffeehouse in Elijah."

I stare up at him in surprise. "You're going to hear Culley play? It's not like you to go slumming." Miles disapproves of Culley's music so much that he wouldn't even attend his junior recital last spring. He'd even called Culley's major professor to express his disapproval over the school allowing Culley to perform rock music rather than classical and had been furious when the professor told him that the school's philosophy was to allow students to explore their own interests rather than be forced into a mold. Of course, it'd tickled me that Miles was unable to bully the professor into changing the whole philosophy of Brevard's music department just to suit him.

To my surprise, Miles's face softens. "He's gotten interested in bluegrass music, surprisingly, and has been playing it a lot recently. Really nice. I don't know what triggered his interest—"

"I do," I interrupt. "It was my suggestion."

Naturally, he pretends he doesn't hear that. "So, I'm anxious to hear him perform in this new venue publicly. I tried to call you earlier to see if you wanted to come with me, but the line was busy. Talking to your new friend, I suppose," Miles says, sneering when he says the word "friend."

"I don't feel up to going." I don't rise to the bait, react to his sneer. Neither do I tell him how much Culley had moved me earlier this week by asking me to come to the coffee-house Sunday evening to hear him play a "gig," as he'd called it, and I'd planned on going. But after our argument today, I'd been so upset I'd forgotten it was tonight.

"Culley said he'd left some music here that he needs for tonight," Miles says, glancing at his watch again, "and I told him I'd bring it. Do you know where it is?"

I shake my head, fighting off a fresh wave of nausea that shocks me with its ferocity. "He must be talking about that book I gave him on Bill Munroe. It might be on the coffee table."

Miles nods, then studies me again. "Well, your coloring is a little better now, but I'm still willing to take you to the hospital if you need to go."

"No point in that. I feel better now," I lie, hoping he doesn't notice the sweat that's popping out on my forehead. Suddenly, I feel fiery hot, as though my skin is on fire.

"Promise you'll call if you need me during the night?" If I didn't know better, I'd swear old Miles is genuinely concerned. His voice has softened, and he's looking down at me with a worried frown.

I figure if I promise, he'll leave, so I agree.

Sure enough, he starts toward the door, telling me that if he doesn't find the book, Culley will have to come over himself and look for it. At the door, he pauses and turns back to look at me. "I hope you don't think you're going to be able to see another man, Corrine," he says. "I told you the other night, you belong to me, and I'm going to get you back, one way or the other. I can promise you that."

And I can promise you that I'll die first, I long to say but don't dare prolong his stay by provoking him. I don't say anything but take the washcloth and place it over my eyes again, shutting out the sight of him standing there leering at me. I wait for the sound of the door closing as a wave of nausea sweeps over me again. As soon as I hear Miles's car leave, I'll make a dash for the bathroom, hoping I can hold off the sickness until then. Instead, I hear a creak of the floorboard, sense his presence standing over me, smell the fragrance of the shaving lotion that's distinctively Miles. Holding my breath, I feel his lips touch my cheek as his hand pushes the damp hair from my forehead. Just as quickly he's gone, and the bedroom door closes quietly behind him.

I wait until I hear the sound of his car on

the driveway before I remove the washcloth and push myself up on the pillows. It took a while before I heard the car, so I assume Miles was looking for the songbook. I wonder if he found it, but when I swing my legs over the side of the bed, all thoughts go flying out the window. I'm violently sick, barely able to make it to the bathroom. I've heard people joke about being "commode-hugging" drunk and realize this must be what they mean. If so, it's nothing to joke about. I throw up so many times that I'm not able to get up afterward, laying my head on the floor. The cool tile feels good to my hot face until I start having chills, then I force myself up, holding on to the commode. I'm able to pull myself upright by grasping the pipes of the basin, then the edge of the sink. By taking baby steps, holding on to first one thing and then another, I start edging out of the bathroom into my bedroom, longing for the warmth of my quilt. I'm so cold . . . so cold. If only I can get to the bed . . . .

The front door slams and I hear banging around downstairs. I've made it into the bedroom by propping myself up on the wall, creeping along, shivering so bad that my teeth chatter. For some reason I think of a story we had in freshman English, the one about the poor woman who goes crazy and tries to get into the wallpaper in her room, where her husband has locked her away. That's me, all right; the poor crazy woman in the yellow wallpaper, stark-raving mad and crawling around and around the room. If Culley could see me now . . . I realize it must be Culley downstairs, looking for his song-book, and I manage to make it to the bed-room door. Panting, shaking violently, I open the door and call down to him. At first my voice is so weak I can't make myself heard, but I take a deep breath and try again. "Culley?"

"I found the book," Culley yells up to me, and I lean against the door frame to keep from falling flat on my face. "So I gotta run. I'm late as it is."

"Culley!" I cry out, realizing he's leaving, doesn't know I need him.

"Don't worry, Mom," Culley calls. From the sound of his voice, he's by the front door, so I've got to stop him quickly, or he'll be gone. "Dad told me that you weren't coming to-night," he continues, his voice ugly. "Please don't think I give a shit, Mom, because I never expected you to come. Matter of fact,

I'm glad you won't be there. It's too fucking late for you to show an interest in me now."

"Culley," I plead, my voice catching in a sob, "please, baby . . . I need you. I need you. . . ." But the front door slams, and I turn to go back into my room. I take two steps before the room goes black, then looms up and swirls in dizzying spirals all around me. I feel the floor moving under me and hear the poor woman in the yellow wallpaper cackling her insane laugh as I fall.

18

Lanier

DAUPHIN ISLAND

IT'S BEEN PURE HELL at the hospital lately. Summers are always bad, both for the patients and the medical staff. Nurses, doctors, receptionists, lab techs, orderlies, even pink ladies and candy-stripers take time off in the summer, and hospitals can be badly understaffed. I tell the SSGs: Whatever you do, don't get sick in the summertime, because you're going to end up on a hospital floor with half the staff you normally have, or—worse—with a staff that's bleary-eyed and exhausted from working too many shifts, since everybody's on vacation. Just another day in paradise.

At the clinic in Reform, Paul and I about killed ourselves in the summer, and we weren't even close to a vacation area. Now that summer's in full swing in Mobile, I'm working a lot of shifts at the hospital, Mobile General, as well as teaching two classes at the nursing school. Like everything else in life, it's a good news–bad news scenario. Good news, I'm finally making some money; bad news, I don't have the time or energy to spend it. Good news, I'm no longer working part-time; bad news, I'm working full-time and part-time both. I'd almost rather be broke than work the hours I've had lately. Good news, Christopher and some buddies came down last week and spent a few days with me; bad news, I hardly got to see them. It wasn't all my schedule, to be fair. Being teenaged boys, they spent their mornings sleeping, their afternoons on the beach, and their nights cruising the hot spots, looking for girls. Good news, Christopher and I are close again—I'm his mommy, and he's my baby boy. Bad news, he's grown up now, off to college in a few weeks. Where has the time gone? I swear, it was just yesterday that he was toddling around in diapers. Yesterday! Now, he's taller than me, with

Paul's curly brown hair and cocker-spaniel eyes and a lopsided grin that—according to his buddies—make him a chick magnet. In spite of his being a jock and somewhat of a good old boy, he reminds me a lot of Paul, the older he gets.

Lindy, now, is the perfect combination of me and Paul. It turned out well for her; she's not what you'd call pretty but is cute as pie, with Paul's hair color and brown eyes and my athletic build—minus the big ass, thank the good Lord. Naturally Lindy doesn't think she's attractive, since she's female and no female ever thinks she looks good enough (except Astor, maybe). I told the SSGs of a study I read about, done with a bunch of college kids. See, they got a group of males and a group of females to rank themselves for their attractiveness, how they saw themselves. Then they got a panel of judges, folks who judged beauty contests, modeling agencies, stuff like that, to rank them. When they compared the numbers, all the males ranked themselves higher than the judges did. And, no surprise—without a single exception, the females ranked themselves lower. Another study I read about, I put in the lesson book. It had to do with teenaged boys body-building and bench-pressing while teenaged girls dieted. I wrote in the lesson book, *Seems to me that males are obsessed with expanding their bodies and females with shrinking theirs, which must have something to do with their self-images.* I observed that in raising my two kids, a boy and a girl. Christopher is confident and competitive and aggressive, while Lindy is insecure and apprehensive, unsure of herself and her place in the world.

When Christopher was visiting, I pumped him for information about Paul and Lindy. Being Christopher, who's not into self-analysis in the least, he gave out only the most basic information. His daddy was still working way too much, he said, putting in longer and longer hours at the clinic. He'd hired Betty Wells (that slut!) to take my place in the clinic, and naturally, she was after Paul, as was an old girlfriend of his, who's moved back to town and is living it up on alimony checks. I told Christopher to tell those floozies that I'd yank their bleached-blonde hair out by the black roots if they took advantage of his sweet daddy. Christopher's buddies laughed and laughed, like I was joking or something, but the clone of Paul just rolled his eyes.

But Lindy, Christopher just shrugged off. "She's weird, Mom," was about all he'd say about his sister. "Stays in her room all the time, writing in her stupid journal." The only slightly hopeful thing he'd said I'd clung to . . . for a while, anyway. "Lindy and some of her nerdy friends are coming to Gulf Shores next week," Christopher told me, and I'd begged him to tell her to call me. He'd shrugged it off but promised he would. The week came and went, though, and I heard nothing from her. Stupid me, after getting home from my shift last Sunday evening, instead of going over to Jesse's I drove to Gulf Shores and rode around, hoping I might spot Lindy. I know the summer homes of all of her friends' parents, so I knew where to look, but nothing. I came home and got drunk and cried on Jesse's shoulder while he patted my back and murmured sweet nothings until I fell asleep, cradled like a baby in his arms.

Coming home from the hospital this evening, I couldn't be hotter, couldn't be tireder. All I want to do is kick my shoes off, get out of my slick, sweaty uniform and into my cut-offs and tank top. Then, I want to open up a bottle of ice-cold wine, walk down to the pier, and watch for dolphins as the sun sets on the bay.

A strange car is parked in the driveway. I look at it, frowning, as I climb the wooden steps to the house. It's classy, a new silver Mercedes with Pickens County license plates, but no sign of anyone. I know it's not Paul—he drives the same beat-up old Jeep he's driven for years. The door to the house is locked; even so, I go inside a little uneasily. Maybe whoever it is walked around the house and is on the deck, waiting for me. Wouldn't expect a serial killer to drive a silver Mercedes, but you never know. After putting my purse and a sack of groceries down on the kitchen counter—fresh tomatoes and the white bread I'd gotten to make me and Jesse tomato sandwiches for supper—I walk over to the glass doors in back. As soon as I open the back door and stick my head out, I see her, standing on the back deck. It's Lindy.

When Lindy stands up and faces me, I can't help it, I fall apart. With a gasp, I run to her and throw my arms around her, not caring that she doesn't move a muscle, doesn't hug me back. Letting her go, I wipe my eyes on the sleeve of my uniform, but every time I look at her, tears roll down my face again. "Oh, Lindy," I cry in a choked voice. "I've missed you so much, baby!"

"Hello, Mama," Lindy says, and her voice is shaky. Even though she didn't hug me back, I notice that she's trembling.

"My God, let me look at you!" I wipe my tears away, this time with a tissue pulled from my pants pocket. Unlike Christopher, who looked tan and robust and healthy, and who'd grown a couple of inches and gained a few pounds, Lindy looks thin and pale. Her best feature is her thick, curly hair, a pretty light-brown color, but today it's not fixed up at all, dull and lifeless and pulled back tight, with a plain old rubber band. She doesn't have on any makeup, and behind her little round glasses are purplish circles under her eyes, making her look tired and sad. She's wearing shorts, flip-flops, and a Reform High School Beta Club T-shirt.

"Christopher told me you were going to be at Gulf Shores," I tell her, "but I thought that was last week."

Lindy shrugs dismissively. "No, it's this week. I came down with the Walkers.

Christopher doesn't know jack." She's always adored her big brother, and him his little sister, but since they turned into teenagers, they go to great lengths to disguise their affection for each other. Guess it's not cool.

"Oh, baby, baby, it's *so* good to see you. . . ." I begin, but my voice chokes up on me again, and my eyes blur with tears. Not wanting to scare her off, since she's being standoffish as she regards me so seriously behind her glasses, I blink, clear my throat, and ask, "That's not your car out front, is it?"

Finally, I get a small smile from her. "Yeah, right," she says. "Mrs. Walker wanted me to see you, so she said I should take her car and come over here. I was scared to drive it, but she insisted."

Karen Walker was not only Lindy's high school counselor but had been one of my best friends in Pickens County. When everything blew up in my face, Karen turned her back on me, like everyone else in town. Her daughter Amy is Lindy's best friend; it was their beach house I'd driven by several times trying to catch sight of one of them. It touches me that, in spite of her rejection of me, Karen made Lindy come over here. One of my main prayers has been that Karen, as a trained counselor, would help Lindy during this time.

"How are you doing? You look great," I lie, trying to keep my voice light and breezy. *It's being so cheerful that keeps me going.*

Instead of looking at me, Lindy turns her head and looks over the bay. It's been a picture-perfect day, the sky high and blue and cloudless, Mobile Bay deep green-gray and still. "I'm fine," she says in a small voice, breaking my heart.

"Remember how we used to go to the pier and watch for the dolphins? I usually do that soon as I get home from work. I've been seeing a lot of them lately," I gush, unable to stop myself. "There's a family of dolphins I see almost every day, a mama, daddy, and little dolphin . . . a-and, ah . . . ." I stop myself, stammering. Not a good idea to bring up a happy family, dolphin or otherwise. "Want to walk down to the pier?" I try instead.

She shakes her head. "I can't stay but a minute."

"Let me get you something. Want a Coke?"

"No thanks."

"Then come in and let me show you how I've fixed the place up," I beg her. Anything to prolong her visit.

To my surprise, Lindy shrugs and follows me into the house. Inside I blabber like an idiot, unable to stop myself, pointing out stuff as if she can't see it. Oh look, honey, there's a chair. And look, a rug on the floor! Lindy nods, polite as always, but barely looks at it. She surprises me by saying, "Looks real pretty. I always loved it here."

"I know you did. Listen, Lindy, why don't you stay with me? I mean, for a couple of days or something? I-I'll take you back, whenever you want to go . . ." But she's shaking her head before I can even finish the sentence.

"I can't," she says. "I'm going to Camp McDowell next week."

"Oh! Father Bob's got you helping again, huh?"

She nods. "I'm teaching a course in journaling to sixth-graders. Be there a couple of weeks."

"That's great, baby." I smile a big watery smile, daring to sit on the arm of the sofa, hoping she'll sit down, too. She doesn't, standing rigidly by the windows, her hands clasped in front of her. I want to go to the bedroom and get my hairbrush, make her sit down next to me while I brush her hair, like I used to when she was a little girl. I want to fix her hair, French-braiding it or pulling it back with barrettes on either side of her pretty little face, like I used to do. I want to feel her silky, curly hair in my hands so bad that I can't stand it.

After an awkward silence, Lindy says, "On the way down? Mrs. Walker stopped in Selma for me to see Grandmama at the nursing home. Daddy took me and Christopher down to see her at Easter, but I hadn't been back since."

Silently, I bless Karen Walker yet again and say to Lindy, "Did Grandmama know you?" Lindy shakes her head, and I tell her, "I haven't been in a few weeks. She doesn't know me, either."

Another silence while I struggle for something to say, something chatty and light that will keep her here. "I hate seeing Grandmama like that," Lindy says with a frown on her face, before I can come up with anything. "Makes me think that getting old kind of like, sucks."

"Yeah," I agree. "Me too."

"Mrs. Walker? She says that the fear of getting old can cause people to do weird things."

I nod. "Scares all of us, I guess." I don't dare look at her, but I feel a tiny glimmer of hope. Has the seed been planted in Lindy's mind that the reason I screwed up so bad has to do with me approaching fifty? That maybe, just maybe, the fear of growing old made me go crazy? Not that I deserve getting off the hook, but if it helps Lindy . . .

Turning her back to me, Lindy points out the window. "Hardly anyone on the bay this afternoon. Don't see but one fishing boat from here." A little quilted purse hangs from her shoulder, and she reaches in and pulls out a set of car keys. "Well, guess I'd better go."

Can't hurt to try again, so I say, "Come on, baby! Let's walk down to the pier before you have to leave. Won't take but a minute." I hold my breath, then try not to clap my hands happily when Lindy shrugs and says, simply, "Well, okay."

On the walk down to the pier, I tell Lindy about the SSG gathering and how Astor was crowned queen this year. She used to love hearing about the SSGs, eager for me to repeat all our stories, making me describe our gatherings in great detail, what everybody said and wore, what we ate, what silly things we did. I always had to censor it, of course, since we're such a bawdy bunch. Now that Lindy's old enough to hear more of our stories, it pains me that she no longer wants to. She tells me about Corrine and Julia calling her in the last few months, but nothing about what they talked about. I'm afraid to question her since they've been working for a reconciliation between us, and she hasn't been receptive to either of their overtures. Instead, I motion for Lindy to sit on one of the benches in the gazebo. She refuses, standing rigidly on the edge of the pier and scanning the horizon instead, several feet away from me. "Maybe we'll get lucky, see a whole bunch of dolphins," I say to her, searching the glassy waters.

But of course, no dolphins this afternoon, and I feel like I've let Lindy down yet again. I eagerly point to every shadow, like a pure fool, saying, "Hey, I think I see one!" But it turns out to be a piece of wood, or a clump of moss from the live oaks edging the shore. "It's unusually quiet today," I tell Lindy. "I don't even see that fishing boat you saw."

She points to the little inlet of live oaks and

palms between our pier and the Picketts'. "It was right over there." Shading her eyes with her hands, she says, with a small smile, "Maybe it was Granddaddy Brewer's ghost."

"If his ghost haunted any place, it'd be here," I say. "He loved it better than any place on earth."

"Seems like he ought to still be here, fishing," Lindy says wistfully.

"He was a fishing fool," I agree. "I sure miss him."

She looks sad and thoughtful. "Yeah. Me too."

I want to ask her about Paul so bad I have to bite my tongue, but no point in pissing on a skunk. The mention of her daddy's name might be enough to make her bolt and run. If we just had a little more time together . . . As casually as possible, I say to her, "Hey, honey, why don't you stay for supper? I'll fix us tomato sandwiches. Or—let me take you somewhere! You used to love going to the Seafood Shack. . . ."

Lindy's still scanning the waters for dolphins. Without glancing my way, she says, "Can't. We're going to The Dock for supper tonight."

"The Dock? That's my favorite place in Gulf

Shores." But it doesn't work. No invitation to join them follows. I try again. "I'm sure if you called Karen, said we were going out . . ."

This time Lindy does look my way, and her face is closed. "No, Mama. I don't want to."

I swallow. "Lindy? Can't we . . . I mean, since you're here, don't you think we could talk?"

She shrugs, turning away from me again. "I really don't want to." Her voice has grown cold and hard. "Mrs. Walker forced me to come here, but now I wish I hadn't."

A lump forms in my throat the size of a baseball, but I make myself say, "Oh, honey, if you knew how much I miss you . . . if you only knew how I'd do anything to make it up to you! To you, and Daddy, and Christopher . . . I know I can't make it up, but . . ."

She turns back to face me, her eyes distant. "No, you can't. You can't make it up to us, Mama. Ever."

I can't stand her looking at me like that, like she hates me. I have to ask her, even if it kills me. "Do you hate me, baby? Please tell me you don't hate me."

She sighs a tired, grown-up sigh. "I don't hate you, Mama. But I do feel sorry for you."

She's moved from where she's been standing and is walking past me, gripping the shoulder strap of her purse. "Guess it'd be better if I go now," she says over her shoulder. Before she can walk away, I rush to her, grabbing for her arm.

"Lindy, wait!" I cry. "Wait a minute, please. Just listen to one thing, okay?" To my surprise, instead of pulling away, she stands still, her eyebrows raised. "Lindy, I don't mean to be this way," I tell her. "I wish—oh, God, I wish I was a better person, that I was the kind of mama that you deserve to have. I asked you if you hate me, but the truth is, I hate myself. I don't want to be like this."

Lindy's expression as she regards me about breaks my heart. She looks old, and wise, no longer a little girl. I've robbed her of her innocence, and it makes me want to die.

"Then *change,* Mama." Her voice is firm but resigned. "My God, you're almost fifty years old, and you don't have your act together yet! What do you think, that you're going to keep on and on, screwing up your life and everybody else's? Long as I can remember, that's all you've talked about, how you mess everything up. But you know what, Mama? All you do about it is *talk.* You, like, talk and whine and say you're sorry and expect everybody to say it's okay. And because you're so cute and funny and lovable, people have always said that it is okay, that's just the way you are. But guess what? It's not okay anymore. So do something to change, how about it?"

Stung, I stand frozen in place as Lindy turns her back on me and walks down the pier at a fast pace. I open my mouth to call out to her, but I can't seem to make my voice work. I want to tell her that she's right, and that I've been so wrong, so wrong . . . but I can't do a thing but watch her walk out of my life and know that if she walks out now, that I've lost her for good. "Lindy . . ." I finally manage to say, but my voice is so choked up that she doesn't hear me. Helpless to stop her, I bury my face in my hands.

Then a sound reaches my ears and causes me to drop my hands away and raise my head. The same sound stops Lindy dead in her tracks. Both of us stare open-mouthed out to the bay, where it's coming from. It's so still that the sound floats over to where we stand, as clear as the bell of a passing ship. In the little cove next to the Picketts' pier, sitting in his old wooden fishing boat, is Jesse.

With his shoulders hunched over, he plays his guitar, playing the heartbreaking ballad that me and him talked about just the other night. From here I can see that his eyes are closed, and he moves his head side to side as he starts to sing. That sweet voice of his floats across the waters and to the pier of Dolphin Cove.

"Oh, my daddy hung the moon so bright," he sings; "he hung the moon to light my path at night. Then my daddy hung the sun, the sun so high; he hung it so I could see to fly. My daddy hung the stars to help me see . . . all to show his love for me. The day I left my daddy behind, the sun it would no longer shine. The day I left my daddy behind, the stars they hid their eyes. The day I left my daddy behind, the moon it fell down from the skies."

Without looking our way, Jesse puts the guitar down, picks up the oars, and begins to row away. Rounding the bend, the boat, outlined in the glow of the setting sun, disappears from our sight. I sink down on a bench, my knees unable to hold me up. Lindy whirls around to stare at me, her eyes wide. "Omigod, Mama—that was Jesse Phoenix, singing my favorite song of his!"

"My favorite, too," I say. "I ain't believing this."

"I've told everybody that he used to live in the house next door to Dolphin Cove," Lindy says breathlessly, "but a lot of the kids in my class? They didn't believe me till Mrs. Walker told them it was true." She stops and eyes me. "You got him to do that, didn't you, Mama?"

I stare at her blankly. "Do what?"

"You got him to come by here and sing that song for me, bet you anything. Didn't you?"

I shake my head with a smile. "Oh, baby, I'd give anything to be able to tell you that I did. But think about it . . . I didn't even know you were coming." Lindy considers what I've said, then nods. "But," I say quickly, "if I'd known you were coming, I'd sure have done it. Remember when I took you to meet him, about ten or twelve years ago now? You were about five, weren't you?"

She smiles the first real smile since she's been here. "Oh, yeah, like I'm going to forget that! Amy and all the girls in my room? They're jealous that I got to meet him in person. I mean, he may be real old, but his songs are still cool."

"Hey, you want to go over and see him? Bet we can get him to sing us another song."

Lindy hesitates, then shakes her head. But I can tell, she almost gave in.

"I guess not. Reckon I'd better go," she says.

This time I don't try to stop her. I stand up and walk over to where she's standing, and I take her in my arms. She doesn't hug me back, but she doesn't pull away, either. When I let her go, she wipes her eyes and looks at me. "Mama? I—well, I didn't come to say all those mean things to you."

"Yes, you did, honey, and it's okay. I'm glad you did, tell you the truth. Remember my lesson book? I'm going in right now and write all that stuff down you said. It'll give me something to think about."

"Hey—I guess my journal is kind of like your lesson book. You think?"

I nod, swallowing, but I can't speak. Lindy turns and runs down the pier, her ponytail bobbing. At the end of the pier, she stops and looks back up at me. "Bye, Mama."

"Bye, baby," I say, and Lindy turns away. With a little wave of her hand, she runs up the path and disappears around the house. I stand where I am, hugging my arms, until the silver Mercedes pulls out of the driveway, and she drives off without a backward glance.

Jesse is passed out sitting at the table, a bottle of whiskey next to him, when I go over that night. It's late, almost nine o'clock. I didn't get over for supper because I called all the SSGs on the phone, telling them about Lindy's surprise visit. It's funny, their reactions. Rosanelle I didn't call, because we're not that close, and she gets on my nerves too bad. I called Corrine first, of course, and Corrine cried. When I told her about Jesse in the boat and him singing the song, she said, "Wait a minute." She left—I figured to pee— but instead, when she picked up the phone again, "My Daddy Hung the Moon" was playing on her CD, and the two of us cried again. "He must have seen me and Lindy together on the pier," I told her, "and heard every word we said. Sound carries on the bay like you wouldn't believe."

After Corrine, I tried to call Julia, but I wasn't able to get hold of her. Julia's hard to reach; always running around doing first lady stuff, but I left her a message. When I reached Byrd, she told me she wasn't a bit surprised, because she'd had me and Lindy on her prayer chain for months, and God always answered her prayers. "Sometimes His answer is 'no,'" Byrd said piously, then got mad at me for saying, "Only sometimes? He *always* tells me no." She spent about an hour fussing at me for losing Lindy in the first place, reminding me that it was all my fault. I finally said, "Byrd, if you're saying this to make me feel better, it's not working" and hung up. Astor was visiting Mose at the nursing home, but she called me back when she got in and got my message. I finally told her the whole story—well, almost. Corrine had said for me not to tell Astor the part about Jesse because Astor would be down here in a New York minute, on him like a honeybee on a big fat blossom. It always takes a while to tell Astor a story, because she's one of those people who interrupt you the whole time to tell you something else before you can finish a sentence. Drives me crazy. Ended up, though, with Astor saying she was thrilled Lindy came to see me, but I shouldn't get my hopes up, because it sounded to her like Lindy still hated my guts. On that cheery note, I hung up on her, too.

Jesse is so out of it that he's snoring,

blowing his boozy breath in my face when I shake him. "Jesse Pickett," I say in his ear, "wake up! I need to tell you something, you hear?"

His eyelids flutter and he blinks, then opens his eyes, looking startled to see me right in his face. "Hey, Lanier," he murmurs, his voice slurred. "Didn't think you were coming over tonight."

"I appreciate what you did this afternoon, Jess. And I'll always love you for doing it."

"I love you, too, sugar," he says, closing his eyes again. "What did I do?"

"You know good and well what you did. You sang! You're singing again, Jess. I'm so proud of you for that."

"If you can call that singing," he hoots, straightening up in his chair and stretching. "More like an old frog croaking. Figured I embarrassed you and your little girl to death."

"Well, you figured wrong. Sounded like the old Jesse Phoenix to me, and my girl was thrilled."

Jess squints as though trying to figure out if I'm shitting him or not. Or so I assume. Instead, he says gruffly, "I couldn't help but hear what your girl said to you, Lanier, y'all standing out on your pier. She sure told you off good. You had any sense, you'd go to Reform and try to get that girl's daddy back."

"He hates my guts!" I cry. "I've tried to get him back, and you know it. But you know what? I'm not anymore. I've decided that he deserves better than me."

His eyes narrowed, Jess thinks about that, reaching over and lighting up one of his stinky cigarettes. Then he surprises me even more by saying, "That's his decision, not yours."

"Make up your mind!" I screech. "First you say I've gotta get him back, then you say it's up to him. Who do you think you are, any-way—Sigmund Freud?"

"You've gotta let him know that you're sorry as sorry can be. If he takes you literal-ly, that you really are sorry . . . sorry as in no good, I mean . . . then he may not want you back. But if he loves you anyway, whether you're a shitty person or not, then you got to accept it and quit beating up on yourself. Best I remember from the days Mama took me to church every Sunday, that's what you call grace. You know, amazing grace and all that stuff."

"Jesse Phoenix gives up songwriting to

take to the pulpit," I say in a mocking voice, sure it's going to piss him off. Instead, he laughs a drunken laugh.

"That'll be the day. Now go on back home, honey. I need to go to bed and sleep this off, and you don't need to be with me tonight, I'm so drunk. But I'm real proud your girl came to see you today."

Before he gets to his feet, I lean over him and kiss his forehead. "Thank you, Jess. Thank you for what you did."

"I didn't do nothing," he says gruffly, then turns away so I can't see how pleased he is with himself.

When I'm almost to my house, making my way in the dark without a flashlight since I've been this way so often lately, I hear my phone ringing. I break out in a run, jumping over ferns and blackberry brambles like I'm jumping hurdles. It's got to be Lindy, calling this late! Maybe she's changed her mind about seeing me. Maybe she got to thinking about our meeting this evening and decided I was right, we do need to talk. I take the steps two at a time, almost busting my ass when I fall down, but I scramble to my feet and run for the phone, panting like I just ran a triathlon. But when I pick up the phone, it's not Lindy after all. It's Corrine's son, Culley, and he starts to cry when he hears my voice.

19

Julia

LAKE MARTIN, ALABAMA

IT IS THE QUIETNESS of the house on Lake Martin that I need most. I stand on the screened porch soaking in the stillness the way someone who has escaped from an arctic winter might absorb the warm rays of the sun. I inhale the sweet smells of the woods surrounding the lake: the sharp, tangy green of pines; the bittersweet incense of the wild ferns growing underfoot; the earthy essence of moss that carpets the forest floor. The lake is dark and murky, as though hiding secrets in its deep-green depths, which appear as inaccessible and impenetrable as underwater caves. The only sounds to disturb the late-afternoon stillness are the occasional trill of wild birds and the gentle lap of the lake water against the rocky shoals surrounding it. The screened porch, like a child's treehouse, is so high over the water it appears to be perched in the leafy oaks edging the lake. On this side of Lake Martin, this hidden, barely accessible area, the vast lake is bordered by high rocky bluffs, unlike the other inhabited places, where sandy beaches stretch out to the pebbles at the water's edge.

Standing on my high-perched porch, I lift a prayer of gratitude for the impulse that brought me here. I don't know where it came from, this sudden, almost overwhelming, need to come here, but I know that I did the right thing. On the ride here from Talladega, I almost backed out, several times. All I would've had to do was tap Cal on the shoulder, say turn around, take me home, I don't know what I was thinking, and I'd been back where I belonged. Even though I don't know Cal all that well, instinctively I know this about him—he would have done so without questioning me, and he would not have said I told you so. Or worse, told Joe Ed or my assistant or the other troopers about my demand that he take me to this place, never mind my responsibilities or the disapproval I would encounter. But I resisted the urge to turn the car around, head home, and do the right thing . . . the thing I've always done faithfully and without question. I forced Cal Hawkins to become my accomplice, my partner in crime, and although he grumbled and cussed and bitched about it, he brought me here, opening himself up to the same criticism due me, and I'm grateful to him.

Cal disappeared into the guest quarters built above the garage as soon as we arrived, without a word to me. I wasn't sure if he was sulking, or angry, or just worried. I felt guilty for including him in my foolish escapade, so much so that I had every intention of sending him back where he belonged as soon as I could. Lieutenant Anne Robinson, one of the female troopers on staff, was usually assigned to me, and I would exchange Cal for Lieutenant Robinson first thing in the morning. Selfishly, I didn't really want to, which made me feel even guiltier. Although I liked Lieutenant Robinson, who was young and athletic, she was a bit talkative, having a tendency to tell me her problems with her boyfriend, a highway patrolman with commitment issues. What I longed for, desperately, was solitude and silence. Cal, I knew from past experience, was a closed, private person, not likely to impose on my space. The night of the so-called terrorist attack, when he and I stayed up and talked, was the only time he'd ever told me anything personal about himself, as long as we'd known each other.

In planning to have Lieutenant Robinson here, it occurs to me that I'm thinking as if I'm going to be here longer than just today. If I stay, I'll either miss the breakfast meeting altogether or I'll have to make Cal get up early enough to take me there. If I return to the Mansion for the breakfast, however, I'll have to make all the endless arrangements to be away, to return here, and just thinking about it gives me a headache. I won't think about it now. I'll deal with it tomorrow.

In an attempt to appease my guilt over bringing Cal here, as soon as I changed out of my suit and heels and into shorts and a loose pullover, I took a grocery bag and packed it for him. I put in a pair of Joe Ed's running shorts—with a Bama logo, of course; a couple of old campaign T-shirts (a simple Stovall for Governor '00, thankfully, instead of one of the cheesy sloganed ones); a pair of flip-flops; and one of the dozens of airline toiletry bags I had stashed away here, filled with necessities. I wrote Cal a note and stuck it in the bag, saying I was sorry that I'd forced him to bring me here but not sorry enough to leave—this with a smiley face drawn next to it. If he'd look in the fridge, he'd find it well stocked with beer and the freezer full of food, I told him. I hoped that he'd relax and do some fishing during his imprisonment here, I added. I climbed the outside steps of the guest house, hung the bag on the door, gave a brisk knock, then hurried back over to the main house before Cal could open the door. I was somewhat disconcerted to hear him talking on his cell phone as I knocked on the door and wondered if he'd called Joe Ed after all. Or maybe Astor . . .

As I stand on the porch and look down at the dark lake, dappled with the shadows of the late-afternoon sun, I inhale the fragrant, fresh air and try to let go of the tension I brought with me. The important thing is, I'm here, and it's as beautiful and as peaceful as I remembered. We don't make use of the lake house as much as I'd like to, coming here only two or three times a year, always accompanied by staff members—advisors and guards and cooks and cleaning staff. Joe Ed finds it too isolated and is restless here. Like most workaholic, driven men, he doesn't relax well away from his natural habitat, a problem when we vacation any-where, much less in a place this secluded. Bethany loved the lake house, but there was always the fear that she might get one of her frequent ear infections or something that would require immediate medical attention, and we were so far from everything, with miles of unpaved, deserted roads between us and a hospital. Years ago I'd had an SSG gathering here, one of the first, but the girls found it too isolated, even creepy in its seclusion, and we never came here again. Those were the very qualities that beckoned to me today, singing a siren song I was unable to resist.

In spite of its isolation, I've always loved the lake house. It's a one-storied, rambling stone house that Joe Ed's daddy bought because it had fallen into disrepair, neglect-ed by wealthy owners who never used it. When Mr. Stovall presented it to us as a wedding present, I expected to find a fishing cabin, much like Lanier's place on Mobile Bay. Instead, I discovered a big, ivy-draped house built of gray river stone, more of a country cottage than a typical vacation get-away like the others that dot the edge of Lake Martin. Joe Ed hadn't told his daddy, not wanting to seem ungrateful, but he'd been disappointed that it was located on the banks of the high shoals rather than the sandy areas of the lake where you could swim and fish. He'd said it reminded him too much of a mountain house in the north Alabama mountains, where he was raised, and I'd said maybe that was why his daddy had bought it. He'd laughed at that, saying his daddy had bought it because it was a bargain, and an investment, bound to increase in value over the years, not for sentimental reasons.

Except for basic repairs on the structure of the house, in the early years of our marriage we'd used it as it was, too busy and preoccupied with starting a family and career to spend any time or resources on it. When Joe Ed ran for re-election to the senate a few years ago, we decided to have a staff retreat at Lake Martin, and I redecorated. Almost instinctively, I sought out furnishings that were made for comfort rather than beauty. Today, as I go through the house and pull sheets off the large pieces of furniture, it occurs to me that this is the only home I've ever had that was even remotely cozy. Joe Ed and I had a modern luxury apartment on the river in Tuscaloosa when he was in law school, then Mother helped me select our starter house in Montgomery, in the right neighborhood. It was a small classy Tudor, with high ceilings and mullioned windows. A few years later Joe Ed was elected to the state senate, and Mother decided our starter house wouldn't do. We had to have an appropriate house, suitable for entertaining. Again, she supervised the selection and restoration of a preconfederacy house in the historic district of Montgomery, within walking distance of the Governor's Mansion, her ultimate goal for her son-in-law. Mother stayed with us for several weeks to oversee the restoration, and the house ended up with all the homey comfort of a museum, just like the Dupont home in Mobile. The SSGs were appalled that I allowed my mother to do that, not understanding that I was in another of the living-dead periods, caught up in the mounting medical problems of Bethany's childhood. Decorating a house was the last thing on my mind.

But the restoration of the house on Lake Martin had been my project and mine alone. My only concession to Joe Ed's career was to take his suggestion that I decorate it in patriotic shades of red, white, and blue, which worked well with the homey, country theme I used. The chintz-covered sofas and chairs I chose were oversized and over-stuffed, the kind you curl up in to read a book, not sit on the edge of to plan a political campaign. I put a long, oval table and a dozen cane-bottomed chairs by the bay windows in the kitchen, rather than having a formal dining room. To accommodate the cooking staff we had to bring with us, the kitchen was large and well equipped with a lot of professional equipment, but I'd deco-rated it like a country farm kitchen, in blue and white, with slate-topped counters, cop-per fixtures, and pickled-wood cabinets. In the bedrooms I'd had the windows enlarged so that every room had a view of the river. Instead of heavy silk drapes and bed cover-ings, I used country quilts and left the win-dows bare, easily opened to bring in the cool breezes of the lake. The crowning glory of the house, however, was my pride and joy— the screened porch. I'd brought in a builder who understood my vision for the old porch and who was able to extend it over the banks of the lake, in the midst of the hickory and oak trees, so that it had the feel of a tree house. I'd filled it with wooden swings hanging from the rafters, wicker chaise lounges, and cushioned gliders.

When I return from taking Cal's bag of supplies to the guest quarters, I go barefoot into the kitchen, and the blue tile floor feels wonderfully cool on my feet. Suddenly, I'm starving. The lunch we had in the cafeteria of the Helen Keller Institute today was not very satisfying, baked chicken as dry and tasteless as paper, hard little pellets of rice, and mushy, overcooked green beans. The lake house is so far from civilization that I've always had to keep it well stocked. Several months ago, when we were here last, on New Year's Day, one of the cooks had brought boxes of Christmas leftovers from the Mansion to fill the freezer. As the first family, we receive dozens of gifts from all over the state, most of which I donate to local charities. But I always keep some on hand, in case the donors pay us a visit and we want to show them how much we're enjoying their generosity. The freezer is stuffed with pies, cakes, and breads from every bakery in Alabama, as well as packages of doves, pheasants, quail, wild turkeys, hams, venison, and containers of barbecue. Pulling packages out and studying the labels, I try to decide what I want. The only thing that appeals to me is a pecan pie from a retailer in Dothan, and I put it out to thaw. I might just eat the whole thing, all by myself.

Closing the freezer, I go to the Sub-Zero and study its contents, chewing on my bottom lip as I try to make up my mind. Then it hits me—I don't want to thaw a precooked package out, I want to cook something. I want to *cook,* by God, instead of consulting with a chef about a menu. I don't want an engraved card on my gold-edged plate that starts out *Soup du Jour* and ends up with *Dessert Tray with Fruit and Cheese.* The staff has stocked the fridge with perishables and basics in plastic containers, labeled and stacked. As soon as I spot the one labeled GRITS, I reach for it.

If I'm going to spend any time walking the grounds, however, I have to do so now, before it gets dark, so I put the grits aside for later. Don't guess I'll starve until then. I dig some walking shoes out of the hall closet, tie them on, and go outside, into the heat of the late afternoon. Although it's well shaded here, the house surrounded by spreading oaks, magnolias, dogwood and sweetgum trees, it's mid-July in the deep South, so it's hot and humid. Nothing is blooming but the orange day lilies and scrubby little daisies I'd planted in the flowerbeds when the redecorating was done, such a contrast to the lush, formal gardens of both the Governor's Mansion and our house in Montgomery. Walking down the dirt driveway, past the garage with the guest quarters overhead, I look to see if there's any sign of Cal. None, although the bag I hung on the door is gone. I'm tempted to throw rocks at the windows, to tease him out of his sulk, but refrain. Don't want to push my luck. When I pass the garage, I take a path that veers to the left, behind the house, cutting through thick foliage to the bluffs. I walk as far as I can along the edge of the lake, several feet below the rocky path. There's no breeze, so the dark-green lake is still as a mirror, except for the occasional splash of a fish or the ripple of a fallen branch.

When I reach the end of the long pathway, I circle around and walk back, coming up behind the house to one of my favorite spots. It's a huge flat area on the top of the shoals, which juts out over the edge of the ridge like an overhang in the mountains. The previous owner had boulders cemented around the edge to form a barrier, to keep anyone from going over the edge, so it's perfectly safe. I'd always loved sitting on it because it provides a wider vista in which to view the lake. When Bethany was twelve, I talked Joe Ed into bringing a photographer with us to take a family picture for our Christmas cards. God, that was over six years ago! It seems like no time at all. I'd gone all out for hokey in the photo, dressing Bethany in a red-and-white Bama sweatsuit and tying her silky hair back with a big red bow. She was so little then; now she's all grown up, out on her own. Whenever she comes home now, it will be more like a visit. My eyes fill with tears and I blink them away, determined not to cry. This is the way it must be, I tell myself, mentally squaring my shoulders. Sitting on the boulders, I look down to the lake below and think of how mother eagles teach their young to fly by pushing them out of the nest. That's what I've had to do with Bethany, push her out of the nest and tell her that the time has come for her to fly.

When we'd had the family photo made, I'd insisted that we sit on the pile of boulders so we could get the autumn leaves in the background, their reflection in the still water on the other side of the lake. Joe Ed and I had one of our rare fights, since he hadn't wanted Bethany anywhere near the ledge, even with him holding her. He'd only agreed because Bethany begged him, then he'd held her so tight she rebelled and struggled against his grip, adding to the tension. Whenever anything was said about a family photo in the years following, Joe Ed would wink at me and whisper, "Just so we don't have to sit on a ledge." *Joe Ed* . . . I was going to have to call him tonight, and he was not going to be happy with me. The occasion of the family photo would be nothing compared to his reaction when he found out where I was.

I rise reluctantly from the ledge, dusting off the seat of my shorts. Atop the bluff on the other side of the lake, the sun has disappeared behind a copse of pines, leaving the sky stained dark red. It's still hot, the air wet and heavy, and I long for the coolness of the screened porch, where slow-moving fans overhead create a breeze. As I round the bend in the trail that comes up in front of the house, next to my flowerbeds of day lilies and daisies, I see Cal. He's jogging up the dirt driveway, dressed in Joe Ed's running shorts and T-shirt, both of which are soaked with sweat. He jogs slowly because of the old football injury, and I stand and watch him with my hands on my hips. Cal, Joe Ed, and some of the other troopers run in the early mornings when Joe Ed's home, on a jogging path he had added behind the Mansion. I've often teased Cal and Joe Ed about it, both of them limping along trying to keep up with the younger guys, in spite of banged-up knees, stiff joints, and aching backs.

Cal spots me and trots over to where I'm waiting, under the shade of a low-branched oak. "I'm dying!" he says, putting his hands on his knees and leaning his head down while he huffs and puffs. "Bury my heart at Wounded Knee."

"With that old injury of yours, Wounded Knee is pretty appropriate," I say dryly.

"It's gotta be a hundred fucking degrees out here," he groans.

"Cal, both you and Joe Ed have got to realize that fifty-year-old men have no business running in this kind of heat! I said the other morning that y'all should go to the gym instead of outside, and what do you do instead? Both of you on the jogging path as soon as I turn my back, running your fool heads off, trying to prove you can still keep up with guys half your age."

"That's because Joe Ed bet us a six-pack that he could outrun anyone on the staff." Cal's attempt at a grin comes looking more like a grimace. His face is deep red and shiny, and he wipes his forehead in the crook of his arm, pushing back his wet hair.

"You look like you're about to have a heat stroke," I gasp, even though I know I sound like my mother. Then I notice his feet. "And to top it off, you're barefooted as a yard dog!"

"You expect me to run in those flip-flops?"

"There's a pair of running shoes here, but I'm not letting you use them if you don't have any better sense than to jog in this heat, you hear me?"

"Yes, ma'am. Anything you say, ma'am."

This time, Cal's boyish grin is infectious, and I smile, too, rolling my eyes and shaking my head.

"All right, I'll stop sounding like my mother. Want me to get you a bottle of water?"

He shakes his head. "Thanks, but there are plenty in the fridge, and I'm heading that way now." He turns and starts hobbling toward the guest house, stopping when I call out to him.

"Cal? Why don't you come over and have supper with me? I'm making a pot of grits."

Cal stops and looks at me over his shoulder. "Evidently I'm so old that I've gone deaf. I could've sworn you said you were fixing a pot of grits for supper."

"A great big pot, with real butter. Nothing finer."

He hesitates for a minute, then shakes his head. "Thanks, but I'll pass. I won't impose on your hard-earned solitude."

"Still mad at me for making you bring me here?"

"Mad as hell. I called Joe Ed, told him he was married to the stubbornest woman I'd ever known."

"You did not," I smile.

"No, but I should have." He turns back

toward the garage. "Enjoy your grits, Julia. And your solitude. Let me know what you decide about tomorrow, okay?"

"I will." I start walking toward the house, calling out to him on my way, "If you change your mind, come on over in an hour. It's obvious you've never had my grits, or you'd be beating the door down."

I open a cold bottle of Pinot Blanc and pour myself a glass, then head to the porch. I've already taken the plastic covers off the furniture and gotten the overhead fans going, getting ready for this time of day. Bad thing about a screened porch in the middle of summer: Its use is limited to twice a day—early in the morning and late in the evening. Otherwise, it's too hot, no matter how shady the porch is.

Fireflies—lightning bugs, I called them as a child—wave their tiny lanterns in the thick foliage under the oaks, and I sink down in a chaise lounge to watch them, enchanted. My brother and I used to chase them through the acres of azaleas growing on the grounds of our home in Mobile. When we caught them, we'd imprison them in jars with holes punched in the top. I'd poke grass and leaves through the holes so my lightning bugs would feel at home, hoping that would make them turn on their magic lanterns. Then I noticed something: Their little lights were not as strong in the jar. Even if I took the jar to the darkness of my closet, the lightning bugs glowed feebly, as though their energy came from the azalea bushes and the night air and the stars, and I had robbed them of the source by putting them in the jar. I'd always end up letting them go, crouched down in the azalea bushes trying to release them in the same place I captured them, sending them home.

When Bethany was a child, her eyes weren't strong enough to see the lightning bugs in the bushes from our porch, so one night I caught one in my hand and, cupping it with the other hand, took it to her. We went into her room, and I motioned for her to follow me into the closet. Inside the closet, I knelt in front of her and held my cupped hands up. "Okay, baby," I'd told her, "I have a firefly in my hands, and you'll know why it's called that when you see it."

Bethany had squealed when I opened my hand enough for her to see the firefly light up, then she begged to hold it. I thought she'd be afraid when she felt the bug crawl from my hand to hers, but instead, she cupped it in her little hands and jumped up and down, thrilled. "I want Daddy to see my fairy-fly!" she'd said. But her daddy wasn't there, away on one of his endless campaign trips. Bethany begged to stay in the closet with the firefly in her hand until her daddy came home so she could show it to him. When Joe Ed called that night and she told him about seeing a firefly for the first time, he cut his trip short and flew back the next day. That night, I watched him and Bethany huddled in the azalea bushes, fair heads bent together, cupping fireflies in their hands.

Seeing Bethany in her new setting must be what has me so emotional today. Unexpectedly, tears fill my eyes, and I wipe them away with my fingertips. I hear a sound and turn my head to see Cal opening the screen door, a frown on his face. "Julia? You okay?" he says.

I try to smile. "Oh, hi, Cal. I'm fine. Just having a delayed reaction to leaving Bethany at the school today, I guess." Fumbling in the pocket of my shorts, I pull out a tissue and wipe my eyes, then sit up straighter in the chaise. Enough! It's not like me to be like this.

Cal stands with his hand on the door handle, a beer in his hand. "Want me to leave you alone?"

"No. I want you to come in and have a drink with me. I want you to make me laugh and forget that I can't stop crying every time I think about Bethany."

Cal hesitates, then walks over to the rattan chair next to mine. He sits on the edge of the ottoman rather than in the chair, as though ready to bolt if I get too teary for him. "If I'm not good for at least one laugh, then you can kick me out," he says lightly.

"It's a deal." This time, I manage a smile. "Ah, I see you found a beer. If you prefer something stronger, Joe Ed has quite a stash in the bar. Help yourself."

Cal shakes his head. "This is fine." I can't help but notice that he's freshly showered, his black hair wet and comb-tracked, and he's wearing the other T-shirt from the bag I hung on the door handle. The running shorts are still quite damp, but I don't say anything. It's impossible not to notice Cal's tightly muscled body in the damp shorts and close-fitting T-shirt, and I avert my eyes uneasily, recalling the erotic dream I had about him a few weeks ago. I should have thought of that before I found myself alone with him in a setting like this. Cal turns up the can of beer, drinks deeply of it, then looks around at the full-leafed trees silhouetted against the fading light of twilight. "Pretty out here, isn't it?" he remarks.

I nod and sip my wine. Glancing over at me and rubbing his hands together, Cal says nonchalantly, "So. What did Joe Ed say when you told him you were here?"

I lay my head back on the cushion of the chaise and look up at the quarter-moon, which has just appeared high above the pines. "I haven't exactly told him yet."

Cal raises his arm and looks at his watch. "They should be in Washington by now. Probably will get dinner before he tries to call. Buy you a little time."

"I don't imagine he'll call tonight, since I just saw him today."

Cal snorts. "I hope not, because he's going to kill my ass when he does."

"Cal? Why do you think Joe Ed wanted you, instead of Lieutenant Robinson, to take me to Talladega?"

He shrugs, glancing over at me, then

clears his throat. "Ah, he said something about Bethany asking to see me."

My eyes sting and I blink, biting my lip. I try to dab casually with the damp tissue at the corners of my eyes, but Cal notices. "Oh, shit. I said the wrong thing, didn't I?" he asks, grimacing.

I turn my head, looking out over the tree-tops. "Oh, wow! Look at that moon. Only a quarter full, but how bright it is. I'd love to see it over the lake when it's full, wouldn't you? Might have to return for that."

"You can count me out."

I dare to look at him. "Cal? I'm sorry I did this to you, I really am."

He shrugs, turning the beer up again and drinking. After a long silence, he says, "You didn't wrestle my gun away and hold it to my head, though I'm liable to tell Joe Ed that you did when he finds out I brought you here. I'm ashamed to tell you how good it sounded to me when you suggested we come here. The schedule has been a night-mare this summer."

"Maybe we both needed some time away from Montgomery," I say. "You know what I'd like to see you do, Cal? After I return home, you should take some time off and come back here. You could take out the boat and fish all day." He and Joe Ed have taken a couple of fishing trips together, so I know it's something he likes.

Cal smiles, watching the quarter-moon, his elbows propped on his knees and his hands cradling the beer. "Sounds good, but I have to save my time off for football season. I think I told you; my son Kyle's a placekicker at FSU, so I try to see all his games."

"You did tell me that. The night of the terrorist attack. Remember?"

He glances over at me, but when his eyes meet mine, he looks away, flushing. "Oh, yeah. I feel real bad, Julia, that I got half-crocked and told you all my troubles that night. Don't know what came over me. I've tried to find a way to apologize ever since, but . . ."

"Oh, hush. I swear, you ex-jocks are all the same. So afraid you might show a smidgen of emotion, and someone will see beneath that tough-guy exterior. You don't owe me an apology, Cal. Tell you what. Let's go inside and cook some grits."

Hands on hips, Cal watches, mesmerized, as I stir a cupful of stone-ground grits into two cups of boiling chicken broth. "It's much better made with heavy cream, but we don't have any," I tell him, measuring a spoonful of salt into my palm and tossing it in. "I was afraid to ask you to stop at a grocery store this afternoon, afraid if you stopped, I'd never get you back in the car. I prayed the whole way that we wouldn't need gas."

Cal chuckles. "You were damned determined to get here, that's for sure."

"Do you like to cook?"

He shakes his head. "Don't know. Rita—my ex-wife?—was a great cook, but one of those who didn't want anyone in her kitchen. Now that I'm on my own, guess I'll have to learn."

"Well, cooking grits is a good way to start, because they're so easy. And so good. Did your mother cook grits?"

I feel Cal's eyes on me. "Naw. She mostly fixed 'gator stew, over a campfire. She tracked the 'gator through the swamp, wrestled him down, killed him with her tomahawk, then skinned him all by herself. Fed the family for weeks."

I stop stirring the grits and look at him. His face is dark, guarded, his eyes fixed on the pot of boiling grits. "Jesus, Cal. You thought I meant that as a put-down?"

When he doesn't say anything, I poke him with my elbow. "Was it good?"

"What?" he says testily.

"'Gator stew. I've never had it."

He cuts his eyes over at me, then his face flushes and he grins sheepishly. "Sorry, Julia. Didn't mean to be so touchy."

"Obviously I hit a nerve. I'd love to hear all about your mama, but now I'm afraid to ask you. Here, take this dried-up head of garlic and see if you can get any garlic out, and we'll put it in the grits."

"Garlic in grits? You're kidding me, right?" Cal frowns in concentration as he pulls the garlic cloves loose from the head, then holds them up to me in the palm of his hand, like an offering. "Here you go."

I laugh and shake my head. "They've got to be peeled and chopped first."

He takes a knife from the wooden block by the stove and squints in concentration as he peels a garlic clove, as though it were a rare, priceless spice that had to be painstakingly extracted. I bite my lip to keep from jerking it out of his hand, smashing it on the cutting board, and throwing it into the grits. When he takes the tiny sliver of garlic left after removing half of it with the peel, puts it on the board, and tries to chop it, my patience leaves me. Grabbing his hand, I say, "Good Lord, Cal—it's not brain surgery. Give it here."

"Do you want me to do this or not?" He pushes my hand away from his, and I step backward, startled. The touch of his hand on mine is like an electric charge, unexpected and unwelcome. Flustered, I reach out for the garlic cloves with one hand and a chef's knife with the other.

"Ah . . . w-watch me and I'll show you how it's done." I pray that he doesn't notice that my hands are trembling as I roll the cloves under the knife to remove the skin, then smash them with the flat side. Scooping up the pungent particles on the knife blade, I dump them into the bubbling grits. "How about bringing me a stick of butter from the freezer?" I ask, making my voice light. Anything to get him away from me.

Cal obliges, frowning. "Hey . . . it's frozen," he informs me. "You still want it?"

I hold out my hand. "Doesn't matter. Watch." I turn off the burner under the grits and drop the frozen butter in, where the bubbling grits melt it into a golden pool. I give it a final stir, inhaling the divine fragrance of garlic, butter, and hot grits. "Ummm . . . you've got to smell this, Cal."

A mistake, I realize immediately, and step back quickly when he leans his head next to mine, his face close to the pot of grits. I've never been this close to him, so I've never noticed before the way his hair picks up the light, like the hidden fire of an onyx, nor had I realized the strong, forceful set of his mouth. He turns his head and looks at me with a slight smile, and I find his black eyes as opaque and mysterious as a primeval forest, and as alluring. "Smells good," he says. "What are we having with them?"

"Ah . . . oh! I guess . . . we'll just have grits. Just . . . grits."

His eyebrows come together in a frown. "Bet there's all kinds of ham and stuff in the freezer."

I hadn't thought of anything else, but I say, "I'm sure there is, but we don't want anything to compete with our masterpiece. You think Pinot Blanc will go okay with grits?"

He grins. "With my grits I usually have a

more robust, full-bodied white, but what the hell."

We fill our bowls and wineglasses, and I motion Cal to follow me to the porch, where we perch on the edges of our chairs, bowls in hand. We don't speak as we eat, and Cal goes back for seconds. "Need anything?" he calls out from the kitchen.

"Look on the counter and you'll see a box with a pecan pie in it. How about bringing me a slice with a scoop of vanilla ice cream on it? Oh—and could you warm it up in the microwave first?"

Cal sticks his head out the door, his eyes wide. "Won't that melt the ice cream?"

I laugh, putting my hand to my forehead. "No wonder Rita wouldn't let you in the kitchen! Warm the pie up for a minute, then put the ice cream on it."

Cal goes back into the kitchen, fiddles around, then sticks his head out the door again. "Pecan pie with ice cream?"

"If it's too complicated for you, I'll come fix it."

"No, I'm just trying to figure this out. I've never seen you eat anything before. What's going on?"

"What do you mean, what's going on? I'm hungry, is what."

Cal eyes me suspiciously but goes back into the kitchen. After what seems like an inordinate amount of time, just as I'm about to go see what's happened to him, he returns to the porch with two plates. He hands me a plate with a quarter of a pecan pie on it, topped with a mound of ice cream. "My God, what did you use to scoop out the ice cream, a shovel?" I gasp.

He sits across from me and digs into his own plate, which looks like it has twice the amount mine does. "Umm, this is great. You said you were hungry. You're never hungry, Julia. I used to think you were anorexic."

Shocked, I sit with my spoon poised over my plate. I raise my head and study Cal curiously. "No kidding? Actually, it's a wonder I'm not, with the mother I have. I was never skinny enough, pretty enough, smart enough. . . . Well, you get the picture. You know my mother."

"She's a tough old broad, that's for sure. Always looks at me like I should be using the servants' entrance, but only if I wipe my feet off real good before stepping on the marble floors." Cal raises a bare foot and laughs. "If she could see me now! Proof that I'm the barefooted savage she suspected all along."

With a pang, I think of Jesus Perez, and how Mother must have made him feel. I look at Cal for a long moment, then say, "I'm sorry, Cal."

He looks surprised. "What for? Not your fault, Julia."

I shrug. "Yes, but . . . well, I'm sorry my mother's the way she is."

"You're not that way, and that's all that matters."

Unexpectedly, his remark, spoken casually, touches me, and I smile at him before turning my attention back to my plate. We fall into a silence eating our pie, except for moans of pure, hedonistic pleasure, but eventually Cal raises his head and looks at me, his eyes troubled. "Okay, Julia, I've got to ask you. What are you doing here?"

"Eating pecan pie. What does it look like?"

"You know what I mean."

"Yes, but I don't know the answer. All I know is, I had to come. Do you remember meeting my friend Corrine, the artist? Lives on Blue Mountain, in north Georgia?"

He frowns. "She one of the Same Old Girls?"

"Same *Sweet* Girls—I've told you a dozen times."

"I've met all your friends, I think, but I can't quite place her."

"A lot of her artwork's at the Mansion, but that's not what I wanted to tell you about Corrine. She has a saying that's her philosophy of life, she claims. She says, when the pupil is ready, the teacher appears."

Cal thinks about it, his dark head tilted to the side. "Sounds like one of my granny's sayings."

I laugh. "My mother has all the old sayings, too. You make your bed, you've got to lie in it; a stitch in time saves nine, stuff like that. But Corrine's saying is more of a Zen thing, unlike the old proverbs. Anyway, what it says to me is this: I must have needed to come to the lake, must have needed to learn something from my time here."

Cal rolls his eyes. "Too deep for a dumb redneck like me. Or redskin, guess I should say."

"You said it; I didn't."

"In the sticks of Florida where I was raised, there wasn't much difference between the two. Except, rednecks were more acceptable than us half-breeds. We were lower than white trash, lower than Mexicans and Cubans, even lower than blacks, which was saying a lot fifty years ago."

"No kidding? That why you have a chip on your shoulder?"

Cal bristles. "Bull. I do not. Want another piece of pie?"

"No. And don't try changing the subject. What was your mother's name?"

"What?"

"Your mother's name . . . what was it?"

"Jesus Christ!" he breathes in exasperation, throwing his hands up.

"Is that a common name among Creek women?"

"Ha ha. Okay, her name was Little Running Deer."

"Come on."

"My mama's name was Faye. Faye Ross. She gave me my old man's last name."

"He was a white man, right? Were they married? Is your mother still alive?"

Cal holds up a hand. "Whoa. One question at the time. Naw, they never married, so I'm not only a half-breed but also a bastard.

Literally as well as figuratively. My mama raised me by herself. In those days, you didn't do DNA tests or sue for child support, so she had a tough row to hoe, all her life. Worked as a maid in a beach resort, long as I can remember. Always thought that's why she died young, working so hard like that. That's my granny's theory, and she's a medicine woman."

"*Is?* She's alive?" When Cal nods, I say, "My God, you're fifty, so she must be a hundred."

He laughs. "She'll be ninety-five this summer. My mama had me young, when she was a teenager. Granny Ross raised me after Mama died. She's quite a character. You'd like her."

"I'd love to meet her. Where is she?"

"Nursing home in Florida. I get down to see her when I go to FSU." He licks ice cream off the spoon and moans, "Oh, God, that's so good."

"Told you," I laugh.

"Matter of fact, Julia, I was going to ask your advice on something, when the time came. I plan on making a big deal out of Granny Ross's ninety-fifth birthday later this summer and was going to ask you what I should get her, since I want it to be something really special."

"Tell you what. I'll do it under one condition: that you invite me to her birthday party."

"Not funny, Julia."

"I'm not teasing about this—I really want to go!"

He shrugs. "We'll see. Joe Ed knows her; maybe he'll want to come, too."

I grin. "Can't you see what the press would do with that? Governor Stovall seeks Native American vote by paying visit to ninety-five-year-old Creek on her birthday."

He chuckles, and we fall into a companionable silence as we finish the pie. I steal a look at Cal, relieved that he's showing no sign of having noticed my reaction when he put his hand on mine earlier. I'd die if he had! It made me understand Astor sneaking out to meet him that night, something I'd been so snooty about before. Cal raises his head and catches me studying him, and I surprise myself by saying, "Cal? I saw you meet Astor that night she stayed with me, on our way to Dauphin Island. The first weekend in June. I've wanted to say something about it, but . . . I heard a noise and woke up, and I followed Astor down the back steps to find out where she was going. She didn't see me, though, but I watched you open the door for her in the back wing."

"You saw me?" he says, his face wary.

"I saw you. Astor didn't say anything to me about it. She still hasn't."

Cal's eyes fill with dismay as we stare at each other. I don't know what made me blurt it out like that. If I'd wanted to hear about it from him, I should've just asked. Cal rubs his face then says, "I'm sorry you saw us."

"Astor's a beautiful, intriguing woman, but she's bad news."

He snorts and shakes his head. "That's for sure."

When he doesn't say anything else, I persist. "You aren't still seeing her, are you?"

His smile seems bitter to me. "Ah . . . no. No, I haven't seen her since that night."

"Good. I'd hate to see you hurt by her, Cal. I love Astor. Like you and Joe Ed, we go back a long time. But . . . I know how she uses people."

He stares at me, as though wanting to say something more. Once he begins, "Julia?" But before I can respond, he shakes his head. "Never mind."

I look down at my plate, chewing my bottom lip, then say, "Please don't think I'm upset with either you or Astor, okay? I know how lonely it can be."

Cal smiles a small smile. "No, I don't think you do, Julia. I don't think you have any idea how lonely it is out there." A heavy silence falls between us. In the semidarkness of the porch, I can feel Cal's eyes on me, then he says, "Well done, Julia. You've succeeded in getting me off the subject of you and why you came here today."

My face flushing, I put my plate—almost empty—on the table where a lamp burns. Rising, I go to the edge of the porch and stand, my back to Cal. "I told you. I don't know why I'm here." Looking down the cliffs, I watch the dark waters of the lake reflecting the lights of the house. The only sounds are insects hitting the screen and the rustle of leaves in the trees. Somewhere deep in the woods an owl calls.

Cal stands, too. "What will you do tomorrow?"

"I've got to decide. Only thing I've decided, I'm not going to the breakfast. I've already left a message for my assistant, for her to send my regrets."

"What do you think Joe Ed will say about that?"

"He'll be okay with it. I've decided to play sick. Sick headache, I said. That way, no one's upset." I don't tell him that I'm ashamed of myself for taking the easy way out, not able to face the consequences of shirking my duties after all. But what would my poor assistant say—the first lady doesn't want to come to your boring breakfast? Sorry, but she simply can't face another one?

Cal comes to stand beside me. "Sounds like the best idea," he says. "But . . . you *are* going back to Montgomery tomorrow, aren't you?"

"No." And as soon as I say it, I know. I'm not going back.

Cal lays his forehead against the screen and closes his eyes. "Oh, shit. I was afraid of this. If not tomorrow, then when, Julia?"

I shake my head without answering, and unexpectedly, my eyes fill with tears. I wipe them away, tired of crying, tired of being tired. "I'm not sure I am."

Cal's head jerks up. "You mean . . . ?" He doesn't finish the thought, doesn't put it in words, and neither do I. A silence falls between us, then Cal clears his throat and says, "Julia?"

"Don't ask me anything else, okay? I don't know what's wrong with me. Oh, God." My voice breaks, choked with tears, and I lower my head, covering my face with my hands.

Taking a step toward me, Cal takes me into his arms. His voice, soft and gentle, shakes me to the core. "You're the saddest woman I've ever known, Julia. I wish . . ."

He doesn't get a chance to finish the thought. As in my dream, my hands move into his hair, and I pull his head to mine. His mouth closes over mine, and his arms, large and strong and muscled, draw me to him. His hands cradle my head, with his fingers in my hair, pulling it down from the tight twist in back. I feel my hair falling on my shoulders, loose, wild, unlike I've ever worn it, and I gasp for breath when he moves his mouth from mine, saying with a groan, "Julia, Julia, no . . ." Before I know what's happening, Cal has gripped my wrists and pushed me away from him. My arms are empty, empty without him pressed against me. I move back toward him in order to regain his warmth, but he pushes me away. "Julia, no," he repeats. "Listen to me! Joe Ed . . . he's one of the best friends I've ever had." His face is dark, and his breath comes in gasps, as though he's been running.

"Cal, please . . ." I murmur, unable to stop myself. I'm drawn toward the warmth of his body as though I've been frozen and am seeking out the searing flames of a fire. "Please . . . stay with me tonight." I know, of course, that that's why we're here, why I've brought him here, forced him to come with me today. I've known, ever since the dream.

But Cal holds my wrists so tight that I can't move, pushing me away from him. He closes his eyes and shakes his head, side to side. "Please, Julia, don't do this to me."

He's right, of course; I can't. I can't do this to him. I cannot tell him that he's the only man who's made me feel this way in so many years that I've forgotten what it's like, that I want him more than he could know, more than he could possibly want me, right now. He's too good a man; I can't do this to him, and I can't do it to Joe Ed. *Joe Ed—my God, what have I done?* I jerk my hands loose from Cal's grip and step backward. Trembling, my knees barely able to hold me up, I reach my hands up to try and pin my hair back as I had it, but it's too late; it's loose and tangled, falling on my shoulders. My lips still burning from his kiss, I raise my eyes to Cal's. The look on his face tears me apart. "Oh, Cal, I'm so sorry," I whisper. When tears roll down my face, I don't bother to wipe them away.

Cal rubs his face with both hands. "We can't stay here, Julia," he says finally, and I nod. No, of course we can't. Here, alone with him, I wouldn't be able to stay away from him, to stay out of his bed.

"We have to go back," I say, and Cal nods, his eyes downcast.

"Yeah. We do," he says hoarsely, raising his head. "Ah—what? What can we do? Okay, what about this?" Shaking, he pushes his hair back with his hands, that coal-black hair that looks coarse but felt like silk in my hands . . . I take a deep breath and tear my eyes from his hands, force myself to think straight. "We can say that you wanted to stay in Talladega and have dinner with Bethany," Cal suggests. "That . . . ah . . . you took her out, we were running late . . ." He stops and looks at his watch. "It's not ten yet. That'll work, won't it?"

I nod, sick at the lie, at using Bethany like this, but what else can we do? Again, I make a futile attempt to pin my hair up, pulling the clasp free that's fallen to my shoulder, caught in a tangle. I say, foolishly, "I—I've got to put my hair back up . . ."

To my surprise, Cal moves close to me and takes the clasp from my hand. His eyes avoiding mine, he gathers my hair into his hands and buries his face in it, breathing deeply. "Goddamn, Julia, you've got the most beautiful hair I've ever seen," he whispers. I stand frozen as he combs through my hair with his fingers, then twists the length of it into a spiral, which he secures to the back of my head with the tortoiseshell clasp. For one heart-stopping second, his hands linger on my neck, then he drops them and steps back, abruptly. "There," he says, looking down at me, his eyes searching mine.

I can't speak, can't breathe, so I turn and stumble toward the door. "Let me get my things," I say, not looking at him, not sure he's heard me. But he too leaves the porch, moving past me in a wide arc to the door.

"I'll get my stuff and meet you in the car," he says briskly, and I nod, heading blindly toward my bedroom in the back of the house.

* * *

Cal and I don't return to Montgomery that night, after all. In my bedroom, I don't change out of my shorts and linen top, since this late, no one will be up at the Mansion to notice that I'm returning disheveled, not dressed properly. I throw my black suit, silk shell, and heels into my overnight bag and reach for my purse. We need to get back now; it's going to be past midnight if I don't hurry. . . . My cell phone falls out of my purse and I grab it, checking to see if Joe Ed's called before putting it away. There's his number listed in the missed calls, showing he called earlier, around eight-thirty. He hasn't called back; must have gone to dinner, or maybe he'd just come in from dinner when he called, before retiring early. With his schedule lately, and seeing Bethany, he's probably exhausted himself. I see that there are several calls that arrived after Joe Ed's, and my breath catches in my throat. Bethany! Why would anyone else be calling me this late, on a Sunday night, unless it's her, needing me? I grab my purse and pull my reading glasses out, peering at the numbers listed on the missed-calls list. It's not Bethany after all—it's Lanier, and I roll my eyes, smiling to myself. Lanier and one of her crises, I imagine, calling to tell me that she's really, really messed up this time. It must be a lulu, because she's called several times. I scroll back to see when she started calling, wondering if she's been calling me all day. There's a number earlier this afternoon I don't recognize at first, then realize from the area code that it's Corrine's. Frowning, I check to see if she's left voice mail, but she hasn't. Odd, for a Sunday afternoon, to have a call from Corrine. Usually, I'm the one to call her, since she says she hates to bother me, with my crazy schedule, afraid she'll catch me in the middle of a meeting or something. Come to think of it, I don't think she's ever called me on my cell phone.

I check the latest voice message from Lanier, but all she says is, "Julia . . . it's Lanier again. Guess your cell phone's out of range. I remember now, this is the weekend you were going to see Bethany at Talladega. Call me when you get this, no matter how late it is." Her voice is frantic, so unlike Lanier's usual, joking banter.

Something's happened, and my fingers tremble as I scroll backward to the first message from Lanier, late this afternoon. I listen as she says, "Hey, Julia, this is Lanier. Can't wait to tell you that Lindy came to see me this afternoon! Call me when you get this, and I'll tell you all about it."

Even stranger, that her first message should contain such happy news and her last message be so upsetting. Could something have happened to Lindy? I press the buttons on the phone that redial Lanier's number, and she answers on the first ring. I can tell immediately that she's been crying. "Julia, thank God it's you!" she says.

"What is it? What's happened?" My knees are too weak to hold me up, and I sink down, sitting on the side of the bed. Suddenly I know what it must be. "Oh, Lord—it's Mose, isn't it?"

"No, no. It's not Mose. It's Corrine." Lanier's voice breaks, and I grip the phone tight as she sobs.

"Corrine?"

"I knew she was sicker than she was letting on, Julia!" Lanier cries. "I knew it, but I didn't act on it. I should have gone there, took her to a doctor myself, made him tell me what was going on with her. I want to go so bad now—"

"Lanier, calm down and tell me what's happened."

"Culley called me. I'd given him my number, made me promise to call . . . he found her, Julia! He said he went to her house to get a book or something, then left. Said he'd just gone out the front door when he heard his mother fall, so he ran upstairs and found her unconscious, on the floor. . . ."

"Oh, my God, Lanier!" I gasp. "She's not . . ."

"No, no, not that. But, it sounds bad, Julia. Bad. Culley was really upset, crying like a baby, he was so scared."

"When did this happen?" I make myself calm down by taking deep breaths, and I hear Lanier on the other end, doing the same thing.

"Just a little while ago. Culley called an ambulance when he couldn't rouse her, then called his asshole daddy, who met them at the Chickasaw hospital. Culley called me from the emergency room."

"Oh, God. What are they saying is wrong?"

Sniffing, Lanier says, "They don't know, is all I can get out of Culley." I wait as she blows her nose loudly. "I'm so tempted to leave here right now, Julia, and go over there. I can't stand the idea of her being in the care of that ex of hers, and Culley was such a wreck, he won't be any good to her. He kept saying over and over that it was all his fault, and I had to bite my tongue to keep from telling the little shit that it probably was. You know how he's always taken up for his screwball daddy over Corrine. I swear, I'm going over there, right now!"

"No, you're not, Lanier. It's too late, and you can't drive all night, then be any good to Corrine tomorrow." I look at the clock on the bedside table. "Listen, I'm closer to Atlanta now than any of the rest of us, and—"

Lanier interrupts breathlessly. "Oh, that's right—if you're still in Talladega, then you're only a couple of hours away!"

"I'll go," I say, not even trying to explain where I am. "I can be there in no time."

"Oh, Julia, that's wonderful!" Lanier breaks down again, sobbing, and I force myself to speak calmly to her.

"Listen to me, Lanier. I'll call and leave you a message when I get there, okay? But don't stay up, and don't leave your phone on. You need to get some sleep so you can come over as soon as we know what's going on, you hear? Because it sounds like Corrine's going to need you."

"Oh, God, Julia—you're great!" Lanier says. "I'll do that. I'll have to work my shift tomorrow because I'm the only one on the floor . . . . everyone's on vacation in the summer, you know. But I'll leave here as soon as I hear from you."

"Great plan," I say. "Now go on to sleep, and don't worry. I'll take care of this." But before I hang up, Lanier says, "Julia?"

"Yes?"

"You remember, don't you, that it was July, twenty-five years ago, when we lost Dixie Lee? I can't stand to lose another one of us."

"Don't say that, Lanier. Don't dare say that. We're not going to let that happen, you hear?"

I bang on the door of the guest house and Cal opens it immediately, a puzzled look on his face. He's buttoning the tan shirt of his uniform, dressed in his stiff uniform pants and highly polished shoes. "I'll wait here for you to put the shorts and T-shirt back on, Cal, but hurry, okay?"

"What the hell?"

"I need you to take me to Blue Mountain.

My friend Corrine? I just found out, she's in the emergency room with an ex-husband from hell and a hysterical son. I said I'd go," I tell him, breathlessly.

If there's anything Cal's good at from his years as a trooper, it's a crisis. He nods. "Let's go, then," he says. "I'll have you there in no time."

20

Corrine
BLUE MOUNTAIN

I'VE ALWAYS IMAGINED THAT ambulances fly through the night with sirens wailing and lights flashing, but when I blink my eyes open and look around, we're moving quietly, at a normal speed. Maybe that means I'm not dying after all. Or more likely, it's the winding mountain roads that are slowing us down. The ambulance attendant sitting on a little stool next to me, a big mountain woman with a long gray braid down her back, is holding my wrist as she checks my pulse, eyes fastened thoughtfully to her huge-faced watch. A blood pressure cuff is on my arm, but no tubes and heart monitors and scary stuff like in the television shows. Without taking her eyes from the watch, the EMT smiles. "You're back with us, huh?"

I nod, not sure I can speak, my mouth is so dry. After a couple of painful swallows, I ask her, "Do I have a pulse?" I feel so horrible, so weak and spent, I can't imagine that much of anything is beating.

I'm not really surprised when she doesn't answer me, scribbling on a clipboard once she gets a reading, then fiddling with the blood pressure cuff, scribbling again. "We're going to get you fixed up, hon," is all she says to me, her calm voice with its flat country twang oddly reassuring. I close my eyes again and drift off, trying to remember what happened. For some reason, I feel no surprise at finding myself in an ambulance, moving through the dark night, although I have no idea how I got here. All I remember is getting bad sick, having hot spells and cold chills, then throwing up about a million times. Miles came by when I was lying on the bed . . . guess he called the ambulance.

"Are we going to Chickasaw?" I ask the EMT, which is a foolish question, considering it has the only hospital on Blue Mountain. Guess I expected her to answer, no, hon, we normally bypass Chickasaw and drive all the way to Atlanta.

"Great little hospital," she says briskly, patting my arm. "They'll take good care of you there."

Suddenly, we're at the emergency room and they have me on a bed-looking thing, rolling me down the hall. I want to tell them that it's okay, they don't have to push me; if they'll let me get up, I'll walk. Or rather, I'll try to walk, even though I'm not sure that I can. It feels scary, riding down the hall like this, looking up at the big lights overhead, and my heart pounds. At least I know it's still beating. I don't like this, don't like doctors or hospitals or any of it. I've never been sick before, not really. Except for Culley's birth, my times in a hospital have been scary, unpleasant stays, brought on by my suicide attempts. I don't want to be here. I want to go home.

I want to go home even more when they put me in an examination room and Miles and Culley show up at my side, Miles being take-charge and in control as always, questioning the nurse who comes in to take my vital signs. I don't know if it has to do with the appearance of Miles or not, but suddenly I'm sick all over again, and the nurse is bustling around, holding a shiny, stainless-steel pan out for me to barf in. Silently, I bless her when she makes Miles and Culley leave the room, but I reach out my hand to Culley when I see the scared expression on his face. However, he doesn't see me, doesn't know that I'm trying to get his attention, to tell him not to worry, that I'll be all right. I start crying and the nurse thinks it's because I'm so sick. She clucks around trying to make me feel better, telling me the doctor will be right in, that I'll just love her, that she's the cutest thing who doesn't look nearly old enough to be a doctor. I lay back on the table exhausted, too empty to throw up, too weak to cry.

The doctor, who looks no older than Lindy Sanders, is a petite Asian girl with a long ponytail and dangling silver earrings. After questioning me, examining me, and ordering a gallon of blood drawn, she disappears for an inordinate amount of time, it seems like. Surely if I were dying, she'd be hanging around. I assume Miles bullied his way in, because after she's gone for several minutes, Miles and Culley come back into the room. Culley lingers by the door, looking so scared that it breaks my heart. I ignore Miles trying to read the monitor they've got me hooked up to, poking around at everything, muttering things like, "Umm . . . Ah, yes. . . . I see," and I motion to Culley to come over. Although he still looks like he's seen a ghost, he moves to stand beside me, taking my hand in both of his.

"You look like Buckwheat with your eyes so big," I say to him, smiling.

His face pale and drawn, Culley doesn't return my smile, just blinks down at me like he's trying not to cry. Suddenly I remember the heated words we exchanged this afternoon, how upset he was with me, and I wonder if he's feeling bad about it. "Hey, baby," I whisper, "it's okay. I'm going to be all right."

He doesn't respond, just shrugging. When the technician comes in to take blood, Culley's eyes get wider and his face paler, if possible. He's always been afraid of needles. "I'll be in the lobby," he mutters, dropping my hand and hurrying out the door.

Miles questions the technician as to what they're checking for, but she shrugs him off, infuriating him, I'm sure. After she leaves, I ask Miles if he was the one to find me after I passed out, and he shakes his head. "No. It was Culley," he tells me. "I couldn't find his damn music, so he drove over to your cabin to look for it. Told me that he'd started to his car when he heard a noise upstairs that sounded like someone falling down. He went back in the house to check and found you unconscious on your bedroom floor."

I remember all of it now, hearing Culley come in, trying to call out to him . . . and the hateful, bitter things he said, yelling up the stairs. No wonder he looks so shaken; he must feel awful. "Did . . . ah . . . Culley say anything else?" I ask Miles. I wonder how much he's told his dad about our argument today.

Standing over me with his hands in his pockets, Miles the therapist says, "You don't need to worry about that now, Corrine. Save your energy for getting well."

"I . . . I don't want him to feel responsible or anything—" I begin, but Miles cuts me off, an eyebrow raised.

"Responsible? Why should he feel responsible?"

"Not responsible, exactly. . . . I meant, I don't want him upset."

"Of course he was upset. He thought you'd tried to kill yourself again," Miles snaps.

I'm stunned speechless, the now-familiar

wave of nausea sweeping over me. I'm cold again, shivering, then hot, drenched in sweat. "Oh, no!"

"It's hardly new territory for him," Miles snorts. "But even so, he was panicked, distraught, full of anxiety, as he always is when dealing with this."

"*This* meaning me and my craziness, of course," I murmur, but Miles doesn't have a chance to respond. The door opens and the little-girl doctor comes in, not quite as perky as before, her face solemn this time. Miles shakes her hand, tells her that he's not had the privilege of meeting her before, even though his mental health clinic is close by, and that it was our son who found me unconscious. By putting it that way, he avoids telling her that he's my ex-husband, so she addresses both me and Miles when she talks. I don't even try to tell her that I don't want him in here, don't want to have to deal with him as well as the sickness, the hospital, and the revelation that my son thinks our argument today was responsible for yet another suicide attempt on my part.

Essentially, the little-girl doctor ends up passing the buck. She says there are all sorts of possible reasons for my sickness, even though nothing is immediately apparent. She's going to admit me so that Dr. Brown can run more diagnostic tests tomorrow. Everything she mentions, CT scans, MRI, GI series, I've had before. When she says they're readying a room for me, I close my eyes, and tears leak out the corners.

"No, no, no," I moan. "I don't want to be admitted. I've had all those damn tests, and I hate hospitals, and I don't want to be here. I want to go home!"

"You could do this as an outpatient, certainly, Miss Cooper," the doctor says, "but you're in no condition to go home. I'm sure I don't need to remind you that you were sick enough to pass out. You were sick enough to be brought here by ambulance. I want to start an IV, since you're partially dehydrated, and your blood count isn't good. Some of the other numbers are causing me concern as well. I would strongly advise you to remain here in order to be monitored closely."

Before I realize what he's up to, Miles has taken the little-girl doctor's arm and propelled her to the door, murmuring, "If I could just speak to you outside, Dr. Lin . . ." And he's taken her out before I can protest. I know what he's telling her, that I'm crazy and unable to make a rational decision. Probably telling her about my past history, the depression and suicide attempts, the hospitalizations. If I could hold my head up, I'd yell at them—the door's open—and tell them that it's *my* body and *my* sickness. But I don't have the energy.

Sure enough, the doctor's expression has changed when she comes back in, Miles behind her looking smug. Glaring at him, I say sullenly, "My ex-husband doesn't make decisions for me, doctor. . . ." But I stop mid-sentence when Culley comes back in the room, standing in the doorway with shoulders hunched and hands in his jeans' pockets. He's still pale and scared, his eyes troubled. Miles motions for him to come in.

"Our son, Culley," he says to the doctor, and they shake hands. "Dr. Lin was just saying, son, that she's admitting your mom in order to run more tests tomorrow."

Culley nods, then glances at me. It's obvious that he's been crying, his eyes reddened and bleary. "It's okay, baby," I say to him. "Everything's going to be just fine."

Whatever they put in the IV for nausea is working. I'm not only feeling better, I'm able to doze on and off, in spite of nurses coming in and out of the room with forms for me to sign, trays of ice water and apple juice, blood pressure, pulse, and temperature checks every few minutes, it seems like. I promise the last nurse who comes in that I'll buzz her if I change my mind about needing something for sleep. I'm weak as dishwater but not sleepy, don't want to take anything. The nurse seems miffed that I turned down her magic pill. I don't even try telling her that I hate to take drugs, hate the groggy way they make me feel, that I'd rather take herbal remedies for sleep if need be. If I did, she'd probably put on my chart that I was being difficult, adding to the little-girl doctor's notes about my past history of craziness. Most likely, I'd end up on the psych ward again. Probably should've taken the damn pill and pretended to swallow it, held it in my mouth until the nurse left the room. She turned out the lights even though I asked her not to, but she did open the blinds next to my bed. I shocked her by asking that the blinds be opened even though it's almost midnight, and I'm sure she'll add that to the chart as more evidence of my advanced stage of insanity.

When the noises on the floor die down, everyone sleeping their pill-induced sleep, I turn on the dim little nightlight over my bed. For some reason I don't want to turn all the lights off and lie here in the dark. When I do, thoughts of the day threaten to overtake me. I can't get it out of my mind. It's not my sickness that troubles me, though, scary as that is. I keep replaying the sharp, bitter words that Culley and I exchanged, over and over, and I recall the awful time leading up to my falling on the floor, when Culley came back into the house and up the stairs, into my bedroom. I can only imagine his horror when he saw me lying there, thinking my argument with him had caused me to overdose. I don't know how I can ever make it up to him. I wanted so badly to talk to him tonight, to tell him that none of this was his fault, but I never got the chance. I was even willing for him and Miles to come with me to the hospital room, but when the orderly arrived to take me to the room, Miles surprised me by saying that he and Culley would see me tomorrow. I called out to Culley, and he returned to kiss my forehead and squeeze my hand. He didn't look at me, however, and didn't respond when I called his name. He was gone before I could catch his eye.

Even though I think I've cried all I can, that

no tears are left inside me, an overwhelming, helpless sadness comes over me as I think about Culley. We'd just begun to relax around each other, and to feel close to each other, and now this! Tears scald my eyes and roll down my face, wetting my hair, which is loose and tangled and spread out all over the pillow. With my free hand, the one that's not hooked up to the IV, I fumble for a tissue, and when I knock the box of tissues off the table to the floor, I cry even harder. Giving in to my weakness and helplessness, I sob loud, gasping sobs that tear at my throat and hurt my chest with their force.

It's then that the door is opened the tiniest crack, and the hall light creeping into the room touches my face. Startled, I turn my head toward the door and see someone peering in at me. It's that damned nurse again, so I swallow my tears and try futilely to wipe them away with the back of my hand. Guess she's come back to give me the pill whether I want it or not. Probably has a monitor where she can hear every noise I make. I see her in the door, outlined in light, see that she's coming toward my bed. And worse—a large, muscular man is with her, an orderly, I guess, who she's brought to make me take the pill if I refuse. Nurse Ratchett is alive and well at Chickasaw Memorial Hospital.

When she gets closer to my bed, I jump in surprise, like a newborn startling in a crib. Instead of a nurse's uniform, she's dressed in a loose, peach-colored tunic and white shorts with tiny pearls in her ears, her pale hair twisted up and held with a clasp. It looks like . . . but it couldn't be! *"Julia?"*

She puts a long, pink-tipped finger up to her lips and says, "Shhh."

The nausea medicine must be causing me to hallucinate. I'm still blinking in shock when Julia leans over me, grabs both of my shoulders, her fingertips digging into my skin, and kisses my forehead again and again. "Oh, thank God, Corrine!" she whispers, her breath hot on my wet cheek. "I was worried to death about you!" She stops and looks around the room, as though making sure no one's around to hear her.

"Jesus Christ, Julia—what are you doing here?" I gasp, still not sure she's real.

"Shhh," she repeats. "You're going to get us kicked out of here."

Looking over her shoulder, I see that a man is standing by the door, lurking in the shadows, the man I mistook for the orderly. "Don't tell me Joe Ed's with you?" I blink up at Julia confused and uncertain. Now I'm sure I'm hallucinating. Maybe I should buzz the nurse and say, "Excuse me, Nurse Ratchett, but the governor and first lady of Alabama are in my room, and I was wondering if you could serve us tea?"

She turns and glances at the man standing in the dark, arms folded, waiting for her. Pushing my damp hair behind my ear, she puts her head next to mine and whispers, "Please don't kill me for bringing him into your room, but it's the only way I could get in."

"You had to tell them the governor was with you to get in here?" I repeat, more dazed than ever. I'm never taking that medicine again.

Still leaning over me, her gray eyes dark with concern, Julia says in a quiet voice, "Of course not. I'll tell you about everything as soon as I hear how you're doing. I didn't plan on coming in, just sticking my head in and seeing if you were asleep. But I heard you crying, so . . ." She stops and shrugs, then asks again, "How are you feeling? What happened?"

Keeping my voice quiet, I tell Julia everything, except the part about Culley and me having an argument. I tell her that the doctors don't know what's wrong with me yet. I lie back on the pillows when I finish, exhausted with the effort. Julia murmurs and strokes my hair, shaking her head. "Oh, Corrine, honey," she whispers, "I'm so sorry. But you're going to be all right. I'm here to make sure of that."

"How did you know I was here?" Talking is an effort, and I swallow painfully. Julia notices and reaches for the glass of water by my bed. After pressing the button to raise the head of the bed upright, Julia holds the straw of the glass steady so I can drink from it, and I slurp eagerly. "Thank you," I say, lying back on the pillows and looking up at her.

"How did I know you were here?" Julia smiles. "Lanier, of course. The Mouth of the South."

I blink. "But . . . how did Lanier know? I didn't call her."

"Culley did, she said. Said he was really upset. Scared her to death."

"*Culley?*"

Julia shrugs. "She said she'd given him her number, begged him to call if anything happened. We've all been so worried about you, Corrine. I'm so afraid . . ." But she stops herself, biting her lower lip. "Listen, I'm going now so you can sleep. Like I said, we wouldn't have come in if we hadn't heard you crying."

I grab her hand. "Please, please don't leave me. I want to hear how you got here." I glance toward the door. "Tell Joe Ed to come on in, too. No point in him standing there in the dark."

"It's not Joe Ed with me," Julia says. "And I sure hadn't planned on doing the introductions tonight, but he does want to say something to you. I'll let him tell you what it is, and maybe it'll cheer you up. Five minutes, though—then we're going. The nurses are liable to come in at any minute, then we'll all get kicked out." Julia turns her head and motions for the man leaning on the door to come over to the bed.

Propped on a stack of pillows, I blink my eyes in the dimness of the nightlight, trying to figure out where I've seen him before. He steps forward hesitantly, obviously ill at ease at being summoned. He's big and dark and dressed in some kind of uniform, and he eyes me nervously. Julia pushes my legs over, sits down on the bed, and motions for the man to sit in the chair next to my bed, the one she's just vacated. He crosses to it, quiet as a panther. I watch as he eases into the chair, then Julia says, "Corrine, you remember Cal Hawkins, don't you? Works for Joe Ed?"

Oh, Jesus, not the bodyguard! I can't help it, I turn my head to stare at Julia in shock. She winks playfully at me, then takes my hand in both of hers. She has to squeeze my hand twice to get me to respond, and even then, I stammer. "Oh! H-how are you, Cal?" My voice sounds like the pitiful mewing of a sick kitten, it's so weak.

He inclines his head, his dark eyes grave and unsmiling. "Better question would be, how are you?" he asks. I like his voice, low and surprisingly gentle, for a man his size.

I lick my dry lips and swallow. "I've been better."

Cal Hawkins smiles a small smile. "I imagine so. I heard you tell Julia that the doctors don't know what's wrong yet?"

I shake my head. "That's right. More tests tomorrow."

Cal winces. "That won't be much fun." I can't stop myself from studying him curiously, since he was such a hot topic at the last

SSG gathering. I remember him from the inauguration a couple of years ago, though there was so much going on that day, it's all a blur. What I can't forget, of course, is Julia and Astor's exchange about Astor's sneaking out to meet him at the Mansion, then Astor denying to me that she'd had an affair with him when I questioned her. Now that I have the opportunity to study him up close, I know Astor was lying like a rug. No way she wouldn't make a play for him. It's not likely he'd escape the kiss of the spider woman when I'm lying here on my deathbed thinking he might well be the best-looking man I've ever laid eyes on.

Julia's squeezing my hand again, and I turn my head to look up at her, blushing that she's caught me lusting after her bodyguard, just like the rest of the SSGs. "Okay, Corrine, I'll tell you what we're doing here," she says, "then we'll go and let you sleep."

"I'm not sleepy," I say, "and when y'all leave, I'll have to lie here and be miserable. I do not want to be here, believe me. But, go ahead. Tell me."

"Well, we flew over here from Alabama after I talked to Lanier, going a hundred miles an hour," Julia begins, and I glance over at Cal Hawkins, wondering how come he's with her, and where Joe Ed is. This was the weekend Julia was visiting Bethany at the Helen Keller Institute, I recall, and I think she said Joe Ed was going to Washington afterward. I turn my attention back to her story. "We figured we could make up something if we got stopped, but we had no problem getting here," she's saying. "No problem, that is, till we arrived at the hospital. I'd called on my cell phone to find out what's going on, and all they'd tell me was you'd been moved from emergency to a room."

"Julia thought that was a good sign," Cal adds. "You going into a room instead of ICU."

Julia nods and continues her story. "So, when we get here, the plan is for Cal to wait for me in the car while I find out where you are and what your condition is. Well! They acted like I was a pure fool, trying to check on you this late. Nobody would tell me *anything,* not even your room number! Guess they thought I'd sneak in to see you if they did, I was being such a pain."

"Now where would they ever get such a silly idea?" I say, and Julia snickers.

"When it became clear that I wasn't going to get any information out of anyone, I went back to the car to get Cal." She glances over at Cal. "And I made him put on his uniform."

I gasp. "What did he have on?"

Julia's eyes widen, and she throws her head back and laughs. When Cal chuckles, too, I can't help it, I giggle, putting my hand over my mouth.

"Poor Cal." Julia remembers to whisper again after her outburst of laughter. "Getting initiated into the SSGs this way." She turns her head to smile at him, a twinkle in her eye, and I realize that they're good friends. I remember now, Cal's been a close friend of Joe Ed's forever. Julia turns back to me. "Cal and I had been at the Helen Keller Institute visiting Bethany, remember, so we were casually dressed. He had on shorts, like me. But once he got into uniform, I dragged him with me so we'd look real official. Didn't know if it'd work or not, but the guy at the front desk—the one who wouldn't tell me anything—told Cal where you were, so we walked to your room big as you please, and no one even questioned us."

"Quite a story," I murmur. "But—surely you're not going back to Alabama tonight, are you?"

Julia shakes her head. "Nope. I'm sending Cal on his way in the morning, but I'm staying here till you find out something."

"Oh, no, you're not. I'm not going to let you do that."

Julia stands up and squeezes my hand again. "Doesn't look like you're in a position to put up much of an argument, my dear." She turns to Cal and motions for him to scoot his chair up closer. "Okay, Cal, now is your chance. I'm going to the powder room. And while I'm gone, Corrine, I want Cal to tell you what he told me on the way over. You'll like hearing it."

Julia goes to the bathroom, and I cut my eyes over to Cal. He's eying me thoughtfully, his elbows propped on his knees. "This can wait, if you don't feel like it," he says, and I shake my head.

"Julia's got my curiosity up now." Not to mention that I can stare at him while he's telling me, I think to myself, glad that Julia's not here to see me blush like a fool.

Cal runs his hand through his thick dark hair and leans forward. "On the ride over, Corrine, Julia began telling me about you."

"Oh, Lord," I sigh.

He smiles at me, his eyes holding mine. I try to look away, but can't. "All good, I promise," he says.

"She didn't tell you that I'm the official crazy of the Same Sweet Girls, did she?"

He wrinkles his brow. "Well . . . she might've mentioned something about that." He holds up a hand when I groan. "No, no, I'm kidding. She didn't tell me you were crazy. Are you?"

I nod. "Pretty much."

He looks skeptical. "I doubt that. See, Julia told me that you were a famous gourd artist, and I said, a what?"

"That's what everyone says," I say, but I don't think he hears me. It's still an effort for me to talk, and the medicine—or something—is making me feel really woozy.

"Julia started to explain it," Cal continues, "but I stopped her. I said to her, wait a minute—wait a minute. I know who your friend Corrine is! And here's how I know."

"How?"

"Well, about a year ago, I go with Joe Ed to Atlanta, to a meeting at the capitol. When he's about to go into one of his meetings, he introduces me to a state senator there, a friend of his. Really surprises me by asking the lady senator to take me to her office while he's in the meeting. I remember what he said, plain as day. He said to the senator, 'Would you take Cal and show him the gourd you bought from Corrine?' Of course, I ask who Corrine is, and he says one of Julia's friends who's a famous artist. Then I ask Joe Ed why he wants me to see a damn *gourd,* of all things, and all he says is, you'll know why when you see it."

I stare at him wide-eyed. "Oh, my God. It was—"

"The Trail of Tears gourd," Cal tells me, nodding. "The senator took me to her office to see it. She even let me hold it," he adds with a smile. "I can't tell you what an impact it had on me, Corrine. I've never forgotten it. So, when I told Julia that story on the ride over tonight, she said if I got a chance to see you, I should tell you that. She seemed to think you'd like hearing it."

"You don't know how much I needed to hear it. But tell me, Cal—why did Joe Ed insist you see the Trail of Tears gourd?"

He shrugs. "Guess because I'm half Creek. Of course, it was the Cherokee tribe on the Trail of Tears, but, hell, Joe Ed didn't know the difference. Most people don't. We're all the same, Cherokee, Creek, Chickasaw, Choctaw . . ."

"The 'C' tribes of the Southeast," I murmur.

"Whatever. Anyway, I wanted to tell you that I'm sorry for the circumstances, but it's such a privilege to talk to the artist who did that gourd. A real privilege."

"Thank you, Cal," I say in a whisper, touched. Julia has returned and is standing next to Cal's chair. I look at her gratefully. "And thank you, too, Julia."

His eyes still on me, Cal asks, "You have more gourds like that one, Corrine?"

I shake my head. "No. I haven't done anything like it since."

"But you have a lot of Native American designs," Julia says eagerly. "When you get well, Cal needs to come to your gallery and do some shopping."

I widen my eyes, knowing she can't realize what an incentive for recovery she's handed me. Oblivious, Julia continues. "See, Cal needs a gift for his grandmother's ninety-fifth birthday, and I realized that one of your Native American–looking gourds would be perfect."

Cal looks down at me as he stands next to Julia. "I thought it was a great idea, too. Sure hope you get well soon, Corrine."

"I hope I will, too." My eyes fill with tears

and I blink, hoping they won't notice. Julia, however, moves quickly, leaning over me and putting her arms around me. "Shhh now," she whispers, her face next to mine. "Don't cry, you hear me? I'm not going to let anything happen to you! Cal, hand me a couple of those tissues."

She takes a tissue and wipes my face, then wipes her tear-filled eyes. Leaning over me, she kisses my forehead. "Try to get some rest, and I'll be back in the morning, okay?"

"Julia, I really don't want you to do this. You've got too much on your . . ." I sob, but Julia shushes me again, pushing my damp hair back from my forehead.

"Hush now. None of the crap I have to do is as important to me as you are. We're going now, so you go to sleep, you hear me?"

"Where will you stay?" I ask, and Julia shrugs.

"There's a Holiday Inn next door. Don't worry about that; just get some rest."

Cal surprises me by leaning down, taking my hand in both of his, and squeezing it. His hands are large and strong, but gentle. "Take care of yourself, Corrine. You've got to get well so I can come to your shop and get my grandmother a real nice birthday gift. Okay?"

I nod. "Okay," I whisper, my voice choked. "And thank you, Cal, for bringing Julia here."

"Glad I could. Let's get out of here, Julia." And with quick little waves, the two of them slip out the door, closing it carefully behind them so no one will hear them.

21

Julia
BLUE MOUNTAIN

TRUE TO MY PROMISE, once I check into a room at the Holiday Inn, I call Lanier's number and leave a message. I tell her that I was relieved to find Corrine in a room, that she was real weak and pale but doing okay. I promise I'll call her from the hospital tomorrow and let her know what kind of tests they're doing, and that I'll try and talk to Corrine's doctor. True to her promise to me, Lanier had her phone off, and I hope that means she's getting some sleep. I want her to get all the rest she can, because I have a feeling Corrine is going to need her. What I don't tell Lanier is, I'm sick with fear. I don't know why, but I have a bad feeling about this.

Maybe I'm overreacting. Maybe it has to do with everything else I'm feeling now, all the confused emotions raging within me. And I thought only men had midlife crises! The SSGs would most likely say what's going on with me has to do with hormones; that is, if I ever told them, which is not very likely. Corrine would be the only one I'd talk to, I realize with a start. The SSGs have all kinds of rigid rules and rituals, but it's the unspoken rules we adhere to. According to those, Astor is my closest friend, and Corrine is Lanier's. I love Astor and I love Lanier, each for different reasons, but for the past couple of years Corrine and I have been getting closer. Once Culley went off to school and freed Corrine from the enslavement to her ex-husband, she began to open up to me for the first time since I've known her. Not that she ever calls; I still have to be the one to initiate it, but when I do, we talk for hours. It has made me realize something, something that still fills me with wonder. Although I've had the SSGs for the past thirty years, for the first time in my life I have the rarest thing a woman can have, rarer than a good man or perfect children. I have a girl-friend to confide in.

I turn off the lamps and collapse in the bed, too exhausted to move. I put on my black velvet eye mask to block out the light around the edge of the heavy brocade drapes, and turn on the white noise machine I never travel without, to drown out the unfa-miliar noises of the hotel. The mattress is too soft, yields too much to the weight of my body, and the stiff white sheets smell like Clorox. It's almost one o'clock in the morn-ing, and my wake-up call is for seven. Even so, I have trouble going to sleep because I can't erase the images of this event-filled day from my mind, and they roll through the dark screen of my closed eyes like home movies. So many firsts . . . Bethany, my baby, away from home for the first time, on her own, learning how to make it without an overprotective father, anxious mother, and wealthy, doting grandparents. Bethany with her first boyfriend! I'd never admit it to Joe Ed, never, and I faked it admirably, I think, but it felt like someone had punched me in the stomach when I saw Bethany with a boyfriend. Joe Ed doesn't hide his emotions like I do mine, but he looked like I felt. What the three of us know, Bethany, Joe Ed, and me, is that Bethany will never have a normal life, with a husband and children. Of course, with her handicaps that's pretty obvious, but in addition, we were told when she reached puberty that she wouldn't be able to have children of her own. What Bethany said in response to the news I will never forget, never. She'd thought about it for a minute, then in her odd, stilted speech, said, "Bound to be lots of kids like me out there that nobody wants."

A day of firsts . . . the first time since the accident that took Dixie Lee from us that the SSGs have had to face that we won't always be together. One of these days, we'll lose one of our six, then we'll be left with five. Then, four. Then . . . No, I can't let myself think that! I can't go there or I'll fall apart. Neither can I let myself picture the fear in Corrine's eyes, the way she tried so hard not to let me see how scared she was, or the way her voice broke when she said she hoped she'd get well. I won't go there, won't think that! I turn over restlessly and pull the big foam pillow close. I should have taken a sleeping pill. Joe Ed and I have a good stock of them for travel, for those times when you can't adjust to a strange bed. I should have taken one tonight so that I could turn my mind off, sink into darkness.

Joe Ed. . . . *Oh, God, what am I going to do?* The rule of the road is, if any of the troopers or aides or staff are with you— which they often are—you put them as close to your room as possible for easy access and communication. I sure broke the hell out of that rule! The night manager, a sweet-faced Indian man, tried not to react when I asked for two rooms on different floors, but his thick eyebrows shot up. I imagine in his business he gets all sorts of strange requests, most of them just the opposite. Cal was parking the car when I got the rooms, or I wouldn't have been able to make such a demand of the night manager. But no way I wanted Cal anywhere near me, even for one night, though we would have been perfectly safe from each other. On the ride over, we reached a resolution: That moment on the porch at the lake house, the kiss that stirred something in me I thought long dead, never happened.

No way Cal and I could ride for two-plus hours in the closed intimacy of a dark car and not mention the incident on the porch, but to give us credit, we tried. After leaving the lake house, we talked of the best route to take to Blue Mountain, as though the future of the planet was at stake. I took the map and tiny little map light out of the glove compartment, then bent over and studied the map so intently you'd think the keys to the kingdom were inscribed in hieroglyphics among the highways and byways of Alabama and Georgia, and I had the code. Muttering to myself, tracing different routes with my finger, I turned the map this way and that, debating the pros and cons of getting on I-59 or I-20, or sticking with back roads. I questioned Cal about every possible pig trot in the backwoods of northeast Alabama, and he got into it, describing every route he'd ever taken, every stop he'd made, and everything he saw on the way, or so it seemed.

When we'd exhausted that topic, we must have spent another hour talking about Corrine. Cal's account of seeing Corrine's best-known work was not only a great story, its telling and my questioning and responses took up a lot of our time. I ended up telling Cal much more about Corrine than I intended, which is not like me. I felt really bad about it afterward, but . . . anything to fill the awkward silences. Like me, Corrine is a very private person and would kill me if she knew I told anyone about Miles and Culley and the awful time she'd had, but I caught myself going on and on, unable to stop. Once Cal realized that Corrine was the artist friend of mine who'd done the gourd he'd found so intriguing, he was interested in hearing everything about her. It didn't occur to me that arriving at the hospital late would create so many problems in locating Corrine, or I'd have kept my mouth shut. It certainly didn't occur to me that Cal would meet Corrine, but at least that turned out to be a good thing. Hearing how much he'd liked her artwork seemed to have made her feel better, if only for a minute.

There was a long stretch of dark highway, heavily wooded on each side, that seemed to go on endlessly before the final lap to Chickasaw. Cal and I fell into a leaden silence in which the car seemed to fill up with our nearness to each other. I was so aware of his presence that I could hear him breathe, could have reached my hand out, ever so slightly, and touched him. I turned my head to watch the tall pines on the side of the road flying past as we sped down the dark road, and I sighed a deep sigh. "Julia?" Cal said to me. "You're really worried about your friend, aren't you?"

I'd stretched and yawned, then rubbed the back of my neck wearily. "I can't help it. Something's been going on with Corrine for a while now, but I haven't faced it. None of us have."

"Didn't you tell me you set her up with a doctor you knew?" Cal was trying to be reassuring, and I blessed him for it. I'd discovered that his abrasiveness was a cover for the soft part of him he kept hidden from the world.

I shrugged. "Well, I don't really know the doctor, just his parents. He's young—they all are now—and Corrine found him to be rather arrogant. Wish now I'd made her go to Emory instead."

Cal had smiled. "*Made* her go? Bet she wouldn't listen, even if you are her best friend. Take Joe Ed. Just the other day, I said to him . . ."

There. It'd been said, finally. Once his name was evoked, Joe Ed's presence hovered in the air between us. It was as though we'd rolled a window down and a surprising shock of arctic air had blown in, coming unbidden out of the warm Georgia night. I dared glance over at Cal when he stopped himself in midsentence and caught his eyes on me. He looked back quickly—we were traveling too fast for him to take his eyes off the road for more than a second—and his jaw tightened.

"Cal . . . listen—" I began, but couldn't make myself go on. I certainly couldn't say what I was thinking, that I wanted him to pull over and make love to me in the darkness of the car, right this minute. I wanted him to tear my clothes off and push me roughly against the cool leather seats of the car. I wanted his mouth over mine, his hands in my hair, my hands on the sweet dark skin of his back. . . . Oh, God, what was I thinking? My face burning, I dared not look his way, afraid that he could read my mind, know the forbidden thoughts that wouldn't leave me alone.

"Okay, Julia, we're going to have to talk," Cal said, his voice harsh.

"You may be the first man in history to have uttered those words to a woman," I said with a small smile.

"Listen, goddammit! Tonight, on the porch . . . I-I really regret what happened—"

"Do you, Cal? Do you regret it?"

He slammed the palm of his hand on the steering wheel, and I jumped, startled. His face was angry, his eyes burning black as he threw me a glance before turning back to face the road. "Don't play with me, Julia," he said. "Don't you dare."

"You think I'm playing with you? Flirting? Looking for a quick roll in the hay? You honestly think I'd do that?" I asked him, stunned.

Cal was silent, then he let out his breath in exasperation. "I don't know what to think," he said finally.

"You know me better than that."

"I don't know anything," he said, his voice curt. "All I know is, since the first time I saw you, I've thought you were the most perfect woman I've ever seen, and Joe Ed the luckiest man alive to have you. But a woman like you, I always suspected, would chew up someone like me and spit him out."

"I can see how you'd think that." He drove for several minutes in silence, then I said, "But I'm not Astor."

Cal hooted scornfully. "You can say that again."

I studied him, his proud profile, his jaw

clenched in anger, eyes fastened on the road ahead, the beam of the headlights cutting through the darkness of the road in front of us. "Astor treated you like that. She used you, didn't she?" I'd suspected as much but had not put it into words until now.

Instead of answering me, he shrugged. I sighed and again rubbed the back of my neck. "Cal, listen to me. I-I'm sorry for what happened between us, I really am. I didn't intend for it to happen, but I don't regret it. I'm going to tell you something that I wouldn't tell you except for that chip on your shoulder, okay?"

"I do not have a goddamn chip on my shoulder," he said in a loud voice, and I smiled, shaking my head.

"I want you to know that something happened between us back there, on the porch at Lake Martin," I said. "And it was something that hasn't happened to me in a long time. Whether you believe me or not, I don't really care, Cal, because I know what I know. And I know what I felt. But I also want you to know that it will never go any further. Because of that nonexistent chip on your shoulder, you'll think I'm avoiding you from now on. And you'll be right. I can't let myself be alone with you anymore, but I want to be sure you know why. I won't ever tell Joe Ed what happened—ever—and I won't tell Corrine or Astor or any of my friends. But I will keep it to myself, Cal, and I will treasure it. I just want you to know."

After a long silence, Cal said in a quiet voice, "Holy shit."

I smiled. "Not only that, you're incredibly eloquent. So. Don't say another word about it, and neither will I. We'll be friends again, like we were before. Deal?"

When he didn't respond, I reached over and put my hand on his arm. "Come on, Cal. Okay?"

"If you say so." We rode in silence for a while, but a more comfortable silence than before. Then Cal cleared his throat and said, "Julia? You know that I love Joe Ed like a brother, don't you? He's been good to me. Nobody's ever treated me like Joe Ed Stovall, nobody. I owe him a lot more than you know."

"Like what?"

"Not money," he said quickly. "I'm the only one on the team who never borrowed a dime from him."

I rolled my eyes. "I would know that without your telling me."

"You think I got a chip on my shoulder now, you should've seen me when I went to Bama, my first time out of the swamps of Florida," Cal said. "If it hadn't been for sports, I'd probably have ended up in reform school, I was such a testy little fuck. Always getting in fights, trying to prove I was as good as everybody else."

"Sounds like the Cal I know," I said, smiling.

"Reason I went to Bama," he continued, "I had such a name on the playing fields of Florida nobody would give me a scholarship. But Bear Bryant did, and he was clever enough to put me with Joe Ed. The two of them turned my life around. Bear wouldn't take my crap, and Joe Ed, well, he was always encouraging me, saying I could make it if I'd just get rid of my attitude. Bear's the one who got me into law enforcement after I bummed up my leg and couldn't play anymore. But Joe Ed's the one who made sure I stayed in and didn't let all the crap from my past fuck me up. I owe him, Julia. Big time."

"Joe Ed's never told me any of that," I said,

studying him. "But it explains a lot. Look—there's the sign to the Chickasaw hospital! Thank God, we're finally here."

This morning the halls of the hospital are noisy, bustling with white-clad nurses, doctors in green scrubs, and aides pushing rattly, stainless-steel carts. Oblivious to the racket, Corrine is sound asleep. I slip into her room and sit down in the chair beside her bed. I'm surprised she's still here since it's eight o'clock, and I assumed they'd have her out early to begin the tests. I tried to get here earlier but was so gluey with sleep I had trouble getting up, then was unable to drag myself out of the hot shower. I discovered I had nothing to wear. In the overnight bag I'd taken to the Helen Keller Institute, I had only my toiletries, undies, and a gown. The Institute had put us in the same guest quarters we'd stayed in when we took Bethany over there, which was so well furnished I'd known I wouldn't need anything else. All I had with me was the beige linen pantsuit I'd worn the first day, the black-and-white checked suit worn yesterday—both with heels and hose—and the T-shirt, shorts, and sandals I wore from the lake house last night. I'd have put those on again except I wanted to confront Dr. Brown and had a notion I'd be more successful if I could throw my weight around a bit. Be much harder dressed in well-wrinkled shorts and a T-shirt, but I'd be damned if I was going to sit in a hospital room all day with a suit and heels on just to impress a twelve-year-old doctor. For comfort, I decided on the pants of the beige pantsuit paired with the black silk tank top from the checked suit; for intimidating the young doctor, I added my heels and pearls.

Leaning over, I study Corrine as she sleeps, longing to push her red-gold curls back from her face, where they cling damply to her forehead. Her eyes are purple-smudged, sunken, and the long lashes sweeping her pale cheeks are wet with tears. The blue-patterned hospital gown has slipped off her shoulder, revealing the sharpness of her collarbone and the whiteness of her skin. Corrine's thinness scares me. She's always been lean and willowy, but today, she looks frail. Unable to resist, I lean over her and pull the sheet up over her shoulders. She looks incredibly otherworldly in sleep, as though transported to far-off faerie kingdoms forbidden to mortals like me. Lanier's always called her Annabel Lee, but today that nickname makes my blood run cold.

When the door flies open, I move back to the chair, and Corrine startles out of her sleep. She blinks her eyes in confusion, and I reach over and take her hand. I can tell the exact moment she remembers where she is, and why, and her face changes, slackens, and sets into resignation. It's also the same moment that my throat constricts, and I know. I know what Corrine knows, what she's known for a while. Something is very, very wrong.

Both of us look up at the doctor who's entered and is standing at the foot of her bed, chart in hand. His identification tag says Dr. Brown, and he's even younger looking than I expected, tall and sandy-haired, with little yuppie glasses. There's an unmistakable Ivy League air about his bearing, his arrogant posture, the floppy cut of his hair. I stand up, extending my hand. "Dr. Brown," I say, my first lady smile full wattage, "I'm Julia Stovall, a friend of your lovely parents." I motion toward Corrine. "I'm the one who insisted my friend Corrine see you, because I wanted her to have the best possible care."

First rule of political savvy: Butter 'em up and leave 'em wanting more.

Without smiling, Dr. Brown shakes my hand politely, then turns to look down at Corrine. "Miss Cooper," he says, an edge to his voice, "you never returned for follow-up tests. Perhaps if you had, this could have been avoided."

Corrine cowers in the bed, licking her dry, parched lips. When she speaks, her voice is weak. "I know. Guess I should have."

Consulting the chart, Dr. Brown says, "I see that you reported a tenderness on the right side to the emergency room doctor. You didn't have that when you came to my office. This is a new development, then?"

Corrine nods bleakly, and I say, unable to keep the excitement out of my voice, "Oh! Then she must have appendicitis. Is that what you think, Dr. Brown?"

"It's not appendicitis, Mrs. Stovall, I can assure you." He turns to address Corrine. "The blood tests have not revealed any definite markers yet, so I've ordered an abdominal CT scan, which should tell us something more definitive."

"That's a CAT scan, right?" I ask. "What . . . ah . . . kinds of things might it show?" The young doctor cuts his eyes at me as though assessing my role here. Evidently I passed some sort of test, because after a moment's hesitation, he answers me.

"It's an imaging test that can reveal any number of problems in the abdominal area, consistent with Miss Cooper's symptoms. One possibility is the presence of a tumor, with possible liver involvement, but I'm not going to speculate until I see the results of the CT scan. In a day or so we'll have more of an idea of what we're dealing with." Dr. Brown removes his pen from the clipboard, puts it in his jacket pocket, and turns to go. Stunned, I take a step after him.

"But—Dr. Brown—can't you tell us anything more? I mean . . . w-why has Corrine been so sick? Why can't she hold anything down? Don't you have any theories?"

His eyes hold mine, and I see for the first time that his are distant, remote, ready to be out of this place of sickness and fear. "I do have theories, Mrs. Stovall," he says coolly, "but as I said, I'd rather not speculate at this point." He nods his head toward Corrine. "Miss Cooper, I'll return to discuss the results of the scan as soon as I have them.

They will be in to prepare you for it shortly. Good day." And he's gone before I can say another word to him.

I turn to Corrine, frowning. "That boy needs to go back to med school. Evidently he flunked Bedside Manner 101."

Corrine closes her eyes and puts her hand on her forehead. "I'm not going through all those horrible tests again, Julia. You heard him—he said tumor, with liver involvement. I know what that means. My mother died of colon cancer. . . ."

"Hush! Don't you dare say that word, Corrine. He said *possible*. Possible, but they won't know anything for sure till you have the CAT scan, and by God, you're going to have it. I didn't break my neck getting over here, going a hundred miles an hour through the backwoods of Georgia, for you to skip out, you hear me? You're going to have it if I have to tie you to the damn gurney!"

Corrine smiles. "You sound like Mama Byrd."

"I swear to God, I'll call in the cavalry if you do this to me. I'll get Lanier and Byrd and Astor and Rosanelle here so fast it'll make your head swim if—"

"Jesus, Julia, don't get your panties in such a wad. I'll do it, okay, just to get you to shut the hell up."

I sit back in the chair, mollified. "Good," I mutter. "Good."

"What'd you do with Cal?" Corrine cuts her eyes to me curiously, and I feel a hot flush creeping up my neck.

"What do you mean, what did I do with him?"

"I meant, where is he?"

"Oh! Ah . . . I left him a note—"

"On his pillow?"

"Corrine! You must not be too bad off, talking trash like that. I left him a note at the front desk of the hotel, telling him I walked over here, early, and I appreciated him bringing me. Said I'd be in touch when I knew more."

"He's nice," Corrine says softly. "Which surprised me."

"Surprised you? Why?"

"He looks tough. Guess that goes with the job, though. Julia—can I ask you something?"

"Of course. But wait a minute." I reach in my purse and pull out my lip gloss, which I dab on her lips. "Your lips are so parched they've got to be hurting you. Want some water?"

Corrine shakes her head. "They took it away right after y'all left. Can't have anything after midnight because of the tests. I—"

We both jump when the door flies open again, and a black man in scrubs comes in, pushing a wheelchair. "Morning, young lady," he says cheerily. "I've come to take you to never-never land."

Corrine groans, and I help her sit up. When the aide puts her in the wheelchair, I ask her, "Want me to brush your hair?"

"Oh, God, yes," she moans. "It's driving me crazy. You got a rubber band?"

I glance at the aide. "Is there time for me to fix her hair?"

He chuckles. "You women, always fixing that hair like you going to a party or something. Be all right if you'll hurry up, now."

I brush the tangles out of Corrine's hair and plait it hastily into a long braid, just like I used to do Bethany's, when the door swings open again, and this time, it's Miles Spaulding. I haven't seen him in years, but I'd know him anywhere. No one looks like Miles this side of Hollywood, with his silvery hair and piercing blue-green eyes, glinting like fine jewels. Corrine stiffens, and I wrap the rubber band around the end of her braid.

Miles is obviously surprised to see me here, but he recovers and holds his hand out to me.

"Ah—Julia! Didn't know you were here." I shake his cool, elegant hand, then lean over to kiss Corrine's cheek.

"There. All ready." I turn my head to Miles. "Corrine has to go. I made this poor man wait until I could get her hair out of her face, but we can't have her running any later."

"Off to the races," Corrine groans, and the aide gets behind the wheelchair to push her out. Before it moves, though, Miles leans down and kisses Corrine right on the lips. I see her recoil, her eyes widening in surprise, and I resist the urge to give the aide a push, to get her out faster. Fortunately, I don't have to, for the aide grins and says, "All right now!" then takes her away.

As soon as they leave, Miles accosts me. "This is *such* a surprise," he says, smiling his chilly smile. "The first lady of Alabama, in person. When did you get here?"

"Last night." I have no intention of telling him anything. The last Corrine told me about her ex, he'd paid her a visit not too long ago and practically raped her. When she'd asked him not to come back to her house again, he'd blackmailed her, threatened to tell their son she wouldn't see him. Blackmail was his favorite mode of operation; that's how he'd gotten Corrine into his bed for years, not letting her see Culley otherwise. One of these days, he was going to pay for that.

"Last night?" His eyebrows shoot straight up to his hairline, which I note with satisfaction is receding. "Must have been late. I was here until ten, I think."

When I don't respond, Miles prods a little further. "Are any of the other women with you, the SSGs?"

I don't know what makes me do it, but I lie like a rug. "They'll be here soon. All of them."

He frowns in displeasure. "I'm not sure that's a good idea. I don't think Corrine needs that much company right now. Are you staying at her place?"

Until now, I hadn't thought of it, but it makes perfect sense. I'll find a way to get out to Corrine's—maybe with Culley, certainly not Miles—and I'll use her car. I'll stay there instead of the hotel next door. I can even borrow a change of clothes from her. "Yes. I'm staying at Corrine's."

"It may be none of my business, but—" Miles begins, but the door swinging open stops him. His eyebrows shoot up even higher, and I bite my lip to hide my smile. It's Cal, dressed in khakis and a denim shirt, with the sleeves rolled halfway up his muscular arms. Freshly showered, his wet hair plastered down, he's scowling, looking darker than a thundercloud. I can see what Corrine meant; he looks tough, not someone to mess with. He dismisses Miles with a glance as he walks over to me.

"You left your briefcase in the car, Julia," he says. "I was on my way out and thought I'd drop it by."

I take the briefcase and put it down next to the bedside table, saying, "Thanks. But don't leave just yet, okay? I need to talk to you a minute."

"I saw Corrine in the hall," Cal says, and out of the corner of my eye, I note Miles's startled expression. "As they were taking her to the elevator. She looked pretty resigned. Said she felt like hell, too."

"Not as bad as she's going to feel, I'm afraid." I know I'm going to have to get it over with, so I nod toward Miles and say, "Cal, this is Miles Spaulding, Corrine's ex-husband. Cal Hawkins." I have no intention of telling Miles who Cal is. Let him think what he will.

The two men shake hands, assessing

each other the way men do. Cal's bound to have his hackles aroused by the contemptuous way Miles is regarding him, his eyes moving over Cal as though he were the garbage man. Cal has heard all about Miles, thanks to my big mouth. His eyes are narrowed and flinty, and he's looking at Miles like a linebacker might regard a tackling dummy. I'd better get him out of here, quick.

Corrine returns to the room late that afternoon, this time on a gurney, asleep. I didn't think it was possible for her to look worse, but she does. I have no idea what they've put her through, but from the looks of her, none of it was pleasant. Her braided hair wasn't my best job, but it wouldn't have come halfway down unless she'd been through the wringer. When I bathe her face with a cool washcloth, I feel like I'm ministering to a political prisoner, just returned from interrogation and torture. She wakes fitfully, and the nurses hook her back to the IV and bring her water, which she gulps thirstily. Afterward, she collapses on the pillow and goes back to sleep. When she wakes, I rebraid her hair, wash her face, and feed her the broth and Jell-O they've brought on a tray. I tell her about talking with Lanier, but I don't tell her that Lanier's coming over as soon as she can find someone to cover her shifts for her. I tell her that I called the others, leaving messages for Astor and Rosanelle, talking with Byrd. I don't tell her, can't tell her, that Byrd cried when I told her what the doctor said about the possibility of a tumor. Byrd broke down and cried like a baby, and I cried with her. I called Joe Ed in Washington and left a message on his cell phone. Corrine listens to my blatherings listlessly, but when I stop, she questions me, asking me things I've already told her. The nurse tells me that she was medicated for the test and that she'll sleep a lot. The phone rings off and on, mostly calls from the SSGs, all saying they'll be over in no time if I need them. Then it's Joe Ed, and my heart thuds in my chest when I hear his voice. His call is perfunctory, however, between meetings and on the run, with no indication that he notices my stammering and stumbling in answering his questions. I stick to the story Cal and I concocted, that I was in Talladega when I got the call about Corrine, and Cal drove me to Blue Mountain. Yes, I tell him, Cal's back in Montgomery now, but before he left, I got him to take me to Corrine's, to get her car, so everything's under control. I don't mention the lake house.

"Miles was here this morning," Corrine says, when she wakes from a fitful nap. I hold a glass of apple juice for her, and her lips tremble on the straw, which breaks my heart.

"He was," I say. "And you'll never guess who he met." She questions me with her large, silver-colored eyes as she sucks feebly on the straw, and I say, "Tickled me good. Cal came in to bring me my briefcase—"

"I saw him in the hall, but I didn't recognize him out of uniform until he knelt down by the wheelchair to wish me luck," Corrine says, taking a shaky breath.

"Well, Miles was here when Cal came in the room, and you should've been here," I giggle. "Miles looked down his nose at Cal like he had cowshit on his shoes or something—"

"Miles looks at everybody like that," she interrupts.

"And Cal looked at Miles like he was a lion in the wild and Miles was his dinner."

Corrine eyes me suspiciously. "You *didn't* tell Cal all that . . ."

I grimace. "Please forgive me, honey, but I

had to find something to talk about on that long ride over here. But don't worry, I didn't tell him everything. Just that Miles had given you a hard time and taken Culley away."

"Instead of talking about me, why didn't you ask him about Astor?"

"I tried, but he wouldn't say much about it. Oh! Look what came for you." I nod my head toward the windowsill, where I've placed two arrangements of flowers and a cascade of Get Well balloons. Earlier this afternoon, I went to the gift shop to purchase an arrangement of flowers from Joe Ed and me and the balloons from the SSGs. When I got back to the room, a candy striper had just brought in a silver vase with pink rosebuds in it. Scribbled on the get-well card was "To Corrine from a fan, Cal H." Evidently Cal had stopped at the gift shop on his way out, which surprised and touched me and Corrine both.

Corrine wipes tears away when I hand her the cards and says, "I'm going to get dehydrated again, just from crying."

"Oh, honey, you cry all you need to. You—"

Yet again, we're interrupted by the door swinging open. I'm beginning to think hospitals shouldn't even bother to put doors up, people come in and out so much. It's Miles again, loaded down with gift baskets, but this time, Culley's with him. Last time I saw Culley was a couple of years ago at an SSG gathering, when he was home from Brevard for the weekend and stopped by Corrine's to get something. Since that time, he's filled out and grown even taller, with more tattoos as well as more holes in his ears. He's a stunningly beautiful boy, always has been. His thick golden-red hair is pulled back to the nape of his neck and tied with a piece of string, and he's dressed in cutoff jeans and a T-shirt with a guitar drawn on it, saying "Will Play for Food."

I nod as politely as I can to Miles, then hug Culley and say the usual grown-up things, how much he's grown, when will he finish school, what will he do afterward. Miles unloads his gifts on the windowsill, pushing the smaller offerings aside for his huge, ostentatious basket of hothouse lilies, which give off a sickening, funereal smell. He has an equally large and expensive basket of gourmet fruit and chocolates, and I roll my eyes. She can't keep a thing down, and he's bringing her fancy food! Culley's leaning over, hugging his mother, blocking off the sight of his daddy at the windowsill, reading the cards that go with the arrangements, but I'd give anything if Corrine could see the way Miles's eyebrows shoot up when he reads Cal's card. He turns his head and looks at Corrine, and I compose my face when he glances at me. Let him think that Cal is more than a fan of Corrine's; do him good to squirm. Corrine had also told me that Miles was trying to get her back. Maybe the scowling appearance of Cal this morning will be enough to make him leave her alone.

Miles goes to Corrine's bedside, bends over and kisses her, then stands with his arm around Culley's shoulders, the doting family at the sick mother's bedside, full of warm wishes. "Will Dr. Brown be around this evening?" Miles asks Corrine. "I'd like to talk to him."

Her face grows even paler, if possible. "He said he'd be back to talk to me about the results of the CAT scan," she tells him, her voice barely audible, and I cringe. Oh, God, that means Miles will stay till then, nosing around in her business. Somehow, I've got to keep him away from her. It's obvious he upsets her; he's bending over her now, touching her cheek with the back of his hand—which would be a tender gesture from anyone else—and she seems to be shrinking into the pile of pillows. I move quickly, going to the other side of the bed and taking Corrine's free hand.

"Dr. Brown talked with Corrine and me this morning," I say, looking first at Culley, then Miles. "He wouldn't speculate on anything until he's had a chance to study the results of the test."

Culley nods thoughtfully, but when he looks down at his mother, his face is troubled, his eyes tormented. I'd give anything to talk to him without Miles around. I'd ask him to come to the cafeteria with me, except that would leave Corrine alone with Miles. Before I can decide what to do, the door opens again, and it's Dr. Brown.

I can tell by his face that he has the results of the CAT scan, and it's not good. My heart sinks, and I squeeze Corrine's hand. Dr. Brown shakes Miles's hand, Miles introduces him to Culley, and poor Culley looks as scared as I feel.

Making the assumption that Corrine doesn't mind us knowing her business, Dr. Brown pulls out a handful of something that looks like large slides or negatives, holds them up for Corrine to see, and takes a pen out of his pocket to point with. "What we have here is a cross-section view of the liver, Miss Cooper," he says, pointing. "The left and right lobes are here." He indicates the area with his pen, then continues. "As you see, we're looking at two different shades of gray." Miles, Culley, and I all move closer in order to see what Dr. Brown is pointing to. "On the right lobe, you can see a small spot, or lesion, about the size of your thumbnail. It's not fluid-filled, so it's not a cyst, and it's a different density. I've ordered a liver biopsy for tomorrow, and we'll have a look at the tissue. Once we get that back, we'll know more. Do you have any questions?"

Corrine blinks, looking too stunned to ask anything. Finally she licks her lips and says hoarsely, "I . . . guess not."

Miles opens his mouth as though to question young Dr. Brown but doesn't. He looks shocked, his face drained of color, which scares me. He knows what all this means, what Corrine is afraid to ask the doctor.

Dr. Brown puts the slides back in the folder and nods toward Corrine, his face devoid of expression, his eyes revealing nothing. It occurs to me that he's not an unfeeling person; he just has to maintain a distance in order to survive having to be the one to bring such bad news. "I'm afraid the biopsy is not very pleasant, but you'll be sedated," he tells Corrine. "Often there's quite a lot of bleeding involved, so you'll have to stay in recovery a couple of hours afterwards. I'll be back to talk with you once I get the tissue results." And without another word, he's gone.

None of us says a word for several minutes after Dr. Brown leaves. Culley shuffles his feet, hanging his head and looking downward, and I hold Corrine's hand so tightly I'm afraid I'm hurting her. Finally Miles clears his throat and says, "Julia, I wonder if Culley and I could have a moment alone with Corrine?"

"Well . . . ah . . ." I look to Corrine for direction, and she nods agreement, though her eyes are wary. There's nothing to do but leave them. "Sure. I'll go to the caf and pick up some supper," I say, with fake heartiness and a cheery wave.

I get a bowl of soup, though I'm too distraught to eat. I wonder what the spot on the liver means, terrified it might be a malignancy. I can't let myself go there now, can't stand to consider the possibilities, and force myself to stop thinking that way until there's a definite diagnosis. After leaving the cafeteria, I stop at a pay phone in the lobby and dial Lanier's number. When I get her voice mail, I say wearily, "Lanier—it's Julia. The doctor told Corrine they found some kind of lesion or something on her liver, and they're doing a biopsy tomorrow. I'll call the others."

22

Lanier

BLUE MOUNTAIN

AS SOON AS I walk into the room and hug Julia's neck, I pull back from her and say, "You're staying at Corrine's, aren't you?"

Julia nods, her gray eyes all puffy and exhausted-looking. "Isn't it obvious?" She turns, modeling an outfit that is so Corrine and so un-Julia that I giggle. Instead of her prissy designer clothes and heels, she has on a long batik skirt and a gauzy peasant blouse, with sandals on her feet.

"Well, get your ass back over there, because the reinforcements are coming in," I tell her. "You look like you need a nap." It's early afternoon, and Corrine's still out of the room, after having the biopsy done. When I called from the car as I drove over, Julia told me they were supposed to have taken Corrine earlier but were running late. I'd said, "Welcome to the wonderful world of hospitals, where everything runs like clockwork."

I expect Julia to argue, but she agrees to go to Corrine's and sleep a couple of hours while I snoop around the floor and see what I can find out. She says she didn't leave until way after visiting hours last night because she was determined to wait Miles out. The nurse had to return twice to tell them that visiting hours were over. Then, she says, she had trouble sleeping once she got to Corrine's cabin because it's isolated and spooky down there at the foot of the mountain. When she tells me that she kept getting up all through the night, I said, "Why didn't you give Miles a call? Bet he'd have been glad to come and tie you to the bedposts."

Julia's driving Corrine's car so she leaves for her nap, and I set out to make friends with the nursing staff. With any luck, I can nose around and find out what's going on. I don't tell Julia, but I'd planned on coming over today even if she hadn't called, that's how worried I was. It was harder than I thought finding someone to take my shift and my nursing classes. But as soon as I could make the arrangements, I was putting the pedal to the metal. Of course, once I heard the words "liver biopsy," nothing could have kept me away. Anytime a patient of mine is having one of those, I *know* what they're looking for.

I case the situation first, strolling down the hall, playing like I'm just stretching my legs after sitting all day in a cramped hospital room. It's not nearly as big as Mobile General; of course, I didn't expect it to be. That could be good or bad, but it's probably bad. Oftentimes, in small towns, the hospitals are cliquish, tight as a nun's crack. Won't give you the time of day. Big hospital now, it's easier to get lost in the crowds. You can nose around and nobody will pay you any mind. Drinking from the water fountain— or rather, pretending to, my lips pressed together since you couldn't *pay* me to drink from a hospital water fountain—I check out the nursing staff. The well-padded black woman studying a chart has got to be the charge nurse, and the stout white woman with the big hair is an R.N. The other hefty women, and the two tubby men, are staff nurses, and the three chunky young women and men waddling around are nurses' assistants. Hot damn! I'm in my territory, the land of the lard asses. I hurry back to the room, knowing now how to get in without telling them I'm one of them. Matter of fact, that might even be best. *Only way to learn anything is to keep your mouth shut and your eyes open,* I'd written in the lesson book once. About time I gave it a try.

I grab my purse and pull out my little notebook (I keep it handy in case I want to jot something down and don't have the lesson book with me), the embroidery scissors my grandmother left me, in a little-bitty case that fits right in my purse, and my purple-inked fountain pen Corrine gave me with the lesson book. Julia told me she'd about thrown up when Miles came in with his big old expensive gifts, so I know where I'm heading. Easy to spot on the windowsill . . . the SSG balloons, a silver vase of pink roses, a basket of summer flowers, Miles's arrangement of lilies, which ought to be in a funeral home, and bingo—the gourmet basket. Undoing the twirly ribbons, I take the cellophane off and grin. Come to Mama, Godiva chocolates, peaches the size of baseballs, and giant strawberries dipped in white and dark chocolate! This was going to be a sacrifice, one that Corrine had better appreciate, because I could sit here right now and inhale everything in this basket. Instead, I remove Miles's card ("To Corrine, with all my love, Miles"), which makes me want to puke. Poking a hole in the card and stringing it on the ribbons, I replace it with my own: "To the wonderful nursing staff of the fifth floor, thank you for the great care you're giving Corrine Cooper in 522! From her girlfriends." I take it down to the nurses' station, where I wait until I get the attention of the . . . ah, very solid head nurse. At first she frowns impatiently at me until I lift the basket from the floor and set it on the counter. "My friends and I," I say humbly, "well, we wanted to do something to express our gratitude to the nurses who've taken such good care of our friend Corrine Cooper. We thought you might enjoy this during your coffee break." She looks taken aback, even suspicious. Then, at the sight of the basket, her face lights up like Christmas. "Oh my, that's so nice of you! Now, tell me your friend's name again?"

* * *

Late that afternoon, Astor and Byrd arrive together, with Rosanelle not ten minutes behind them. Byrd falls apart when she sees me and runs into my arms. "Oh, Lanier," she says as I hold her, her tears wetting the front of my polo shirt, "has Corrine got a tumor? Please tell me it's not true!"

I release her and eye her suspiciously. "Who the hell said anything about a tumor?"

"Julia!" she sobs. "Julia said . . . I forget how she worded it, but *something* about a tumor."

"Some of her symptoms suggest that possibility, which is all that Julia said," I assure her, then turn to Astor.

Astor steps forward and hugs me, then kisses my cheek. I swear, she's going to have every doctor on this floor making up some excuse to come to this room, once they get a load of her. *Girl, what were you thinking?* You'd think she'd have sense enough to dress comfortably for the hospital, but she has on a black halter top, backless except for the crisscrossing of thin straps, and an extremely short denim skirt. Three-inch platform shoes lace up around her calves and make her tall as an Amazon. Her hair is loose on her shoulders, held back by pink-tinted sunglasses pushed up on top of her head. "No need to sugarcoat things for me and Byrd, Lanier," she says, patting my shoulder. "We know it's bad."

"Probably. But we don't know anything for sure. Until we do, we've got to be optimistic. The power of positive thinking and all that crap. You hear me, Astor? And you, Byrd?" I point to each of them like a schoolmarm, wagging my finger. "We're going to pretend that y'all came over just to cheer Corrine up, *not* because we're worried. Nobody say pea-turkey about being worried, and I mean it!"

Byrd nods, dabbing at her eyes with a tissue. "I've got to pull myself together before they bring her back to the room, then."

"You sure do," Astor tells her. "You look like Tammy Faye with your mascara running down your cheeks."

"Oh, God," Byrd moans. "Where's the john?"

I point and Byrd hesitates. "Isn't Julia in there?"

"Julia's at Corrine's, taking a nap," I tell her. "We're all staying at Corrine's while we're here, by the way. No point in paying for a hotel."

Astor sniffs. "Corrine's place is so small.

And not even air-conditioned! I've never stayed there in the middle of the summer, but I imagine it gets pretty hot."

"Then get your royal ass over to the Holiday Inn," I say, peevish, not in the mood for Astor's crap. "I can't afford a hundred bucks a night, myself."

Snorting, Astor gives her head a toss, flinging her long hair about. "Oh, please. Don't give me that, Lanier. Paul's a successful doctor."

I glare at her. "What does that have to do with the price of doo-doo in Denmark? I'm not getting anything from Paul, and you know it. And besides, everything Paul makes goes back into the clinic. He may be successful, but he's certainly not rich."

She studies me, eyes narrowed. "How long are you going to remain in limbo, Lanier? Get a divorce and get it over with. Then you'll be sitting pretty."

Before I can answer, the door to the hospital room creaks open, and we both whirl around, expecting a gurney with Corrine on it. Instead, it's Rosanelle, poking her head in. She scans the room, her overly-made-up eyes resting on the empty bed, then she looks from me to Astor questioningly. I motion for her to come in, and she whispers, "Sure it's okay? Is Corrine here?"

I shake my head. "She's still out, probably in recovery. And this is a hospital room, not a library, Rosanelle. You don't have to whisper."

She comes in, preceded by waves of her strong perfume, and hugs both me and Astor. I steel myself for her hysterics, remembering how she freaked over Corrine's pallor at the SSG gathering, but she surprises me. When Byrd comes out of the bathroom, pulling up her britches, she and Rosanelle hug, and Byrd puts a balled-up tissue to her eyes. "Lordy," Byrd sighs. "I've got to quit boo-hooing! Don't know what's wrong with me, unless it has to do with it being twenty-five years ago this very month that Dixie Lee died."

Rosanelle is watching Byrd, head tilted to the side. She's been to an alumni meeting in Huntsville and insisted on coming by the hospital on her way back, when I talked with her last night. I'd tried to discourage her, saying it was hardly on her way back to Brierfield, but Rosanelle said she'd be in a college car and could count the mileage. "After all," she'd reasoned, "it *is* an alumni function." I didn't even try to argue with her about that. As usual, Rosanelle is all made up and dressed to the nines, in an expensive-looking lime-green pantsuit and open-toed sandals with low heels. Proves to me neither Rosanelle nor Astor has a lick of sense. "*I'm* not that worried about Corrine because I've turned that worry over to the Lord," Rosanelle is saying when I tune back in to her. "He never puts more on our shoulders than we can bear."

"Then the Lord must of mistaken some of us for linebackers," I mutter. "But actually, Rosanelle, I'm glad to hear you say that, because we need that kind of optimism. I was telling Astor and Byrd before you got here that we've got to stay upbeat for Corrine."

"It's being so cheerful that keeps us going," Byrd murmurs, then we all shut our mouths and turn toward the door. Wheeled in on a gurney, Corrine is returning to the room.

I always tell folks, if you're not sick going into a hospital, you can bet your booty you will be when you leave. Corrine is wiped out, her eyes sunken and glassy, her already-pale complexion pasty looking. There's a compress on the biopsy site to keep the bleeding in check, which I inspect as soon as the nurse goes out the door. Nothing more fun than a liver biopsy, where they take a long needle, insert it in the liver, and extract tissue. Feels as good as it sounds, too, even with the patient sedated and semiconscious. Corrine sleeps on and off, waking every now and then to find one of us standing over her, wiping her face with a cool washcloth or smoothing back her hair. I get tickled when she wakes up and her eyes fall on Astor, sitting beside the bed (hogging the only comfortable chair, naturally) and patting her hand. Corrine looks like she's seen a ghost, and gasps, *"Astor?"* Must of thought she was having a nightmare. But once the room comes into focus, she murmurs, "I'm glad y'all are here," before falling back to sleep.

Julia's back when they bring in Corrine's supper, and the aide is so nice to us that the SSGs flip out. "What a great hospital," Byrd says. "I've never seen nurses so friendly!" When a CNA comes in to check Corrine's vitals, I ask if there's any chance we could have a couple of more chairs. As with most small hospitals, the room is a pretty good size. It contains a recliner that Astor claimed immediately and a typical hospital-issue chair, squat and padded with orange vinyl. Falling all over herself to be helpful, the stocky nurse's assistant rounds up a buddy, and they bring in two more chairs. When they ask if we need anything else, the SSGs exchange amazed glances. I plop my butt on the foot of the hospital bed, and the girls pull their chairs in a circle around it. I hate to do it, but I wake Corrine up. One reason's she's so weak is she's had nothing to eat or drink. I'll feed her, get a nurse to take the compress off, then get her in the shower. They've brought her a semi-solid diet, and if she can hold it down, she should begin to get her strength back.

After food—well, if you can call it that—a shower, a fresh gown, blow-dried hair, and a touch of lipstick, Corrine looks like a different person. I roll the head of the bed upright, fix her pillows just so, arrange her clean hair to curl around her shoulders, and sit back, admiring my work.

"You look like a little girl playing with a Barbie doll, Lanier," Byrd says, laughing. I spread the word to everyone when Corrine was showering: upbeat, upbeat, upbeat! Anybody says *one* word about Corrine looking bad, or us being scared, and I'll smack 'em.

"I never played with doll babies," I tell her. "For Christmas I got things like footballs and tennis rackets and basketball hoops."

"Why does that not surprise me?" Astor murmurs.

"Y'all should not be here," Corrine says, scanning the room, looking from Julia to Astor to Byrd to Rosanelle, then resting her gaze on me. She tries to look aggravated, but I can tell she's happy to see us. All of us, even Rosanelle and Astor. "I just can't believe y'all are really here."

"Some of us would do *anything* to get the crown," I tell her. "Julia thinks she's got it sewed up for next year, coming over here the other night, prissing around being so sweet. Huh! She thinks we're going to sit back and let her walk away with the crown, she's got another think coming."

"I'm just having some tests run," Corrine says, laying her head back on the pillows as though talking exhausts her. "It's not like I'm about to croak or anything. . . ." She stops and looks at me suspiciously. "Unless you know something I don't. Lanier? Have you talked with the nurses, or . . ."

I roll my eyes. "Believe me, I would if I could. But there's a thing called HIPPA, which is a new privacy act, and they're not allowed to tell me jack."

"They're the *nicest* nurses I've ever seen," Rosanelle gushes. "I just love them."

"Yep," I whisper to Corrine, "and if old Miles brings another hundred-dollar basket, they'll be even nicer." Julia and Corrine are the only ones who know what I'm talking about, and both gasp and turn to the vacant spot on the windowsill. Julia giggles, and Corrine rolls her eyes.

"What?" Byrd's looking from one of us to the other, eyes narrowed, neck stuck forward like a great blue heron about to plunge for a fish. When we giggle instead of answering her, Byrd pulls herself up from the orange plastic chair and goes to the windowsill. Squinting, she reads the cards, then whirls around to smile at Corrine. "Oh, how nice—you got flowers from a fan!" Leaning further, she says, "Can't read the writing . . . looks like Sal or Cal or something."

Astor's head shoots up, and Julia says, "Must be the nice lady who buys a lot of your gourds. Right, Corrine?"

Corrine's looking a little flustered, as Byrd

reads the other two cards. "Umm . . ." she says. "Don't see anything here from Miles but the lilies." At that moment the door opens and Corrine mutters, "Speak of the devil."

And there he stands, in all his splendor, the Prince of Darkness himself, his eyebrows shooting straight up as he surveys the room in surprise. I'm thrilled to see that his long elegant fingers are wrapped around another huge, cellophane-wrapped basket.

Once Miles steps into the room, poor little Culley lurks behind him, looking like he stepped off the cover of a punk-rock album. His baggy britches look like they're going to fall off—when he turns around, bet you can see his crack—and he's wearing a skimpy black T-shirt with "Duck Off, Fude" written in silver letters. I'll never tease Christopher about being a dumb jock again.

Miles is not pleased to see us. "My God, Corrine," he says in a cold, disapproving voice, "looks like you're having a party in here." Yeah, buddy, I think to myself. One you're not invited to.

"The SSGs came to cheer me up, Miles," Corrine says in a small voice, and I want to shake her, thinking she owes him an explanation. Miles's eyes sweep the room, and he speaks to each of us briefly, though it's obvious he doesn't remember anyone's names, except for Julia and Astor. He doesn't call me by name, just nods curtly in my direction. I haven't been around him all that much; it's always been obvious that he doesn't approve of Corrine's friendship with me. Corrine's never said so, but I can tell. When they lived on top of the mountain in that glass house, which had all the warmth of an ice castle, I visited a couple of times but told Paul afterward I'd never go back when Miles was there, he made me so uncomfortable. He was totally obsessed with Corrine, watching her every move, demanding all her attention. No wonder she went wacko half a dozen times. Been me, I'd have spiked his coffee with rat poison. Now, even with me sitting on the foot of the bed as close to her as I can, Miles heads straight to Corrine. She tries to move her head, but he takes her chin in his hand and kisses her lightly on the mouth, obviously not caring that the SSGs are watching.

Culley comes forward, hugs his mama, then says in a low voice, "You look good, Mom. Feeling better?" Sure enough, when he leans over the bed I see his crack, and

Julia and I exchange amused glances. Julia, who's sitting by the head of the bed, jumps up and pats her chair, saying, "Culley, sit here so you can visit with your mother, honey." But Culley shakes his head and stands awkwardly by Corrine's side. He holds her hand but doesn't look at her. Something weird going on there.

"I've talked with Dr. Brown, but nothing from the biopsy yet," Miles tells Corrine. I bite my tongue to keep from saying, Oh, you talked with Dr. Brown, huh? Has the good doctor never heard of HIPPA? "He says he might know something tomorrow," Miles adds. Surely Corrine had better sense than to get one of Miles's cronies for a doctor! I swear, Corrine, like most women, has such a bad problem with self-esteem, letting Miles pull her strings like she does. I could just shake her. Yet the answer is right in front of her, blazing on Culley's shirt in silver letters: Duck Off, Fude.

Miles moves away from Corrine's side long enough to put the basket he's carrying on the windowsill. (Hot damn—looks like expensive cookies, crackers, and cheeses!) He scans the room and scowls, no doubt wondering where the basket he brought yesterday disappeared to. A puzzled look on his face, he inspects Julia from head to toe, and I cover my mouth to keep from snickering. Guess he figures skinny little Julia ate the whole basket of goodies, all by herself. Then Miles turns around, takes reading glasses from his shirt pocket, and reads the cards on the flowers. He studies the card on the bud vase, then, peering over the top of his glasses, eyes Corrine sharply. Can't wait to ask Corrine what that's all about. Why should Miles be so blame curious about some woman who buys gourds from her?

Standing in front of the windowsill, Miles says to the room in general, in a rather loud voice, "I hope you ladies won't keep Corrine up too late. She needs to get her strength back, you know."

Rosanelle, the dummy, is the one to respond. "Don't you worry about that, Miles. Matter of fact, I was thinking the same thing. We should leave in a few minutes and get some supper, don't you think, girls?" She directs this question at us, then turns her head up to look at Miles, standing next to her. "Is there a nice restaurant in town?"

His brow wrinkled in a frown, Miles appears to be thinking about her question, then he raises a finger high, as though an idea just occurred to him. "Tell you what. The Chickasaw Inn downtown has a fabulous new chef I've been dying to try." (Don't let us stop you, I think to myself.) "Why don't I take you ladies there for dinner? It will give me the opportunity to become better acquainted with Corrine's friends and allow Corrine to get her rest."

"What a great idea!" Rosanelle says, standing and smoothing down her pantsuit. "I'm about to starve."

Astor rises from the recliner, too, then stretches her long limbs like a cat lying in the sun. "A lovely plan, Miles. I'm hungry, too." When she holds her arms straight up in a stretch, as though reaching for the ceiling, her halter top rides up, revealing her smooth, flat midriff. Her skin's such a rich caramel color that, even as tanned as I am, it makes the rest of us look washed out. Miles's eyes look like they're about to pop out of his head as they travel slowly over Astor's long, shapely body. I wink at Julia, and she manages to keep a straight face. Old Miles is staring at Astor like a fat man outside the window of a candy store.

Byrd picks up her purse and stands as

well. "I haven't eaten anything all day. Glad you suggested this, Miles," she says.

"Coming, Culley?" Miles asks his son, but Culley shakes his head.

"Can't, Dad," Culley says, glancing down at his mother. "I'm going over to the coffee-house to practice for Sunday night."

Corrine raises her face to him, her crystal-colored eyes shining and a flush of color appearing high on her cheeks. She sure adores that boy, even though he's sided with his daddy through it all. Proves that love is blind. Me, I think Culley needs a wake-up call. Corrine has tried to shield him from knowing what a louse his daddy is long enough.

"Culley was supposed to play in a coffee-house last Sunday night," Corrine tells the SSGs, "but I messed his plans up by getting sick." Culley keeps his head down and doesn't meet her eye, kicking at something on the floor, hands deep in the pockets of the low-slung britches. My palm is itching to get up and slap the shit out of him, then say that he can at least by-God look at his mother when she talks to him.

The SSGs are making moves to leave, Byrd coming to kiss Corrine good-bye,

Rosanelle with her gold compact open, applying another heavy coat of bright red lipstick, and Astor twisting her body from one side to the other like a corkscrew. Julia catches my eye frantically, and I incline my head toward the bathroom. "Ah, Julia," I say loudly, "come to the mirror and I'll show you how to use that clip to keep your hair up." It's the only way I can think to get her alone. Both of us are sending the same eye signals to the other: No way in hell I'm going to dinner with Count Dracula!

In the bathroom, I say real loud, "Stand so you can see in the mirror," then go through the motions of unfastening the heavy tortoise clip from Julia's ponytail and letting her great-looking hair fall to her shoulders as I comb through it with my fingers. Sotto voce, I say, "Sorry, Julia, but you've gotta go with them."

Julia's eyes widen and she winces in pain as I twist her soft silky hair around my hand so I can pin it up. "Easy, Lanier! I'm tender-headed," she says, loud enough for the others to hear. Then she whispers to me, "I don't want to go! One of the reasons the SSGs came today was to keep the son-of-a-bitch away from her, not to become palsy-walsy with him."

"Well, it's working, isn't it? He's not only leaving, he'll have to pick up a hefty tab for everybody's supper. Spread the word to everyone to order the most expensive thing on the menu, along with several bottles of the best wine Chickasaw Inn offers. You go, and I'll stay here and see what I can find out from the nurses," I whisper back. Then, loud voice again: "All righty! Looks mighty pretty." Actually, it's lopsided, but I don't want to delay getting Miles out of here any longer. In the mirror I can see that he's returned to Corrine's side, and he's leaning over, stroking her hair. I nudge Julia with my elbow and she goes flying out the door, saying with a fakey sweet smile, perfected by her years of being queen: "Okay, folks; let's go now."

A couple of weird things happen after they finally leave. Only thing I agree with Miles about, I, too, want Corrine to get some rest since she's been through pure hell lately. I know how those tests wear you out. Miles is pissed when I say I'm not going to dinner with them. "I hope you'll keep in mind, Lanier," he says, an edge to his voice, "the reason we're leaving now is to allow Corrine to sleep."

"I thought the reason you were leaving was to eat dinner," I can't resist retorting.

He shrugs. "That, too, of course. But please don't tire Corrine out. She'll need her strength for tomorrow."

Corrine stirs on her stack of pillows. I hate to admit it, but old Miles has a point; she has wilted like a flower in the hot sun, after looking so good just a few minutes ago. "Lanier's a nurse, Miles," she says, and I cheer her on because it comes out sounding pretty hateful. Especially for Corrine, who's real soft-spoken, not a loudmouth like me. "She's not going to tire me out. She's spent most of her life taking care of patients," she adds.

Miles's expression tells me that he wouldn't trust me to take care of his hamster, but I don't care. Main thing is, everyone finally clears out, and it's just me and Corrine. "I'm glad we have some time together, Lanier, because I want to talk to you."

Oh, shit, I think, she's going to ask me about the liver biopsy, and I don't want to tell her what they're looking for. I can't sit here looking at the best friend I've ever had and say, casually, a lesion on the liver? Oh, shoot, that's nothing! Probably nothing but a metastasis. Nothing, that is, except cancer that's advanced enough to have spread to the liver. Who'd be silly enough to worry about a little thing like that?

Instead, Corrine says, "Miles said something to me that scared me, Lanier."

"What was it—Hello?"

"I've been meaning to tell you so you can put it in the lesson book. Not too long ago when he was at my house, he told me there was something he warned his patients of. He said, your biography becomes your biology."

I snort. "Honey, if that's the truth, then you're a dead woman."

"That's exactly what I told him."

"Guess he didn't admit the part *he* played in your biography, right?"

Corrine smiles a small smile. "Now what do you think?"

Before I can hear more of Miles's words of cheer, the phone rings. I answer it, hoping it's not him calling to see if I've left yet. "Hello?"

"Is Julia there?" It's a man with a real deep but sort of hesitant voice.

"Joe Ed?" I've heard him give a hundred political speeches, but this doesn't sound like him. Maybe he's got a cold.

"Ah . . . no," he says, even more hesitantly. "Julia's been here all day, but she's gone now." I almost drop the phone when he says, "Could I speak with Corrine?"

"One minute." I hand Corrine the phone, shrugging. Corrine blinks curiously, clears her throat, and says, "Hello?" in a little bitty voice.

She listens a minute, then her face changes. "Oh, hi. How are you?" She listens again, her eyes not meeting mine, though I'm about to break my neck, eavesdropping. "It's really nice of you to call. I'm still having tests run, but I don't know anything yet." Listens again, then says, "Why, thank you. No, I won't forget that you're coming to the studio, soon as I'm well." Silent a minute, then says, "I'll look forward to that, too." She turns her head from me because I'm breathing down her neck, and she's about to get tickled. "Of course you can call back tomorrow. I should hear something by then." Silence, then, "Thank you for calling. I really appreciate it." And she hands me the phone to hang up.

Of course as soon as I put the phone back on the receiver, I jump her. "Who was *that*?"

Corrine shrugs. "Nobody."

"Nobody, my ass! Mr. Nobody sure has a sexy voice. You better not have a boyfriend and not have told me. No secrets between roomies, remember?"

"I don't have a boyfriend. It's just someone who's coming to the studio when I get out of the hospital."

"Oh." I'll admit, I'm disappointed. "Too bad, because the only way you'll get rid of Miles is to start seeing someone."

Corrine shakes her head. "I don't want to see anyone, Lanier, I've told you a dozen times. I'm off men, remember?"

"I must be the only woman in America who still likes men." I sigh, and Corrine manages a weak smile.

"You know, Lanier, I don't think that Miles will ever leave me alone, no matter what. He married someone else, remember? Didn't last any time. Soon as she left him, he started coming back around me."

"I was proud of you for standing up to him tonight, reminding him that I'm a nurse. But you know what? The old boy did have a point. I'm going to leave you now because you're about to drop off to sleep." I can see that she desperately needs to recuperate. She protests my leaving and begs me to stay, but by the time I kiss her good-bye, write another note from the SSGs, attach it to Miles's gift basket, and head out the door, she's already fallen asleep.

When delivering the basket to the nurses' station, I ask if there's any coffee on the floor. Unless they're the only nurses on the planet to do otherwise, there's always coffee brewing in the lounge behind the nurses' station, and they invite me back. Even though I force down a cup of black, nasty coffee while chewing the fat (so to speak) with a couple of staff nurses, I don't get much information. They're plenty friendly, thrilled to pieces with the goodies in the basket, but I can't pry anything out of them that I didn't already know. I say my thank yous and good-byes and leave. Damn—I should've eaten the gift basket myself.

I'm heading to my car when the second weird thing of the night happens. At first I'm disoriented, not remembering exactly where I parked when I arrived this afternoon, being in a strange place. Unlike so many hospitals nowadays, Chickasaw Memorial is in a really pretty setting, with wide green grounds overlooking Blue Mountain. Seems like I parked in a lot next to the emergency room, so I cut across a grassy patch to get there quickly. In the dark, under a willow tree, is a picnic table (who on earth would want to picnic at a hospital, I wonder) and I see that a pretty young girl is sitting on the table under the weeping willow, weeping, appropriately enough. Bless her heart, somebody must have died. Just as I hurry past her, something catches my eye and I stop in my tracks. It's not a girl after all, in spite of the long red-gold hair and earrings. It's Culley. His face is buried in his hands and he's squalling like a little boy.

"Culley?" I put my hand on his shoulder gently, so as not to scare him to death, me coming up on him in the dark. He jumps, startled, and looks up at me, his face all red and wet. Soon as he recognizes me, he throws his arms around me, crying even harder. I stroke his hair and murmur to him as I would Christopher or Lindy . . . as I've done with Christopher and Lindy, a million times. When their dogs or cats died, when they didn't make the team, when they got their feelings hurt, when they fell and scraped their knees, they ran to Mama. I recall when Culley was born and I came to visit Corrine, loaded down with presents, and I held Culley for the first time. He was a beautiful baby, plump and pink, with soft fuzz on his perfectly formed little head. If only Corrine had taken that baby and left Miles Spaulding's house right then, never looking back, she'd have saved herself a lot of heartache. And this boy, too. Many times I've wanted to knock Culley into next week, but it's been hard on him, too.

"Your mama's going to be okay, Culley," I tell him. "It'll turn out to be nothing, you wait and see."

Culley dries his eyes on the hem of his T-shirt, then rubs his face. "This is all my fault," he says. "Reason I'm out here, I was waiting till everyone left, then I was going back and tell her I'm sorry. I lied about going to the coffeehouse."

"Of course it's not your fault, Culley! That's bull—" But he stops me, holding his hand up.

"You just don't know. You don't know what I did." He hangs his head, not looking at me, wiping his eyes on his arm when he starts crying again.

"Then why don't you tell me?"

"You'll hate me."

I nod. "Yep, I probably will. I didn't make any mistakes at your age, so I'll probably hate you for making one. What'd y'all do, have a fight, and you think that made her sick?"

He shakes his head. "Worse than that. I said the worst things I could say to her, the meanest things I could think of."

"What?" I dare ask, holding my breath.

"I said she was a psycho, and that I hated her stupid gourds, and I felt sorry for Dad, having to put up with her all these years."

"Jesus! Is that all?"

"I hate myself, Lanier. I swear I've been thinking about killing myself, I feel so bad." He sighs with a trembling shudder.

"Oh, that would make her feel much better," I say dryly, sitting beside him on the bench.

"I love Mom," he says, his voice breaking. "But you know what? I don't remember ever telling her. I must have, when I was a little kid, but since I've been old enough to remember, I haven't. What's wrong with me, Lanier, that I can't tell her how much I love her? You think I'm some kind of weirdo or something?"

I look at him, at the nose rings and ear-rings and tattoos and obnoxious T-shirt, the britches falling off his skinny little butt, and I wonder if I'm really supposed to answer that. Instead, I put my arms around his neck and hug him. "Oh, honey, it's not that. Your mama has tried so hard to keep things from you because she doesn't want you to be hurt. Like all mamas everywhere, she doesn't want you to ever be miserable or upset or torn apart. She thinks she can protect you from knowing that life can hurt you in all the soft places, you know? Like she can be some kind of shield between you and the bad part of life. I wish she could be . . . just like I wish I could for my kids. If only it worked that way."

Wiping his eyes and nose on the back of his hand, Culley sniffs and sniffs, then raises his head. After a long silence, he says, "Lanier? When I was a kid, I thought Mom loved her stupid gourds more than me. I thought she didn't want to live with me and Dad because her art was the most important thing in the world. Know what? I'm beginning to think that Mom's art must be like my music is to me. I couldn't live without my music; I swear I couldn't. If I lived in one of those Taliban countries or someplace where they wouldn't let you have music, I'd wither up and die. I know I would."

"Culley, listen. As important as your mom's art is to her, *you* are more important. The art may be her soul, but you're her heart. Her heart, honey! I can't tell you how she's suffered all these years because of the big gulf between the two of you, or how she's despaired that y'all would never be able to reach across it."

Culley puts a hand over his eyes. "I'm so scared! I'm scared it's too late, that she's going to die without knowing how sorry I am."

I pull his hand from his eyes and make him look at me, leaning down and staring at him, right in the face. "Don't let that happen. You hear me, Culley? You can tell her now, but once she's gone, you can't. You can't do it then, so it had damn better be now. You know what I'm saying, don't you?"

He nods. "Yeah, I think I do. Should I go up there now and see her?"

I think a minute then say, "Tell you what. She's asleep, half doped up from the stuff they gave her during the biopsy today. But I don't want you to wait, so here's what I think you should do." I reach in my purse and pull out my notebook and the fountain pen. "Your mama gave me this pretty little pen," I tell him, smiling. "Let's go over to the light where you can see. Take this and write her a nice note, telling her all the stuff that you've told me. Okay? Can you do that?" Culley nods, and I get up, motioning for him to follow me. "When you finish, take the note up to her room and put it on her pillow. It'll be the first thing she sees when she wakes up in the morning, and I can promise you, it will be the best thing she's ever read. She'll be able to get through tomorrow so much easier, just having read it first thing in the morning."

"You think so?"

"I know so."

Culley scratches his head and frowns. "I'm not sure if I can say all that stuff, Lanier. I feel kind of . . . you know . . . fruity saying it. Mom and I have never talked much. What I was saying to you—it sounds pretty hokey, doesn't it?"

"Just say what you can, sugar. It's going to take a while for you or your mom either one to say what you need to say to each other. So just say what you feel like you need to for right now."

"Okay." Leaning on a car, he starts to scribble away, but I stop him.

"Maybe you'd better go in the lobby in case this is the mayor's car you're writing on and he or she doesn't appreciate it." I pull out several more sheets from the notebook and hand them to him. "In case you mess up. That way, you can take your time and say what you want to."

He nods, then gives me a tight hug. "Thanks, Lanier. I really appreciate this. I'll go in the lobby right now, okay?"

I give him a kiss on the cheek and a pat on the back, then turn to try again and find my car. I haven't taken but a few steps when Culley calls me. "Hey, Lanier?"

I stop and look over my shoulder at him. "Yeah?"

"Mom's going to get well, isn't she? I mean, you're a nurse and all. . . . You don't think she has like cancer or something, do you?"

His question throws me off, and before I can respond, his face falls, and his eyes go wide. "Oh, God, you do, don't you, Lanier? You think it's cancer, don't you?"

"No, of course not! I—don't know what she has, honey."

He takes a long, trembling breath, and I make myself say, "But whatever it is, Culley, she's going to need you now. So go on and write your note. It will mean more to her than you can ever know. And I promise you this, it will go a long way toward helping her get well, whatever she has."

The SSGs are back from the dinner at the Inn by the time I get to Corrine's cabin. Everyone is pushing and shoving in the bathroom, trying to take off their makeup, put on their night cream, brush their hair and teeth, and get ready for bed, the way we always do in October, when we have the fall gathering here, fighting for space in the lone bathroom. Over the years we've discussed having the fall get-together elsewhere, renting a larger cabin nearby or some rooms in the many inns around, but we always end up back here. The only one who complains is Astor, and she's always shouted down. We've worked out our sleeping arrangements over the years, and nobody messes with them. Kind of like Dolphin Cove, the living area is one big room, with a kitchen and eating space. Instead of the back wall of windows like I have at my place, everything here is arranged around a huge stone fireplace, which we all love. Even though Corrine's bed is upstairs in the loft, we usually pile quilts on the floor in front of the fireplace and sleep there. Astor hogs the sofa, but the rest of us—even prissy Rosanelle—love sleeping in front of the fire.

"Okay, out with it. How was dinner with that sweetheart of a man, Miles Spaulding?" I ask as I stand in the doorway, leaning on the frame, arms folded.

Rosanelle is brushing her teeth and she spits and gargles Listerine with enough gusto to make me gag. Leaning toward the mirror over the lavatory, Julia is patting some kind of gel on the purplish circles under her eyes, and Byrd's face is white with cleansing cream, which she rubs into her skin as she eyes herself in the mirror. Rosanelle has on a long white cotton gown and robe set, embroidered with little pink flowers—exactly what you'd expect her to sleep in. I wouldn't sleep a wink in something that uncomfortable. As usual, Julia is drop-dead gorgeous in an ivory silk gown that looks like a slip, and Byrd's wearing shortie pjs with Bama elephants on them. Funny what our sleepwear says about us. I sleep butt-naked, except for the SSG gatherings, when I bring one of Paul's old XXL T-shirts to wear so I won't gross anybody out.

Her eyes on mine in the mirror, Julia makes a face. "I couldn't eat a thing. But I ordered crab cakes, lobster Newburg, chocolate torte, and two fifty-dollar bottles of wine."

I laugh and high-five her. Byrd wets a washcloth and begins washing the greasy white crap off her face, saying, "Be glad you didn't go with us, Lanier. Miles would've made you so mad! It was obvious he only invited us to go so he could pump us for information about Corrine."

"I hope you didn't tell him anything." I turn from Byrd in order to stare daggers at Rosanelle, but she surprises me.

"Don't you look at me like that, Lanier. You'd have been proud of me. I know what Miles did to Corrine, getting custody of her little boy, not letting her see him, so I wasn't one bit friendly to him. Was I, girls?"

"She's right, Lanier," Byrd agrees. "You'd have been real proud. And she ordered more than Julia! We've got doggie bags full of stuff for tomorrow, so we won't have to eat cafeteria food. Think those nice nurses will let us use their microwave?"

"I can promise you they will," I tell her, yawning and stretching. "Especially since I delivered another gourmet basket to them, courtesy of the Prince of Darkness."

Byrd and Rosanelle both turn to look at me in surprise until they realize what I'm talking about, then they giggle. "Miles asked Julia what happened to the basket he brought Corrine yesterday," Byrd tells me, "and it was so funny! You should've seen his face when Julia told him how much she enjoyed it. Then she ordered all that food, and his eyes almost popped out of his head."

Julia laughs. "And when I got up to go to the bathroom, Miles told the girls that it was so strange someone as little as me would eat like a field hand. Byrd said she about choked on her scotch."

"I ordered a thirty-five-dollar shot of single malt," Byrd tells me proudly. "Never had it before, but it's Buster's favorite, so I knew what to ask for. Only thing, I don't like scotch so I had to order a Coke to mix it with. That's when you should've seen Miles's face!"

We laugh again, then it occurs to me that someone's missing. "Astor gone to bed already?" I ask them.

The three of them exchange glances, and Byrd says, "I'm going to be perfectly honest with you, Lanier, we thought this a tad strange."

"'This' being . . . ?"

"Astor going over to Miles's house," Rosanelle answers, and I screech, *"What?"*

Julia explains it to me. "Since we're being honest, I'll admit we may have contributed to it by making sure that Astor sat by Miles and talked to him, since none of us wanted to. And they talked a lot, didn't they?" Rosanelle and Byrd nod in agreement, and Julia continues. "And, to be fair to Astor, we were able to overhear a lot of it, of course, sitting right there at the same table, and they talked mostly about Mose's artwork. Miles told Astor that he wanted to add another of Mose's paintings to his collection and said he'd like her advice on which one he should get. Astor said she'd have to see where he planned on putting it before she could say for sure. So after dinner, Astor agreed to go to his house and see where he plans on putting a new painting."

I frown, chewing my bottom lip. "Hmm . . . I know what Corrine would say about that, don't y'all?"

The three of them nod, and Julia smiles, shaking her head. "Oh, I know for sure what she'd say! But the thing is, it was a legitimate reason for Astor to go. Only thing we thought a tad strange was Miles's insistence she go tonight and Astor's willingness to do so. I tried to say, it's too late tonight, you should go tomorrow instead, but they ignored me."

"Oh, God, he's not going to be bringing her back over here, is he?" I ask, and Julia shakes her head, telling me, "She followed him in her car, so we don't have to worry about seeing him again tonight."

"Bet he'll be back in the hospital room tomorrow evening, though," I say, "when the doctor's liable to return with a report from the biopsy."

That sobers us up, and everyone gets real quiet. To make them feel better, I tell them about the encounter with Culley on the grounds of the hospital, and Julia puts her hand to her throat and closes her eyes. "Oh, thank God, thank God!" she says. "Sounds like the first step of their reconciliation. Too bad he had to wait until she got sick. I just hope it's not too . . ." But her voice falters, and her eyes darken.

Byrd says, "Lanier, get your nightgown on—"

"I don't have a nightgown," I snort.

"Then get whatever you sleep in on, get

your face washed and your night cream
on—"

"I don't have any night cream."

"Obviously. I've been meaning to tell you,
Estée Lauder makes an excellent emollient
for maturing skin, which you need to try with
that sun damage you have. Now. Everyone
get ready and let's meet downstairs."

Downstairs, with everyone in their nighties
and me in my huge T-shirt, Byrd says we
should stand in a circle and hold hands as
we pray for Corrine. Byrd's eyes narrow
when she looks at me. "Don't you dare make
fun of me, Sidney Lanier Sanders, and I
mean it. This is important."

"What do you think, that I'm a heathen as
well as a fuck-up?" I say indignantly. "I'll have
you know I pray all the time. I may not do it
the same way you do, but I have an agreement with God. If He'll listen to me, I'll listen
to Him in return."

"Why, Lanier—how nice," Rosanelle says,
smiling at me.

"Okay, girls, let's hold hands and bow our
heads," Byrd orders.

It's hard for me not to giggle, though,
because Byrd has a green gooky mask on

her face, which looks like Halloween make-up and is supposed to exfoliate her skin when she rinses it off. All you can see of Byrd besides the green stuff is the big round holes where her eyes are, and the slash for her mouth. The green mask looks even funnier in contrast to her snow-white hair, which is wet and sticking up on top of her head. She looks like a green-faced cockatoo.

"Shouldn't we wait for Astor?" Rosanelle asks. She's coated her platinum hair with conditioner and wrapped plastic wrap around her head, telling us that after our prayer meeting, she'll heat a towel in the microwave and wrap that around, too, before she washes it out. She offered to do mine as well, but I told her and Byrd to concentrate on their own dry hair and mature skin and leave mine alone, thank you.

"No," Julia replies. "No telling when Astor will be back." I eye her kind of funny, but she won't look at me. I can't wait to get her away from Byrd and Rosanelle later on and ask her if she thinks Astor is going to screw Miles. We've already decided: Julia and I'll sleep together in Corrine's bed, Rosanelle and Byrd on a pallet, and leave the sofa for Astor when she gets in.

But all thoughts of Astor, Miles, and everything else go out of my head when Byrd starts praying for Corrine, praying that the Lord will see fit to heal her. Byrd starts crying, which gets all of us started, too, and dropping our hands, we end up with our arms around one another, huddled together and asking God to please, please not take another one of us.

The next morning brings more prayers, but this time, we don't get a chance to huddle together and try to draw comfort from one another. As I expected, before the doctor arrives—the charge nurse had let me know he'd be coming by this morning with a report—Miles and Culley show up. Guess Miles must've checked with the doctor as well and knew the lab results were back. Because Julia and I have claimed the places closest to Corrine, Julia in the chair at the end of the bed and me sitting on the foot, Miles is forced to stand leaning against the windowsill, his arms folded. I scoot over and pat a place next to me on the hospital bed for Culley, and he sits next to me. I'm surprised to see that he's cleaned himself up for the occasion, dressed in a faded but clean pair of jeans and a plain navy-blue T-shirt, his hair pulled from his face in a tight pony-tail. Miles has a suit on, so I guess he's going to work from here, and Culley will leave to run Corrine's gallery.

When Miles first arrives, I can't help myself; I watch Astor for her reaction. None of us heard her come in last night, and no one questioned her this morning, we were all so anxious to get to the hospital and find out if the doctor was coming. But Astor stares straight ahead without looking at Miles, even though he's standing by her chair. She, too, looks a lot more presentable this morning, with black capris and a tight white T-shirt, flat sandals instead of the platforms. Byrd is gnawing her finger-nails, and Rosanelle has her eyes closed and head bowed, getting in an extra prayer, I reckon.

I didn't have a chance to ask Corrine about the note from Culley, but I can tell she got it by the way her pale face lights up when Culley comes in the room. She doesn't take her eyes off him, and I see them smiling shyly at each other after he kisses her cheek, then sits down beside me. Neither one of them says a word to indicate that anything's different between them, but I can feel it. Already, a prayer answered.

Dr. Brown seems startled to see such a room full of people, and he tries for a touch of humor, although he doesn't strike me as a fun kind of guy. "Well, Miss Cooper," he says, "glad to see that the gang's all here."

"My friends and family have been wonderful," she says in a soft voice, her eyes leaving Culley to look at the doctor as he approaches the foot of her bed. "You've got the results of the biopsy, haven't you, Dr. Brown?"

Dr. Brown opens the chart he carries, not going any closer to Corrine than the foot of the bed, and not meeting her eyes. Uh-oh. My heart thuds and my breath catches in my throat. I know what that means, when the doctor can't face the patient.

"The tissue is back, and it shows that the lesion on the liver appears, unfortunately, to be cancerous. What we have is a metastasis, which means we're not looking at liver cancer. Instead, the malignancy has metastasized to the liver from another site. Sometimes, the tissue doesn't help us, doesn't indicate where it comes from. In that case, it becomes our job to find the primary." He closes his mouth in a thin line when he finishes, waiting for Corrine's reaction.

"F-find the primary?" she echoes.

"We'll need to locate the primary source of the malignancy in order to know which chemo protocol to use," he tells her. "In other words, how best to fight it. So I've ordered another series of tests, among them a brain MRI, colonoscopy, and mammogram. After looking at the results of those, we'll decide where to go from there, what protocol to proceed with. Are there any questions?"

It's as if everyone in the room is holding their breath, it gets so quiet. None of us look at each other, all eyes plastered on the young doctor. I dare glance over at Corrine to see if she's going to ask anything, but she's staring at the doctor white-faced, her eyes stricken. After a long silence, the only thing she says is, "Cancer," in a small, shaky voice. It's not a question.

"Not the death sentence it once was," Dr. Brown says sternly, sounding almost mad. "No point in saying it like it is." Yeah, you get it, buddy, I think to myself, and see what you say then. Even though it's not a death sentence anymore, it still scares the crap out of everyone who gets the diagnosis, I don't care who they are. Dr. Brown continues, "I can assure you that we'll do everything possible for you, Miss Cooper. You'll have the best care there is. Now. They will be in to take you out so we can start a new round of tests, then I'll return in a day or so to discuss treatment." With a nod of his head to the room at large, but not meeting anyone's eyes, he leaves.

In the stunned silence that follows the doctor's departure, Culley is the first one to react. Jumping to his feet, he bolts out of the hospital room, the heavy door slamming after him. Corrine cries out, "Culley!" and both Miles and me move to go after him, Miles a couple of steps ahead of me since I have to jump down from the high hospital bed, and he's already standing. He closes the door in my face, but I quickly overtake him and pass him in the hall. One thing I'm sure of, a former track star can beat an old fart like him in a foot race, any day of the week. Sure enough, I reach the elevator first and hurriedly close it in Miles's red, angry face, even though he looks like he's going to grab the doors and hold them open. I'll be damned if I'll let him work his poison on Culley before I can get to him, try to explain what Dr. Brown was saying. I imagine that, like most family members, once Culley heard the word "malignancy" he didn't hear another word spoken.

Culley outsmarts me and his daddy both. I can't find him in the lobby, can't find him in the parking lot, don't see him on the picnic table or any other place I look. I figure, too late, that he must have run down the stairs rather than taking the elevator to the lobby. I see Miles looking all around, too, then watch as Miles gets in a fancy car and hightails it out of the parking lot. Guess he's going home to look. Nothing to do but wait, give Culley a chance to pull himself together. One thing I know, he'll be back. I wouldn't have been so sure yesterday, but after last night, I know that he will.

While I'm outside where my cell phone picks up, I take it out of my pocket and call Jesse. I promised him I'd let him know when I heard something. It rings about fifty times before he answers, and his voice is sleep-filled and slurred. I know with a sinking heart that he's hungover. Bet you anything he's been drunk the whole time I've been gone. I tell him about Corrine, and he's as sweet and sympathetic as can be, but I wonder if he'll even remember that I called, once he gets good awake. *If* he gets good awake . . . before I came on the scene, he told me he often drank all day and all night, many days not knowing what time it was, whether it was night or day. "Come home soon, baby," he murmurs before hanging up. "I miss my little girl."

"Write me a song like you promised, Jess," I tell him, "and I'll be home."

I don't know what makes me do it, but when I get in the lobby, I turn around and go back outside. Dialing again, I call the Pickens County Medical Clinic in Reform, Alabama, and tell the receptionist to get Paul on the phone. She sputters around, insisting I tell her who's calling, and I say that it's Dr. Brewer, calling from UAB, that it's imperative I talk to Dr. Sanders immediately. After a long wait, Paul is on the phone. "Dr. Brewer? Dr. Sanders here."

"Paul? It's Lanier," I say. "Don't hang up

until you hear me out, okay? I'm at the hospital in Chickasaw with Corrine. She's sick, Paul. She's real sick. . . ." I don't mean to, but I break down, crying.

"What's wrong with her, Lanier?" Paul says, and his voice, that wonderful, soothing, calm voice of his, threatens to be my undoing. I start squalling so bad I can hardly hold the cell phone in my shaking hands. It's not much bigger than a matchbox, anyway.

"A lesion on the liver," I finally manage to tell him, "but it's not the primary."

"Have they located the primary?"

"No. No . . . but they're about to do the follow-up, the MRI and so forth."

"Sounds like colon to me. Maybe breast. Possibly stage four, if it's metastasized to the liver." Paul takes a deep breath, and I can tell he's shaken up. You'd never know unless you knew him well enough to catch the slight tremor in his voice. Paul's always adored Corrine, and she him. She thinks I don't know she's been trying to get us back together, but Christopher told me about the letters she'd written, begging Paul to reconsider his decision to drop-kick me out of his life.

"Yeah, that's what I'm thinking," I say.

"Listen, I was hoping you might call her doctor here, tell him you're a family friend—"

But Paul stops me. "You know I can't do that, Lanier. He can't talk to me unless I'm a consulting physician." I know Paul well enough not to even ask him if he'll pretend to be. Saint Paul would never do anything unethical. But he adds, "Tell you what, though. I'll ask around, see if anyone knows anyone there. Chickasaw, you say?"

"Chickasaw Memorial. Paul?"

"I'm sorry about Corrine, Lanier. Real sorry. Damn! You know as well as I do that's not a good diagnosis."

"I know." I swallow and try to say how good it is to hear his voice, but can't.

"Will you let me know what you hear about the primary, and the chemo protocol?" His voice goes right back to its professional tone.

Unable to speak, I nod, like a dummy, but when Paul says, "Lanier? You must be on your cell phone because I think we're losing our signal," I say thanks and good-bye and hang up. Oh, Paul . . . we lost our signal a long time ago, didn't we? I sink down on the steps of the main entrance of the hospital and have a good cry, my head in my arms. Then, exhausted, I raise my head and dry my eyes on the sleeve of my T-shirt. I've got to pull myself together before I go back to Corrine's room, because one thing I know for sure: She's going to need me like never before.

23

Corrine

BLUE MOUNTAIN

BEFORE THEY LEAVE BLUE Mountain, the SSGs are full of advice for my cure. Rosanelle arrives in my hospital room all dressed up for her return trip, where she'll attend an alumni barbecue in Dothan, Alabama. As usual, she looks every inch the former beauty queen/pride-and-joy of The W. Even though her red, white, and blue pantsuit is perfect for a picnic, my first thought is, oh, honey, *no*. "Corrine," Rosanelle says as she grabs my hand and kisses my cheek, flooding me with gardenia perfume, "just say the word and I'll stay. The Dothan group will be sick with disappointment, but they'll get over it."

I shake my head while trying to retrieve my hand. All I need on top of everything else, every bone in my right hand crushed. "No, no," I say. "Lanier and Julia are going home with me for a few days, so I'll be fine. No reason for you to disappoint the alumni of Dothan."

"Well, I'd hate to, but I'd do it for you, honey," she smiles, kissing my other cheek. "I'm not the best cook in the world, but I can open a can of tuna fish and make you a good sandwich. And I can sure wait on you hand and foot."

"I don't want anyone waiting on me hand and foot . . ." I begin, and from the foot of the bed, Lanier pipes up, "Good thing!" "I'm going to be fine, Rosanelle," I continue, ignoring Lanier. "You heard what the doctor said, that things will be better now, with me on the nausea medicine. I'm already feeling much better."

Her eyes narrow as she looks me over, and I can tell by her expression that she's thinking, you may *feel* better but . . . Giving my poor hand another bone-crushing squeeze, she straightens up and smooths down the front of her white pants. "Well. Soon as I get back to the office, I'm sending you a copy of that diet I told you about. Best way to fight cancer is with nutrition. Consume an unbelievable amount of beta-carotene and antioxidants, and next thing you know, those little boogers will overtake the cancer cells and just gobble them right up. I'll send the testimonies that go with the diet, and you'll be amazed! Never read anything like it. One poor woman, the doctor gave her six months. Six months, can you imagine?" She shudders. "Pancreatic cancer. She fought it with broccoli, beets, and green peppers, and that was ten years ago. Guess she showed that doctor, and you can do the same."

Lanier mutters under her breath, "Holy mother of God," and Rosanelle turns from me to smile at her. "Have you ever heard such an amazing story? That's one you won't find in the medical books." Turning back to me, she says, "Okay, I've got to hit the road now. But say the word, and I'll be back in a heartbeat. Or, tell you what! You want me to come back here on my way home, spend a couple of days with you?"

"No, no," I say hastily. "I'm running Lanier

and Julia off in a few days, soon as I get my strength back. I'm going to need some time alone to think things over."

Leaning over me and putting her face close to mine, Rosanelle says in a whisper, "Don't want Lanier to hear me say this, but I hope you'll decide against the chemo. You'll be sick as a dog, your beautiful hair will fall out, and your mouth will be full of sores. All that, and absolutely no guarantee it'll work, as your doctor said. Just promise to try the beta-carotene, okay?"

"I promise I will, Rosanelle," I say. "Now, run along because I'd feel awful if you were late for the barbecue in Dothan, all because of me."

After she leaves, Lanier is fuming. "I heard that, Corrine. I know you've got better sense than to think you can cure yourself with one of Rosanelle's diets."

Byrd's chair squeaks when she pulls it closer to the hospital bed. "It's a combination," she tells us earnestly, looking from Lanier to Julia. "I hope that Corrine will decide on a combination of chemo, nutrition, and prayer. That's the only way to be healed. In the bookstore? I bought a healing tape, Corrine, that I'm leaving with you. Listen to it every night and it will direct your prayers. It has subliminal messages, too, that continue to send healing messages to your brain as you sleep."

Julia is at the windowsill, getting the flowers ready to be taken home once an aide arrives with my wheelchair and release papers. She's poured the water out, and now she's wrapping the vases in tissue paper. "So sweet of Paul to send flowers," she says over her shoulder to Lanier. "Don't make any decision, Corrine, until you hear my proposal," she says to me. "Joe Ed has a fraternity brother who's an oncologist at Duke, and I'll not only take you there, I'll stay with you through the whole thing if you decide on one of their experimental programs."

"This from the woman who gave you the ever-smiling Dr. Brown," Lanier drawls. "Here's what I want you to do, Corrine. Paul sent you flowers, so being the pukey-sweet person you are, call to thank him. While you have him on the phone, ask him what he recommends. What would he tell one of his patients in your place?"

This voicing of opinions has been going on since last night, when Dr. Brown returned with the final word. After several days of endless

testing, the tests had one thing in common—
they all came back negative. The primary
could not be located. One day there was a
surprising scene that took place at the foot
of my bed, when Dr. Brown and another doctor, whose name I've forgotten, had an actual argument about the location of my "primary." Dr. Brown was so convinced it was
somewhere in the colon that he got visibly
upset when the other doctor couldn't find
anything. The other doctor, who'd come in
with Dr. Brown to show me the disgusting
pictures of my innards as though I wanted to
see them, waved the pictures in front of Dr.
Brown's face and practically shouted, "I can
tell you one thing, Roger, it *ain't* the colon."
Lanier got so tickled she buried her face in a
magazine, but I could see her shoulders
shaking. Of course, once the SSGs found
out Dr. Brown's first name, we immediately
nicknamed him Jolly Roger.

Dr. Brown's pronouncement last night,
that the primary couldn't be determined, got
me released from the hospital but faced with
an agonizing dilemma. All-purpose chemo,
which "might" destroy the cancer cells but
would do a lot of damage to healthy cells as
well; surgery to remove the lesion, which

would almost surely return since the primary couldn't be removed; or all sorts of experimental treatments, such as a catheter of chemo threaded through a vein in my leg directly to the tumor. During that fun time, I'd be virtually hog-tied into a reclining position for seven agonizing days, bodily functions tended to by all sorts of tubes and stuff. The only option *not* open to me, according to Jolly Roger, was to do nothing. That was absolutely not a consideration, he warned, because once it gets to the liver, it can spread very rapidly. I was to go home and regain my strength, take some time (but not too much, for obvious reasons), and think about my options. He didn't say get my affairs in order, but I could see it in his face. Make out a will. Get your insurance policies all paid up. Say good-bye. . . .

Astor arrives late, after Byrd has said her tearful good-byes and left for Birmingham. Byrd had planned on staying longer, but one of the grandbabies was having a birthday party, and I insisted she not miss that since I'd have both a nurse and a first lady who'd been queen more than anyone else to take care of me. Lanier got furious with Byrd because Byrd burst into tears when she said she'd see me this October, at the fall gathering. Lanier stomped out of the room, and Byrd kept wringing her hands and saying, "I know you're going to be fine, Corrine. I'm not a bit worried about you, I swear I'm not. I don't know why I'm crying!" It ended up with me comforting her, hugging her neck and telling her that she was right, I was going to be fine, and I'd see her in October, at my place. But when Byrd left, with her wet face and tear-stained eyes, I cried, too, with Julia holding my hand and sobbing as well. I couldn't help but wonder if I'd see any of them in October.

I've signed everything, and Julia and Lanier have gone to the car with a load of flowers, dirty clothes, and fun stuff from the room—the plastic bedpan and water pitcher—while I await the aide with the wheelchair. Astor comes breezing in, her face composed, her silky hair loose on her shoulders. She's looking particularly leggy in the short denim skirt (long legs that lead straight to heaven, Astor told us Mose had declared on meeting her), and a black V-neck top. Last night, after everyone but Lanier had gone to my house to bed, Lanier told me about Astor going to Miles's place to help him decide where to hang one of Mose's paintings. "Astor's trying to sell as many of Mose's paintings as she can," Lanier'd said, "because the nursing home costs so much. I'll admit I wondered if Astor and Miles got it on. . . ."

Weak and wiped out as I was, I'd grinned in sheer delight. "Such a thought would never enter my mind."

"Well, Julia and I were suspicious enough to say something to Astor about it," Lanier'd continued, "but she put our mind to ease. Astor doesn't like Miles any more than the rest of us; she's just being nice to him to help Mose out."

"Just like Astor," I said, "always thinking of others."

Astor's bearing gifts, more stuff for Lanier and Julia to have to tote to the car. She gives me a quick hug, then plops her fanny down next to me, pushing me over. I'm sitting on the side of the bed in a loose gauzy sundress Julia brought me to wear home, one I'd forgotten was hanging in my closet. It's perfect, not only being soft as a nightgown, but also loose enough to hide my new skinniness. Funny, how we women are always saying we want to be thin as scarecrows, yet if it happens this way, things sure look different. Should I beat this, I'll never think about dieting again.

"Gifts for you, Lady Corrine," Astor says, pushing a strand of hair behind one ear. "Thank goodness I had these in my car. Just what you need." She pulls a video from a huge black tote. "You haven't seen this video, since I haven't marketed it yet." Sure enough, there's Astor on the front, in black leotards, arms arched high above her head as she stands on one foot, the other foot resting on her thigh. Her head's thrown back in a dramatic pose, her long ponytail against her spine. "Astor Does Yoga," the caption reads. So much for catchy, original titles.

"Good picture of you," I murmur politely. One thing we've had to do consistently over the years is critique the promotional photos of Astor for her various projects. Astor pulls out a mat, a pair of leotards, and a head roll, all in her signature black.

"You can have the tote, too," she says, thrusting it at me. "But the main thing's the video. Follow it religiously, and I promise, you'll get better. I'm not saying that yoga will cure cancer, but it does help your body build up its natural defenses." She puts an arm around my shoulder and gives me a quick hug. "Oh, I wish I could stay with Lanier and Julia to help take care of you! I would if I didn't have those damn dance recitals coming up." Silently I bless the timely recitals. If I had to go home to Astor's ministrations, I'd just as soon stay in the hospital.

Since I'm in a weakened condition, I have no intention of mentioning Miles to Astor, getting into all that with her yet again, but she surprises me by bringing it up. "Oh! I don't think I told you," she says coyly, "that I may have sold another of Mose's paintings. Since he hasn't been able to paint for the past few years, our income's nothing like it was when we first married, not to even mention the fortune it costs to keep Mose at St. Mary's. I was thrilled to hear that Miles plans on buying a new painting. I think he's coming over next week to pick one out."

There is a God after all. Miles can't be in Birmingham and Blue Mountain at the same time, so I'll have a reprieve from his solicitous visits. I don't want Astor to know I care one way or the other, so I just say, "Miles has plenty of money, so don't let him short-change you."

Again, Astor reaches up to push a loose

strand of dark hair behind her ear, and I notice something odd. "What'd you do to your wrist?" I ask her, pointing. The diamond bangle bracelet she's wearing looks too thin to have rubbed her wrist raw, and I'm immediately suspicious.

Astor's face flames, and she reaches down to pick up her purse. "Oh, nothing! Just a little scrape. Guess I'd better be on my way now since I'm already running late." She leans over and kisses the air by my cheek, patting my shoulder. "I'm off! Let me know if the yoga helps, okay? I'll be glad to send another one of my tapes. See you in October!"

Coming in the door as Astor goes out is the aide with the wheelchair. In spite of my dire prognosis, I'm wheeled out of the hospital with a big smile on my face. I can't help it; the image of Astor and Miles together cheers me up more than any medicine.

I almost fall apart when I get back to my house. I feel like I've been away from home for several weeks rather than several days, and I walk around touching everything in gratitude—the few possessions that I really treasure, pictures of Culley, of the SSGs, of some of my favorite gourds, with citations and awards. Also, the artwork I've collected over the years, one of Mose's paintings (a small one) as well as other artifacts from artists whom I've had dealings with at various galleries and art shows. "Home sweet home," Julia says, putting one of my floral arrangements on the mantel.

"Oh, yes," I say, smiling up at her as I plop down on the sofa. "It sure is."

Since it's past noon, Lanier's in the kitchen fixing us an omelet for lunch. It still surprises me that Lanier's a good cook. As soon as we got here, she went to the garden to gather some of my poor scraggly herbs to make an omelet. For the first time in weeks, I'm actually hungry. The nausea medicine's at work, plus I've had no solid food for days. Odd thing is, except for a dizzying weakness, I feel so much better than I did before going into the hospital. If I didn't know better, I could pretend that I was cured. I went to the hospital, was put through the wringer, and surprise! Miraculously cured. If I didn't know better. . . .

Julia picks my feet up by the ankles, slips

off my clogs, and puts my legs straight out in front of me on the sofa. "Lie down," she orders. "Lanier's the cook, and I'm the physical therapist. We're here to make you take care of yourself."

I groan but obey her, propping up on a stack of pillows. "Thank y'all for this, Julia. I feel so guilty about keeping you away from your duties as first lady."

Julia rolls her eyes, pulling up a stool to sit beside me. She looks more like herself today, dressed again in her clothes, beige linen pants and a black silk top. It's been so strange seeing her in my clothes the last few days. At first I was so out of it with the tests, and being medicated, that I thought I was hallucinating. What surprised me was the change it made in Julia, being out of her designer clothes and into my artsy-fartsy stuff. Made her look so soft and vulnerable, not the poised, confident Julia I've always known. "Duties be damned," she scoffs. "When I leave here, Corrine, leaving you all by your lonesome to decide what you're going to do, I'm not going back to Montgomery."

I must have stared at her in astonishment because she laughs lightly, tossing her head. "No, I'm not running away from home. Or maybe I am. I'm going to spend a couple of days with Bethany in Talladega, then I'm going to our lake house at Lake Martin, maybe spend the rest of August there. I need some time by myself, too."

"I'll bet you do." To me, Julia's life as a public figure would be a nightmare, all that political stuff. I'd hate it. "One small problem," I ask her. "How are you getting there?"

With a flutter of her hand, she waves it off. "Oh, I'll just rent a car. By the way, Cal called me and wanted your home number, so I gave it to him. Was that okay?"

"Sure," I shrug. "He's been real sweet about calling the hospital, checking up on me. Once Lanier answered the phone, thought I had a boyfriend."

Julia tilts her head to the side, and her eyes light up. "You and Cal? Hmm . . . I like it! Two of my favorite people, both of whom deserve a little happiness."

I shake my head. "You can stop playing cupid. Cal's really something, I'll admit, but . . . I can't even think of anything like that."

"Actually, I believe it'd be just the thing for you to think about now."

"Julia!"

She holds up a hand. "Okay, okay. I won't push you, but I do need to ask you something else. You've made it clear that you want me and Lanier to leave so you can be on your own to decide about the treatment, but I'm not sure that's a good idea. I mean, wouldn't you rather talk about it, bounce some ideas around?"

"I don't think I can now. I'm still in shock. I haven't taken it in yet."

"Omelets ready," Lanier calls from the kitchen. "Y'all want me to bring them out there, or should we eat at the table?"

"Bring them in here," Julia answers her, then turns back to me, her face soft, her lovely gray eyes sad. "I can't stand the idea of you going through this alone!"

"I'm not alone. I have you, Julia, and Lanier, and even Byrd and Rosanelle and Astor. Only good thing about this . . . I'm not facing it alone."

We're sitting on the porch that evening, glasses of wine in hand, watching the sunset and crying. Each of us is trying to fake it, keep our tears from the others, wiping an eye while pretending to push our hair back, tighten a loose earring. Lanier's swinging in the wooden swing, her bare feet kicking the floor lazily, her hands resting on the chains suspending the swing from the ceiling. Sniffing, she rubs her face, then brushes the tears from her eyes with the tips of her fingers. Julia and I are sitting side by side in the rocking chairs, our faces to the setting sun, which has turned the dark trees and the slow-moving Shoal Creek a shocking shade of pink. Julia stops her rocking and coughs, wiping her eyes hastily with a tissue. We'd all promised each other we wouldn't cry anymore once I got home, a promise that hasn't lasted out the day. I have to turn my head from the sunset, it hurts me so bad. How can I stand to leave this place? It's fed my craving for beauty all these years, all year round. In the spring and summer, it's the surprise of the blooming trees and bushes that gets to me. Now, in summertime, the heavy pink blossoms of the mountain laurel look like fruit hanging from its thin branches. Wild blueberry bushes, bright with berries, line the path leading down to the stream, and fields of brambles have replaced their delicate white blooms with clusters of fat, sweet blackberries. Spring almost breaks my heart, especially when the dogwoods are in bloom, draping the mountains with lace garlands. Autumn is my favorite, when the summer-green leaves change to fiery shades of gold and crimson.

But the snow-dusted treetops of winter speak to me in a different way, calling out to that part of me which will always be drawn to the cold and dark part of life. I think I'd prefer to die in winter, when the earth is frozen and the woods are bleak, like my soul will be, to have to leave this.

"Morbid thoughts, Corrine?" Julia says, startling me out of my reverie. "You have a strange look on your face."

I glance at her and smile. "I was thinking it'd be easier to die in winter when everything's all dark and gloomy anyway."

Julia nods, turning her face back to the sunset and sipping her wine. "I think you're right."

"Godalmighty," Lanier screeches and puts her hands over her ears. "I'm not listening to this!"

"I meant, wintertime in general," I explain

to her. "I'm not planning on kicking off this winter if I can help it."

"Well, don't talk about it then. It tempts the gods." Lanier's scowling, kicking the floor hard enough to send the swing veering crazily.

"Take your hands away from your ears, Lanier," I say, raising my voice. "I need to say something to you and Julia both."

"No. I don't want to hear it."

"You don't know what I'm going to say."

"Yes, I do. You're going to say how much you love us, and how you want us to be brave and carry on and take care of Culley and all that crap. I'm not listening to it, so don't even start," she says in a loud voice.

"Lanier!" Julia says, with a frown. "If Corrine needs to talk about this . . ."

I hold up my hand. "Whoa. That's not what I was going to say." Lanier's crying now, wiping her eyes furiously with the back of her hand, and I continue. "Don't say anything, just listen, okay? I just want to ask the two of you . . . I mean, I want you two to promise me . . . if I get to where I can't do it, I'll need someone to pull the plug. I don't want y'all, and Culley especially . . . to watch me die like I had to watch my mama, not the way she suffered, and I mean it. But, in case I need some help doing it—"

"Shut the fuck up," Lanier moans, and Julia gasps.

"Lanier," she says, "I know exactly what Corrine is saying, and I'd want someone to do for me what she's asking us to do for her."

"Well, you have fun doing it, Julia," Lanier snaps, "because I'm not having a thing to do with this." She gets up and storms into the house, leaving the swing to flop sideways. Julia and I look at each other, and Julia leans over and takes my hand.

"What you want me to do, hon? Put a plastic bag over your head? Feed you sleeping pills mashed up in applesauce?" Her voice is light and playful, but her eyes are steady.

"Whatever it takes," I tell her, squeezing her hand.

Julia sighs a deep sigh and sinks back in her chair. "I'm going to be perfectly honest with you, Corrine. I'm not sure I could do it, once push comes to shove. But I meant what I said to Lanier. I'd want someone to do it for me. When Bethany was born, and we didn't know if she was going to be a vegetable, or totally blind, or deaf, or what,

Joe Ed and I had a similar discussion. I said that was no way to live, and if I ever got that way, I'd want him to pull the plug on me. Joe Ed reacted pretty much like Lanier did, but then he admitted to me that he'd want someone to do it for him. But the question remains, could any of us actually *do* it? I'm not sure I have the courage." She turns her head, and her eyes, dark and troubled, hold mine. "Think you could you do it for me, Corrine?"

I think about it, then shake my head. "I have no idea. Theoretically, I could . . . but, to actually *do* it? I don't know, either." A silence falls, and I glance back over at Julia. "Guess I'll have to get Astor to, then."

Julia looks startled, then her face breaks out in a grin. "As long as we can joke about it. . . ."

"It's being so cheerful that keeps us going!" we both say together, laughing.

Lanier pokes her head out the door, frowning, the phone in one hand and a glass of wine in the other. "I can't imagine what you two sickos are finding to laugh about. Here, Corrine." She thrusts the phone out. "It's for you."

"Is it Miles?" I mouth, frowning, and she shakes her head.

"It's Mr. Nobody. The one with the sexy voice," she says, and plops back down on the swing. "And I'm sitting right here and by God listening to every word."

And she does, her eyes narrowed and fastened on me. "Hi, Cal," I say into the phone. Julia beams while Lanier cups her hand over her ear playfully, listening.

"Am I calling at a bad time?" Cal says. "Sounds like you women are having a party."

"We're celebrating my homecoming. And talking about fun things, like when is the best time to die. What do you think, Cal? Spring, summer, fall, or winter?"

"Jesus! And I thought I had a sick sense of humor," he groans. "Who's there, all the Sweet Old Girls?"

"Only Julia and Lanier. You've met Lanier, haven't you? My roomie at The W?" I'm doing this mostly to aggravate Lanier, whose eyes are about to pop out of her head. She keeps mouthing, Who? Who is it? until Julia gets up, sits beside her on the swing, and, in a low whisper, tells her the story of her and Cal coming to my hospital room, Cal and I talking about the Trail of Tears gourd, and his plans to come to my studio to pick out a gourd for his grandmother's birthday. Lanier eyes me slyly once Julia finishes and moves back to her rocker. I have to turn my head away to keep from getting tickled, because Lanier begins leering at me and making loud smooching noises.

"Hang on a minute, Cal," I say, putting my hand over the receiver. "Cut it out, Lanier," I whisper. "I'm trying to have a serious conversation." I remove my hand and say, "We don't let Lanier out too often, Cal, because she embarrasses us when she gets around people."

"You sound so much better than you did in the hospital," he says.

"That's because I feel better than I have in a long time, which sounds so odd, considering. But I'm taking a miracle drug that controls the nausea, and I think once I get my strength back, I'll feel even better."

"Still weak?"

"Yeah, but that's better, too."

"Did . . . ah . . . the doctor put any time line on your making a decision about your treatment?" he asks. He'd called last night, and I'd told him about not finding the primary, and the options the doctor gave me.

"Just said not to take too much time, for obvious reasons."

"Doesn't sound like he gave you much direction," he says after a moment.

"No," I say quietly.

"How long will Julia and Louise stay with you?" he asks me, and I chuckle.

"It's Lanier, not Louise. Unusual name, isn't it? That's because she's such an unusual person—" Startling me, Lanier jumps up from the swing and jerks the phone out of my hand.

"This Cal?" she says into the receiver, gruffly, and Julia and I exchange glances, Julia rolling her eyes to the ceiling. "Hey, Cal, honey! This is Lanier, and my feelings are hurt that you don't remember me from the inauguration, since I about wore myself out flirting with you. I could tell it was turning you on, too." She listens a minute, then laughs. "Oh, you are *so* bad. How's the bodyguarding business?" She wags her head from side to side mockingly as she listens to his response. "Okay, okay, excuse the hell out of me," she says. "How am I supposed to know that you don't like to be called a bodyguard? I thought that's what you were, but I reckon 'security officer' does sound a bit more dig-

nified." He says something to her that causes her to throw her head back and laugh,
then she says, "Listen, Cal, Julia told me that
you were going to buy a gourd from Corrine
and give it to your poor old grandma for her
hundred-and-fiftieth birthday. . . ." She stops
and listens, then says, "Well, I just wanted to
tell you that's the worst pickup line I've *ever*
heard."

I gasp, and Julia comes to the rescue,
wrestling the phone away from Lanier. "Cal?"
she says, while Lanier giggles. "This is Julia."
She listens a minute, then shakes her head
sadly. "You're right; the Same Old Girls are
all crazy as loons, and I regret introducing
you to any of them. I know, I know, if I were
a true friend I'd never have done so." She listens a minute then says, "I'll call you from my
cell phone in a couple of days to discuss
that, okay? I've got to look at both mine and
Joe Ed's schedule first. Now, I'm handing the
phone back to Corrine."

I'm blushing like mad, not daring to look at
Lanier, who's smirking again. Cal surprises
and touches me with what he says next.
"You're lucky to have such great friends,
Corrine."

"I know," I say, and again, my eyes flood

with tears. "I couldn't make it without them, crazy as they are."

Julia and Lanier have gone, returned to their lives, and I'm alone again. In order to get Lanier to go home, I had to pretend to feel a whole lot better than I do. But I discovered something weird: I was able to convince myself as well as Lanier. In faking it, getting up each morning and fixing my own breakfast, showering and dressing myself, putting on makeup and doing my hair, even going to my studio and piddling around for an hour or so, my strength started coming back.

It's not that I wanted Lanier or Julia to go; the opposite, really. Funny thing is, I was scared for them to leave me alone. I'm ashamed to say now that I talked Lanier into sleeping in the bed with me the first night I was home from the hospital because I was terrified to be alone at night, in the dark. Lanier insisted on staying with me the next night, too, even though I tried to get her to sleep on the sofa, telling her I was over my silly fear. Julia left a couple of days before Lanier did, then Lanier slept on a pallet on the floor, as though to wean me from having someone with me day and night. I wonder if that's a natural part of the illness. It's so unlike me—I've always preferred being by myself, not being one of those people who have to be with others all the time. Miles almost smothered me to death when we were married.

Culley, though, is another matter. I don't ask him, but I want him with me now, more than ever. The day before I got the diagnosis, he'd torn me all to pieces by leaving a note on my pillow. All it said was, *I didn't mean all that stuff I said, and I'm sorry for saying it. Please get well, Mom. You don't know how much you mean to me. Love, Culley.* Julia seemed disappointed that's all the note contained—he could've at least said he loved you, she declared—but not me. After years of nothing, Culley's writing the note spoke more to me than the few sentences it contained. He comes by the cabin every single day after closing the gallery, where he's busy training a young artist to take over running it in a couple of weeks, when Culley has to return to school. Although he doesn't stay long or say much on those late-afternoon visits, his presence tells me a lot. I'll wait until he's ready to say more. But for now, at least I know I have a reason to wait, and to hope.

Hope. That's all I have, I guess, but not very much of it. One reason I don't want Lanier and Julia to go, I'll be forced to look at Jolly Roger's options then. None of the above, I wanted to yell at him when he outlined my choices. I wanted to scream and cry and beat my hands on the wall and say No! No! No! I don't want to fill my body with poisons; I don't want a ghastly, painful operation to remove a spot that's just going to return; I don't want to be a guinea pig without knowing it'll be worth it. Believe me, I appreciate the irony of me fighting for life, not wanting to die. I want to live more than I've ever wanted anything. I have to wonder if this is what happens when you reject the gift of life. Though I've tried a couple of times in the past, I haven't been able to find a successful way of offing myself, so my body obliges me. Looks like old Miles was right. My biography has become my biology, after all.

Funny, but I feel better every time I go back to my studio, even though I'm not working, haven't been able to work for a while. Just going into the studio is all it takes to lift my spirits. I hope that soon I'll be able to pick up where I left off with the kettle gourd, the one I still haven't named. First day I went back, when Julia and Lanier were still here with me, I went to pieces, soon as I walked in the door. Thank God I'd convinced Julia and Lanier to let me go by myself! I'd hated for them to witness my coming apart. It was a double whammy, of course. I was back with my life source, my gourds and paints and tools, but also, it was the scene of that awful time with Culley, the day I got so sick. It was too much, and in my weakened state, I sat on my work stool, put my face in my hands, and cried for a good five minutes. Afterward I stumbled to the sink, washed my face, and pulled myself together. When I recovered, I went to each of the gourds that I had spread out on the shelves in various stages of completion and held them close, swearing I'd be back to finish them one of these days. I promised the funny, odd-shaped gooseneck that an ugly duckling could be turned into a swan, just wait and see. The gigantic African bushel would be made into a vessel worthy of its size and dignity, and the long dipper wouldn't be just another plain old dipper, not when I got through with it. Cupping the mini-sennari in the palm of my hand, I promised it'd be so delicate and lovely that my customers would fight to take it home with them.

Reaching for the kettle gourd I'd been working on the day I got sick, the day Culley caught me cuddling it, I again took it to the bank of windows in order to see if it had the same effect on me it'd had before I went into the hospital. Yet again, the strange design, the concentric circles and vines, worked its magic, and I held it in my arms, pressed close against my body. I whispered that I'd be back to finish it soon.

Before Julia went home, an odd thing happened with the kettle gourd. Julia wanted to see what I had in my studio, and in the process of going around to the various gourds, we came to the unfinished kettle. Julia gasped and put her hand to her throat. "My God, Corrine," she said. "I've never seen anything like that."

I handed it to her, but because it's so big and bundlesome to hold, she seemed afraid to take it, holding it away from her like a basketball. Funny to me how people think gourds are made of glass. Once in the gallery a customer dropped one and actually screamed and jumped back, expecting it to shatter at her feet. "I haven't painted it yet, as you can see, and I have no idea what the design is," I told Julia, "but I like it, too." I don't tell her what an understatement that is, that the gourd has cast some kind of spell on me. I'm drawn to it every time I enter the studio.

"The design's Native American, isn't it?" she asked me, her fingers tracing the circles and ovals, traveling up the ascending vines.

"Well, that's the inspiration. Came to me from studying some pictures from one of my old textbooks. You know, the course I took on Native American art."

"What does it mean?" Julia asked me, and I shrugged.

"Nothing. Art doesn't have to *mean* anything, you know."

Julia rolled her eyes. "Please. I had an art history minor, remember? I meant, what does the design mean?"

"I have no idea, which is the strange thing about this gourd. The gourd and the design came together in a way I can't even begin to explain."

She tilted her head to the side. "This would be the perfect gourd for Cal to buy for his grandmother, don't you think?" She held the kettle this way and that, studying it.

I frowned. "Ah . . . I kind of doubt it. Gourd that size, with all the work I've put into it, I'll have to sell for a pretty penny. Bet Cal doesn't have a whole lot of money."

"That's for sure," she agreed.

I showed her a whole shelf of smaller ones I had in various stages of completion, all with Native American designs. Some of them were really nice, with beading and inlaid jewels. I'd expect an elderly lady in a nursing home, without much space, to prefer one of those, anyway, and Julia agreed. Then she held the kettle gourd close to her, cradling it like a baby, as I'd done so often. "Sell this one to me, Corrine. I've got to have it!"

I'd laughed before realizing Julia was serious. She was as taken with this gourd as I was. "Come on, Julia. You have a dozen of my pieces. Joe Ed'll divorce you if you bring in another one."

"Doesn't matter. I want this one. There's something about it. . . ." And I'd gotten goosebumps, a rabbit running over my grave, Mama used to say. The kettle was having the same effect on Julia that it had on me. That's when I knew that I couldn't sell it, not even to Julia. It would have to stay with me.

It's important to me to return to the studio with Culley, once I feel well enough and have my strength back. It's like getting back on a horse after getting thrown. Both of us have to do this, I'm convinced; so a week after Lanier has gone home, I purposely go to the studio and wait for Culley at the time he normally comes here after closing the gallery at five. I hear him calling me, walking through the house, and I call out to him, telling him I'm in my studio. "Can't you come to the house?" he says, and I smile, calling out for him to come to my studio instead. I know he doesn't want to, but . . . He appears at the door hesitantly, and I put aside the gourd that I've been holding.

"Come in, Culley," I say, when he stands at the door without entering.

He shrugs, his head lowered. "Naw, that's okay. I just wanted to see how you were feeling today."

"Just for a minute. Please. I've got some green tea over here." I go to a table under the windows and pour me and him both a glass of iced green tea, part of Molly's cure.

She'd joined the forces looking for my cure, of course, bringing me all sorts of herbal concoctions.

Culley appears uneasy, gulping down the tea as he tells me about the gallery, how the new assistant is working out. It's already late August, and he's going back to school next week. I can hardly stand to think about it. Where has the time gone? "Culley, listen," I say. "I . . . ah . . . never did tell you how much your note meant to me."

His face flushes, and he shrugs again, turning to look out the window. "No big deal."

"It was a big deal to me, Culley-bear," I say, the pet name I'd given him as a baby slipping out unbidden. I haven't used it in years, but he shows no reaction. "Listen, I know things haven't always been good between us—" I begin, but Culley puts his glass down with a loud clank, stopping me.

"Could we talk about it another time, Mom?" He won't meet my eyes.

"Okay, okay. I won't say anything else, then, except this. Why don't you write me when you go back to school? And I'll write you back."

He frowns. "*Write* you? You mean, like a letter?"

"I realize that's a totally foreign concept to your generation, but yeah, like a letter. I used to write you all the time, when you first went off to college, but you never answered my letters."

"Sorry," he mumbles, ducking his head.

I hold a hand up. "I wasn't saying that to make you feel bad. I just think, since we've got a lot to say to each other, it might be easier on both of us if we put it in writing."

Culley considers it, then his face changes. He glances at me cautiously, swallows hard, and says, "Sounds like a good idea. But I need to know, will you answer my letters?"

I open my mouth to say I'm not the one who's had that problem in the past when it dawns on me what he's really saying. "Oh. Oh, honey, I'll answer every letter I can, okay? I promise you that. I'm really feeling a lot better now."

Culley nods, then before I realize what's happening, he lunges forward awkwardly and throws his arms around me. "Okay, Mom," he says in a choked voice, hugging me so hard I almost lose my balance, "we'll write to each other. That's a good idea."

I hold him close in a way I haven't been able to do in years until he pushes away, turns without another word, and scurries out

the door. Poor Culley-bear; the way he's
handled things his whole life, by turning and
running. Only way he's been able to handle
an overpowering, controlling dad and a
wacko mom, I guess. Since my sickness, our
relationship has been two steps forward and
one step back. I just hope and pray that my
time doesn't run out before we're able to get
in step and stay that way.

Like Julia did, and using almost the same
words she used, Cal Hawkins holds the kettle gourd in his big rough hands and studies
it appreciatively. Unlike most people, he
doesn't hold it as though it's fragile, however. "Godalmighty, Corrine," he says with a
sharp intake of breath. "I've never seen anything like this one. It's something, isn't it?"
    I smile, touching it lightly with my finger-
tips. A caress. "It's something," I repeat.
    Almost the end of August, and I'd told Cal
a couple of days ago that it'd be fine for him
to come over and select a gourd for his
grandmother today, since he was going to be
in this area, picking Joe Ed up from the
Atlanta airport. What I didn't tell him was,
Culley had left for Brevard and I was having
such a difficult time that I needed a distrac-

tion. (Yeah, right—some distraction, Lanier had teased me, giggling.) I haven't told Lanier, Julia, or anyone else the other reason I need a distraction now. Thanks to the wonder drug, the nausea is under control, but the weakness has returned with a vengeance. Jolly Roger warned me that as the tumor grew, I'd get more and more exhausted, for complicated reasons having to do with the liver and red blood cells, which I tuned out. It's a good news–bad news scenario. Good news, the nausea's gone; bad news, exhaustion and a knee-buckling weakness have taken its place.

Following my lead, Cal traces the design with his fingertips, holding the gourd high to see if the design is on the bottom. He raises an eyebrow when he sees it originates there. "How did you do that, lay down under it?"

"Trade secret," I smile.

"You know, it's completely different from the Trail of Tears gourd, but it has its own power. Do you think?" When I nod, he asks me, "What's the design?"

I shrug. "I was hoping you could tell me."

"*Me?*"

"The inspiration came from a design in a textbook of Native American art, but it's really different from the other iconography. Guess I was hoping you'd tell me it was some ancient Indian image that I'd re-created subliminally. Or maybe the symbol of a fierce old Creek god that your ancestors worshiped."

Cal hoots. "I wouldn't know an ancient Creek god if he bit me on the ass. And the only ancestors of mine who worshiped anything were Freewill Baptists."

I eye him curiously, the black hair and eyes, the sharp planes of his face, the erect carriage, and I see the unmistakable mark of the proud Creek features caught in the photos and paintings in my textbook. The original inhabitants of this land, whose heritage my ancestors had come close to obliterating forever. I wonder if Cal is proud of his ancestry or if he's grown up feeling like a second-class citizen in a place and time where that feeling is all too common for anyone different, whether black, brown, yellow, or red.

"So you aren't especially interested in your Creek heritage, huh?" I ask, and he thinks a minute before answering me.

"You know, Corrine, it's been weird." Cal puts the gourd down, replacing it on the little bed of nails that holds it upright. He leans against my work table, arms crossed, a frown on his face. "Julia asked me a similar question, and as I told her, I grew up in a day and age when my people were considered lower than blacks or white trash. In the sixties and seventies, though, we were suddenly cool. We weren't Indians anymore, we were Native Americans. Big deal, right? The last few years have made us politically correct, and we're back to being Indians again, I guess, but now we're American Indians." A look of disgust on his face, he crooks his fingers to indicate quotation marks around the last two words. "I've had people treat me both ways, and I don't know which one I hate more—folks who look at me like I should be wearing a loincloth and war paint, or folks who fall all over themselves genuflecting and kissing my ass because I'm half Creek. It's all fucked up to me."

"Ha. I'd like to see you in a loincloth." I raise my hand to my mouth as a flush scalds my neck and cheeks. "Oh, Jesus! I didn't mean that like it sounded," I cry. Oh yes you did, Lanier would say if she were here. Thank God she's not, or I'd never live it down.

Cal throws back his head and laughs. "Now we're both red," he says.

Mortified, I turn quickly and grab the kettle

gourd again, holding it against me like a shield. Wish I could hold it in front of my face. "I—ah—I'm glad you like this one so much," I stammer lamely.

"Julia told me about it, so I was anxious to see it," he says. "But she says I can't have it for Granny Ross because she wants it herself."

"Well, Julia can't have it, either, because I've decided not to sell it."

"Can't blame you for that. Doubt I could afford it, even if you did."

I put the kettle back down. I have yet to paint it, and it breaks my heart to leave it unfinished. "Tell me about your grandmother, Cal, and I'll show you what else I have in the studio that she might like."

"Oh, Granny Ross is quite a character. But her health's really fading now, and she's gotten pretty feeble. Probably not going to have her around much longer."

Something she and I have in common, I think to myself, but to him I say, "If you don't see anything here you think she'll like, you can go to my gallery and look."

"I'd love to see the gallery, too." Tilting his head to the side, Cal studies me like he'd done the kettle gourd a minute ago. "You feeling okay, or not?"

I shrug, lowering my eyes. "Well, much, much better than I did when I saw you last. But I've been really tired lately."

"Doctor can't give you anything for it?" he asks, and I shake my head.

"Evidently not." I turn away and reach for a sennari with a gemstone inlay. "Okay, look at this one . . . This motif is based on shells found in a temple mound in Moundville." I point to the design with my fingertip. "When I was there a couple of years ago, looking for ideas for designs, I sketched it."

"Hey, cool," Cal says. "Eagles, maybe?"

"Stylized eagles, I guess. And this one over here your grandmother might like, too. See the tiny ears of corn, suggesting the green corn ceremony? I was thinking something small might be nice, since you said she lives in a nursing home. Probably doesn't have much room."

Cal chuckles. "You were thinking small fits the size of my budget, I imagine. And you're right, except when it comes to getting something for her. She's more like a mother to me than a grandmother, since she raised me after my mama died, so I don't mind splurging."

"Then we have to make sure to get the

right thing. And don't worry about the price; I'll work with your budget. Tell you what, why don't I give you directions to my gallery, and you go there and look as well? That way, you'll have seen everything before making a choice." I reach for a piece of paper and pen from my work table to write the directions on, and Cal watches me. When I hand him the paper, he folds it and puts it in his shirt pocket.

"Thanks. I'll do that," he says, patting his pocket, and I walk him to the door. When he starts out, though, he hesitates, looking at me almost shyly with those black, intense eyes of his. "Ah, Corrine? I don't suppose . . . I mean, it'd be great if you'd show me around your gallery, but if you don't feel like it, I understand."

I put my hand to my throat in surprise. "Oh! You don't have to go to the Atlanta airport?"

He looks at his watch. "Not until nine-forty. Won't take but a couple of hours to get there, will it?"

"If you drive like the night you brought Julia to the hospital, it won't take that long," I say with a smile. "Well, sure. I'll go to the gallery with you."

He looks pleased, then says, "Maybe we could grab a quick supper afterwards."

"Supper? Thanks, but guess I'd better not. I haven't been eating much lately."

"Oh. Well, sure—sure! Just thought it might do you good to get out of the house," he says, looking down and shuffling his feet. I'm surprised at how shy and uncertain he is, being such a macho-looking guy. "I wouldn't keep you out long, since I've got to leave shortly, and you could order something light, like soup. But . . . hey—never mind. Bad idea."

"You know what?" I say, then blush when his eyes meet mine. Both of us, awkward as newborn calves. "You're right," I tell him. "It'd do me good to get out, and soup sounds perfect."

Going into town for dinner turned out to be the best thing I'd done in a long time, for more reasons than one. It ended up with Miles seeing Cal and me leaving Chickasaw Inn, which triggered another of Miles's jealous fits. Unpleasant as it was, it made me realize I'd been a fool to try and have any kind of amiable relationship with him, that

Miles would never settle for anything less than my complete subservience. One thing being sick made me realize: Time is too precious to squander it on someone like Miles.

As Cal and I were coming out the heavy oak door onto the street in front of the Inn, a sleek black car came to a stop in front of us with such a squeal of brakes that Cal and I both jumped back. Instinctively, Cal's hand shot out to grab my arm, pulling me behind him, and my breath caught in my throat. I saw then that it was Miles in the driver's seat, leaning over and glaring daggers at us. "Oh, Lord," I murmured, and Cal tightened his grip on my arm.

"Who's that creep?" he asked me, keeping his voice low.

"My ex-husband, the Marquis de Sade. Let's get out of here before he finds a parking place. He's the last person I want to run into tonight." It'd been such a lovely evening I didn't want to spoil it by an encounter with Miles.

In the darkness of the car, Cal glanced at me as he pulled onto the street. "So, what's the deal with your ex?"

"He wants us to get back together," I admitted.

Cal nodded. Over dinner (after careful prodding on my part), he'd told me about his ex-wife, how devastated he'd been by their divorce. He admitted that he had hoped they'd get back together, until recently, when she'd told him firmly to get on with his life since she now loved someone else. "That what you want, Corrine, to get back with your ex?" he asked.

I shook my head. "No. I don't want that, although at one time, I loved Miles more than anything. Looking back, I see that he always found a way to make me feel bad about myself. I didn't have sense enough to see it at the time. I didn't think I deserved any better." I pointed out the window, leaning over. "There's my driveway. It's hard to see at night." On the long, dark drive down the mountain to the cabin, I glanced over at Cal. "Know what I read once? That we can only truly love people who make us feel good about ourselves."

"Makes sense to me," Cal responded. "It's been hard for me to admit, but I wasn't much of a husband to my wife. No wonder she left me."

She must've been an idiot letting some-one like you get away, I thought to myself.

But to him I said, "I sure wish I'd left Miles long before I did."

Parking the car, Cal asked me, his voice carefully casual, "Surely you haven't been letting your ex harass you, have you, Corrine? I remember him being in your hospital room."

I lowered my head. "Yeah, I guess you could say that Miles harasses me, though I hadn't thought of it that way."

Cal studied me, then said, "I'd be glad to have a little talk with him." When I looked at him skeptically, he grinned. "Jesus, I didn't mean beat him up or anything. Believe it or not, I've had some training in handling guys like him. Bet I know what to say to make him leave you alone."

I laughed, picturing that encounter. "Miles is not exactly your typical harassing ex-husband, Cal. He's a therapist."

Cal snorted. "No wonder he's so fucked up, then." When he turned off the car, his eyes fell on the clock on the dashboard, and he groaned. "Oh, man, look at the time! I've got to go, fifteen minutes ago." He jumped out and hurried around the car to open the door for me, but I stopped him, the two of us standing on the dark driveway.

"Wait here, Cal," I said, putting a hand on his arm. "You're right; even going a hundred miles an hour, you're barely going to make it to the airport in time. But give me one minute, okay? I'm going to run in the house and get a birthday gift for your granny."

"No need for you to do that," he protested, but I didn't wait to argue with him. Leaving him scowling by the car, I went around the house to my studio, took the kettle gourd off the bed of nails, and put it in a big paper sack, the kind with handles that I kept handy for carrying my gourds. I put my face to the kettle gourd one last time and nuzzled it. I wasn't sure exactly why, but suddenly I knew I was supposed to give it to Cal's grandmother.

At first Cal refused to take the kettle gourd, holding up both his hands in protest. Stammering awkwardly, I tried to explain why I was giving my treasured gourd away, but Cal looked at me like I was crazy. I couldn't blame him; it was one of those weird things that you know instinctively but can't explain, and I knew my attempts to do so sounded like a bunch of New Age mumble-jumble to someone like Cal. Finally, he had no choice but to take the sack and leave, since he had a little over an hour to make a two-hour trip to Atlanta.

After watching the lights of Cal's car disappear in the darkness, I was so exhausted and weak that I barely had the energy to climb the steps to my porch. But the night wasn't over yet. Just as I reached out to open the front door, I heard the sound of a car in the driveway and turned my head. Had Cal forgotten something? The gaily wrapped box with the inlaid sennari he'd bought at my gallery for his granny was in the backseat; I'd seen it when I got out of the car. My heart sank when I saw the sleek black car pull into my driveway and heard a car door slam. It was Miles.

Unable to stand on my feet any longer, I sat on the top step, which still held the warmth of the day, and leaned against the log railing. I not only lacked the energy to pull up a chair, I didn't want Miles joining me, sitting companionably in a rocker. I didn't feel up to this encounter with Miles, but it couldn't be helped. Might as well get it over with—it was certainly long overdue.

Miles towered over me, glowering as he stood on the step next to me, and I had to look up at him. "Let's go inside and talk,

Corrine," he demanded as soon as he reached the top of the steps. His jaw was tight, his anger barely under control.

I shook my head. "No." I shook my head even more forcefully when he motioned toward the porch chairs, and I said, "If you want to talk to me, you're going to have to do it right here."

Miles stared down at me, his full lips drawn in a tight line. "I couldn't believe my eyes when I saw you coming out of the Inn tonight, Corrine. You have no business being out on the town, gallivanting around. You are a very sick woman."

"Miles, listen to me—" I began, but he interrupted me, his face flushed.

"And I don't know *who* that man was you were with," he said, eyes flashing, "but for Culley's sake, you should let me run a background check on him. Anyone looks like that probably has a record."

"It's absolutely none of your business who I go to dinner with," I snapped, my face burning. "How dare you come over here saying such things to me?"

"Tell me this—is he Italian?"

"*Italian?* Why on earth would you ask

something like that?" Hand it to him, Miles was still able to surprise me.

Glaring, Miles says, "Because I suspect that muscle-bound boyfriend of yours is Mafia. When I braked the car after seeing the two of you coming out of the Inn, I recognized the gesture he made."

"What he'd do, Miles, give you the finger? Only Italians do that?"

Miles's face flushed. "I saw him reaching in his breast pocket, as though for a gun."

I wasn't able to suppress a giggle, it was so ridiculous. "Oh, Lord. What you saw was the instinctive reaction of a law enforcement officer who thought a car was running us down."

Typical of Miles; even that infuriated him. "Law enforcement, huh? Might have known. Most of them are nothing but hooligans with badges."

"I'd keep that observation to myself, if I were you," I said with a sigh. "But for now, I want you to listen to me, Miles, and listen to me good. This is the last time I'm allowing you to come here and harass me."

"Harass you?" His face twisted in a sneer. "That's an outrageous accusation, Corrine. I'm concerned about you, is all. And I want you back. I've made no secret of that. Culley is thrilled at the idea that his parents might be together again."

I stared at him in astonishment. "Surely you haven't put that idea in Culley's head!" But I knew he had, knew Miles well enough to know he would do such a thing. A good deed never goes unpunished . . . that was what I got for trying to have a friendly relationship with the father of my son. I pulled myself up and faced Miles. "For Culley's sake I've tried to be nice to you recently," I told him with a trembling voice, "because I never wanted Culley to find out the kind of man his father is. Now that he's an adult, he'll find out anyway, in spite of all I've done to shelter him. And you know what, Miles? Culley will have to deal with it, like all of us who've had shitty parents have done. Culley won't be the first kid to have to overcome that."

"He's certainly had to with you for a mother," Miles said, eyes narrowing meanly.

"He sure has," I agreed. "And he'll survive having you as a father."

Miles reached out for me, and I took a step away from him. "Let's don't do this, Corrine," he said, his voice rising. The look of panic on his face surprised me. "Surely you know how much I love you."

I looked at him long and hard, and I felt nothing but pity. "Actually, that's not true, Miles. The problem is, you can't stand the thought of me not loving you."

He took a step backward as though I'd slapped him. "But—you've never loved anyone but me, Corrine. You can't deny that!"

I shook my head and folded my arms, my exhaustion heavy as a hot cloak. Too tired to be having this conversation. "That was then, and this is now. Now that I might be dying, Miles, I'm looking at things differently, and—"

"We're all dying," he interrupted me, and I sighed in exasperation.

"Truer words were never spoken. But tell me this, Miles. How would you like to swap places with me?"

"I want you to let me take care of you, Corrine. I want you to let me love you and cherish you, for whatever time you have left. I don't want you to die!" For the first time since I'd known him, Miles broke down. His shoulders shook, and he covered his face with both hands, sobbing.

Years ago, when I loved him, his tears

would have moved me. Now, I just wanted him gone. "I'm not real crazy about the idea, either," I admitted. "But for whatever time I have left, I want to be with the people I love and who love me. That no longer includes you. I'm sorry to have to say that, but it has to be said. I don't love you, and I don't want you around me."

Miles pulled a handkerchief out of his back pocket and mopped his face. When he composed himself, his reddened eyes were hard and angry. "What a cold and unforgiving woman you've become!" he spat out. "If I leave here now, Corrine, be warned: I won't be back. My love is a gift, and I have no intention of throwing it away on someone who doesn't value it."

I smiled at him. "Good for you, Miles. I wish to God I'd done the same."

Leaving him standing with a stunned look on his face, I turned and went into the house, closing the door firmly after me. For the first time, I didn't worry about him following me. After several seconds, I heard his heavy sigh, then his footsteps going down the steps. I stood with my hand on the light switch until I heard the sound of his car leaving. Once it was gone, I turned off the light and took a deep, cleansing breath. Even though I was weak, exhausted, and facing a dire future, for the first time in many years, I felt free as a star.

24

Julia

LAKE MARTIN

IF ONLY I'D DISCOVERED the fine art of lying much sooner, my life would've been easier. I see that now. Not that I'm a George Washington; it's a bit more complicated than that. Over the years, I've developed a fondness for, and perfected the art of, the sin of omission. Commission always seemed a far greater sin. As a recovering Catholic— I became an Episcopalian when I married Joe Ed—I know better, but that's the way it feels. I can feel truth-filled and pious and self-righteous when I manage to avoid actually telling a lie by diverting the truth instead. It's like holding a mirror up to a beam of light, catching its image, and defracting it to shine elsewhere. With a lifetime of practice, I've become an expert at it. Maybe the SSGs have been right about me—they've always said I should have run for office instead of being content to be the spouse of a politician. With a skill like that, I'd have made a great one. Maybe because of my strict upbringing in the church, it's always been difficult for me to face anyone and tell what I know to be a bald-faced lie. Divert or twist the truth, certainly, but to look someone in the eye and lie without even blinking? That's not me. Lately, however, I've done it, and often enough to get good at it.

I've lied to the SSGs; I've lied to my assistant and to the staff at the Mansion; I've lied to my parents and my in-laws; but most of all, I've lied to Joe Ed, the biggest lie of all. And here's what kills me: With each lie, it becomes easier. I guess it's like any repetitious motion; when you do it over and over, you begin to do it by rote, without even thinking. It comes naturally. And the other thing is the way one lie builds on another, the old thing about the tangled web we weave. The lies keep building, trapping you deeper and deeper within them, until you're so knotted up in the web that you can't free yourself. Because I'm new at it, however, I have to learn the inevitable outcome of getting in so deep: Almost always, you end up getting caught.

Sitting on the porch with a cup of coffee in hand, I raise my face to the sun and breathe the fresh-scented air. All morning, a line of a song from *The Sound of Music* has been running through the back of my mind, haunting me. I can't get all of it, just the phrase that won't let go of me, something about my days in the hills coming to an end. It's true for me; my days here are coming to an end, and I have no idea what I'll do next. All I know is, I'm tired of being me. At an SSG gathering not too long ago, Lanier said, "I'm sick of looking in a mirror and seeing *me* look back. I'm sick of my clothes and the food I eat and my day-by-day routine and silly little habits. I'm so tired of myself I can't stand it." I know exactly how she felt. Rising and stretching, I go back into the kitchen for another cup of coffee. While I'm there, I slice a thick piece of bread, slather it with butter, sprinkle it with sugar, then reach for the cinnamon. I put the bread in the toaster oven to make myself the greatest comfort food ever, cinnamon toast. This morning, I need it.

Might as well take the phone back to the porch with me, start my daily web-weaving. But when I go back to the porch, the phone sits silent on a table next to me, and I stretch out on a chaise lounge, pulling my robe up and over my legs. Munching cinnamon toast and sipping coffee, I look around at this place that I've claimed as my own: the tall treetops, the deep dark lake, the sparkle of the sunlight on the water. I can almost pretend there's a touch of fall in the air, since it's the end of August. Truth is, it will be another month at least before we begin to feel that delicious coolness that fall brings, so welcomed after the stifling heat of another miserable summer in the deep South. Funny how I've spent my whole life in the South when, like so many of its sons and daughters, I'd planned on leaving it as soon as I could. I wonder if I'm nothing but a cliché, a middle-aged woman who's escaped from her life and spends her days rehashing it, going over the regrets and what-ifs and if-onlys. You'd think it were me instead of Corrine who's facing a life-threatening illness. Life-threatening . . . it's true; my whole life is threatened, though not from an outside force.

I almost don't answer the phone when it rings, forcing me back to my life. Sometimes I wish I could take all the multilined phones surrounding me, and all the compact little cell phones, and the fax machines and the computers with their modems and e-mail connections, and throw every blasted one of them into the lake. Guiltily, thinking it might be Corrine, I pick up the receiver and press TALK. It's Cal. He's the only one who knows the web of lies that have gotten me here and kept me here the last two weeks.

"Ah, Cal, my partner in crime," I say, smiling and picking up my coffee cup. "How was your visit with Corrine?"

"Good, I think," he says. "Interesting, seeing her studio. I've never been in an artist's studio. It was really cool, the way she does the gourds. I learned a lot."

"Never too old to learn. How was she feeling?"

Cal hesitates, then says, "I'm not sure. Not sick anymore, she said, but tired. Real tired."

"I haven't asked if she's made a decision about treatment yet, but her time's running out. Did she say anything about it?"

"No. She didn't seem to want to talk about it."

"I think it'd be good for her to talk, but . . ." I shrug. "Know what I like, Cal? That you and Corrine have become friends. Who'd ever have thought it, that night we went flying over to the hospital?"

"Yeah, it's strange for me, too," he chuckles. "Never had any women friends, you know? But Corrine's great, and I'm enjoying getting to know her."

"Better watch out. Hang around with the SSGs too much, and we'll turn you into a sensitive guy. Before you know it, you'll be connecting with your inner teddy bear."

"That'll be the day."

"Which gourd did you get for your granny?"

"That's what I'm calling to tell you—something weird happened. I bought a little one with lots of beading and stuff on it. Pretty, you know? And I talked Corrine into going to dinner with me—"

"Oh, Cal, how nice!"

"It was, even though her asshole ex-husband saw us, and it upset her." I sigh, annoyed at Miles for stalking her, but Cal brushes it aside. "No big deal," he continues.

"He's nothing but a bully, because he high-tailed it when he saw me, like he could tell I was itching to get my hands on him. I took Corrine back to her house after dinner, where the weird thing happened."

"You hang around Corrine much," I tell him, smiling into the phone, "and you'll get used to all sorts of strange things."

He chuckles, then continues. "I couldn't stay because I was running late to pick Joe Ed up, but Corrine told me to wait, she wanted to send something to my granny. I told her I already got her gift, but she said for me to wait. She went inside and came back with a sack, and in it was that big gourd you liked so much."

"She gave it to you but wouldn't give it to me?" I say indignantly. "Why, that hussy!"

"She insisted that I take it, even if it's not finished. Or so she said, though I couldn't tell the difference. Said something had been compelling her to make it, so she decided it was supposed to go to a Creek medicine woman on her ninety-fifth birthday. According to her, it was synchronicity that I showed up to get a gift for my granny when she was trying to decide why she made that particular design, what she should do with the gourd, stuff like that. Listen to this—it gets even weirder."

"Corrine does weird well."

"Corrine said something told her to send the gourd to Granny after I put my hand out in a protective gesture—that's what she called it—when her ex almost ran into us. Hell, I told her, that was nothing but instinct with me. I'm a state trooper, remember? But she said, no, it meant something to her."

"Oh, Cal," I say, touched. "That's really sweet. No one's ever protected Corrine from Miles, so of course she was grateful and wanted to do something in return."

"Nope, it's not that. Are you ready for this? Corrine said when I did that, she understood what the design was, that it symbolized the protective ring her friends formed around her. Told her it looked like a bunch of circles to me."

I throw back my head and laugh. "You know when I said it was nice that you and Corrine had become friends? Now I see that it's beyond nice; it's amazing. You're such opposites."

"Well, I tried to tell her I couldn't take her prized gourd, but she wouldn't listen, just kept saying please take it. And wouldn't take a penny for it, either. I was running so late I couldn't stay and argue, so I decided I'd take it to Granny Ross, tell her Corrine's story, and when Granny—ah, dies, I'd give it back to Corrine. What do you think?"

I can't even voice my fear that Corrine might not be around then, so I force myself to make my voice light. "Tell you what. If your granny doesn't like it, bring it to me."

He laughs. "Granny Ross will like both of the gourds, I'm sure. I always take her robes and slippers, stuff like that, so these gifts will be different, if nothing else." Cal's a straight-talking guy, skilled at keeping his voice even and expressionless, but I can tell by the change in timbre that he's pleased with him-self. I don't even try telling him how much his devotion to his grandmother moves me.

Instead I say, "Tell me again when the big event is?"

"Couple of weeks. I'm taking a few days off, going to Kyle's game while I'm there."

There's a silence, then I say, "Sounds like fun." Recently I'd released him from his promise to take me to his grandmother's party. Guess it wasn't such a good idea, I'd said casually, and Cal had agreed. Now I'm planning on dropping hints for him to take

Corrine instead. I hope and pray that she feels up to it. I was serious when I told Corrine it'd do her good to get involved with someone now, in spite of her illness. Or maybe because of it, to help her focus on something else. What I can't tell her, of course, is how close I came to taking my own advice. Corrine would be the only one I'd tell, but I swore to Cal I'd never mention it, and I owe him that much.

"Listen, Julia," Cal says, bringing me back from my wandering thoughts. "Another reason I called. Joe Ed was asking me some questions on the ride back from the airport."

"What kind of questions?"

"You know, how come you're still at the lake house, if I'd talked with you, things like that. Said he was worried about you."

"Worried?"

"Yeah, that he was afraid Corrine's illness, coming so soon after Bethany's going to school, was having an effect on you."

"Bound to," I agree. "Is that all he asked?"

"Pretty much. But he sounded . . . I'm not sure. Kind of funny."

A silence falls, and I thank him for letting me know, then hang up. Poor Joe Ed! No wonder he's sounding funny. I'd been surprised when he bought my story so easily, even though it sounded lame to my ears. When I left Corrine's, I rented a car and drove to Bethany's, spending a few days with her at her school, taking her shopping for fall clothes in Birmingham, and treating her and the new boyfriend to expensive dinners at every nice eatery within a hundred-mile radius of Talladega. Then I returned to Montgomery, but only long enough to pack a larger suitcase, cancel everything on my schedule, and get my car. Joe Ed was overworked and stressed out, even though the legislators were in summer recess, usually a less hectic time for him. He'd hardly reacted when I told him the plans, that the SSGs and I would be staying at the lake house so we'd be closer to Corrine and could visit her easier. If he thought it strange when I told him Corrine didn't want us staying at her place because she needed her space, he didn't say so. (Oddly enough, the only part of my story that was true!) "The lake house is still quite a ride to Chickasaw," was all Joe Ed said. "Why don't you rent a place somewhere on Blue Mountain instead?" Because I love staying at the lake house, I'd responded, and there, I could work on my new book in the Bethany series. Plus, I'd found some back roads that got us to Chickasaw in a couple of hours. He'd shrugged and said best he remembered, the SSGs didn't like staying at the lake house, but if that's what we wanted to do . . .

Lies on top of lies. When I told Lanier I was going to the lake house after my visit to Bethany, she'd said, "I thought you told me when you and Joe Ed took Bethany to St. Thomas in May, that was your vacation." It was, I'd replied. And her point was? Her point was, it was good Joe Ed could take that much time off; she was just surprised to hear it. When I told her Joe Ed wouldn't be with me, she'd flipped out. "Don't tell me you're staying at that spooky place on the other side of nowhere by yourself!" Of course not, I'd responded. She knew better than that, didn't she? Since he'd become governor, neither Joe Ed nor I could go anywhere without half the damn staff tagging along. In order to remain at the lake house alone, I had to spin more and more lies, and it was only a matter of time before I got caught.

* * *

It happened the last part of August, and in a way I wasn't prepared for. It was late afternoon, and I was returning from the walk that had become part of my routine. In the time I've been here, I've fallen easily into new habits. I sleep late, something I never got to do at the Mansion, and I fix myself whatever I want for breakfast, once having strawberry shortcake without feeling guilty about it. (I've gained a few pounds since I've been here and don't even care.) Without the morning meetings with my assistant and the staff, I'm free to do whatever I please, so I clean the house, rearrange furniture, rehang pictures, and work on the domestic project I've started since being here, refinishing an old dresser. After whatever I want for lunch— plain old lunch, not a luncheon!—I take a nap, then spend the rest of the afternoon working on my new book, *Bethany Goes Away to School*. My sunset walk gets me back in time for my glass of wine on the porch and whatever I want for supper (not dinner!), and the rest of the evening I spend reading or talking to one or another of the SSGs on the phone. Uneventful days, planned *by* me, not *for* me.

I walk past the ledge where we'd had the family photo made and take the path leading up behind the house. At almost the exact spot where I was the time Cal and I were here together and he came jogging up the drive, I stop, startled by a sound I haven't heard once in the last two weeks. A car is approaching, rounding the curve in the driveway. It's so thickly wooded here that you can hear a car before seeing it, until it clears the curve. Now it appears, a big black Lincoln with the state of Alabama seal on the doors. It's Joe Ed.

The car pulls up to the garage and my first thought is, thank God it's Don Thompson and not Cal with him! The previous governor's right-hand man, Don has retired from the state troopers since Joe Ed came into office, but he still works occasionally, filling in for Cal and other troopers as need be. Of the old school, Captain Thompson jumps out of the car to open the door for Joe Ed, who seems surprised to see me standing in the driveway. Unsmiling, Joe Ed, dressed in his usual dark suit, walks over and kisses my cheek, taking off his sunglasses. I haven't seen him since I've been here. It's been several years since Joe Ed's caught me in such a disheveled state, dressed in paint-splattered shorts and T-shirt, neither of which is any too clean. I have no makeup on, and my hair is tied back carelessly. "What are you doing here?" I say to my husband, after greeting Captain Thompson. For his benefit, I smile widely and say, "Such a pleasant surprise!"

Joe Ed eyes me. "Wouldn't be a surprise if you'd ever check your voice mail," he says, an edge to his voice. "I left you a message. Since I'm giving the summer commencement address at Jax State, I'm staying here." When Captain Thompson pops the trunk of the car, Joe Ed takes an overnight bag out. "Just leave those, Don," he says, indicating his briefcase and a portable file. "Don't need them tonight."

My mind's racing, but I can't think fast enough to come up with a way to cover my tracks. If only I'd checked the answering machine instead of letting it fill up! But I hadn't done so for a couple of days, since my assistant had started calling me with corrections and additions to my fall schedule. I couldn't face it and had planned on pretending the machine was broken, knowing the SSGs could reach me on my cell phone if need be. More lies! I could've at least played the messages; didn't mean I had to answer them. More often than not lately, I'm not thinking straight.

Don Thompson has been here before. He takes his overnight case from the trunk and heads for the guest quarters without saying a word. Stony silence is his usual demeanor, which makes him ideal for his job. "You're traveling light," I say to Joe Ed as we start toward the house. It isn't often he's without his aides or more of the troopers. I don't dare ask him where Cal is.

Joe Ed shrugs. "Summertime," is his only response. Once we get inside the house, he stops before heading down the hall. "Guess it's okay for me to take my suitcase to our room." I'm so surprised that my mouth drops open, and Joe Ed chuckles, the only light moment since he's arrived. "I just wondered if some of the SSGs have taken over our king-sized bed," he explains.

"Oh! No, no . . . they're . . . ah . . . not staying in our room. They're using the guest rooms," I say brightly, passing him in the hall-way. Trying to do so casually, I close the doors to the guest rooms—which are obviously unoccupied—as we walk down the hall to our room. I dare not look at Joe Ed to see if he notices the emptiness of the guest rooms, but just in case, I say, my voice too loud and cheery, "The girls wouldn't want you seeing their stuff strewn everywhere!"

"Like I care," Joe Ed says. "Anything new with Corrine?"

I shake my head, opening the door to our room. "Nothing yet."

"Where is everybody?"

Oh, God. Gone shopping? Gone to see Corrine? And how will I explain it when night comes, and no one returns to the house? If only I'd checked my messages, I could say everyone cleared out because he was coming, so the two of us would have some time together. Should I try that anyway? I could say—let's see—that I'd gotten his message and knew he was coming, I just didn't realize it was today. Thought it was tomorrow. So the girls left. . . . Unable to think it through, find the holes in the story, I say, "Oh, they'll be back," until I can come up with something better.

Joe Ed doesn't seem to notice, pulling off his tie and coat and throwing them on the bed as soon as he enters the room. "Godalmighty," he says, taking a deep breath. "It's great to be here. It was a hundred fucking degrees in Montgomery yesterday. Soon as we turned off the highway, I could feel myself relaxing." He loosens his belt and pulls his shirt out of his pants, and I watch him, sick with guilt. He looks wiped out, his face sagging, his eyes bleary.

"Get into some shorts and come out to the porch," I say. "The fridge is full of beer and wine, so grab something cold." I scurry out of the room, closing the door behind me, then go to the office at the opposite end of the house, where I've been working on my book. Closing the door, I go to the desk and play the answering machine, hitting the skip button when my assistant comes on. There's not only a couple of messages from Joe Ed telling me that he's coming here, there's also one from Cal warning me of the plans. "Don't think it means anything," he says in a low voice, "but he's leaving me behind to catch up on paperwork, bringing Thompson with him instead. Let me know."

I've already talked to Lanier and Corrine today but wonder if I should call them, just in case. And say what? Don't call me tonight;

Joe Ed is here and I don't want him to know what a lying sneak I am, telling him that the SSGs are staying here with me. Oh, I lied to y'all, too? I can hear the jokes they'll make. Know how you can tell Julia's lying to you? Her lips are moving. Except, I don't think any of the SSGs—even Astor, whom Corrine swears is a consummate liar—would think my becoming one is funny.

Sitting on the porch, Joe Ed and I make small talk, him with a beer and me with a glass of wine. I excuse myself to thaw out a couple of the chef's dinners in the microwave, one for us and one for Don Thompson, and I remember cooking garlic grits, with Cal at my side, watching. When I recall the electric moment that our hands touched, I lose my grip on a wineglass, and it shatters on the tiled floor. "Julia?" Joe Ed calls from the porch, and I reply, "It's okay—I just dropped a glass." After sweeping up the shards of glass, I stick my head out the door. "Joe Ed? Should I ask Don to join us for dinner?"

Joe Ed is stretched out on the hammock, beer in hand, eyes closed. Without opening them, he says, "You can ask, but he won't do it. Probably rather take it and warm it up in the microwave over there. He's fishing now,

anyway." My heart sinks, because I'd counted on Don's silent presence during the meal
as a buffer between me and any questions
Joe Ed might throw my way.

Joe Ed's questions come, but not till after
dinner. As we eat, I tell him—again—about
my efforts to get Corrine to a national cancer
center, or to Duke to try an experimental
program, or anything that might help her.
Joe Ed's input is good, but my heart sinks
when he says he'll give Corrine a call, try to
see if he can talk her into it. So far, I've
avoided flat-out lying to Corrine, because of
her condition. God, have I sunk so low that
I'm thinking it's okay to lie to a friend, unless
that friend has cancer? In that case, revert to
the sin of omission. Just don't tell her that
you've used her, told your husband that
you're staying here in order to be near her.
What has happened to me? "I'm sure
Corrine's doing all sorts of New Age crap,"
Joe Ed continues, "that might do her more
harm than good. Maybe an outsider like me
can make her see reason."

"You're hardly an outsider," I tell him, smiling. It's true; Joe Ed's the only SSG husband
who has known us almost as long as we've
known each other. Except for Buster, but Joe

Ed still has a few months on him. As we often tell him, he's our official sweet old boy.

After dinner, Joe Ed watches a Braves game on TV—a rare treat for him—then announces that he's going to bed. "Go ahead," I call out from the porch. "I'll join you in a minute." I breathe a sigh of relief once he's gone, collapsing on my favorite lounge. The answer had fallen into my lap when we were having dinner, and Joe Ed had said, "You know I don't like the SSGs going to Corrine's and leaving you by yourself. It's too isolated here. Folks around here know we own this place, and there are a lot of crazies everywhere. I don't want you staying here by yourself." Without raising my eyes from my plate of fettuccine, I told him that I'd planned on going to Corrine's and joining the girls but changed my plans when he arrived.

"If you need to go, do so," Joe Ed had said. "You don't have to baby-sit me."

Still poking at the fettuccine, I'd shaken my head. "No, no. I'll go tomorrow after you leave."

It's early when I ready myself for bed, but Joe Ed has the lights out and his back to me, apparently conked out. I'm not surprised, since he looked so exhausted. As soon as I crawl into bed and pull the sheets up, however, he turns over. "Julia?" he says, and his voice is hoarse and sleep-filled.

"Go back to sleep," I say in a whisper. "I didn't mean to wake you."

Instead, Joe Ed sits up and turns on the lamp beside the bed. Then, to my surprise, he puts a hand over his eyes and sighs a ragged sigh. "Oh, Julia," he says, and my breath catches in my throat.

"What? What is it?"

"Why don't you tell me?" he says softly.

"Joe Ed, turn off the light and go to sleep. You're exhausted and I am, too." I close my eyes and poke at my pillow, my heart thudding.

"I tried to sleep. I tried to let this go, to let you work out whatever it is you're going through," he says. His voice is filled with pain, and it scares me. "I shouldn't have come here. As long as I was away, I could pretend everything was fine, that you were really here to be near Corrine. But once I got here, I saw that my suspicions were right. No one else is here. You're not staying here with the SSGs, and I doubt that you're staying here to be near Corrine."

"I cannot believe what you're saying!" I cry,

sounding properly righteous and offended. "That's so unlike you to accuse me of something like that. Now turn off the light and go to sleep. You're just exhausted, or you wouldn't be talking like this."

Joe Ed's hand shoots out, and he grabs my wrist, pulling me toward him. I dare to look up at him, and his face is dark and troubled, his eyes bleak. "Don't pull that crap on me, Julia. Something is going on with you. You can't even look me in the eyes anymore. God, if you could've seen your face when I drove up today! Whatever it is has been going on for a while, but I've thought it was Bethany, and lately, I've tried to convince myself it's Corrine. I've known better, but I couldn't deal with it. Tell me the truth, Julia . . . are you seeing someone else?"

"How can you even ask me—" I begin angrily, trying to pull my arm from his grasp, but the pain in his eyes stops me. "No," I say, lowering my voice. "I'm not seeing anyone else. But I'll admit this, Joe Ed: Lately, I've wondered if you are. You've been so distant. . . ."

Joe Ed drops my wrist in surprise. "Is that what this is about? You think I'm having an affair?"

I shrug. "I don't know why you've been so distracted, so I figured that might be it."

"Jesus, Julia—why haven't you said something?"

"I even wondered about you and Astor. . . ."

"Astor?" He snorts. "I'll leave that to Cal."

I dare to look at him. "You know about them, then?"

Joe Ed sighs. "Cal didn't tell me, if that's what you mean. The night she stayed at the Mansion, before y'all went to Lanier's? I was coming in late from my meeting and saw her sneaking out, saw Cal let her in the back wing. I'm pretty sure it was nothing but a one-night stand, even surer it was initiated by Astor. She caught Cal at a vulnerable time, is all. You know how she is, Julia, better than anyone! I'll admit Astor and I have always flirted a lot, and we kissed once when both of us were about half-drunk. But I wouldn't have an affair with your best friend! Jesus—is that what you think of me?"

Flirtations with best friends was not a subject I have any business bringing up, so I shake my head. "No, of course not. I've just been so confused lately, about a lot of things. I have suspected you of having affairs before, though. Truth is, I wouldn't even blame you."

"Listen to me, Julia." Joe Ed places his hand on my chin and turns my head, making me look at him. When I lower my eyes, he tightens his grip, saying, "At first . . . when you cut me off . . . I'll admit that I had a couple of one-night stands. I'm not proud of it, believe me. It was nothing but sex, and I've never wanted you to know. It's you I love, and you only. I have from the first day I saw you."

Joe Ed releases me and leans his head back against the headboard as I wipe my eyes with my fingertips. After a silence, he releases a deep sigh. "I'm sorry I've been distant, Julia. It's not you, I swear. It's just all the stress . . . everything lately. I wish we'd talked before now." He rubs his face and smiles a weak smile. "God, you had me scared to death! But if it's just my distance . . . well, I won't let that happen again."

When I don't respond, Joe Ed leans over and kisses my cheek. "Let's get some sleep now, okay? I'm glad we had this talk, and I think things will be better from now on." He turns off the lamp and settles down in his mound of pillows. The only light is the moonlight, pouring through the windows across our bed. Ironically and painfully, bitterly so, it's a full moon, round and golden and so lovely it breaks my heart.

I put my hand over my mouth to try and stifle my sobs, but it's no use. Turning my back on Joe Ed, I fumble on the bedside table until I loosen a handful of tissues from the box. I cover my eyes with the tissues, which quickly become sodden with my tears. Joe Ed's hand is tentative on my shoulder. "Julia?"

When I'm able to talk, I swallow several times and say hoarsely, "Please go to sleep, Joe Ed. I'm fine." But when his arm moves around me, I stiffen, my breath catching in my throat. Joe Ed is motionless for a minute, then he removes his arm with a sigh. I turn my head to see him propped on the pillows against the headboard, rubbing his face wearily.

"You're not fine, are you, Julia? Not really."

"No."

"So it's not really my preoccupation that's bothering you, then?"

"No. It's not you at all, Joe Ed. It's me."

"Can you tell me what's wrong?" The pain in his voice cuts through me like a knife. He knows there's more wrong with me than just the distance that's developed between us.

I shake my head. "I'm not sure I know, Joe Ed," I say so softly that he doesn't hear me, and I have to repeat it. "I don't know what's wrong with me."

After a heavy silence, he says, "Do you love me, Julia?"

I'm crying again, my face in my hands. "I don't know. I don't know how I feel about . . . anything anymore."

"Did you come here to get away from me?"

I can't answer him, my throat is so tight with tears. Finally I'm able to say, "That was part of it. I needed to be alone. I needed some time to . . . think."

"About us?" Again, the fear in his voice shakes me. I nod because I can't speak, and I feel his eyes on me in the white moonlight outlining our bed.

"I'll resign, Julia. I'll resign tomorrow. I'd rather give it up—all of it—than lose you."

I reach for another handful of tissues. "Absolutely not," I say in a choked voice. "You can't do that. You're doing too much good. I believe in what you're doing . . ."

"It's just me you no longer believe in, then."

I can't stand for him to think that, and I put my hands over my ears. "No, no! Don't say that, Joe Ed. You know better than that."

"Then tell me what I can do, Julia. Tell me what I can do to keep from losing you!" He leans over and grabs my arm. His hand feels cold to my bare skin, as cold and desolate as my heart. "This—this *job,* or whatever the hell it is, it's killing me, too, Julia! No way I'm going to run for re-election. Maybe if I changed my work habits—"

But I stop him, shaking off his hand. "Listen to me, Joe Ed. It's not you. It's *me*. It's me, and you know it. I lied to you, I lied to my friends. . . . I can't go on like this." I can't be me anymore, I want to tell him. But it sounds so stupid, I can't say it. How can I make him understand something I don't understand myself?

After a heavy silence, Joe Ed says, "There's nothing I can do, is there, Julia? You're thinking about leaving me, I can tell. And there's nothing I can do to stop you." He sounds so resigned, which hurts me almost as much as the pain I heard in his voice previously.

"Joe Ed, please . . . you're exhausted, you've got to give a speech tomorrow . . . please, please let's not do this tonight."

"Oh, God! If I lose you, Julia . . ." But his voice breaks, and he puts his hands over his eyes as though to stop the tears.

I lay a hand on his shoulder, but I can't think of any words of consolation. I'm too confused about my own feelings to console him, offer him any hope. Instead, I say softly, giving him a shake, "Joe Ed, listen. Listen to me! We can't do this now, not with you getting up in the morning and going to Jacksonville. You can't do it; you're already worn out. Next weekend, Labor Day's coming up, and you'll have some time off. Why don't you come back here, spend a few days? We can talk then, okay?"

He turns his head from me, as though to hide his grief, and tries to wipe his eyes on the edge of the pillowcase. "Joe Ed?" I say, shaking his shoulder again.

"Yeah, okay. Whatever," he says in a muffled voice, his back to me.

I'm silent for a long, painful minute, then I say, "I'm going to get you one of our magic sleeping pills. You have to sleep or you'll collapse. Will you take one? Please?"

He shrugs but doesn't answer. I go to the bathroom and get the pill and a glass of water and take it to him. Kneeling beside him in the dark, I hold the pill in my palm like an offering. "Come on, honey," I whisper.

"Leave it," he says hoarsely, closing his eyes as though to shut the sight of me out. "I'll take it."

"You promise?"

He nods, and I put the pill and glass of water on the bedside table. Going back to my side of the bed, I sit down, rubbing my face. But I can't lie down beside Joe Ed and go to sleep. His pain is too raw, radiating from his inert body like a burn. Grabbing my robe, I slip out of the room and tiptoe to the porch, sinking in my lounge chair and pulling my robe close against the coolness of the night.

I haven't brought any tissues with me, so I soak the edge of my robe by holding it over my eyes as I cry. If I ever make it to heaven, which is looking more doubtful by the day, I intend to have it out with God. Why does it have to be so painful? Are the cynics right— you're born, you hurt a whole lot, then you die? Why does none of it make any sense? Why am I so miserable, when I have everything and more, things so many people are denied? Why can't I just be grateful, and happy? *What's wrong with me?*

I cry so much my eyes are swollen and my throat raw, until my tears dry up. Laying my head back on the lounge, I think about my inability to love, to feel passion, to allow Joe Ed—as good a man as I've ever known—to love me. Something died in me the day, so many years ago now, when I got a glimpse of that black-haired baby as she was carried away from me. I was so young, and so naive, that I don't even know if I loved Jesus Perez or not. He, too, was a child, a child in a man's body, as sheltered and innocent as me. I never tried to find out what happened to the baby or Jesus. Instead, I let that part of me dry up, the part that loved Jesus Perez so completely that I gave myself to him without a thought of the consequences. I deserted the baby, leaving her to whatever fate befell her because I couldn't face the pain of claiming her. I accepted Bethany as my cross to bear, the punishment for my sins, and I used Joe Ed because he let me do it, allowed me to use his love and give him nothing in return.

Ah, am I finally facing the truth about

myself? Now I have to wonder if I turned to Cal because something about his exotic looks struck a memory buried somewhere deep within me and made me think of Jesus Perez. Jesus was the first and only one to touch the part of me that has long since died, and evidently I was using Cal in an attempt to resurrect it. I close my eyes as that realization sinks in. The only other time I've felt it, besides the times with Jesus Perez, and more recently, with Cal Hawkins, has been in my dream life with Joe Ed. It's the only time and place, when Joe Ed sleeps and I press myself against him, falling into a dream where we're lovers, where I'm able once again to feel the desire I discovered in the arms of Jesus Perez.

My thoughts are in a turmoil, but I'm so emotionally spent that I doze fitfully on the lounge, my robe with its tear-dampened hem pulled up to my shoulders. I wake with a crick in my neck from the awkward angle of the way I fell asleep, my head lodged by the hard, striped cushion of the lounge. Stirring, I try to pull my thin silk robe closer, longing for warmth. I'm cold and miserable and suddenly afraid. So afraid, and so cold! I don't know how long I've slept, but rain clouds have covered the face of the moon, and the porch is dark and shadowy. I don't know what woke me up, but I'm overwhelmed with a terrible sadness, a sense of loss unlike anything I've ever felt.

I gasp and get to my feet. When I do so, my robe slips to the floor, but I don't stop to pick it up. I walk barefoot across the porch, moving through the shadows to the door, and go quickly down the dark hallway. Opening the door to the bedroom, I check to make sure Joe Ed's asleep, and then I slip into the bed beside him. He's turned away from me, as I left him earlier, clutching his pillow and snoring lightly. Carefully, I ease myself next to him, curving my body to fit against his back. With the side of my face pressed tight against his shoulder, I put my arm around his waist and he stirs. I freeze and hold my breath, not wanting to wake him. When he's still, I know that the pill has worked its magic again. Closing my eyes, I relax and sink into the warmth of the bed, back into the dark land of sleep.

In my dream Joe Ed turns to me, opening an eye in surprise, saying "Julia?" in a hoarse voice.

"I tried not to wake you," I whisper, and he

replies, "I'd fallen asleep, but I didn't take the pill. I was waiting to see if you'd come back to me."

"Oh, my darling . . ." I murmur, shivering as his arms close around me, warm and strong and comforting. "I got so cold on the porch," I tell him, my arms going around his neck. "And I felt so alone."

"You're not alone, Julia," Joe Ed says, his breath hot in my ear. I turn my face to his, my hands moving into his hair. His mouth covers mine, and he pulls himself heavily on top of me. My legs go around his waist when he enters me, his breath coming hot and fast, my body arching toward him. "Julia," he says again, in a choked voice, "My God!" In a free-fall, a whirling spiral, we cry out together, my fingers digging into his shoulders. I gasp, my mouth on his, and I tell him what came to me in the cold darkness of the night.

"I can't stand the thought of losing you, Joe Ed," I say, half-strangled on my sobs. His hands are on my face now, those big, capable hands that held our daughter so tenderly when she cried out for him in the night; those hands that reached out to stop me when I struggled to get up yet again, worn out from caring for her, our baby girl, who couldn't even hear her own cries. My tears wet his hands, and Joe Ed says, his voice not sleep-filled but *real,* oh so real: "You haven't lost me, Julia. I'm right here."

25

Lanier

DAUPHIN ISLAND

JESSE'S HOUSE IS A mess, looking like it did the first night I found him here, almost three months ago. I stumble over stuff, kicking whiskey bottles and beer cans out of the way, cussing as I go. On the counter and the coffee table are burning candles, wicks half buried in melted wax, which has spilled over the sides of the candles and collected in a puddle around them. Still miraculous that he hasn't burned the house down. I thought I'd hidden all of the candles, afraid of this—that he'd get drunk as a skunk and leave them burning when he passed out.

"Jesse Pickett," I yell, heading toward his

bedroom in the back, "don't make me come up there! You'd damn better *not* be passed out in your bed."

But of course he is, butt naked. He's sprawled facedown, thank God, his guitar on the floor, as though he was playing it and dropped it. Worse, he puked all over himself before passing out, and I lose it. "Goddammit!" I shriek. "I ain't believing this! I'm gone two weeks and this is what happens. You are beyond fucked-up, Jesse—you're beyond help. I give up! I just plain give up!"

I go to his bathroom, kicking wet towels and dirty clothes out of the way, and turn on the shower, getting it scalding hot. Going back to the bed I grab Jesse by the arms, yanking him off the bed. He raises an arm to cover his face, like a prizefighter about to be creamed. He looks scared until he sees it's me, then his face lights up. "Hey, baby," he says, slurring his words so it comes out sounding like "Ali Baba." "Didn't know you were back."

"Aw, no shit. Come on, get up!" He staggers as I pull him to the bathroom, bent over like an old man. It's like dragging a sack of wet cotton, but I get him into the shower.

"Whoa, honey," he groans, "what you doing?"

"Cleaning your sorry ass up," I snap, pushing him into the shower and pulling the curtains. "So don't you by God move until I get back."

I pull the stinking sheets off the bed—the bedspread is wadded up on the floor—and take them to the laundry room, muttering to myself the whole time. This is the final straw. As soon as I get him cleaned up, I'm taking him to the hospital. A few weeks ago, I copied down the name and phone number of his manager in Nashville, and I'm calling him, soon as I leave here.

I put clean sheets on Jesse's bed, throw all the whiskey bottles in the trash, and go to the back room to check on the progress of the shower. As I feared, Jess is dry as a bone, slumped in a corner under the showerhead avoiding the spray of water. "Jesus Christ," I mutter, pulling my T-shirt over my head, slipping out of my shorts and panties, unhooking my bra, and kicking off my sandals. Flinging the curtains back, I get in beside him, grabbing him by the arms and holding him upright until the water is hitting him full in the face. Reaching behind him, I grab the soap and lather him all over. Jess's eyes fly open when I get to his privates, and he moans, "Hey—that feels pretty good."

"Shut up," I snap.

"Look at that, would you?" he murmurs. "You're turning me on, baby. Pretty, ain't it?"

"Oh, bull. I'm a nurse, and I've seen a million of them. They all look alike."

His face falls. "You mean . . ."

"Don't even go there, Jesse. You'll get your feelings hurt. Now, lean down so I can wash your hair."

With all that water pouring over him, it doesn't take long before Jesse sobers up somewhat. I lather up my hair after finishing his—might as well, since I'm in here—which seems to sober Jesse up quicker than anything. Eying me, he says, "If I'd known what a great body you have, Lanier, I'd have gotten you naked long before now."

I hold my head back and let the stream of hot water soak my hair. "And to think, all you had to do was puke all over yourself and pass out. Can't accuse you of not being romantic."

He helps me rinse my hair, his long calloused fingers perfect for massaging my scalp until it's squeaky clean. "Umm . . ." I murmur, forgetting how mad I am with him, "you missed your calling."

"Looks like I missed a lot of things," he mutters, and I open my eyes to see him looking me over from head to toe. Guess it's been too long since he's seen a naked woman.

"You can quit your staring," I tell him, reaching up and turning off the water. "I'm through with you." Out of the shower, I throw him a towel. Once I've dried off and gotten dressed, I get Jesse's toothbrush and put toothpaste on it. "Get rid of that stinky breath while I find you some clean clothes, then shave, if you think you can do it without cutting your face off. I'm taking you to the hospital."

"Hospital!" He groans, but I shut him up by poking the toothbrush in his mouth, leaving him leaning against the sink, half-ass brushing his teeth. I return with a clean pair of shorts and a T-shirt.

"Couldn't find any underbritches, but you don't need them. They'll just take them off when they get you in a hospital gown. Here." I throw the clean clothes at him. "Get dressed and come on."

Jess falls on the floor when he tries to step into his shorts, and grabbing his arm, I pull him up. "Must've slipped," he mutters.

"You didn't slip," I tell him, making my voice hard and mean. "You're too drunk to stand up. Here. Hold on to my shoulder so you can get your britches on."

"I'm not drunk," Jess protests, swaying. "I swear! Don't be mad at me, baby. I wrote you a song."

"Bullshit. You haven't written anything, Jesse-goddamn-Phoenix, and you know why? Not because you're washed up. You won't write again until you get sober, I see that now." I take a small towel and, motioning Jesse to bend over, dry his long hair, which is now a lot more gray than brown. Hard living will do that to you. He flinches when he tries to comb it out, it's so tangled.

"Seen the scissors?" he asks, opening the door of the medicine cabinet.

"You're not cutting your hair! Drunk as you are, you'll end up looking like Rod Stewart." Before I can stop him, Jesse has pulled out a pair of scissors and whacked out a huge chunk right in front. "Dammit, Jess—have you lost your fool mind?" I screech. "Give me those scissors, and sit on the pot. But for God's sake, put the lid down first."

I've never cut anyone's hair before, but I don't tell Jesse that as I chop away. When I finish, he about breaks my heart by staggering over to the mirror, rubbing the steam off, and studying his ugly mug with bloodshot eyes. "Thought if I looked prettier, you might like me again," he says mournfully. "But I see it didn't work."

I can't help myself; I go behind him and put my arms around his waist, laying my head against his back. "Oh, Jesse, honey," I sigh. "What am I going to do with you?"

He turns around and puts his arms around me, kissing the top of my head. "Come listen to your song," he begs. "Please?"

"Okay, okay. But then we've gotta talk, and I mean it."

I don't turn on any lights on the porch because Jess says his eyes hurt (can't imagine why!), so we sit in the moonlight. The silver moon's almost full, hanging high over the bay, its twin dancing a jig on the water beneath it. Jess sits in an armless wicker chair with his guitar in his lap, and I pull up a stool at his feet. He tunes his guitar, muttering that it must've fallen off the bed, and I prop my elbows on my knees, watching him.

"I wouldn't have gotten so wasted if I'd known you were coming home today," he says, glancing at me sheepishly. "Thought you said tomorrow."

"I told you today. You just got drunk and forgot," I snap.

"Don't be mad at me," he pleads. "I feel worse about it than you do."

"It makes me sick, Jess! You were doing so much better. You were so sweet, singing to Corrine over the phone the other night, and she loved it. I thought you were going to be okay now, I swear I did. Shows how naive I am. You're not going to get well until you get into a program." All summer I'd thought I could help Jesse, just being a friend, being there for him. I'd gotten him cooking again, and crabbing, taking the boat out, but most of all, singing. Yet first time he's by himself, it's back to square one.

"Well, you can forget that," he says, long fingers moving up and down the guitar strings. "I'll be goddamned if I go into one of those programs again."

"Again?"

"I didn't stutter. I've been dried out before," he says grumpily, not meeting my eyes. "See where it got me. I ain't going back, I can promise you."

And I can promise you that you are, I

think, but I don't argue with him tonight. He's going, and that's all there is to it, if I have to hog-tie him. Tomorrow I'll call his manager, see if I can get him to come here and help me get Jess into a good place. But for now I say, "Thought you'd written me a song."

He plucks on the strings, frowning, but the guitar still sounds twangy, out of tune. "Don't know what's wrong with it," he grunts.

"Tell you what. Why don't I go, let you get to bed and sleep this off? We'll try again tomorrow, okay?"

Jesse hangs his head, his fingers stilled. "Don't know how come I can't remember your song, honey. . . ."

"It's okay." I take the guitar from him, putting it on the wicker swing next to us. Then I take him by the hand, helping him to his feet, and lead him back to his bed.

"Stay with me, Lanier, please," he starts pleading, soon as we start the now-familiar walk down the hall. "I'm real scared tonight, for some reason."

I get him in bed, and he passes out by the time his head hits the pillow, without waiting for me to get into my usual position next to him, snuggled up till we both go to sleep. Worked out without me having to tell him that I wasn't going to tonight, anyway. I push his still-damp, choppy hair back from his forehead, then lean over him, my cheek next to his. Don't know how I'm going to do it, but I've got to get him some help or he's going to drink his fool self to death, something I can't stand to even think about. He stirs, and his eyes fly open. "Hey, little girl," he murmurs, "I was dreaming about you."

"Go back to sleep," I whisper, but Jess surprises me. Moving faster than I ever imagined a drunk man could, he grabs me and kisses me hard, a real kiss instead of the usual brotherly one, and it sends a thrill all the way down to my toenails. Even though I'm about to melt into the mattress, I make myself push away from him. "What do you think you're doing?" I say, gasping for breath and wiping my mouth with the back of my hand.

"The damndest thing has happened, Lanier," he says in a hoarse voice, his bloodshot eyes glowing. "I've done gone and fallen in love with you."

"Don't you dare say that, Jesse Pickett. Please don't say that."

"I'm writing a love song about me and you. It's called 'I've Come Home to You.' And I'm gonna sing it for you," he says and moves to kiss me again. But I pull his hands away and scoot off the bed, leaving him hugging a pillow instead.

"Sleep it off," I call out from the door, "and I'll hear the song another time." I back out the door quickly, closing it behind me, and hurry home, fast as I can get there.

My answering machine's blinking when I get home, and I'm afraid it might be bad news, a call this late. When I hit the playback button, my mouth falls open and I stare at the machine in disbelief. It's Paul. He doesn't say anything much, just that he's calling to check on Corrine. He has never called me here before. With shaky fingers, I dial his number, and when he answers, my heart goes to my throat. "Paul?"

"Hello, Lanier," he says formally, as though we're business acquaintances. It's still the same for me; every time I hear his voice—he called twice when I was at Corrine's—I feel like I've been socked in the stomach. At least he's talking to me again. "When I didn't get you," Paul says, "I called Corrine, so you didn't have to call me back."

"Y-you called her tonight?" I stammer.

He chuckles. "No, I called her tomorrow morning."

I smile, twisting the cord of the phone around my fingers. "Stupid question. Did Corrine say anything? All I can get out of her is, she's going to think about it for a while longer."

"That's all she'll tell me, too. I told her not to wait too long, making up her mind."

"I'm glad you said that. I've wanted to but haven't quite been able to. Don't want her to know how fast things can move once it gets to the liver."

"You should've talked to her more frankly, Lanier," Paul says sternly, in his best doctor voice. "A patient can't make an informed decision without all the facts."

"But it's not a patient! It's Corrine, who I'm closer to than my own sister."

His voice softens. "Yeah, I know. Makes a difference, doesn't it?"

"Paul? What do you think her chances are? I mean, even with treatment?"

He hesitates, then says, "Not good. But you know that as well as I do."

"Know what she asked me?" I tell him indignantly. "She actually wanted to know if me and Julia would help her . . . you know . . . *off* herself, if she got too bad. Made me furious, her even thinking we'd do such a thing!"

There's a long silence, then Paul says, "Spring break, I took Lindy and Christopher to Selma, to see your mother."

"Lindy told me. Last time I visited her, she didn't know me from a Georgia bulldog. Like a fool, I took her a plant, and she started eating it."

"She had one lucid moment while we were there," Paul continues, as though I hadn't interrupted him. "We were leaving the room, and she called me back in. Making sure the kids were in the hall and couldn't hear her, your mother asked me if I'd give her an overdose."

"Mama did that?" I shriek.

Paul's voice is as calm as if he were giving a weather report. Only time I've ever seen him lose his cool was the day he told me to get out, that he never wanted to see me again. "I told her that I wished I could help her. If she were lucid, it'd be different. If she's ever lucid long enough to know that's what she wants, I told her, then we'd talk."

"What?"

"No one should live like that, Lanier, and you know it."

"Of course I know that. It's pathetic, seeing her like that. But—but—that doesn't mean I'd ever *do* anything—" I sputter, flabbergasted. "She may no longer be aware of it, Paul, but she is my mother!"

"Yeah, that makes a difference." His quiet voice is thoughtful. "I've never been able to with a family member, either, and don't know if I could."

I sink to the nearest chair, my legs no longer able to hold me up, and I have to swallow two or three times before I can speak. "Did you just say what I think you said?"

"Think about it, Lanier. Even you said that Bud Wilson went so much faster than anyone dared hope."

"Mr. Wilson?"

"Didn't you think it weird that I cleaned up the IV afterwards, not letting you or the home-health nurse touch it?"

Bud Wilson was an elderly neighbor who'd been like a grandfather to Christopher and Lindy, until he got Parkinson's so bad that he couldn't swallow without choking, waving his hands frantically as he gasped for breath, the fear in his eyes horrible to witness. He'd lived right next door to us, and me and Paul and a home-health nurse took care of him so he could remain at home, not spend his last days in a hospital. Paul signed his death certificate, with me and the nurse as witnesses. "Who else?" I ask faintly.

There's a long silence, and I hope to hell that he's not counting. Finally he says, "Think about it, and you can figure it out."

"Probably Mrs. Dawson," I say, breathing a deep sigh and closing my eyes. "And maybe Andy Parker . . . Jesus Christ, Paul! All this time, I was married to Dr. Death."

He laughs his great big Paul laugh, and I picture him throwing his head back, like he used to, his eyes crinkled. "I swear to God, I thought you knew, Lanier, and just didn't say anything. When you said that about Corrine, I realized you didn't."

I don't tell him that I've never been so shocked, even more so than I was by the way he reacted to my cheating on him. And I thought I knew Paul better than anybody.

"Lanier?" Paul asks. "You're awfully quiet."

"I haven't taken this in yet. Oh, Jesus. Andy Parker!" I'd gotten so upset that I hadn't been any help when the hospice nurse called me and Paul to Andy's side, and I'd lost all my professional detachment. A kid, he was Christopher's age, gone blind with a brain tumor, so maddened with pain that he'd almost bitten his tongue in two, painkillers barely dulling the agony. The tips of his fingers were torn to pieces where he'd clawed the bedposts. And then I remembered something, something I'd forgotten until now. Outside Andy's room, I'd grabbed Paul and shaken him as I sobbed. "Do something, Paul," I'd yelled as I shook him, the hospice nurse averting her eyes. "Don't leave that child in such awful pain!"

"Andy Parker was the first, wasn't he, Paul?"

"I'd never had the guts before, though I'd wished I had, many times," he says. "But I decided that night—if I got caught, I'd gladly spend the rest of my life in prison, knowing Andy Parker was out of his misery."

"Jesus, Paul. I'm in a state of shock."

"Obviously. And disapproval. Disgust, even?" Asking me such a thing, Paul's voice maintains its steady, even tone, with no fear that I might hate him or turn him in. One thing about Paul and his high-minded principles: If he thinks something is right, the rest of the world be damned. The opinion of others has never influenced him, one of the things I admire about him. The SSGs like to think I'm like that, too, that I don't care what anyone thinks, but they're wrong; I've always been much too easily influenced by other people's opinions.

I think about it, then say, "No. Not disgust or disapproval either. Just a lot of admiration for your courage." And saying it, I know it's true, although I haven't admitted it till now. "Many times, I've wished I could do it, but I was too scared. What might happen to me was always more important than someone else's suffering." Then the thought occurs to me, and I gasp. "Paul! You didn't tell Corrine all this, did you?"

"Godalmighty, Lanier. It's hardly something I go around telling people."

"I was just afraid . . . that Corrine might have asked you to help her, like she did me and Julia—"

"I think there's a bigger concern with Corrine. She's had a couple of suicide attempts—"

"Oh, my God!" I say with a shudder. "I hadn't even thought about that."

"Well, you should. Seriously, Lanier. We've

both seen some botched attempts, and you don't want Corrine going through that, on top of everything else." An annoying beep interrupts him, and he says, "Hang on." When he comes back on the line, he says briskly, "Emergency call. I've got to go." And he does, without another word.

I sit with the phone clutched in my hand, trying to decide what to do, too worried about Corrine to rehash Paul's conversation or to decide if his calling me is a hopeful sign. Corrine has asked Julia and me, and the rest of the SSGs, to let her have some time to herself, which we've done. I'd been prepared to quit my job if need be and stay with her through all this, the chemo or whatever treatment she decided on, but she wouldn't hear of it. Not now, she'd said. Probably will come a time when I need you, she'd told me when I left her.

In bed I can't sleep because I'm so worried, and I get up to get a glass of wine. Only one thing I can do to keep from worrying myself sick that Corrine's going to get so down about this, and feel so hopeless, that she might do something to herself. I'm going to stay with her. Surely she won't close the door in my face if I show up, suitcase in hand. Soon as I can work it out with my schedule, I'm going back to Blue Mountain, by God! Heading to my bed, I stop by the window and look out into the dark night, checking to see if Jess's lights are still out. Another worry. And added to it, damned if Jesse hasn't gone and fallen in love with me. The call from Paul, and the worry over Corrine, blocked that out of my mind, so it hasn't sunk in yet. Now why'd the fool go and do something like that, turning my insides to mush kissing me and all? I ran from that temptation like a scalded cat, hightailing it as far away from Mr. Jesse Phoenix as I could get, knowing where I'd have ended up other-wise. Then damned if I didn't have the first hopeful sign from Paul, him calling me here. Before turning out the lamp, I get out the lesson book and write: *I think I'm holding on to a limb to keep from falling into a hole, but the limb turns out to be nothing but a twig, and the hole looks like the Grand Canyon.*

I cry like a baby when I finally hear the song Jesse wrote for me. All the next week, when I'm doing lesson plans for my classes so that someone can fill in for me, and training an inexperienced nurse to take over my shift at the hospital, Jesse works at getting his act together. I'd stuck by my guns and called his manager, who'd promised to come down and take Jess to Nashville, back to the last place he'd been sent to dry out. But his manager made the mistake of alerting Jess to his plans, which was all it took to get Jess to clean up his act, trying to show us that he'd be able to control his drinking. He sobered up and started behaving himself again, crabbing and fixing the house up, spending his evenings cooking and his nights playing his guitar and working on his love song for me. Labor Day, he lugged out the barbecue grill and cooked ribs, so proud of himself he could hardly stand it. Every night the week following, he had supper cooked for me when I got home from work, and he said that in a couple more nights, my song would be ready.

I didn't know Jesse had finished my song when I go over to tell him that I'd packed up the house and was leaving. I'm surprised to find him looking better than he has the whole time he's been back in my life. When I got home from work, he'd left me a message saying he had fixed supper, to come over as soon as I get in. When I arrive, he's set the glass-topped table on the porch for two, with candles burning on either side of a florist's arrangement of tea roses. "Here, baby." As excited as a little boy, Jesse hands me the card on the roses. "I got them sent here instead of your place because I wanted to see your face when you read the card."

My hands shaking, I read it, the words blurring as tears fill my eyes. "To Lanier, the only woman I've ever written a song for, with gratitude. I love you, Jess."

"My way of telling you that the song's ready," Jess says, grinning his goofy, lop-sided grin.

"Oh, Jess . . ." I begin, but he pulls out a chair for me with a bow.

"Can't hear it till we eat, though," he says, kissing my cheek as I sit down.

"I can't stay. Actually, I didn't come to eat supper . . . I came to talk to you."

"Talk later. I made the best she-crab soup you've ever tasted! Pour us some of that wine, baby." And he darts into the kitchen before I can stop him.

"How come you're holding on to your pocketbook like that?" Jess asks when he puts my soup in front of me, then sits across from me with his own bowl.

Looking down, I realize I've got the lesson book clutched to my bosom, like an old lady with her purse. I've brought it over to read something to Jess, but for now I say, "Oh. It's sort of like a journal. I want to read you something in it."

"Read it later," he says, slurping his soup. "I'm about to starve to death."

I don't think I can eat a thing, but I'm so tired and hungry that once I have a taste, I gobble it up and ask for another bowl. I steal glances at Jess as I eat, noting that, in spite of his attempts to clean up, his hands are still shaky, his eyes bleary, and he's drinking several glasses of wine. I have a bad feeling that when I leave Dauphin Island, he'll be right back where he was.

"What you looking at?" he says suspiciously.

"You," I answer. "How cute you are."

"Aw, shit," he says, but flushes with pleasure. "Okay, time's come to move to the swing."

"I never guessed you were so romantic," I say, when he lights another candle on the table by the swing and moves the roses next to it.

"You're gonna find out how romantic I am,"

he smiles, and I lower my eyes guiltily. He doesn't know I've come to say good-bye.

To my surprise, Jess plays the guitar and sings like the Jesse Phoenix I knew before, doing a couple of his old songs to start with—"Lost in a Land Called Lonesome" and "My Daddy Hung the Moon." I applaud appreciatively, but I can't meet his eyes when he picks up a candle stub, pretending it's a microphone, and says, "This next one is a new song, ladies and gentlemen, first song I've written in years. It's dedicated to the girl next door, who goes way back with me. I been around the block a few times, but I've never written a song for a woman before. But there's never been one like Lanier."

The tune sounds like a ballad—haunting, I imagine the music critics will call it—and it about breaks my heart because it's so beautiful. Looking right into my eyes, Jesse sings, "I left home when I was a little boy, searching for fortune and fame. My mama cried, and something in my daddy died, the day I left them both behind. I found my fortune, and I found my fame, but I never found my way home again. Now Mama's gone, and Daddy, too, but when I came home, I found you. You took my hand, you called my name, and I forgot my search for fortune and fame. The path that led me back home led me to you."

When I put my head in my hands, Jess lays the guitar down and comes to sit by me on the swing. Taking me in his arms, he holds me while I cry, soaking the front of his shirt as he pats my back helplessly. When he kisses me, it tastes like the salt of my tears. "Who'd ever have thought when you was a little girl pestering me," he says with a smile, "that one day, you'd save my life?"

"I didn't . . ." I begin, but Jess puts his hand over my mouth.

"Would you just shut up and listen? You know how restless I've been, all my life. You know about me breaking my mama's heart, but bet you didn't know that I didn't change my name so I'd have one that looked better in lights. I changed it because I knew how much it'd hurt my daddy. God, I've been *so* lost, Lanier! I've had more women than I can count, even marrying a couple of them. Looking for something . . . that's all I've done, my whole life. Look for something. Didn't know what the hell I was looking for, until now. Now I know—it was you."

"Oh, Jess. I was afraid of this," I say in a choked voice, my head against his chest. "And I'm so, so sorry. I came over tonight to say good-bye to you."

Jess lifts my face, looking down into my eyes. "Hey, baby, it's okay. I know you're going to stay with your girlfriend for a while. That's one of the things I love about you, how you take care of everyone. But you know what? I'm gonna take care of *you* from now on. I want to spend the rest of my sorry life taking care of you."

I sigh a deep sigh. "Oh, Jess, honey. I've loved you my whole life—"

"I love you, too, baby."

I put a finger over his lips. "I loved you before you became Jesse Phoenix."

"That's another thing. You and me, we know each other, yet we like each other anyway."

"I know. But you've gotta stop making this harder than it already is! I told you, I came over to say good-bye—"

"I'll be here when you get back," he says, his eyes aglow.

I lower my head. "I'm not coming back, Jess."

His arm falls from my shoulder, and he

jerks away from me as though I'd shot him. I can't look him in the face, can't stand to see his pain. "Not coming back?" he repeats.

I swallow back tears. I can't keep on crying or I'll never do this. "I started out training someone to take my shifts and my classes and ended up turning in my resignation instead. I've already packed and closed up the house. I'm leaving first thing in the morning."

"Damn! You're moving in with your friend?"

I shake my head. "No. I'm not even going to Blue Mountain. I called Corrine to tell her that I quit my job and was heading her way. She got real upset, saying she didn't want anyone with her at this point—"

"But you're going to anyway?"

Again, I shake my head. "Will you shut up and let me tell you? Unless she gets sicker, I'm not going until our weekend in October, because that's what she wants. She's determined to have our get-together at her place like we do every year and to make it on her own till then."

Jesse frowns. "So—where you going, then?"

"I'm going home."

"Home?"

"Remember me telling you that I've called Lindy, my little girl, several times since she's been here? Last time I talked with her, for the first time she said that she missed me, and it about broke my heart. After Corrine said she didn't want me to move in with her, I called a friend in Reform to see if her mama's house is still vacant. She rented it to me, Jesse. When I leave here in the morning, I'm going back to Reform."

He stares at me in shock. "You going back to your husband?"

I shrug, looking down at my feet. "No. But I do hope he'll take me back, eventually. I know this now, Jess. I should not have come here when he kicked me out. I should've stayed and fought to get him back. Most of all, I should've stayed for my kids. It was a bad thing I did, leaving them. Leaving Paul was one thing, but leaving my kids . . ." I shake my head. "You told me that yourself, remember? Christopher's gone, but I can be there for Lindy. It's my last chance to be with her before she goes off to school, too."

A silence falls, and when I finally look at Jesse, he's wiping tears away. Without a word, I go back into his arms, resting my head on his chest for the last time. We don't say anything as he sinks back into the swing, cradling me and swinging slowly, back and forth, back and forth. With his chin on top of my head, Jesse clears his throat and says, "Lanier? You're doing the right thing, honey."

"Thank you for saying that," I say, my voice choked up. "And thank you for my song. You'll never know how much it means to me."

"Only song I've ever written for anybody."

"I want you to do something else for me, too, Jess. When your manager gets here, I hope you'll decide to go with him and get yourself straightened out. You know you can't go on like this, don't you?"

He doesn't answer me, so I let it drop. I can't make him go and neither can his manager. It's something he's going to have to do for himself. After a while, I say to him, "I hope one day you'll give another concert and you'll sing my song."

We swing, holding on to each other, until Jess says, "Tell you what. If you promise me that you'll come to it, I'll give one more concert. And I'll sing your song, first time anyone except you hears it. How about that?"

"You got yourself a deal," I say, smiling through my tears.

*   *   *

Back at the cabin, I realize I didn't read to Jess from my lesson book. I'd liked what I'd written, thinking it might be something he could use for a song one day. But now, reading it over, I'm glad I didn't show it to him; it makes me so sad. I'd written, *Love's been called everything from a wildfire to an earthquake. But what if it's more of the feeling you get when you come home after a long absence?*

26

Corrine
BLUE MOUNTAIN

WHEN I LEAVE MY studio and go back into the cabin, the phone's ringing. I stand by it, but I don't pick up the receiver. Instead, I sit down on the couch and count the rings until the answering machine comes on. Four . . . five . . . six . . . I've set it to ring as many times as possible, hoping the caller will get discouraged and hang up. I've never had caller ID but don't really need it; the gallery and a few select customers, the SSGs, Culley, Miles (who had to have it when Culley was living with him), and now Cal, are the only ones who have my private number. One good thing: I know it's not Miles. After our long-overdue confrontation the night he saw me and Cal together, I haven't heard from him. According to Astor, he's been making frequent trips to Birmingham, still trying to decide on a new painting. When she told me that, I put my hand over the receiver so she wouldn't hear me snickering. If Miles and Astor have finally found each other, at least I know there is a God of Just Rewards.

The answering machine comes on: "Hi, this is Corrine. I'm working in the studio now, but leave me a message and I'll call you back, soon as I can."

It's Byrd. "Hi, honey. Hope you're feeling okay this morning. Listen, I'm calling to see if you still want to have the SSG gathering at your place. Are you sure? I know you keep saying it gives you something to look forward to, but I'm worried it's too much for you. Well . . . let me know. And I'm so glad you're working! Call me back tonight."

For several days, all the SSGs have called with similar messages. The truth is, I'm not working at all, and they know it. I'm tired, bone-tired in a way that I never imagined anyone could be. But that isn't the reason I'm not working. In order to buy my solitude,

I've been pretending to be engrossed in finishing the gourds I'd left in various stages of completion when I got sick this summer. It's all an elaborate ruse, which everyone is going along with. (Except Culley—to keep him happily involved in his final year at school, I've led him to believe I'm working night and day.) It's necessary for me to have this time to myself, whatever I have to do in order to get it. At first everyone tried to smother me, couldn't stand to leave me alone, until it became clear that I needed this time of solitude more than I needed their solicitation. I would need that later; right now I had to have a time of mourning. I think of a quote I saw once, attributed to Chekhov: "I am in mourning for my life." Although I've been determined not to feel sorry for myself, it's hard to stay off the pity pot. *Just when I was beginning to make some sense of my life. . . .* But I can't think that way, either. Going down that path leads to nothing but despair, and I can't afford the luxury now. I don't have time.

My days have fallen into a pattern. Each morning I spend in my studio. Instead of working, however, I mostly sit and hold each of the gourds that I haven't finished. The bigger ones I hold in my lap, like small children who need comforting. I tell them I'm sorry I didn't finish them, and that their lives, like mine, will never be complete. Late in the afternoon, after my now-necessary nap, I walk in my garden where the gourds are hanging ripe on the vines. My beautiful gourds, which will never become more than they are now! They'll ripen and dry on the vines and on the trellises that Culley made for me, but they won't be picked and left to cure in my studio, as is my habit. They'll never be brought to harvest. Another thing that I will leave unfinished.

After my daily pilgrimage to my garden, I sit on the porch and watch the sunset, as I've done for so many years, but it's a different experience now. I refuse to rhapsodize and carry on like a pure fool about the metaphorical meaning of the sunset—I can't do it without making myself gag—so I just sit and enjoy the cooler September evenings as I sip the one glass of wine I allow myself. When I told Julia that, she asked if the doctor approved of me mixing alcohol with the nausea med. I didn't tell her that I hadn't talked to Jolly Roger, even though his office had called a couple of times. To put them off, I'd left a message that I hadn't decided what to do yet. The nurse said I should come in for another CT so they can determine the "progression" of my illness, but I'm not. I know instinctively what my progression is, and I'm trying to prepare myself.

Part of my preparation came about accidentally, based on a conversation with Paul Sanders, whom I've talked to several times since I got sick. Last time we talked, I'd called to ask what would happen to me if I didn't take the chemo or the other horrible treatment choices, and he'd said that the outcome wouldn't be very desirable.

"Come on, Paul," I'd said. "Me and you go too far back for you to talk to me like a doctor. Tell me like a friend, okay? Put it in SSG language."

And Paul had responded, "Well, putting it that way, it will suck a big one. You won't be crowned queen at the next gathering because you won't be there. And you sure as hell will not be the same sweet girl you've always been."

I sighed, then said, "What would you do if you were me, Paul?"

"I'm not sure, Corrine. I'd probably try the chemo."

"If I do, you think I have a good chance of being crowned queen next year?"

He hesitated just long enough for me to know the answer, even though he insisted I had a better chance with the chemo than without. Without it, I didn't have the chance of a fart in a whirlwind. Just to feel him out, I said, "Paul? I've joined the Hemlock Society. Are you familiar with them?"

"I am."

"They've provided me with some good information. When the . . . ah . . . time comes, it's much easier if you have someone to help you. I shocked Lanier by asking her if she could."

"So she told me."

"I felt real guilty afterwards. Guess it was too much to ask of her, close as we are."

"Most people couldn't do it."

"But . . . let's just say she did. Could she get into trouble?"

"You mean besides spending the rest of her life in jail? I'm sure you know what you asked her is illegal as hell."

"Yeah, I know. I wish I hadn't mentioned it to her."

After a silence, Paul said thoughtfully, "Don't waste your time worrying about it, Corrine. You and I know Lanier better than anyone, and we both know she couldn't do it." That was the extent of our conversation, but it told me a couple of things: one, that I was as unlikely to survive this as I'd feared, and two, that I was on my own.

Late Sunday afternoon I wake up from my nap to the sound of banging on my front door. If I hadn't been startled out of my sleep, I probably wouldn't have gotten up. I stumble off the couch, almost falling on the floor, and push my tangled hair out of my face. When I open the door, I blink in the light, trying to place the man who's standing there, silhouetted by the sun. "I'm so sorry," he says with a grimace, putting a hand over his eyes and peeking through his fingers. "I woke you up."

"Cal!" I say, startled wide awake now. "What are you doing here?" I look over his shoulder, recognizing the dark sedan parked in the drive, the one he drove last time he was here, to get the gourd for his grandmother. I remember he said even though he was picking up Joe Ed at the airport, he was driving his own car rather than a state car because he was coming to my place first. We'd laughed about it, imagining the state auditor's face if the extra mileage was listed as "picking up a gourd."

"I tried to call . . ." Cal says apologetically, and it's my turn to grimace.

"Oh, dear. I took the phone off the hook last night and forgot to put it back. No wonder none of the SSGs have called." I hit my forehead with my palm. "Crap. Now they'll think I've kicked the bucket."

Cal smiles, standing with his hands on his hips. He looks different, dressed in an FSU T-shirt and jeans, a baseball cap in his hands. Different, but good. Really good. I must be at least half-alive after all. "Naw, they'll probably think the same thing I thought," he says. "Kept getting a busy signal, so I figured you were home, talking to the Sweet Old Girls."

I motion toward the living room. "Want to come in?"

"I can't stay, but . . . I did want to talk to you. I took the gourds to Granny Ross."

"Oh! You mean—*when*?"

"This weekend. I'm on my way back from Tallahassee."

"Oh, my God," I gasp. "Come in, then. I want to hear all about it."

As soon as Cal enters the living room, I'm embarrassed by the mess, newspapers strewn everywhere, empty glasses on the end tables, a hastily kicked-off quilt on the floor by the couch. I pick up the quilt and fold it, trying to think what I've got to drink besides my so-called therapeutic green tea, which I've consumed by the gallons lately with no noticeable improvement. The SSGs left a couple of beers in the fridge, so I say, "How about a beer?"

"Sounds great, but I'll get it." He puts out an arm to stop me. "Don't want you waiting on me—"

"Don't you dare say in my condition," I warn him. He grins sheepishly, ducking his head, and I decide I'm more like three-quarters alive. "Besides, I'm getting myself some tea anyway," I add.

Before I get the tea and beer, I sneak into the laundry room and brush my hair, which looks like a rat's nest. My makeup's upstairs, but I remember the heroines in old English novels pinching their cheeks to give them color, so I pinch away. Then I bite my pale lips, grimacing at my reflection in the mirror.

Oh, well, didn't help much. I still bear a striking resemblance to Madeline Usher after she clawed herself out of the tomb. When I come back into the living room, Cal's looking at the things I have on the mantel, holding one of my bottle gourds in his hand. "Some that you didn't see when you were here in August," I say, handing him the cold beer.

He takes the beer and eyes me curiously. "How have you been, Corrine? I've been worried about you."

"When you were here in August? I just thought I was tired. Now it's a Jurassic tiredness."

"Last time we talked, you hadn't made a decision on the treatment. Julia was telling me the other day that you still haven't."

"Not true," I tell him. "Julia just doesn't know what I've decided."

"Ah. Want to talk about it, or not?"

I nod toward the couch. "Let's sit down."

Sitting by me on the couch and putting his beer on a pottery coaster on the coffee table, Cal turns his head to me, eyes narrowed, and says, "Okay. Tell me what you've decided."

I hold up a hand. "Instead of talking about such a depressing subject, I want to hear what your grandmother—Granny Ross, right?—said about the gourds."

His face changes, lights up, his eyes glowing like coals. "Oh, man. It was great. That little one, the whachamacallit—"

"Mini sennari."

"Yeah, that one. She absolutely loved it. Everybody did."

"Everybody?" Cal and I have become friends, but I don't know a lot about his family. Over dinner at the Inn, he told me he didn't have any siblings, just his granny, his ex-wife, and a son who played football in college. I connect that with the T-shirt, and say, "Wait—you told me you were going to your son's football game the same weekend as the birthday thing with your granny. He's at FSU? Did they win?" Beaming, he nods, and I say, "Okay, go ahead. You had a big family bash for your granny's birthday, right?"

He nods. "Not much family left, just a few ancient great-aunts and cousins, but we all got together at the nursing home on Friday because me and Kyle—my son—had to be at the game on Saturday. I gave Granny Ross the little gourd at the family thing, then spent Saturday at the game, taking my son out afterwards. This morning, before I left, I spent the morning with Granny Ross, just me and her. That's when I gave her the big gourd, the one you made me take to her. Which is what I came all the way up here to talk to you about."

I gasp, my hands flying to my mouth. "Don't tell me! The design . . . did she say it was some kind of ancient icon that I—" The look on Cal's face stops me.

"Oh, please," he groans. "Not that again."

"Cal!"

"I have to tell you, Corrine, I've never heard such a crock in my life. I don't mean to hurt your feelings, but you've gotta admit that's *way* out in left field."

I'm trying really hard to be insulted, but I can't help it; I smile instead. "Guess it sounds pretty stupid, huh?"

He surprises me by placing a hand on my arm. "Hey. I didn't mean to sound like a jerk. Actually, it's a neat idea, crazy as it sounds. I liked what you said about that protective circle thing."

"You don't sound like a jerk; it's me that sounds foolish. Julia or anyone else can tell you that I'm notoriously crazy."

He studies me. "No, you're not." I look at him skeptically, and he amends it. "Well, maybe you're a little crazy, but in a nice way. Know what I mean?"

"It's okay," I tell him. "Don't feel like you have to say that just because I'm sick."

"I mean it, but that's not what I came to tell you." Cal picks up the beer and drinks deeply of it, then puts it back on the coaster. He doesn't meet my eyes when he says, "Granny Ross sent that big gourd back to you."

"She did what?"

"She wouldn't keep it. She sent it back," he admits. "I've got it in the car. I wasn't going to bring it in till I had a chance to explain."

I put my hands on my hips, leaning away from him. "You wouldn't let her keep it, would you? Bet you told her that I didn't want to part with it! Dammit, Cal—"

He holds a hand up to stop me. "Whoa. I'm caught in the middle between two stubborn women. I told Granny Ross about you, but I certainly did not tell her you didn't want to part with the gourd. Know why? Because she's stubborn, too, and she wouldn't have taken it. I figured if she'd done that, you'd jump me, which you're doing anyway."

"Sorry," I mutter, somewhat mollified.

"Granny Ross sent a note to you, if you'll

let me go get it." He pats my hand and says to stay put, that he'll go to the car and get it. I try not to speculate on the message, but I can't help it. In spite of Cal's warning, I'm hoping against hope that an old medicine woman was able to interpret the design based on primeval Indian lore. Or maybe some long-forgotten Creek legend that she'd forgotten about until she saw the gourd.

Cal returns with the sack I sent the gourd in, and I reach for it eagerly. I've missed it more than I'd realized—something I'll keep to myself. "I told Granny if she sent it back, you'd worry that she'd call you an Indian giver," Cal grins, taking the gourd out of the sack and handing it to me.

"Not funny," I say. I don't hold the kettle gourd as close as I'd like, so Cal won't think I'm even crazier, but I keep my hands on it.

"If you promise not to freak, I'll show you a couple of symbols Granny mentioned." He points to the cross within a circle that I'd etched on the very top. "Symbol of the sun," he says, "but you probably knew that. It's used in a lot of Indian craft." With the tip of his finger, he traces over the tasseled oval shapes near the bottom. "She said those could be ears of corn, maybe having something to do with the green corn ceremony. They look more like sprouting seeds to me." Taking hold of the gourd's stem, Cal takes off the lid and studies the inside curiously. As with my other gourds, I've sanded it smooth as a polished stone; had it been finished, I'd have painted the inside as well.

"Here's something that's different about this gourd," I tell him. "I've never made one with a lid before. Don't know why it needed one . . ." I stop myself before saying that it spoke to me and told me the lid was a necessary part of it. I can only imagine his reaction to that.

"Granny Ross put the note in a sealed envelope so I wouldn't read it," he said, frowning as he withdraws what appears to be a notecard in a small square pink envelope, like a society lady might use to RSVP to a fancy party. Playfully, Cal tries to read over my shoulder, but I turn my back to him. I have to hold the note close to read it because the writing is small and shaky, what you'd expect from someone her age.

"Dear Corrine Cooper," the note says.

"Thank you for the gourd. My grandson says you want me to have it. I appreciate it but I'm sending it back. You have to finish it. When you do, you'll know why you made it. It is not for me but for you. When it's finished, that will be clear. Signed, Mary Ross. P.S. Cal said you hoped I could say what the design is. My eyesight is bad now, but I can see what it is, plain as day, and so can you."

My eyes wide, I hand the note to Cal. "I don't get it," I tell him after he reads it and looks at me quizzically.

"There's a reason for that," he says with a snort. "Nothing to get. All she said was, you need to finish it."

"Yeah, but why?"

Cal shrugs. "Hell if I know. But if I were you, I'd do it and see. Maybe once you get it all painted, it'll spell out the winning lottery numbers or something."

Rolling my eyes, I reach over and pick up the kettle gourd. Holding it up to the light, I turn it over, this way and that, studying the spirals and intertwining vines. Then I put the lid back on it, shaking my head as I sit it on the coffee table in front of us. "Did you tell your granny what I said about the protective circles?" I wonder why she didn't say something about that idea, which I'd thought was a pretty good one.

"I didn't tell her anything. I'll admit, I was curious to see what she thought about the design. I asked her, and all she'd say was it was obvious. I said, what'd you mean, obvious? What is it? She said *I* couldn't see it, but *you* could. Guess she was wrong."

"Guess so," I say, disappointed.

Cal eyes me curiously. "You going to finish it?"

I lower my eyes and sigh. "I can't, Cal. I haven't been able to work anymore."

He looks startled, and leaning toward me, places a hand on my shoulder. "You're really sick, aren't you, Corrine? And here I've been keeping you up, talking, drinking a beer . . . what a thoughtless jerk I am. You need to lie down?"

I shake my head. "No, no. That's not it. Except for the tiredness, I don't feel sick. Dr. Brown told me I wouldn't until . . . things progressed further, the way he put it. So it's not that I don't feel like working; it's more like . . . oh, I don't know. I just can't."

Cal tilts his head to the side. "Probably help you if you could. You know, get your mind off things." He picks up the beer can and finishes it off, then turns to regard me. "Seriously, Corrine, sounds to me like you're more depressed than anything else."

"Depression is my native land," I admit.

"Not that you don't have reason to be," he says quietly, and I nod. A silence falls between us as Cal appears to be deep in thought, rubbing his chin and frowning. Just as I'm about to ask what he's thinking, he takes me by surprise. Standing up, he reaches for my hand, pulling me to my feet. "Pick up the gourd, Corrine," he says in a no-nonsense voice, inclining his head toward the kettle gourd on the coffee table. I lean over, pick it up, then look up at Cal questioningly. He jerks his head toward the front door. "Come on," he says, picking up his Braves cap and snapping it open. And taking my elbow, he leads me out the front door.

"Where are we going?" I ask, once we start down the front steps, him halfway pulling me.

"To your studio. Where *you* are going back to work." And he marches me to the back of the house, throwing open the door of my studio with a flourish.

"I told you I'm not working anymore!" I protest, but Cal pulls out the chair at my work table, and putting his hands on my shoulders, forces me to sit down.

"Then it's no wonder you're so down in the mouth, doing nothing but sitting around thinking about dying," he says.

I look up at him openmouthed. "How do you know—"

"Give me a break. What would anyone in your position do but think about it, day and night? You not taking any treatment is nothing but a bunch of crap, you ask me." He raises his hand to stop my protest. "Okay, nobody asked me. But you've got to fight it, Corrine. Surely you won't give up without a fight!"

"You sound like the SSGs," I mutter. "Everybody minding my business, telling me what I need to do." I look up at Cal, standing over me with his hands on his hips. "I'm not a fighter like you, Cal. It's your profession."

"Damn right you're not like me," he says, and his eyes blaze. "Anybody with tough enough skin and a hard enough head can do what I do. But you, Corrine—you're an artist! Not everybody can do that, because it's a gift. Can you imagine what it takes to move a guy like me to tears? That's what happened when I saw your Trail of Tears gourd. Like to have embarrassed myself to death." He points to the kettle gourd, which, out of habit, I'd placed on the bed of nails. "So by God, you've got to finish that one."

I look at the gourd, etched but not painted, badly in need of finishing. I raise my eyes and look up at the shelves above my workbench, where the other unfinished gourds sit on little squares of nails. Reaching in his pocket, Cal retrieves a card, scribbles something on the back, and hands it to me. "My cell phone and my home number. Call me when you finish it because I want to come back and see it. I want to see what Granny Ross meant by her note."

When I don't take the card, sitting in the chair without moving, Cal sticks it among my brushes. Then he kneels in front of my chair, elbows propped on his knees, and looks up at me. "Okay, I'm going to leave you now so you can get to work. I've got to get back to Montgomery before dark, anyway."

"Better haul ass, then."

"As you know, that's no problem. You gonna work when I leave?" His smile changes to a stern frown, and I shrug.

"I don't know."

He searches my face, then says, "Know

something, Corrine? I have another motive for wanting you to finish the gourd."

I look at him suspiciously. "You do?"

"Yeah. I'd like an excuse to come back here and see you again."

"Why would you want to do that?" I blurt out, then blush like a fool.

Cal laughs. "Come on, Corrine. Don't make this harder on me than it already is. I've never been any good at this kind of thing. I feel like such a fool."

"What kind of thing?"

"Jesus! You don't really think I came all the way over here just to look at a bunch of damn gourds, do you?"

My eyes wide, I stammer, "A-actually, I did."

"First night I saw you, I thought you looked like an angel lying there in that hospital bed, that hair of yours spread out on the pillow," Cal says dreamily while I stare at him in disbelief. "I was so blown away I could hardly say a word to you. But I can't tell you what a jerk I felt like, smitten by someone sick as you were that night. Made me feel like a pervert or something, so I kept it to myself."

Pressing my hands to my burning cheeks, I say, "But . . . I thought . . . I mean, you've said several times that you like us being friends. It never occurred to me you'd think of me as anything other than a friend."

Cal shrugs. "I only said that because I couldn't imagine a woman like you would ever be interested in someone like me. Not that anything's changed," he adds hastily, "but I decided to go ahead and tell you how I felt, anyway."

I'm too flabbergasted to say anything, so Cal gets to his feet and picks up his baseball cap, his eyes averted. "Okay, I've had my say, so now I'm hitting the road," he says, red-faced. "Sorry about blurting out all that silly stuff, Corrine."

"I wouldn't call it silly, exactly."

"Oh?"

I shake my head. "No. I thought it was nice. It was . . . nice." What I can't tell him is, no one's ever said anything that romantic to me. Miles swept me off my feet with passion and sensuality, but the thrill and sweetness of romance? I have never experienced it, not once in my pathetic life.

Then, the loveliest thing of all. Reaching over, Cal takes my hand, which I've clenched nervously into a tight fist. He opens my fingers and presses his lips to my palm. His lips on the palm of my hand are more erotic than any kiss I've ever had, leaving me speechless. Then, with great care, he closes my hand back into a fist, his eyes holding mine. "Take care of yourself, Corrine. I've been looking for you all my life, and I don't want to lose you now," he says, releasing my hand. But before I can say anything, he's gone, closing the door of the studio behind him and leaving me startled and dreamy-eyed.

I don't tell Lanier or Julia about the conversation with Cal. They're the only SSGs I'd tell anyway, but I find myself wanting to keep that moment close and secret, like a cherished memento, a flower cut and dried in an attempt to preserve its brief life. Even if I never see Cal again, I'm grateful to him for offering me such a fine gift, a surprising moment that everyone should have at least once in a lifetime. Maybe he didn't mean a word of it; it's not very likely that I'll be around to find out, but nevertheless, I floated around in a daze after he left me that day.

My bemused state of mind was not the reason I didn't do as he'd insisted, however, and go back to work. I wasn't able to work on the kettle gourd again until it became clear to me what its purpose was. Once that happened, I worked feverishly, night and day, as though obsessed, until I finished it. And then, exactly as Granny Ross said in her note, I knew. I knew what it was.

It happened about a week later. I had a restless, upsetting night, unable to sleep because of strange new sensations in my body. I wasn't sure what was going on, but something was, and it wasn't very pleasant. In a lot of ways, it was a repeat of the time I got so sick and alternated between feeling ice-cold and burning hot. I shivered and shook and pulled blankets over me, then sweated and burned and kicked them off, soaking wet. I wasn't so much sick as feeling odd, a sensation like floating in and out of consciousness. I wondered if I was dying and decided if I was, it wasn't as bad as I'd feared. Scary, but not painful. My last night in the hospital, Jolly Roger had painted all sorts of dire pictures of what can happen to the brain when the liver goes, how you can hallucinate and rant and rave and basically go bonkers. I told him since I was already crazy, nobody would know the difference, which he didn't think was particularly funny.

But I wondered if that's what was going on with me now.

One reason I couldn't sleep that night was the brightness of the moon. It bathed my room in a ghostly white light, which seemed almost eerie in my restless state. But I didn't want to get up and close the curtains, because I didn't want to be in darkness, either. Moonlight, too bright; no moonlight, too dark and scary.

I fell into a fitful, troubled sleep where I dreamed I was in my garden, walking along the dirt path. On either side, the vines were full of gourds of all kinds. Since it was a dream, there were gourds I'd never grown before, maranka and crown-of-thorns and luffa, all growing on the same vines. Another thing that could only happen in a dream: There were blossoms, both yellow and white, among the full-grown gourds, and dried gourds hanging with green ones. Gourds of all kinds and in all stages grew in my dream garden. I went deeper and deeper into the vines, like going into a forest of vines, and suddenly there was a clearing. A woman was there, bent over like an old witch, with her back to me. When I got closer, she turned around. I saw that she was Native American, dressed like an Indian princess in the movies, with fringed buckskin and beads and feathers, her hair in long black braids. I knew she couldn't be Cal's granny because his granny's not a movie-star Indian but is old and bedridden, in a nursing home in Tallahassee. This woman was both young and old, her body bent and withered, but her face smooth and ageless and pretty. She was holding my kettle gourd in her hands, and she handed it to me when I walked up to her. It was finished, painted and perfect, more beautiful than any piece I've ever done. When I took it from her hands, she smiled at me. Her smile was sweet and kind, but it scared me, and I took a step backward, away from her. I held the kettle gourd close so she wouldn't take it away from me, but instead, she turned and walked into the forest of gourd vines. It was like she disappeared, swallowed up in the thick vines. When I was sure she was gone, I looked down at the kettle I held in my hands.

Finished, the kettle gourd was so beautiful it took my breath away. The spirals and circles and intertwining vines were painted in all the colors of the gourd-vine forest, every shade of green, gold, yellow, and brown imaginable, with pure white blossoms scattered among the vines. There was no beading, no inlay, no jewels, just the colors and shapes of the gourd vines, and I knew then what the design was. I felt like such a fool for not seeing it before; it was so obvious a blind person could see it. Cal's Granny was right: Now I knew what the design was. Amazing that I didn't see it before, see how it duplicated my gourds in all their different stages. But its purpose? The size, the shape, the lid—there was a reason I was compelled to make it as I did, but I still didn't know what it was.

In my dream the wind began to rustle through the vines, a cool wind that chilled me to the bone. Even so, the kettle gourd I held felt warm against my body, and I pressed it closer. I grasped the stem to remove the lid because the warmth was coming from inside, as though a fire burned there. Lifting the lid off, I looked inside, looked at what was inside the gourd, and then I knew. *I knew.* I thought they'd be blacker, sootier, but they were gray, the color of the sky between night and dawn. Even though they were warm, still smoldering, I put my hand in without getting burned. Instead of being coarse and scratchy, they were velvety to the touch, as fine and delicate as crushed butterfly wings. Turning and walking down the path, I started tossing the ashes among the vines, and the cold wind picked them up and scattered them. They were lifted by the wind until they turned the entire green gourd-vine forest a pearly shade of gray.

The last weekend in October, and the Same Sweet Girls are reclining around the fire, our faces taking on the glow of the dancing yellow flames. We're such a subdued group I'm beginning to wonder if the body snatchers have invaded north Georgia. Everyone's here, now that Lanier has gotten in. Propped on a stack of throw pillows, she's chosen a place away from the rest of us. The flames reflect in her pale brown eyes as she stares into the fire, and from my place on the sofa,

I study her to see how she's holding up. She's wearing a new sadness that doesn't fit her, like a child draped in a heavy cloak that drags on the floor.

Lanier drove straight here from the memorial service, so she's dressed in black, which I've never seen her wear before, a black turtleneck sweater with pinstriped charcoal slacks. Maybe that's why she seems so different. This morning she was up at sunrise, scattering Jesse Phoenix's ashes on Mobile Bay. Without setting a clock, I woke up at the same time, just as the sun was coming over the mountains, sending pink fingers of light into the morning sky. Turning my face to the window, I looked toward the rising sun and said a prayer for Lanier and for poor Jesse. Lanier is eaten up with guilt, blaming herself for leaving him, for going back to Reform. She blames herself for sending Jesse's manager to check on him without telling Jesse first, convinced that if she'd only done so, the manager would have found Jesse the way she'd left him, rather than dead of alcohol poisoning. Lanier thought that because she was making such an effort to stop her self-destructive patterns of behavior, Jesse would, too. I could have told her different.

When the pupil is ready... I had to come down with a deadly disease before I could see that, and Jesse never did, drinking himself to death like that. If we refuse to learn the lessons life sends our way, we'll find ourselves heading down a path of self-destruction that can only end one way.

My mama used to say that deaths always come in threes, which naturally makes me uneasy. A week before we heard about Jesse Phoenix, Cal's Granny Ross died. Unlike poor Jesse's death, which the news reports called "tragic and untimely," Granny Ross's was peaceful, Cal told me. Poor Cal; he keeps calling and asking if he can drive over and see me, and I keep refusing to let him do so. I think he understands, though. His daily phone calls, full of his dark humor, make me laugh and cry and have become one of the bright spots in my days lately. I'm not sure how successful I've been in letting him know that I'll always treasure the gift he's given me. I'll hold it close, and I'll take it with me.

Lying in front of Lanier, her long legs draped over a footstool, is Astor, in her usual tights and leotards, a paisley shawl tied casually around her shoulders. Unlike the rest of us, who wear the SSG pin over our hearts, its gaudy rhinestones glittering in the light of the fire, Astor has hers pinned to hold the shawl together. Her hair is spread out on my braided rug like a sheet of black silk, and her arms extend over her head in an arch. She, too, is staring in the fire, and I have a chance to study her unobserved, her face turned in perfect profile to me. I'll never figure Astor out, and having accepted that, I'm able to let it go. It's been almost an obsession with me, I realize, from the first day I met her. A possibility hits me like a splash of cold water. Maybe there's not that much to figure out. Could it be that I've made Astor more mysterious and intriguing than she actually is? Once I gave her a T-shirt that had a picture of Snow White's wicked stepmother looking into a mirror and saying "It's All About Me, Isn't It?" Astor's astonishing self-absorption could be all there is to know about her. Maybe the other traits that have mystified me, her lying and conniving and manipulation, are simply by-products of her egotism. Maybe it's that simple after all. Queen Astor, the role she was born to play.

My gaze travels from Astor's prone figure to those of Byrd and Rosanelle, lying next to each other, propped up on a hassock that they're sharing, faces turned to the fire. Byrd is, as usual, the one being nice to Rosanelle, making her feel a part of the group. Truth is, however much we might bitch and moan, Rosanelle will always be one of us. Maybe no one else could have stepped in to fill the gap in our group except her, being so different from the zany and fun-loving Dixie Lee. Frozen in time, Dixie Lee will always be twenty-five years old, bright-eyed and rosy-cheeked. Unlike the rest of the SSGs, she will never age, fighting wrinkles and sagging skin and creaking joints. Makes me feel kind of sorry for Rosanelle, trying to replace someone like that. "Hey, Rosanelle," I say, breaking the silence that has fallen over the room like a pall, "I like your new do." As usual, Rosanelle has done something different with her hair, which is flipped behind her ears, showing off heavy gold earrings. Even though she's lying on the floor, head propped up, her platinum hair is motionless, not fazed by the position she's in. "Why, thank you, sugar! How *sweet* of you to notice," Rosanelle says, and Julia cuts her eyes to me and winks.

The only one of us who's sitting in a chair

rather than on the floor, Julia is rocking, holding my kettle gourd in her hands as she studies it. I can't get over the difference in Julia now that she and Joe Ed have moved back to their home in Montgomery, out of the Governor's Mansion. Joe Ed's still governor, of course, and they still use the Mansion for entertaining, but Julia told me she couldn't live there anymore. She's having their house redecorated, fixing it up like *she* wants it, not her mother, she told me. The other SSGs, even Lanier, think that's why Julia's looking so serene and happy now, but I know better. A few weeks ago Julia called to tell me the astonishing news: After all these years, she had fallen in love. I almost dropped the phone until, shyly, she told me that the damndest thing had happened: She'd fallen in love with her own husband. "Well, that's convenient," I'd said, and we'd both ended up laughing.

Julia has already taken the predictable teasing about rocking the kettle gourd to sleep. A couple of weeks ago when I finished it, I brought the kettle from my studio and put it on the stone hearth, the only place it fits, since it's the size of a pumpkin. Byrd described the kettle perfectly when she arrived and saw it, next to the fire. "Would you look at that," she'd cried. "Corrine has made a *gourd* gourd." And that's what it is, now that it's finished—a gourd depicting the life cycles of my gourds. I've started referring to it as the gourd-vine gourd, and it's become the object of much curiosity among the SSGs since I told them its story.

Hard to think this way with any degree of humility, but I admit the gourd-vine gourd turned out as beautiful as the one in my dream. I got up that very night of my dream and went to my studio. Even though I was so sick I could hardly hold a paintbrush in my hand, I started working on the unfinished gourd, mixing paints feverishly to match the colors in my dream. I'd either fallen to sleep or passed out while working on it, my head on my work table, my sweat-soaked night-gown speckled with paint, all shades of green and gold and brown. Each day follow-ing, I worked on painting the gourd to look like the one in my dream. In some ways I was afraid to finish it, because I interpreted the dream to mean that finished, it would be ready to use as my funeral urn. Tearing open the envelope of the note I'd written to the SSGs, I added that I wanted my ashes put into the gourd-vine gourd until some were scattered in my garden, some in Shoal Creek, and the remainder in Mobile Bay. I resealed the envelope and put it back in the box where I'd told Lanier to find it when the time came. As I worked I remembered a myth I'd heard once, something about a craftsman who was ordered by the gods to make his own crypt. Naturally, in no hurry to finish it, he dawdled along. Since it was never finished, he became immortal, but I wasn't counting on that happening to me.

A strange thing happened as I worked on the gourd-vine gourd. At first I could only work a few hours a day. I was too weak, and the new sickness that had come on the night of the dream worsened. Some days I could hardly hold my head up as I sat at my work table, couldn't keep my shaking hands steady enough to guide a paintbrush. It was only when I got so transfixed by the intricate painting of the gourd that I would lose myself and would come out of my trance to realize I'd managed to paint for a whole hour. The next day, two hours, and the next, even longer. Before I realized it, I'd worked a whole day without being sick. I'd gotten up from my work table, gone into the house, and made myself a grilled cheese sandwich. It was the first solid food I'd had in days, since I'd only been able to hold down broth, yogurt, or Jell-O. The next day, I felt well enough to have boiled eggs with toast and apple butter for breakfast. I stopped drinking the tasteless green tea and brewed black tea leaves instead, drinking it strong and hot, with lots of milk and honey.

As my strength came back, I worked longer. The day I finished the gourd-vine gourd I felt well enough to go to my gallery for the first time in weeks, where I discovered only three of my gourds remained to sell. I went home right then to finish the rest of the gourds in my studio. I'd slept hard at night, waking up refreshed and eager to get back to the studio. Again, I was forced to persuade the SSGs and Culley and Cal to stay away until I finished my work—only this time, it was the truth. I assume everyone agreed to let me be because they thought it was keeping my mind off my illness. They had no way of knowing my work was my path out of a long, dark tunnel instead. For the first time in weeks, I felt *alive*. It came to me that I was being handed a reprieve, a chance to finish my work, the only thing I've ever had to offer God in exchange for all that's been given me. Some sort of repayment for the beauty I've been privileged to experience, in a way. Despite the awful irony, I'm grateful that I've gotten to the point I can think like that, to let go of the awful depression and mourning and appreciate the beauty of life instead. My beauty disease has come full circle.

"You've hogged that big gourd long enough," Byrd says to Julia, sitting up and holding out her hands. "Hand it here and let me look at it." The others chime in, asking Byrd to pass it around. As the gourd-vine gourd is handed from one to the other, their reactions are predictable, and from my position on the sofa, I smile watching them. Rosanelle shudders and says, "I cannot imagine why anyone would want to be cremated. The Apostles' Creed at my church says we believe in the resurrection of the *body,* not the ashes."

Julia eyes her incredulously. "Please tell me you're not serious," she says, and Astor throws her head back and laughs, clapping her hands together.

"Corrine—I have an idea." Astor turns to me, her face glowing in the firelight. "Think you could make one of those urns for Mose? Instead of a design, could you paint a picture of me on it? Mose would *love* that."

Sitting quietly by herself until now, Lanier turns her head to look at Astor, her eyes wide. "I must not have heard you right, Queen Astor. I could've sworn you said you wanted a picture of yourself on Mose's funeral urn. That's the tackiest thing I've ever heard."

I'm the one who starts the giggling, but soon everyone's joined in, even Astor. "Oh, honey, *no,*" Byrd howls, holding her sides, and Julia provides the next line: "Girl, what are you *thinking*?" We laugh until we exhaust ourselves, then fall back into our places, wiping our eyes.

I push myself up. The home-health nurse turned the big old sofa into a bed for me when I refused to let her bring in a hospital bed, and it's surprisingly comfortable. "Lanier?" I say, catching her eye. "Would you get the cider?" Nodding, she jumps to her feet and heads to the kitchen. I scoot up far enough to reach into the drawer of the pine table at the head of the sofa, which I have to do quietly, since none of the SSGs will let me lift a finger. Since the Jurassic exhaustion has almost overtaken me, I don't have the energy to protest their waiting on me hand and foot. But this, I want to do myself.

Lanier returns with a wooden tray holding six wineglasses and a bottle of apple cider, ice cold and beaded with water. Julia stopped on the mountain and bought the cider from an old farmer, and it looks wonderful, golden-brown and murky, sold in a corked bottle. I pull a sack out of the table drawer, but the drawer creaks when I close it. "What are you doing, Corrine?" Julia gasps. "Why didn't you tell me you needed something from the drawer?"

"You need something? I'll get it for you," Byrd says, scrambling to sit up as she smooths down her hair, which is sticking up like little white feathers in the back. Her plump cheeks are flushed and rosy from the heat of the fire.

"I've got it," I tell them, though I have to lean back and take a deep breath before I can continue. Watching me nervously, everyone gets real quiet. Rolling my eyes, I say, "If I'd known dying was all it takes to get this group to shut up, I'd have done it long before now."

Nobody laughs, and Lanier glares at me. "Dammit, Corrine, crack another joke like that and I'm leaving," she warns, pointing a finger at me.

"Okay, okay." I clear my throat and sigh. "I do have something to say, though."

Julia stops me this time. "No good-bye speeches, either," she says. "I don't know about the rest of you, but I cannot take it."

Everyone chimes in, which gets Byrd sniffling and dabbing at her eyes. I wait for the clamor to die down, then hold up a hand. "I have something to give everyone, is all. Then let's have our apple cider toast."

"Apple cider!" Astor says, making a face. "What about the rum punch?"

"Way to go, Astor," Julia says dryly. "I brought cider because Corrine can't drink rum."

"Doesn't mean the rest of us can't," Astor mutters, but Julia's look shuts her up.

"Since I hardly *ever* drink liquor, I much prefer cider," Rosanelle says piously.

I hold the paper sack up and motion to Julia. "Would you take this for me?" Leaving the rocker, she comes to the sofa, taking the sack from me and peeking in. "Just pass them out," I tell her. "There's one for each of you. Doesn't matter who gets which." Without a word, Julia puts her hand in the sack and brings out five miniature gourds. Stepping around the room, she hands each of the SSGs one, and they hold them in their palms. I've cut the tops off the gourds to make little lids, and Rosanelle lifts hers, peering inside.

"Eeek—there's a bug in here!" she screeches.

"It's not a bug, it's your gift," I say. "As y'all know, I've been real busy lately finishing up my artwork. . . ."

"That's an understatement," Lanier snorts. "Day and night, that's all you've done."

"These miniatures are so pretty I decided not to do anything but clean them out and cut the tops off," I continue. "So, if you'll look inside, you'll see a seed." Each of the SSGs takes out the seed and puts it in her hand, studying it curiously.

"Looks like a pumpkin seed," Lanier says, picking hers up. "I almost ate mine."

"No, they're the seeds of ornamental gourds," I tell them, "and no two are alike. You can't look at the seed and predict the size or shape of the gourd it produces. You plant it, then take what grows. May not be what you wanted, but . . . it's what you get. It'll be unique, and in its own way, beautiful.

I won't make everyone gag by pointing out the obvious metaphorical meaning of that."

"Too late," Lanier mutters.

"But—what do we do with them?" Rosanelle asks, wrinkling her nose as she pokes at hers with a long red fingertip.

"Well, next spring, I want you to plant it. Hopefully, in your garden . . ." I pause and look at Astor, the city dweller, "or a pot on the patio will do. It'll be fully grown by the get-together next October, when everyone should have a plant full of gourds. Best to let them dry on the vine, by the way. I thought it'd be like . . ." I clear my throat, blinking my eyes rapidly, "ah . . . having a part of me here, even if I'm not."

As I feared, a heavy silence follows. Julia lowers her head and cuts her eyes over to Lanier. Astor coughs; Rosanelle's big blue eyes grow round; and all the color drains from Byrd's face. The speech has taken all my energy, and I collapse back on the pillows. Then quickly, before any of us can get upset, I say, "Queen Astor, could you pour me a glass of that apple cider?" No chance of Astor being so upset by the thought of me not being around that she can't do it, I figure.

But I'm surprised to see that Astor's hands tremble as she brings me a glass of cider, and she averts her eyes, not meeting mine. I gulp the cold cider, my throat parched, then motion for Astor to pour for the others. Astor surprises me by holding up a hand in protest.

"I'll let everybody pour their own while I get something," Astor says, removing the paisley shawl from her shoulders and tying it around her hips. "Be right back!" And she scurries to the place by the front door where everyone piled their suitcases on arriving this morning. I try to raise up to see what she's doing, but before I can get the mound of pillows stacked up, Astor has returned, and everyone is on their feet, applauding. When I see what she's taking out of her black tote bag, I put my hands to my face and shake my head.

"Oh, Lord," I say, laughing. "I *knew* I'd get the crown eventually." The hideous rhinestone crown sparkles in the glow of the fire as Astor holds it high, twirling it so it sends out facets of light over our upturned faces. Then, with one of her dramatic flourishes, Astor reaches into the tote bag and pulls out the purple satin cape. When she gives it a smart snap to unwrinkle it, ostrich feathers float to the floor like purple snowflakes.

"The cape's just the thing with your ragged old flannel nightgown," Byrd says brightly. Julia comes over to the sofa, taking the cape from Astor and draping it around my shoulders. Bending over, she kisses my cheek. "Some of us would do anything to get the crown, wouldn't they?" I whisper. When Julia gives me a playful punch on the arm, she smiles a big smile, but her eyes glisten with unshed tears.

Rosanelle and Byrd, the two camera buffs, squat next to the sofa, cameras raised, but Lanier cries, "Wait—something's missing!" at the same moment Astor brings out the scepter. Julia takes it from her and lays it across my chest, moving the purple and gold streamers aside. Astor puts the crown on top of my head, but Lanier says impatiently, "Hurry up and take your pictures and get that thing off her—it weighs a ton."

Lanier's right; the crown feels like a stack of bricks weighting down my head, but I pose and smile obligingly as flashbulbs flash. "Okay, that's enough," Lanier says, leaving her place by the fire and heading toward me. "I'm getting that crap off Corrine before it sinks her right through the sofa."

Everyone agrees, but I hold up my hand to stop Lanier before she reaches me. "Wait, Lanier. I want to wear it a little longer," I say. She looks surprised but stops and gives me a curtsy.

"Whatever you say, Your Majesty," she says, then turns toward Astor, who's standing in one of her poses at the end of the sofa. "Go ahead and pour the cider, ex-Queen Astor, while I get Corrine's meds. It's past time for them." Starting this weekend, Lanier will be taking over for the home-health nurse who's been with me. She and Julia plan on staying after the others leave.

From my perch on the pillows, I watch everyone, holding their glasses out with cries of "Oh, this looks so good!" and, "What a great idea, Julia, bringing the cider," as Astor pours. However, no one proposes a toast or cracks a joke. Instead, they focus on the pouring of the cider as though it were the only thing that mattered. Watching them, my throat is tight and my heart heavier than the crown on my head. I try to think of something to lighten the mood, to make us laugh and joke again, but instead, the room blurs as my eyes fill up with tears. Byrd and Rosanelle hold their glasses out as Astor pours the fizzy cider, and Rosanelle sniffs her glass before asking, "This won't make me drunk, will it? Smells like it's fermented!" Julia and Byrd exchange glances, and Julia giggles. "If you get drunk on *apple cider,* Rosanelle Tilley," Byrd drawls, "you've got to forfeit the crown for the next fifty years."

Lanier returns to my side with a glass of water and a handful of pills, and I try to wipe my eyes with my fingertips before she catches me. Taking the pills has become a production since it's gotten more difficult for me to swallow, but I finish the task and lean back on the pillows. Lanier straddles a footstool perched next to the sofa and leans toward me, pushing my hair back from my damp forehead. "Ready to take off the crown now?" she says, raising her voice to be heard over the clamor of the SSGs. When I shake my head, Lanier protests, "I'm afraid it's too heavy."

I shake my head again, looking up at her, unable to stop the tears that trickle down my cheeks. "It is," I say. "But I don't want to take it off."

Lanier puts her face next to mine, her arm

around my shoulders. "Then keep it on, honey," she says. "You keep it on as long as you want."

I feel so silly keeping the crown on, but it's no longer heavy, like it was when Astor first put it on my head. It feels like a cloud on my head, light as air, even though it's weighted down with gaudy jewels and rhinestones which sparkle and shine like strobe lights. Lanier asks me again if I want to take the crown off. She asks me if I want to take off the cape, take the tacky scepter out of my hands, but I shake my head, tightening my grip on the scepter, with its cotton bolls and purple and gold streamers. "Corrine? Corrine?" Lanier says, leaning over me, her tear-damp face next to mine. "Are you sure it's not too much for you?"

I shake my head, trying to tell her that I don't want to let go of anything, the crown or cape or scepter, but even as I open my mouth to say so I can feel my grip loosening on the scepter, can feel it falling from my hands.

"It's okay, honey. Just let go. You can let go now." It's Julia, leaning over me, on the other side of the bed. The other SSGs have gone home, but Julia and Lanier have been with me for several days, through the awful darkness that came on me more suddenly than expected.

"Julia?" I say, swallowing painfully, trying to make myself heard. "I'm scared."

Julia's hand is cool and gentle on my hot forehead. "Don't be afraid," she whispers. "Lanier and I are here, honey. We're not going to let you be afraid."

I swallow again, but this time the words won't come out. Finally I'm able to say it. "Where's Culley?" They don't hear me, Julia and Lanier. Their heads are bent together, and I hear them whispering. Lanier's saying something about Paul, how she couldn't do this without Paul's help, but I shake my head again, trying to let them know that it's not Paul I'm asking about. "Where's Culley?" I repeat.

Julia leans over me, and she wipes my face with a cool cloth. "It's okay," she says again and again, like a broken record. "Don't worry; Culley has gone now. There's no one here but us." And I remember then. Culley was here. He was here before the darkness came, but thank God, he's gone now. Cal was here, too, but he's gone also. I don't want either one of them to see how silly I look in the crown, with the cape around me, and me holding so tight to the scepter. They'd tease me if they were here. "I don't want Culley to see me with the crown on," I say.

They don't hear me. Julia is whispering, asking Lanier something, but Lanier's fiddling with the IV that she brought with her. Lanier says her hands are shaking too bad to do this, that she has to pull herself together. "What did Corrine say?" she asks Julia.

"She thinks she has the crown on," Julia whispers to Lanier, and I laugh. "Lanier? Julia?" I say, laughing louder in an attempt to get their attention, to tell them to open their eyes, that I *do* have the crown on! But they're whispering, not hearing me, even though Julia's holding my hand so tight she's about to crush it. I want to tell them that they're just jealous that I'm wearing the crown and they're not, but for some reason, they can't hear me. I want them to see that I'm laughing, playing with them, no longer afraid. It hurts me to see Lanier's face so grim and Julia so pale, like a ghost floating around in the darkness.

Suddenly the sun has come out, and it streams in the window over my bed like a waterfall of light. It's so bright that I try to turn my head away, try to close my eyes, but I can't move, can't get away from the startling brightness of the sun. Raising my head, I see that it's not coming through my window after all; it's reflecting off Mobile Bay. The SSGs are on the pier at Dolphin Cove, and I'm the queen, holding the scepter and wearing the crown, the long flowing cape over my shoulders. We're all there, Julia and Lanier and me, Byrd and Astor and Rosanelle. The light in my eyes is coming off the bay, but it's also coming from the sparklers everyone is waving in the air, sending long streaks of fire through the sky, like jet streamers.

There's music, too, music floating across the water, and I raise my left hand, the hand not holding the scepter, to shade my eyes. A small wooden boat floats on the blue, blue waves, and I see that Jesse Phoenix is in the boat, playing his guitar and singing. I try to get Lanier's attention, try to tell her to look—it's Jesse! He's playing a song for me, just like he did for her and Lindy. But Lanier has dived into the bay and is swimming, her face bright and her eyes shining. "Lanier!" I call out to her, but she doesn't hear me. "Look at that fool Lanier," I say to the others, and we laugh together, waving at Lanier as she swims past us.

Julia comes to me, her lovely face serene, and she takes the crown and cape and scepter from me. At first, I protest, but Julia says, "It's better if you leave it all behind." Without the heavy crown, I'm so weightless now that my feet barely touch the pier. Julia reaches out, takes my hand, and leads me to the end of the pier. I float along beside her, the sun still so bright as it reflects off the waters that I squint and turn my head to the side so I can see to follow Julia. At the end of the pier, bobbling in the waves, is the wooden boat, but it's empty now.

"Where's Jesse?" I ask Julia, but she doesn't answer. Instead, she puts her arms around me, hugging me tight. "It's okay, honey," she says, kissing my cheek. "You can go now." Hesitating only a moment, I leave Julia standing on the pier watching me as I climb the rickety ladder down to the boat. When I sit down, I see that the boat's not empty after all. Inside, next to the oar, is my gourd-vine gourd. I turn my head back to the pier and call up to Julia, "Wait! I don't know how to row."

Julia points out to the horizon. "It's okay. Just follow Lanier," she says. And there's Lanier holding on to the fin of the silvery dolphin, waving at me as she flashes through the water. I pick up the oar and start to row, not sure where I'm going. I head toward Lanier, and the boat moves smoothly, as though pulled along by unseen currents. A bend lies ahead, and when Lanier disappears from view, I turn to look over my shoulder. Behind me is the pier, and I see that Lanier's back now, no longer swimming with the dolphin. I don't know how she got back so fast, but there she is. She's standing next to Julia, their arms locked together. Next to them are Byrd and Astor and Rosanelle, their hands raised, waving good-bye.

The boat rounds the bend, and the pier at Dolphin Cove is no longer in sight. There's nothing around me but water, blue-black and scary-looking, as far as I can see, and I'm afraid. My hands tremble so hard that I drop the oar, but the wooden boat glides on, as though I were still paddling through the water. I'm on an ocean that's so vast that for one scary minute, I can't even see the horizon. Suddenly, the water is calm and blue again. The other shore looms before me, and I breathe a sigh of relief.

As the boat moves closer, I see the dark line of the shore and the silver outline of a tall pier jutting out into the water, much like the pier at Dolphin Cove, except it's silhouetted against the sun. A crowd waits for me on the pier, and like the SSGs on the other shore, they're waving, hands held high. Someone begins to run down the pier as the boat draws nearer, and I shade my eyes against the blinding sun behind the pier, trying to see who it is. Oh, God, it's been so long that I would never have known her! It's Dixie Lee, who is as young and as radiant as when I saw her last, all those years ago. She holds a child by the hand, a child who seems to be edged in light, and they're moving down the pier hand in hand, coming toward me, waving and waving.

When the boat floats beneath the pier, I stand up and look for a rope or something, since there's no ladder leading upward to the pier. I know I'm supposed to be on the pier, know that the crowd there is waiting to welcome me, but I don't know how to get to them. I look down, searching the bottom of the boat. At my feet is the gourd-vine gourd, which I'd forgotten was there. I reach over to pick it up, then I step back in amazement. The vines I so carefully drew and painted on the sides of the gourd spring to life. Right before my eyes, they leave the gourd and they spill over the sides of the boat. I shade my eyes and watch as the vines climb up the posts of the pier, toward the sky, forming a leafy green path. Leaving the wooden boat behind, I start to climb.